I0639827

KEPT
IN THE
DARK

ARJAY LEWIS

MIND
BENDER
PRESS

Kept In The Dark
Copyright ©2018 Robert J. Lewis

Cover Design: Marianne Nowicki, PremadeEbookCoverShop.com
Editing: Libby Broadbent

ISBN-13: 978-1545504499
ISBN-10: 1545504490

Published by:
Mindbender Press
474 South Main Street
Phillipsburg NJ 08865
www.mindbenderpress.com

DEDICATION

To the talented Marianne Nowicki,
an extraordinary artist and designer
who makes all my book covers look good.

"People will do anything, no matter how absurd, in order to avoid facing their own souls. One does not become enlightened by imagining figures of light, but by making the darkness conscious."

— *Carl Jung*

"Darkness cannot drive out darkness: only light can do that. Hate cannot drive out hate: only love can do that."

— *Dr. Martin Luther King Jr.*

PROLOGUE

It's been over two decades since I first crossed paths with Jake Hurd. I never imagined it would take me this long to tell his story, but now, finally, the time has come. I was his therapist and the hours we shared were unlike any I'd ever experienced—marked by strange revelations and culminating in his mysterious disappearance on the very first day of the new millennium.

Looking back at 1999, the fears we had—of computers crashing and technology causing the world's end—now seem almost laughable, quaint, and misguided.

How wrong we were.

We stood on the brink of an apocalypse, one that could have wiped out humanity and handed our world over to ruthless, shadowy creatures. It was a disaster averted by one man—a single warrior—branded mad by a skeptical society.

Now that I am retired and my children have grown I feel safe enough to share what happened. What follows is my account of Jake's life drawn from everything he confided in me, colored by the creative freedom to reconstruct dialogues between him and those he encountered.

You may dismiss this as mere fiction—perhaps believing I was hypnotized or drugged during that strange period. That might be the only way to accept the existence of the creatures that haunted Jake's every step.

But I assure you: these creatures were real.

October 2020
Doctor Samuel J. Lucas, MD, PhD
Board Certified A.B.P.P
Retired

JAKE

1. MEETING JAKE

....

"Doctor Lucas!"

The words shattered the stillness of a chilly November night in 1999, ripping through the dimly lit sanctuary of my office.

I was buried in stacks of paperwork, the monotonous rustle of paper my only company when the frantic shout pulled my attention.

Heart pounding, I yanked open the door.

Standing there was Nurse Althea Winters, her broad frame heaving with ragged breaths, wild strands of hair escaping her nurse's cap. Her usual composure was gone—replaced by raw, palpable fear.

"It's Jake," she gasped, voice barely more than a strangled whisper. "He's... gone mad."

Althea Winters was a legend at Greystorm Psychiatric and Teaching Hospital. She had stared down the worst in human madness and come out unshaken, a rock amid the storm.

But now something had cracked that foundation. Her wide eyes darted, unsteady. I knew the gravity the moment I saw her.

"You gotta come quick, Dr. Lucas," she urged. "There's blood —everywhere."

We stepped into the corridor. The overhead bulbs struggled against shadows pressing in, the flickering light creating grotesque shapes on the peeling walls. Althea moved swiftly for a woman so big—almost frantic—and an icy knot tightened in my stomach.

"How bad is it?" I managed to ask.

She hesitated, breath hitching. "Dr. Benning gave him a sleeping pill. But some damn fool forgot to turn on his light for the night shift…"

I stopped her with a sharp look. "You charged up to my office because somebody didn't have their night-light?"

Her glare was fierce enough to cut glass. "There's blood everywhere, Dr. Lucas! You don't understand." She wrenched free from my grip and pressed forward.

Then came the scream—primal, guttural, a howl ripped straight from the abyss of madness. It echoed down the hall, twisting the air with despair, rage, and an ancient terror I hadn't felt in years. My skin crawled and my pace quickened.

Rounding the corner the scene hit me full force. Three men grappled with a figure bathed in shadows and smeared crimson. Two hefty orderlies—one black, one white—strained to hold him down, while a tall, gaunt man with wild white hair and a trembling mustache fought desperately.

Blood soaked the man's white gown blooming in dark, twisted flowers across his legs, face contorted with pain.

But it was his eyes that froze me: icy blue, wild and void of humanity, shining with a feral insanity that made me stumble back.

I shouted, desperate to pierce the chaos. "What's wrong? Tell me!"

The man's gaze snapped to mine. In that moment a flicker of recognition flared in those maddened eyes.

"I need light," he rasped, voice raw and broken. "Please."

I pulled open the nearest door—an examination room usually locked down—and slammed the switch. Harsh fluorescent bulbs sputtered to life bathing the room in a relentless glow. I flipped on several intense lamps focused on the metal table.

"We're not supposed to use this room," Althea warned, voice low and tense.

I ignored her. "Sit. Stay here under the light while I take a look."

He muttered under his breath: "The scalpels... it tried to kill me."

The words sent a shiver down my spine but there was no time for hesitation. "Nurse Winters! I need a wound kit, stat!"

The orderlies lifted the man onto the table as the bright light seemed to tether his fraying sanity.

Slowly I peeled back the soaked fabric, revealing the full horror. Bruises bloomed in angry purple across his legs. His wrists were wrapped in tattered bandages. Scars crisscrossed his body—some jagged and raw, others unnervingly precise like ritual markings.

I swallowed hard, forcing the shock down my throat. Pulling on gloves I began cleaning the new wounds—deep, vicious slashes from what looked like scalpels. Blood welled up again and again but as the light hit his skin, his tremors quieted.

"How did this happen?" I asked, voice steady though my heart hammered in my ears.

He leaned closer, voice a cracked whisper: "They did this to me."

"They?" I pressed, my skin prickling.

"The things… hiding in the dark."

This was my first encounter with Jake Hurd. What I thought was a shattered mind spiraling into psychosis was something far darker. Something that would drag me into a nightmare bleeding beyond the boundaries of sanity and into terror itself.

I didn't know it yet—I would soon learn Jake was worse than crazy—and knowing him would make my world a much more dangerous place.

2. GRAY NOVEMBER

"Heard you had a bit of excitement last night," Bill Benning said, his voice carrying that familiar mix of amusement and curiosity. He was settled comfortably on the corner of his cluttered desk, his ample frame seeming almost to spill over its edges.

Bill was the administrator of Greystorm Hospital—the most notorious state-run asylum in the East—and also an old friend, more mentor than anything.

Short, maybe five-two, and nearly as round as he was tall, he looked every bit the picture of a man in his sixties who'd let life's pressures settle deep into his stomach. His shirt was slightly rumpled beneath the loosened tie, the heavy jacket draped over his chair like a cape abandoned miles from battle.

"A little, yeah," I said.

"Thanks for patching him up."

I nodded. That night's chaos replayed in my head with unsettling clarity. "Have you examined him properly? He's covered in scars."

"All in places he can hide when dressed," Bill's thick, dark eyebrows twitched as he leaned forward.

"Is he a cutter?" I asked, using the term for people who harm their own body as a way of coping with emotional stress. The medical term for this was 'non-suicidal self-injury.'

"It's likely," Bill said, voice low, "but it's the dark. That's what really terrifies him—"

"And the things hiding there?" I added.

Bill looked at me squarely. "You actually talked to him?"

"Briefly. Enough to get a glimpse into his psychosis."

Bill nodded slowly. "His case fits right into that research paper you wrote."

I rubbed my eyes sensing the weight behind his words. "My paper was on sleep deprivation."

"Sammy," Bill said, using the old nickname he never failed to remind me I'd earned over twenty years ago. "Here's insomnia mixed with a crippling anxiety. He could be your next comprehensive study."

Bill had a way of dropping crumbs, then pressing until you took the bait.

"He's been involuntarily committed," Bill said finally, "after slitting his wrists. I think you're the one who can help him."

I felt that old familiar tug—the responsibility and the dread. I'd known Bill for two decades: from drunken nights to endless clinical debates, had seen his daughter grow up, and counted him among the few who truly understood the burdens we carried.

"Bill," I said, running a hand through my thinning hair, "I have a busy private practice now. I don't have time."

"This one's different," Bill insisted. "You spoke to the man—he sees things."

"Tell me, Bill," I said incredulously, "how many patients do you have who see things? This guy's just scared of shadows."

Bill scoffed. "Don't talk to me about primal fear. This goes deeper."

"How?" I asked, already sensing his answer was about to blur lines I wasn't ready to cross.

"He speaks in riddles. Feels you out. He's a lot smarter than he should be. Stable, too."

"Stable?" I scoffed. "Last night he sliced his leg open with a scalpel."

Bill's lips quirked into a smile that didn't reach his eyes. "Okay, this is an important case."

I crossed my arms. "There's money, isn't there?"

Bill sighed. "There's always money. A security company is footing the bill."

"Security?" I frowned. "Did he steal something?"

"No. The opposite. He works for them." Bill's tone dropped. "He's a night guard."

I hesitated. "You mean, like a night watchman?"

"Yes, but he's more than that. He's an inventor—alarms, motion detectors. The man built a fortune for them."

I snorted bitterly. "Perfect job for a paranoid."

"And they want him back. They want him well."

I paused. "How much would this fool's errand pay?"

Bill laughed. "Double your rate."

I stared. "You're kidding."

"That's what the company agreed to. I was thinking of analyzing him myself."

"Bill, you're an administrator."

"For the last decade." He pulled himself up, bristling. "Sammy, I have more hours with patients than you are even close to."

I rubbed my temple. "Alright. I'll consider it."

Bill's grin was triumphant. "Good. Take the weekend to decide. My best to Marcie."

I left the office and stepped out into the November gloom. The sky hung low, heavy with clouds that threatened rain but never delivered. The cold air bit into my skin as I walked to my car—an ominous stillness settling over the world.

It was Friday night—Shabbos. Perfect timing of course. The Jewish Sabbath begins at sundown, when the days are short and shadows stretch long.

Anything that makes it more inconvenient.

I was born Jewish though I never much cared for the rituals. It was Marcie who insisted we join a synagogue, drag the kids to services, and walk this path.

After our children arrived the special Friday night dinners started: the prayers, the candles, the blessings. I humored it all—for her sake. I didn't believe any of it, but wasn't that what a therapist would suggest a husband do?

I slid into the driver's seat and fished a couple of Tums from my stash in the glove box. Bill's request from earlier had triggered my stomach into a slow boil—the acid gnawing up my throat like a watching predator. Forty-four isn't old, but a taxed stomach sure makes you feel it.

I backed my black Mercedes out of the lot and headed toward the exit, flicking on the headlights to cut through the gloom that wrapped the world like a leaden cloak.

The roads from Greystorm to Denville often snarled with traffic but tonight I slipped through side streets and made it home quickly.

Pulling into the garage the house looked empty, silent, cold even before I crossed the threshold.

Out of nowhere, a fierce weight tackled me from behind—my six-year-old son, Rueben. His small arms clamped around my legs.

"Aha! A Rueben sandwich!" I teased, hoisting him up and making eating noises on his stomach. He wriggled, giggled, and told me laughingly to stop.

Rachel appeared then, my twelve-year-old daughter, slipping a quick kiss onto my cheek. So mature, so composed, silently observing the dance of family life.

Marcie emerged from the kitchen, her smile clipped and blunt —what I call the 'therapist grin.' It's an expression that hides everything, revealing nothing—a mask so subtle you barely notice its coldness.

"You're home. Just in time to light the candles," she said, voice steady but distant.

I nodded, setting Rueben down gently. Marcie immediately took hold of him, smoothing his white shirt, adjusting his black-and-gray clip-on tie.

She shot me a sharp look. "Get dressed. We're about to start."

"I'm wearing a suit," I replied.

"Dress nice," she countered, "it puts you in the mood. Wash up. Dinner's soon."

I turned and climbed the stairs, annoyed I had to do this one more task. I changed into a clean shirt, buttoned my navy-blue suit jacket, dabbing water on my face.

The mirror reflected a man hollowed by stress—rounded stomach, slumping shoulders. I have to hand it to Marcie; two kids and she's kept her figure.

Downstairs, the table was set immaculately—white linens, nice dishes, two braided loaves of challah nestled beneath a cloth embroidered with Hebrew letters.

I sat at the head of the table, opening the small book that had the blessings written out.

Marcie chanted the blessings with effortless grace, her voice rising and falling. The kids followed, Rueben solemnly covering his eyes, Rachel more like a distant observer.

When the last 'Amen' faded, I smiled at Marcie, and for a fleeting moment, she returned it—a smile, genuine and warm, rare these days.

"Read the blessings," she encouraged.

I placed my hands on each child's head, reciting words I barely believed, then kissed them softly. Then the verses praising my wife —and she responded with a psalm in my honor.

The climax was the Kiddush—the silver cup overflowing with wine. The formal part ended with washing hands and breaking the bread, blessings threaded with tradition and the weight of expectation.

Dinner stretched on; I savored the wine's warmth, the richness of food grounding me. Marcie kept the kids in check, deflecting their bickering with soft authority.

Later I helped clear dishes. No television on Friday nights— Marcie's rule—and so we played board games, the flickering candlelight carving jagged shadows over the room. Finally bedtimes came and the house grew hush.

Drunk on wine and the faint comfort of ritual, I climbed the stairs with Marcie. As we changed into pajamas she broached the topic that had been quietly gnawing at her.

"Have you thought any more about the mezuzahs?"

I scoffed. "Aren't we doing enough?"

"They belong on every doorpost."

"Superstitious nonsense," I muttered.

Her eyes flashed with frustration. "That's a fine way to speak of our traditions."

"You can take those things too far," I said, voice heavy.

We slipped under the covers, darkness wrapping around us.

"Are we going to make love?" she asked softly—a tentative question. "It's a mitzvah on the Shabbos."

"I could get in the mood," I replied uncertainly. "What about you?"

"If you want, tonight would be the choice. Next week..." she trailed off.

Her period and the week following it were off-limits for intimacy—a rule she insisted on since the children came along.

"There was a time that didn't matter," I reminded her quietly.

She sighed. "Sam, let's not start."

"I'm not starting. Just discussing."

"And don't play semantics."

"I'm a psychiatrist. It's what I do."

We lay there, the silence stretching thicker than the bedcovers.

"So," she pressed, "do you want to or not?"

I pulled her close, kissed her. Her lips responded, warm but hesitant. I caressed beneath her nightgown.

The whole thing lasted ten minutes between undressing, caressing, and coupling. She even made little noises of appreciation. Afterwards we lay together in the darkness of our marriage bed.

"Why don't we go away for a few days?" I suggested, grasping for something—anything—to break the pattern.

"Sam, I just started at St. Clare's and I have no vacation time. Besides, the kids have school."

"Without the kids. Just you and me, a quiet hotel. You could wear that blue, frilly thing."

"The last time I wore that, I ended up pregnant with Rueben."

"I guess it worked," I chuckled.

"We don't need another baby," she said, voice gentle but firm. "Rueben's finally in first grade. I'm practicing again."

"We don't need the money."

"It's not money. I'm a therapist. A good one."

"I know."

"Are you trying to keep me barefoot and pregnant? Rachel was finally old enough for school—BAM!—we go away, and you forget condoms."

"You weren't on the pill then."

"I've supported your career. I need you to support mine."

Her logic struck me down—sharp, unyielding. Life was black and white to her. But what about the shadows in between?

"Of course, honey," I sighed, defeated. "I love you."

"Me, too," she whispered. "Besides, this was fine, wasn't it?"

3. A New Kind Of Crazy

The next morning after Marcie took the kids to temple, she returned and caught me off guard with a question that immediately set my nerves on edge.

"So, what's this new case Bill has you working on?" she asked, a hint of curiosity—and something else in her voice.

I froze, suspicion tightening my chest. "New case? What are you talking about?" I replied cautiously.

"The night guard," she said, folding her arms. "Can you even talk about it yet?"

My emotions flipped from surprise to anger in an instant, my jaw clenching. "I haven't accepted that case," I said sharply.

Her cheeks flushed an awkward pink. "Oh. I just thought it might fit well with your other work." There was a hesitation in her tone that only made the air heavier.

I stood abruptly pacing toward the bathroom. My fingers fumbled for the Maalox bottle on the counter as I fought down the rising urge to throttle Bill until he gagged. Marcie followed quietly behind.

I stopped and squared my shoulders, forcing myself into a calm, therapist-like voice. "Marcie, I haven't made a decision. But I honestly resent the fact Bill went behind my back to call you—my wife—to push me about this."

Her posture stiffened; I saw her hand go to her hip. "Don't be so dramatic," she said sharply. "No one's pushing anything on you."

I took a long swig of Maalox, the chalky liquid thick going down my throat. "Then why did he tell you at all?"

"He didn't call me about your case," she said smoothly, switching into her rational mode. "It just came up—I work in the same field you know."

I scoffed, voice low and tight. "Bill manipulates. This is just another variation."

Her eyes narrowed. "And you react like this every time I mention therapy. You never take me seriously. If someone talks to me, you think they're trying to influence you."

"I know Bill. This is a tactic."

A sharp sigh escaped her lips. "You're paranoid. Really, you are."

Before I could respond she stormed out of the bathroom, leaving the tension thick. For the rest of the weekend the silence between us was loud, broken only by the laughter and chaos of our children who thankfully needed most of our attention.

That Sunday night I swallowed my pride and apologized. "I do take you seriously," I said quietly and Marcie's demeanor softened.

Later, lying in the dark, she spoke softly. "We should go for couples' counseling."

I hesitated. "Is that really necessary?"

She turned to face me, shadows playing across her features. "We don't fight well. Never have. Maybe we could learn some new techniques. It might help."

I took a deep breath, the sinking feeling settling deep in my gut again. "If you want to."

Her voice sharpened instantly. "Don't patronize me. I'm serious."

I tried to keep my temper in check but failed. "So am I!" My voice was louder than intended, tinged with frustration. I quickly exhaled. "Sorry. You're right. But can we at least pick someone we don't know?"

"Should we go out of state, too?" she said, dripping with sarcasm.

"Good idea," I shot back.

We lay there, the fire of anger cooling slowly into thoughtful silence. Finally she murmured, "You know... we could go to a couples workshop and say we're there to learn techniques for our patients."

I nodded. "Sounds plausible. And hey, it's even a tax write-off."

Marcie shook her head in the dark. "Always the mercenary."

"Just practical."

For the first time all weekend, the tension eased.

Driving back to Greystorm on that gray Monday the sky remained stubbornly overcast—no rain, no sun—just a dull slate of clouds that felt like the endless twilight of an Alaskan winter.

I couldn't shake the eerie feeling it gave me like being trapped in one of those towns where darkness drapes the streets for months on end, suffocating and relentless.

People need sunlight like fuel; it kick-starts our bodies to churn out the chemicals that keep us sane. Without it, the days shrink and the shadows deepen—creating more cases of depression..

On the positive side, that was good for business.

But today, despite the gloomy weather, my thoughts were hotter than the summer sun. I clenched the steering wheel tighter, forcing my breathing slow and even.

Anger-management techniques: deep breaths, counting backwards, imagining a calm lake. I couldn't just barrel into Bill's office flinging all my frustration at him like daggers.

No, I owed the man plenty. Yet I followed his sly moves like a seasoned hunter stalking prey—every step deliberate, every word a trap to be sidestepped.

The administration building loomed ahead, dull and serious as the weather. When I stepped into his office there was Bill—smiling like a jolly, clean-shaven Santa Claus but plumper, booming with exuberance that cut through the gloom.

Damn it. I wanted to be mad at him but he made it impossible.

"Sammy!" Bill's voice rang out, warm and inviting. "Come in, sit down. I've been waiting for you."

I lowered myself into the chair opposite him, trying to keep my temper in check. "About this case—"

Bill's eyes twinkled. "I thought it would intrigue you, my boy." He pushed himself up to his full, though diminutive, stature. "Did you speak with Marcie about it?"

That needle pricked my skin. "No, Bill. But it annoyed me that you did."

His brow furrowed in faux innocence. "Discussed the case with Marcie? I can't recall… I spoke with her about a few things. It might've come up."

"Don't play dumb with me," I snapped, heat rising to my collar. "You told her so she'd sell me on it."

Bill's smile wavered. "Sammy, you cut me to the quick. It was just shop talk. And he is a fascinating patient."

I saw it. That jovial, plump innocence designed to disarm me. And damned if it didn't work. Bill seemed genuinely pleased just to have me in the room.

"Why fight it?" I shrugged, the fight draining out of me. "Let me see the file."

"That's the spirit," he said, clapping me on the back. As if fate had sealed the deal, he handed over the folder.

As I tucked the file under my arm I couldn't hold back one last jab. "Your meddling blew up my relationship with Marcie."

Bill's expression softened with concern. "I'm sorry. You two should get away for a weekend."

"I keep suggesting that. Marcie says it's not logical."

Bill's eyes sparkled. "Sometimes you have to throw logic out the window. That's how Helena and I have lasted forty years. Occasionally I just sweep her off her feet."

The mental image of Bill, as hefty as he was, hoisting equally large Helena in his arms made me choke back a laugh.

"Maybe you should pass that advice along to Marcie," he suggested. "And to sweeten the pot, I'll send her flowers—with your name on them."

I rolled my eyes. "First cajoling, now bribery. Where does it end?"

"Read the file, Sammy. I promise you, it's fascinating."

Back in the tiny office I shared with the visiting doctors I flipped on the green-shaded lamp, casting a dull glow over the patient's folder. The name at the top in bold block letters stared back at me: JAKE HURD.

His notes revealed a man gripped by paranoia—he insisted on leaving the lights on in his room at all hours, terrified of the dark.

But surprisingly, Bill's notes diagnosed no depression. Odd considering Jake arrived at Greystorm with two neat, amateurish slashes across his wrists. Those weren't the desperate cuts of someone determined to die; a true attempt would sever the artery.

This was more a cry for help than an actual goodbye.

Bill had placed Jake on Navane, a strong antipsychotic. From the dosage I saw, I knew the patient wouldn't be hallucinating any little creatures in the near future.

However, his speech would slow and fragmented, a side effect Bill considered a worthy trade-off. Bill came from a school of thought that believed pills could fix nearly all mental ills.

I found the transcript of Bill's interview with Jake shortly after admission. The patient's words were guarded, cryptic, layered. He played with meanings like a chess master, making me wonder if he was testing us.

The admission report told a grim story.

Jake was found in the darkest corner of his sprawling workplace, wrists slit, barely conscious. An EMT working security stopped the bleeding just in time.

From there, Jake spent a night in Morristown Memorial before quietly being transferred to our custody under involuntary commitment—the paperwork meticulous, giving us between twenty days and three months to decide his fate.

I combed through results: IQ tests, Rorschach inkblots—all confirming Bill's claim Jake was intelligent, perhaps a genius.

"Not smart enough to stop himself from slitting his wrists," I muttered under my breath.

His physical exam showed a history of self-mutilation—old scars peppered his limbs—consistent with patterns seen in many cutters who test the waters before targeting wrists.

The contradictions gnawed at me. Physically battered yet psychologically guarded. Or maybe just cunning; maybe this was a game to Jake, a psychological chess match with life and death stakes. Playing us for fools would mean ego, but self-harm hinted at a deep desire to destroy that ego.

And a terrifying fear of darkness—how could someone so sharp be trapped in such primal dread?

My first meeting revealed none of the brilliance. Jake was simply afraid. Raw and exposed.

Bill believed this case could yield a paper tying my sleep deprivation studies into delusion research.

I closed the file and popped two Tums, chewing thoughtfully. Damn Bill. He always knew exactly which buttons to press.

And now I was hooked.

4. Taking the Case

I swore under my breath never to let Bill finagle me again—only to instantly recognize the futility of such a vow. Bill had an uncanny way of twisting situations, and I knew well that outrunning his manipulations was a losing game.

Shaking off the frustration I walked to my temporary office, the faint hum of fluorescent lights greeting me.

The folder lay heavy on the desk as I perched myself in the creaky chair. I needed answers and the thread to pull was obvious: Jake's company, Security Information Systems.

If I could get the inside scoop from his coworkers and especially the man who had found him—perhaps I could piece together the puzzle.

The number was straightforward, given the company and supervisor details right there on the folder. I dialed letting two rings throb through the silence before a brisk, personable voice answered.

"Security Information Systems."

"Frank Delaney, please."

Clicks echoed mechanically over the line before another ring pierced the quiet.

"Delaney here!"

The intensity in his voice was sharp enough to make me wince. It was so loud, booming, I had to yank the phone away from my ear. He spoke with the over-the-top enthusiasm of a used car salesman desperate to close a deal.

"Mr. Delaney, this is Dr. Lucas. I'm the specialist Dr. Benning brought in regarding Jake Hurd."

"How's the old boy doing, Doc?" His voice bounced with jovial warmth, but there was an edge—like he was sizing me up.

"It's too early for a complete evaluation," I said carefully. "But I was hoping you could tell me more about him."

"Jake?" He chuckled. "Great guy. Good man. But honestly I don't know him too well."

I pressed on. "What do you know?"

"Well, most times I see him he just drops in after meetings," his voice dropped conspiratorially. "He's eager to show off one of his little tinkers."

"Tinkers?" I echoed, intrigued..

"Yeah, that's what he calls them. His inventions—surveillance gear, state-of-the-art stuff he cobbles together in his basement lab. It's wild stuff—computer-driven, motion detectors, tiny cameras. You wouldn't believe half the things he builds. Every month or two he swings by with something new."

"That's unusual for a night guard, isn't it?"

Delaney laughed. "That's because Jake's not just a night guard. He's the site supervisor. And he still works a site because he wants to—not because he has to."

I frowned, sensing an incongruity. "What do you mean?"

"These inventions? The company mass-produces most of them. And Jake's getting a cut, a hefty one at that. Made a fortune off those things—more than I ever will." His voice reverberated with a mixture of admiration and envy.

Suddenly their investment in Jake made sense. He might be a paranoid—but he was a productive one.

"Jake's work put this company on the map," Delaney continued. "Old Man Hurley, the president, even gave Jake a commendation last year. Came with some impressive remuneration. We used to be a small-time outfit, just guards at corporate sites. Now? Full home security systems—top tier. They even install 'em free if you sign up for monitoring."

I tugged at a memory—a radio ad I'd heard promoting such wares. I'd ignored things like that—until now.

"Say, Doc," Frank's tone shifted into salesman mode again, "ever consider the peace of mind an alarm system could offer? Considering you deal with all kinds of crazies—"

"Maybe another time," I cut him off trying to stay on track.

He chuckled. He just couldn't help himself.

"Could I speak to Jake's coworkers?" I asked.

"Sure! Go to his site. Every security officer there knows Jake. Especially the midnight shift; they work with him."

My brow furrowed. "Hold on... he's site supervisor but works midnights? I expected—"

"That's what he wants." Frank's volume dial turned up, impossibly louder. "If Jake wanted some cushy exec gig they'd hand it to him. But no. Midnight to eight, same shift he's worked forever. Beats me why."

A chill ran down my spine. Control of his environment. All the signs of advanced paranoia, possibly obsessive-compulsive behavior. Jake wrapped himself in a world of control and order.

Delaney warmed to the topic. "He works at Bellcant Innovations out in Whippany. Easy to find. Best time to catch folks with stories is shift change, around eleven-thirty. Those guys will spill plenty. Jake's a character, no doubt about it."

"I'm sure," I said, trying to mask the knot of anxiety tightening in my chest. "If I needed access to Jake's personnel records—"

Frank's tone dimmed. "Can't really do that legally. But his state stuff? Public record. Clearances, disciplinary history—that sort of thing. But, hell, look at the time. Gotta run. Doc, you call me anytime you need help with ol' Jake."

"I will," I said, but it was too late. The line went dead.

I sat back, the echo of Frank's booming voice still ringing in my ears. Jake Hurd was more than a paranoid night guard. He was a man entangled in layers of invention, control, and something darker I was only beginning to grasp.

5. Scene Of The Crime

Before leaving Greystorm, I deliberately halved Jake's prescription. Bill's dosage would muddle his mind, and I needed to speak with Jake sharp enough to understand. The conversation was urgent—delicate. I couldn't risk jumbled thoughts.

The day ahead found me in my Denville office, nestled in one of those sterile buildings known as a 'Doctor Complex.'

The term sounds like a Freudian joke.

But no—it was plain real estate jargon. A mere hill away from Saint Clare's Hospital, the complex was designed to concentrate medical professionals and labs in one monotonous location.

The building itself didn't break the mold: a three-story brick box with the charm of a filing cabinet. Inside everything dared to be beige—walls, carpet, elevator doors, even the muted amber-glass windows that never opened.

The relentless beige seemed intent on draining color from the day.

My office sat on the second floor. I stepped through the electric sliding doors, my footsteps sinking softly into the padded carpet as I punched the elevator button, feeling like a ghost in a sanitized mausoleum.

The monotony grated. The sterile environment was a sharp, suffocating contrast to the raw humanity I dealt with.

Inside, my assistant, Anne awaited. She was a rarity—a vivacious breath of life in the dull beige tide. Originally from England, Anne came to America dreaming of Broadway stardom, a dream Broadway cruelly snatched away.

Yet, she carried herself with a grace that would have lit a stage. Warm, grounded, and utterly genuine, she was the perfect anchor in this antiseptic world. Our relationship was purely professional; neither chemistry nor desire were present. She was an exotic presence in my daily grind, a bird too free to be caged.

The day dragged on, each patient blending into the next—a parade of mundane cases, their troubles skimming the surface but never diving deep. I leaned in, coaxing, probing gently, searching beneath the rehearsed answers for a flicker of something raw, something real.

But today the walls held firm. No breakthrough. No sudden revelations that could shatter the monotony.

Between patients Anne informed me a fax came from Delaney approving my meeting with Jake's coworkers for that night, with directions.

After that, I packed up and headed home to a quick weekday dinner that I prepared—a simple repast, nothing lavish, but I called the shots and tried, however fleetingly, to reclaim some control in a day that felt otherwise stalled.

Marcie had group therapy, Rachel battled her Hebrew lessons for her upcoming Bat Mitzvah, and I tucked Rueben in with no drama.

When Marcie arrived home, I told her I accepted the case, which gave her a chance to flash her 'I-told-you-so' look. She followed it with a 'thank you' for the flowers which Bill sent to her office.

By 11 PM I was on the road heading toward Bellcant Innovations—a sprawling fortress of glass and steel off Route 10 in Whippany to interview Jake's coworkers.

The campus stretched over acres, a city unto itself, with machine shops, gyms, cafeterias, and even a gift shop. The sheer scale was daunting.

By 11:30, I stepped through the revolving doors into a vast lobby where bland decoration and color-coordinated art hung like silent sentinels.

Before me loomed a massive black-stone reception desk behind which eight stern figures shuffled, all clad in matching camel jackets. Their eyes pinned me down with the cold suspicion of gatekeepers guarding secrets.

Instinct urged me to raise my hands or brandish ID, but I simply nodded and spoke calmly. "I'm here to talk about Jake Hurd."

An older African-American man with a grizzled face and several missing teeth peered at me sharply. "Who're you, and what do you want?"

"I'm Dr. Lucas," I answered, flashing my Greystorm ID. "Jake's doctor."

His eyes twinkled with a mixture of recognition and skepticism. "Well, I reckon we all know Cap'n Jake."

A tall, dark-haired woman stepped in, exuding quiet authority. She was a living warning—strong enough to knock me out with a single blow if she chose.

"Is this an official investigation?" she asked, voice low but steady.

"No. My visit's unofficial. Off the record."

"What's this about?" the old man pressed.

"He's a shrink checking on Jake," she answered, her eyes flickering to my ID. "Frank Delaney contacted me. Told us to cooperate."

Relief flickered beneath my professionalism. "Good," I said, attempting calm. These were formidable people—all tall, all poised, the kind you wouldn't want to cross. "Who's known Mr. Hurd the longest?"

"That'd be Charley," said the woman, nodding toward the toothless man.

"Near on ten years," Charley confirmed.

"Lieutenant Fran Neiman," the woman introduced herself. "I've covered Jake's shifts for almost a year now."

"Thank you for your assistance," I said, not knowing what else to say.

"That's Jerry," she added, indicating a lanky white man with a buzz cut. "Found Jake after the accident."

Just then a large black man approached, his presence seeming almost incongruous against his soft-spoken voice: "Is the Cap'n gonna be all right?"

"It's too soon to say. We aim for a full recovery. That's why I'm here." I kept my voice steady even as my heart thudded in my chest.

"Talk to Jerry first," Fran suggested. "He's going off duty. If you want privacy go in there." She pointed toward a modest waiting room.

Jerry and I settled into plush black leather chairs in the room, and I pulled out my yellow legal pad and mechanical pencil—the tools of my quiet trade. "Tell me about finding Captain Hurd. When did it happen?"

He exhaled, gathering himself. "Last Wednesday night. Graveyard shift. Cap'n Jake likes to keep a presence—does a tour every shift." His words were punctuated by a nervy string of 'y'knows,' a nervous tic that revealed unease beneath his tough exterior.

"On that night?"

"Yeah. He took Post Six, the early one at one AM, though I'd normally do it. I covered the main desk."

"When did you know something was wrong?"

"Around two, two-oh-five. I heard screaming over the radio. Not like anything I wanted to hear."

"Captain Hurd?"

"Yeah. I was shouting over the mic, calling out to him, but responses were all wrong. Other guards were scrambling."

"Chaos," I murmured.

"Hell, yeah. Charley covered the desk, all of us running to Building Two. I raced to the basement—last place he'd be at that hour." His voice cracked slightly.

"Why the basement?"

"Shift ends at two-ten. Last key's right outside. Thought he'd be heading out. We were calling, searching."

"And you found him?"

"In that basement room—which is nothing but storage, furnaces, and ducts. He was lying there with his wrists slashed."

I swallowed. "You stopped the bleeding?"

"Had some training back in the National Guard. Tore my shirt, made a tourniquet. Probably saved him."

The image slammed into me: battered and vulnerable.

Jerry hesitated, then spoke of what Jake had been wearing—a black SWAT-style vest with battery packs, broken lights lying shattered nearby. "Like some kind of armor he made."

My mind scrambled to piece together the fragments.

I asked if I could see the spot. Jerry checked with Lieutenant Fran. Once cleared we proceeded down twisting hallways and stairs to a subbasement. The vast space was cold and silent—no windows, just steel beams and thick dust hanging in the air.

A chill—not from the temperature—gripped me.

As we walked through the door, I thought I saw a person out of the corner of my eye. I gasped, but it was only a six-foot-tall toy soldier wearing a plastic grin.

It stood next to dirty boxes marked 'Xmas decorations' and parts of a giant fireplace.

Jerry saw my reaction and said, "Oh, yeah, him. I guess I'm used to him. Scared me the first few times, y'know."

"I just didn't expect..." I mumbled, my cheeks hot with embarrassment.

"Yeah." Jerry chuckled and gazed at the toy. "The guys who work here keep putting him in different positions. Some of them kind of, y'know, vulgar."

I forced myself to focus. Ten feet from the door the concrete bore rusty red stains—a grim testament that the place had never been truly cleaned. Jerry's voice faltered with anger. "Police called it attempted suicide. Cap'n Jake wouldn't do that."

I knelt, eyes narrowed. "You think someone attacked him?"

Jerry nodded fiercely. "Bruises on his face—no way he did that to himself. Somebody came at him."

I remained silent. I was familiar with patients who hit themselves or violently threw themselves against stationary objects resulting in bruises.

Jerry added, "He's been nervous lately. Excited, too. Folks around here jittery with the Millennium Bug on the horizon."

Writing it all down, I knew the picture was far from clear.

Back in the lobby I spoke with Fran and Charley together.

"To the best of your knowledge did Jake show signs of mood swings or depression?"

Charley chewed his lip as he considered my question. He leaned back in his chair with his chin on his tie. "I can't rightly say he was any more upset than normal. Fran, you know about anything upsetting the Cap'n?"

"Well, those things he built. He was spending a lot of time on something." She chuckled at a memory. "They gave him a workshop here on site."

Charley nodded his head. "Thass right, he come here early to work on it."

"After sundown," Fran added. "He said he liked to be here once it got dark."

Charley laughed. "Yep, and it gets dark early come November."

I turned toward Fran. "Do you know what he was working on?"

Fran shook her head. "He's pretty tightlipped."

"Like an oyster," chimed in Charley.

"Yeah," said Fran. "I heard Bellcant offered him a job, but he turned them down."

"Don't that beat all?" Charley added. "Only finished high school, but he's as smart as the big-brains they got working in the labs."

I nodded to acknowledge their statements while I turned to the second page on my legal pad.

"Anything personal you noticed?" I asked. "Mood swings, depression?"

Charley shook his head and glanced up with a look both sad and annoyed. "He weren't one to talk about hisself. I knew he had a daughter and had hisself one messy divorce, years back. I've known a lot o' men to complain about their ol' lady, but he didn't say nuthin' 'bout it 'cept how tough it was."

"Every conversation I ever had with him was about the job," Fran told me with a shrug.

I made a few more notes and thanked them for their help. I gave Fran and Charley my business card and told them to call me if they remembered anything important.

It was well past one in the morning when I finally returned home and slipped through the front door, every creak in the floorboards threatening to announce my return. I moved like a shadow, barely daring to breathe, but fate had other plans.

Twice—twice! My ankle slammed hard into the edge of some unseen piece of furniture lurking in the pitch-black living room. I gritted my teeth and cursed quietly, the sudden sting radiating up my leg. My breath hitched; pain pulsed stubbornly beneath the skin, refusing to fade.

Careful now, I limped down the hall to the bathroom. The faint hum of the water running masked the quiet rustle as I peeled off my clothes and slipped into my pajamas.

Drawn like a moth to a light I drifted toward Rueben's room. Through the slightly ajar door the soft, steady glow of his nightlight outlined his still form.

He lay motionless as if frozen in time, wrapped in a bubble of complete peace. His face, bathed in ethereal light, looked so untroubled—so fully surrendered to sleep. A pang of longing tightened in my chest.

Oh, to lie there like that, untouched by whatever demons haunted me.

I made my way to my bedroom, every step hesitant. The darkness was absolute, pressing in on me, swallowing my figure whole.

I stumbled again though more gently this time, before sinking onto the bed. I cradled my throbbing ankle under the covers, grinding my teeth against the pain.

From the far side of the bed Marcie's soft, rhythmic snoring whispered reassurance—a steady anchor in the night.

I closed my eyes, unaware the nightmare had only just begun.

6. JAKE'S PROBLEM

The next morning I woke after the seven AM alarm buzzed for the third time.. No matter how many times the alarms screamed at me I couldn't break through the fog that clung to my mind.

I stumbled around the house like a restless zombie, barely conscious, while Marcie orchestrated the morning chaos with military precision, hurrying the kids out the door for school.

I dressed in a daze, every movement mechanical and slow. My mind was murky; I felt like I was wading through thick molasses.

Despite my usual disdain for early starts I had an appointment with Jake at eight o'clock sharp. Jake—the man I'd met just once —and now the reason I was dragging myself from bed hours before my normal nine-thirty. Apparently he insisted on early sessions because he only slept during the day.

I stopped at the nearest coffee shop, desperate for a jolt of caffeine to banish the haze. As the bitter liquid burned its way down I felt the first stirrings of clarity. But time was slipping away.

I arrived at the Greystorm office with barely a minute to spare. My heart pounded as I shuffled through papers, trying to pull myself together.

The caffeine kicked in fully and I forced a calm smile, reminding myself this was just another day.

At 8:03 an orderly entered, escorting Jake into the room. He wore a hospital gown and a paper-thin bathrobe, both sterile and unyielding.

Bands of fresh bandages wrapped around his wrists and legs reminded me of the night I'd first met him. Though tall, perhaps once towering, Jake hunched a bit and now stood roughly six-foot-one—still imposing but diminished.

His hair surprised me. Thick and mostly intact, buzzed an inch on top and closely shaved on the sides, it was the kind of neat uniformity I envied without wanting to admit it.

According to his file he was fifty-nine—but age hadn't been kind. Deep, swollen bags hung beneath his eyes, shadows heavy and permanent.

His cheeks and nose were blotchy, red from some mild Rosacea flare-up—or maybe from something harder to pin down. I suspected alcohol might be a factor.

The orderly was a large African-American man named Carl. He reminded me of a football player both in build and demeanor, complete with a full beard.

Carl nodded to me. "I'll be back in an hour, okay, Doc?" His deep voice rumbled through the quiet room.

"Thanks, Carl," I replied, my voice steadier than I felt. As Carl closed the door behind him his eyes locked briefly on Jake who seemed almost unaware of him.

I smiled and extended my hand. "Nice to see you again, Jake —this time not in an emergency. I'm Dr. Samuel Lucas, but please, call me Sam."

Jake's eyes flicked to my hand, then back to my face with a blankness that made me question if he even recognized me. Finally he reached out, his grip weak, his handshake limp as if I was holding onto a ghost.

"Would you like to sit down?" I asked gently.

His eyebrow quirked. "Aren't you going to put me on a couch?"

I chuckled, masking the tension. "Only if you want to. You could sit right here." I gestured to the chair beside me.

Jake stared at it as if it were some foreign object. After a pause he nodded. "Alright." He shifted carefully, adjusting the thin robe that refused to cover his legs properly.

"May I call you Jake?"

He hesitated before nodding. "I don't mind." His voice was low, wary, eyes darting. "What I mind is this robe. Could I get a pair of pants?"

"I'll see what I can do."

Seated across from him, I pulled out my leather portfolio— soft brown leather opening like a book with a cover that snapped shut to keep patient notes private. I cleared my throat. "I understand you've been having some troubles."

"That's what they tell me," Jake replied, his tone flat.

"Who tells you that?"

"The doctors, the nurses… even the orderlies. There was a man from my security company who came by—said all they wanted was for me to get well."

"Is that a bad thing?"

Jake's expression darkened. "You all think I'm crazy."

"How does that make you feel?"

"Like you think I'm crazy," he grinned bitterly. "Dr. Benning asked me how I felt. Are you just going to repeat all of his questions?"

I snapped my portfolio shut and traced the silver metal trim with my finger, buying time. Tension prickled like static.

Shifting tactics I said, "Okay, what do you want to talk about?"

He studied me, then said, "You like football?"

"Sure. Football works." I allowed myself a genuine smile.

Our conversation was more one-sided than not—I talked, trying to draw him out. His coworkers were right: Jake was tight-lipped, closed off. But football was safe. Impersonal. We talked about the latest games, the teams we liked or loathed. I wasn't a fanatic, but I knew enough stats to keep the thread alive.

Slowly Jake became animated. His eyes brightened. A spark, brief and fragile, but there. It felt like progress.

Fifty minutes later a sharp knock rattled the door frame.

"Doc," Carl's booming voice filtered through, muffled, "you 'bout done?"

"Just a minute, Carl." I stood and extended my hand toward Jake.

Surprise flickered in his eyes. "But we didn't talk about why I'm here."

"No, I suppose not," I said, with a lighthearted tone. "But anytime you want to I'm here to listen. We have another session tomorrow."

Jake's gaze flickered suspiciously, then rested on the clock. It was 8:57.

"Yeah, besides, I've got to sleep."

"How is it, Jake? Sleeping during the day?"

He shrugged, eyes downcast. "You get used to it."

The day's brief spark of life dimmed as we approached the door where Carl waited.

"Hey, Jake," Carl asked, "how'd it go?"

"Alright," Jake muttered.

"We talked a lot of football," I added.

"Yeah? Jake likes that. Don't ya, Jake?"

"I guess," Jake said with a reluctant nod.

Carl led him out. I sat down, drained my now-cold coffee and chewed a Tums to settle my stomach.

This first session was just a beginning. I'd cracked his shell if only slightly. Maybe I'd coax him to open further next time.

I leaned back and stared up at the ceiling shadows—deep, shifting shapes that seemed to crawl across the plaster like creatures just beyond sight. I understood Jake's fear. Anyone could mistake those shadows for lurking threats.

I caught myself gazing at the corner where darkness pooled, turning it over in my mind.

Glancing at the clock—9:15—I jolted. Had I really been sitting, lost in those shadows for ten minutes?

Shaking off the eerie spell I grabbed my things and hurried out, determined not to be late for my 9:30 appointment at my private practice.

I drove faster than usual, the weight of the morning pressing down on me. Bursting through the door of my office, papers and laptop bag slung over my shoulder, I paused only to catch my breath.

Anne was already at her desk, her British precision apparent in the way she organized the space. She looked up and grinned.

"Good morning, Doctor," she said, her accent drawing out the word like a melody—'doctuh.'

"Morning, Anne." I glanced toward the waiting room, desperate for a moment to steady myself. "Is Mr. Simmons here?"

"No, he's running a tad behind," she replied with a sly smile. "As it appears, are you."

I blushed. "I got held up," I stammered. How could I explain that I'd been stuck staring at shadows in another office?

Anne's lips pursed with mock severity. "It is rather difficult to tell patients to be punctual when you are late yourself, Doctor."

"Of course, Anne," I sighed. "I'll do better tomorrow. I've got a new patient at Greystorm I'm seeing every day. I'll leave earlier."

"Veddy good," she said, polite but unyielding.

I walked past the row of chairs into my office, feeling the gray skies pressing down like a weight through the window's dull, clouded view.

Just then, my desk phone buzzed. I pressed the intercom. "Yes?"

"Dr. Lucas," Anne's voice came clear, "Mr. Simmons is here."

Simmons has been one of my most enduring patients—a prisoner in a cycle that seems endless. At twenty-eight he lived with his mother, planning to break free, apart from her suffocating hold.

But every time the thought became real, the guilt crushed him, triggering crippling anxiety attacks that tethered him even tighter to her. A decade passed. Now, at thirty-eight, I saw no signs he'll ever muster the courage to change.

This is the lifeblood of therapy: to listen intently, to weigh each word, to probe beneath the surface and gently suggest alternative paths.

I float in the currents of hope and despair that swirl around those who walk through my door—searching for light in their personal labyrinths.

The hour with Simmons slipped away like sand through my fingers, then the next, and the next—each session blurring into the last. By 12:30, the familiar burn in my chest started whispering warnings. I popped one of the hidden Tums, then another, but the gnawing acid pain clung stubbornly until five o'clock, a constant reminder of the emotional toll of the day.

It had been a 'good enough' day—no breakthroughs, no heroic vows to claw out of neurosis. Just the steady grind of people circling their own wounds.

Driving home my thoughts flickered to a late-week round of golf, maybe a chance to escape the weight of it all.

Pulling into the driveway, Rueben ran to meet my car. His small arms immediately enveloped me in a fierce, joyous embrace. It was Tuesday—Rachel was watching over her little brother until I arrived.

Marcie sacrifices long Mondays and Tuesdays on the parenting front convinced I'll handle the cooking. Monday nights? I can whip up a decent meal. Tuesday? I admit defeat and call for delivery.

As soon as I stepped in Rueben bounced excitedly, shouting, "Pizza Hut!"

"Dad," Rachel called out, breezing past me toward the door, planting a swift kiss on my cheek. "I'm going to Jennifer's."

"Are you eating there?" I asked, watching her dash out.

"Yeah, I'm fine!" she called back, the door clicking closed behind her.

"Pizza Hut!" Rueben pleaded again, spinning in anticipation.

I shook my head, trying to mask the exhaustion. "Not tonight, Rueben. I'm… not really in the mood for Pizza Hut."

His hopeful face immediately fell but before the sadness could settle a new spark ignited. "Domino's!" he yelled, eyes brightening again.

"Come on, big guy," I said, a grin creeping in. "Tonight's Man's Night."

"Man's Night!" he roared with delight—six years old clinging to the promise of grown-up adventures even if he didn't quite know what that meant. "What are we gonna do for Man's Night, Dad?"

I chose my words carefully as I would in a session. "We don't have to do what the girls want for once."

"Yeah!" Rueben cheered.

"And we can get whatever we want for dinner."

"Yeah! Domino's!"

Pizza still reigned supreme.

"We can even hit the food court at the mall," I suggested, trying to steer him toward plans that suited me.

"The mall? We're going to the mall?" His victory dance resumed, full throttle.

"Get your coat," I directed.

He twirled for the finale and grabbed his jacket like a prize.

The drive to Rockaway Mall was a familiar journey into an endless maze of commercial excess—a concrete jungle, an ode to capitalism's ceaseless appetite.

Inside bright lights and endless shops blurred past: coffee stands, sneaker boutiques, and the cavernous food court called FoodWorks.

Rueben wasted no time selecting his favorite pizza slice from the Italian kiosk while I settled for a steak sandwich from Steak Escape.

After our meal we wandered together, a father and son on a small adventure. At the toy store Rueben's excitement shifted gears as he reminded me Hanukkah was just a month away.

It was a rare pleasure, just listening to his concerns over trivial battles—as a father might, offering only gentle affirmations, no attempts at solutions.

By 8:00 PM we picked up Rachel on the way home. The familiar routine resumed: putting the kids to bed, pouring a drink —a splash of whiskey over ice chased with Maalox—and then turning to Jake's case study until drowsiness claimed me well before Marcie's late return.

But sleep found me restless.

I dreamt a strange hospital held me captive.

Its walls whispered of long ago—nearly a century past. I moved sluggishly down endless halls, as if dragging through molasses. Two nurses passed—dressed in stiff white gowns and caps that recalled nuns more than clinicians. Gas lamps flickered casting uncertain shadows on decayed walls and grimy tile floors. Overhead mold spread like a slow poison.

From a shattered green room came a chorus of moans—a symphony of misery rising from sickly men lined in beds. Their suffering was vast and raw, a living orchestra of desperation.

The stench was unbearable—a nauseating blend of urine, ammonia, and feces. Yet beneath the rot was something else: the unmistakable, suffocating odor of despair.

This was no mere hospital. It was a prison for the shattered minds, a madhouse where patients were tied down, bound in straitjackets and left to rot.

In the room's corner a figure sat on a stool wrapped in canvas and leather restraints. His head hung low, but the familiarity struck me like a blow.

Jake Hurd—looking exactly as he did in my office.

"Jake?" I whispered. "What are you doing here?"

"Don't you know, Sam?" His voice was soft, resigned. "I'm crazy."

The moans swelled into a chorus as I surveyed the room. "I have to get you out of here."

"Why?" Jake asked calmly. "Isn't this where I belong?"

"You're not crazy. Not like them," I said as I unbuckled his restraints.

"I'm crazy in a way you don't understand," he said with a chilling smile. "Yet."

Suddenly the patients stirred. The straitjackets slipped away, and the wild-eyed men rose—stumbling toward us like predators on the hunt.

Jake, still bound, remained unnervingly calm.

"We have to get out now!" I urged, terror tightening my throat as the mass of deranged figures closed in.

"They're not the ones to fear," Jake mumbled.

"What do you mean?" My palms slick with sweat, heart pounding.

From the floor a dark viscous liquid spread—a sickly black stain that surged forward like a wave of oil. I tried to scream but no sound escaped my throat.

The substance swallowed Jake whole—encasing him in a suffocating, rubbery veil that clung tightly, veins bulging on his neck as he gasped for air. In a final desperate breath, the black tide surged down his throat.

The madmen's screams exploded around me.

Another black puddle lapped at my feet, then climbed my legs, slick and cold. I screamed, joining the chorus of madness.

I jolted awake, thrashing wildly as if clawing away an unseen monster.

A voice pierced the darkness. "What?"

I fumbled with the bed sheets as Marcie flicked on the light.

I was back in my room in pajamas, and the grotesque chorus of lunatics had vanished.

"Are you all right?" Marcie's voice was breathless.

I struggled to steady my breathing. "Yeah, yeah. Just... a nightmare. I'm fine."

"You were screaming. You woke me."

"Sorry. I just need a drink."

She exhaled deeply. "Can you have it downstairs? I've got to get up early with the kids."

"Yeah. Of course." I swung my legs over the bed, stiff and uneasy.

As I descended to my den the dream's haunting images twisted in my mind. I immediately turned on a lamp. My hands trembled as I poured a scotch, the amber liquid swallowing the shadows within.

I finally sank into my recliner, eyes fluttering shut with the light still burning—a lone sentinel against the dark.

7. WILLING TO SHARE

T he next day, the nightmare still lingered heavily as I stepped into Greystorm.

My nerves fluttered with unease—half-expecting to see Jake dragged in still bound by the straitjacket from my dream.

But reality steadied me. Carl escorted him through the door, wrapped not in restraints but in the rumpled bathrobe he'd worn yesterday. I made a silent note to arrange better clothing for him.

We fell back into the usual rhythm trading words cautiously—sports scores, weather complaints, mundane scraps of conversation that Jake clung to.

But beneath it all I wanted to speak about the nightmare haunting my mind, to crack open the dark door and face whatever lurked behind it.

When Jake left, I didn't return to my office. Instead, I headed to my appointment with Janice Franklin, my therapist for the past two decades.

Janice—sixty-something, an earth mother with roots deep in the hippie sixties, feminist seventies, and New Age eighties—was a steady beacon in the storm of my life. A psychiatrist by trade, but a damn good one.

After I recounted the dream, she murmured, "Interesting."

"Interesting?" I shot back, biting back impatience. "That's all you've got? You sure you're not just humoring me?"

A soft grin curved her lips. "Not at all. Lately I've had a surge of patients claiming they 'see things in the dark'—visions, shadows, that sort of thing."

I blinked, incredulous. "You're kidding."

She raised a hand solemnly. "Honest. I'm wondering if this is some strange side effect of the new millennium or Y2K panic."

Since it was the later part of 1999 the world was in a panic that the computers would all breakdown because they could not work once the year ended in 00. The apocalyptic media frenzy predicted planes falling from the sky, power grids failing, societal collapse.

"Can we stay focused on my dream?" I pressed.

Janice pursed her lips. "Maybe it's just your mind replaying vivid details about Jake. Sometimes the brain just throws up images without deeper meaning."

"That's no help."

She shrugged. "Sometimes a cigar is just a cigar."

"Thank you, Dr. Freud," I muttered, already restless.

We circled the topic but ended nowhere. I left her office still clutching that uneasy feeling like a stone in my gut.

Back in my office I wasted no time. I found a local men's store and ordered a dozen jumpsuits for Jake, wanting to preserve his dignity the best I could.

The following morning, a cold gray filtered the world through the car windshield as I drove to Greystorm. The air sharper, clinging with a wintry chill.

At eight sharp a knock echoed on my door and Carl ushered Jake in. He occupied his usual chair, alert and more focused than before—the reduction in his medications already making its mark.

Jake wore one of the new jumpsuits. When I asked how they felt he replied dryly, "A lot better. Nice not having my butt hang out for everyone to see."

His joke caught me off guard and laughter bubbled uncontrollably from my chest.

He smiled, nodding. "You're in a good mood today, Sam."

"Yeah. But I'd rather talk about what you're feeling. Or we could stick to sports and small talk if you're not ready."

I held my breath. This felt like a crossroads—the moment a patient sees their doctor not as an interrogator but as an ally.

Jake's gaze bore into me, intense and searching.

"We don't have to," I quickly added, easing back into my chair keeping my expression calm. "Only if you want."

"You're different from Dr. Benning," Jake said quietly. "He just asked questions like he wanted to find a problem and crush it." His face softened, a flicker of relief. "But you... actually seem like you want to know."

"I do, Jake. As much as you want to share. If you want to tackle a problem, I'm here. Otherwise we're just two guys talking."

He considered my words. The silence thickened—it was so quiet I could hear the muffled footsteps in the hall, the hum of the heating system. If anything was to be said, Jake had to speak.

Finally he dropped his chin and locked eyes with mine. "You really want to know? The entire story? Everything?"

"Whatever you want to tell me," I said softly. "I'm listening."

He nodded, swallowed hard. After a pause he began, "I'll tell you what happened. You can decide if I'm crazy or not."

I asked gently, "Do you think you're crazy, Jake?"

A deep sigh escaped him as if years of bottled-up frustration fell loose. "Sometimes I thought I was. But not now. I'm sane. It's a part of my life that's crazy."

"You're safe here, Jake."

He shook his head. "Safe? I'm not safe anywhere. None of us are." He glanced away, not wanting to meet my eyes. "You'll think I'm raving."

"I've heard raving before," I said, leaning forward with elbows on knees. "Most people I work with aren't insane, just troubled. When desperate, people do things that seem irrational—even destructive."

I sat back letting the words sink in. "Talking helps sometimes. It shrinks problems down, makes them manageable. That's what I want to offer you, Jake—a chance to see your story from another angle."

He looked at me, searching. "Are you willing to share my problem with me?"

"Of course," I replied firmly.

He nodded as if deciding. "Then I have to start at the beginning."

As he spoke I felt the journey ahead—a path twisting into darkness I might never emerge from. A story I wasn't sure I was ready to hear, but couldn't turn away from either.

1960

8. PEGGY

I n the summer of 1960 America stood at a crossroads—stepping out from the sunlit innocence of the fifties into a decade charged with possibility, promise, and just a hint of unease.

At the Democratic National Convention that year the young and charismatic John F. Kennedy ignited imaginations, his youthful energy a beacon to a new generation hungry for change.

Meanwhile, rock 'n' roll and doo-wop filled the airwaves and seventeen-year-old Jake Hurd felt the pulse of it all throbbing in his veins.

Jake had long carried a secret thrill: his shortwave radio. Fascinated by the magic of voices crackling out from unknown places he taught himself electronics with a soldering gun in hand, piecing together a ham radio by the time he was sixteen. He'd passed his novice license exam on a dare, proud of the certificate that hung above his cluttered workbench.

By day, Jake kept himself grounded in the small town routine. To save for college he worked evenings and weekends at the local Gulf station, pumping gas and patching tires.

Mr. Benson, the owner, was a gruff but kind man who appreciated Jake's knack for fixing what others deemed broken. Yet the job left Jake with hands forever smeared in oil and grime —a fact that gnawed at him more than he admitted.

Peggy wasn't fond of it either.

Peggy Clune was Jake's sweetheart, a term from a time when the word still held the weight of quiet devotion.

They'd grown up side by side on Main Street in Mendham, New Jersey, and since dating in their senior year, she'd become his world.

They graduated in 1959—Jake with a head full of dreams, Peggy with aspirations beyond their sleepy towns.

Between odd jobs and mowing lawns, Jake scraped together enough cash to buy his pride and joy: a battered 1952 Lincoln. It was a black behemoth, solid and heavy, a four-ton relic with a V8 engine that growled to life like a restless beast.

The car still carried itself with understated dignity—its large, bowed fenders and rounded roofline a nod to a bygone elegance. Like a grand dame past her prime, the Lincoln held on to class, even as her paint chipped and chrome dulled.

At twenty-five cents a gallon, the Lincoln guzzled gas like a thirsty beast, but Jake could still pour five dollars into the tank and drive nearly a hundred seventy miles—a luxury for a working kid on a budget.

Mendham was quintessential small-town America, far from the bustle of nearby Morristown—the latter's gleaming Bambergers with its shiny escalators a world apart from Main Street's cluster of mom-and-pop shops: the hardware store, the ice cream parlor, the newspaper stand.

Jake's father, Alan Hurd, owned the town's pharmacy—a business passed down through generations—yet he regarded Jake's year off with cautious hope. Alan expected his son to enroll in college come fall, to study pharmacy and eventually inherit the family store.

Peggy's dreams pulled her in a different direction.

Raised on a modest farm between Mendham and neighboring Chester, she rode the bus every day into Morristown to attend beauty school.

She wanted more than the dirt and toil of rural life—a better, cleaner future. She scolded Jake often about his blackened fingernails and the faint but stubborn smell of gasoline that clung to his skin.

"I don't want you holding me unless those nails are clean," she'd say, voice narrow with longing and impatience.

So each night Jake labored over his hands in the bathroom, scrubbing with gritty Lava soap until his skin was raw, brushing beneath his nails until they shone. A ritual born of love—and pressure.

"Jake," Peggy snapped one evening, her nasal Jersey accent sharp with frustration, "that gas station job—there's no future there. You'll never have time to study like that. You need something clean. Something that lets you breathe."

On his nineteenth birthday, Jake went the extra mile. Hours before Peggy came over for dinner, he took a long bath, washing his hair twice and scrubbing every place grease might hide until his hands gleamed as if new.

Peggy joined his family for dinner, and his mother had baked a cake, the scent of vanilla and frosting filling the small house where his mother and father sat around the table, laughter mixing with the clink of silverware.

After dessert, with the summer sky spilling indigo twilight, Jake and Peggy piled into the Lincoln for a drive.

"I know a spot," Peggy said with a sly smile. "Bernard's Mountain. Best view for miles around."

Jake knew exactly what that meant—a quiet place for couples to steal a few precious moments.

He eased the Lincoln up the winding road, forcing himself to keep the speedometer steady, well below sixty despite the roar of the V8 beneath the hood.

At the summit, he killed the engine. The car's radio crackled softly, murmuring Elvis Presley's soulful "Are You Lonesome Tonight?" across the stillness.

Jake reached for her, but Peggy pulled back, eyes sparkling with mischief. "Present first," she giggled.

She handed him a plain box stamped with the Bamberger's logo. Jake peeled back the paper to reveal a silk tie, striped diagonally in deep blues and reds.

"They call it an Oxford," she explained, "like the college in England. It's real silk." Her voice was a mix of pride and hope.

"It's beautiful, Peggy," Jake breathed, leaning in to kiss her tenderly.

Her laughter bubbled up, bright and daring. "You might need it. Look what I found." She produced a carefully clipped newspaper ad, the edges sharp and neat:

Security Officer
If you have a D/L, a High School Diploma, and a car,

you can enter the exciting world of security.
Up to $2.00 p/h; nights and weekends available.
Call 555-1200
Security Information Systems

"Security?" Jake's forehead creased. "What's that about?"

Peggy's eyes shone with possibility. "A night guard job. Clean work, Jake. You work the overnight shift, and you can go to college during the day—maybe Garden State University, right in state. Two dollars an hour—that's double what Old Man Benson pays you. And no grease on your hands."

Her fingers twitched at the buttons of her blouse, slowly and deliberately.

Jake's breath caught. "Peggy—what are you doing?"

She smiled, mysterious and sultry. One button slipped free... then another. The soft swell of skin at her chest came into view beneath the fabric, and Jake's eyes darted quickly around the nearly deserted parking lot before settling back.

She slid his hand into hers, pressing it lightly. "I love clean hands, Jake. They don't feel dirty... not near me."

"Oh, Peggy..." Jake whispered, heart hammering.

Their lips met again, urgent yet hesitant. Peggy's fingers found the clasp of her bra at her back, undoing it with a deft flick. She let him feel, guiding his hands beneath soft cloth, murmuring, "Easy. Be gentle."

Her head tilted back, breath coming in uneven gasps.

"Peggy," Jake groaned, lips trailing along her neck.

Suddenly she pushed his hands away and then his face, pausing their kisses.

"Calm down," she panted. "Just... let me lead, okay? It's your birthday. I promise it'll be one you won't forget."

Her hand slipped into his lap, deft fingers finding the opening in his pants. His pulse thundered in his ears as she reached inside, exploring. "Give me your handkerchief, Jake."

Hands fumbling, Jake pulled the white cloth from his back pocket and handed it over.

She kissed his palm with a whisper of warning. "If anyone finds out…"

"I won't tell," Jake breathed, his voice hoarse with emotion.

Peggy smiled, dark and knowing. "Good. Now, you just let me know before anything happens. If any of that stuff gets on me—I could end up with a baby."

Ten frantic, charged minutes passed. It was not quite like a Hollywood love scene, but raw, clumsy, and real. She covered him with the handkerchief when it was over, holding it tight as his groans faded into labored breaths.

"Hush now," she whispered in his ear. "Someone might hear and call the cops."

The night air was thick with heavy silence as Jake tried to steady his racing heart, the weight of the moment settling deep inside.

Peggy straightened, buttoning her blouse, cheeks flushed. "Happy Birthday, Jake."

She handed him back the handkerchief, now slightly stained, and leaned close.

"Maybe with that nice clean job, you'll get to touch my girls more often."

The morning sun spilled through Jake's bedroom window but he barely noticed. His mind buzzed with a restlessness he couldn't shake.

By mid-morning he was already spinning excuses to Mr. Benson, careful to keep his tone casual, noncommittal, while his heart pounded with a mix of nerves and excitement.

He needed to get to Morristown—the Security Information Systems offices—before the day slipped away.

Wearing his new tie he drove to the address. The building was a far cry from the sleek, modern images Jake imagined. It sat squat on South Street, an aging structure showing its years: cracked paint peeling from the walls, dirt streaked corners, and an air of neglect hanging thick in the stained reception room.

In front of a pair of closed office doors a woman sat behind a small beat-up desk, chewing gum with a distracted laziness. Her fingers hunted slowly and deliberately across the keys of a battered typewriter, the clack of each letter painfully loud in the quiet space.

Without looking up, she slid a stack of mimeographed forms toward Jake.

He settled at a rickety desk, one leg barely holding it upright, and began filling them out. The uneven wobble made him grab for steadiness more than once.

After finishing he deliberately smoothed out his driver's license and vintage Mendham High School diploma—his only trophies —and handed them over.

She rose and vanished through one of the doors.

Jake's gaze flicked to a closet in the corner, the door forced open just enough to reveal a chaotic jungle of dark blue uniforms, tightly packed and cocooned in dry cleaner bags. They looked official—police-like—but the dust on the bags dulled their once crisp authority.

The secretary returned, resuming her painstaking typing with all the urgency of a snail on a sidewalk, barely acknowledging his presence.

Minutes stretched unbearably.

Finally a broad-shouldered man emerged from the back office. His tailored shirt and polished shoes couldn't hide the power restrained in his thick arms and imposing height.

Standing, Jake offered his hand which was met with a firm grip.

"Good morning. Dan Hurley," he announced, the smile broad and surprisingly warm.

"Jake Hurd, sir," Jake replied, voice steady despite the fluttering in his chest.

"Sir? Manners, I like that. Very important in this line of work," Hurley said, pulling open the door to his office. "Come on in."

Inside chaos ruled. Stacks of papers teetered on every surface threatening a collapse. Hurley took his place behind the cluttered desk with the calm certainty of a man who thrived in disorder.

"This company's new, Mr. Hurd," Hurley began, tone firm but fair. "I was a cop before this. Three rules I believe in: timeliness, thoroughness, discipline. Self-discipline, meaning you're on the job whether you feel ready or not. You follow?"

"Yes, sir."

"Good. You're a student I see. Education's the best way for a man to improve himself. When can you start?"

Jake's throat tightened. "I... I could start immediately, sir."

Hurley nodded approvingly. "Good, then. There's an opening on the midnight shift at Murray Hill. Can you do tomorrow night? Midnight start?"

Jake's pulse quickened; the chance was real. "Yes, sir. I can."

"Alright. We start new guys at a buck-fifty an hour."

Jake blinked, surprised. "But the ad said two dollars per hour —"

"That's 'up to' two dollars," Hurley cut in smoothly. "You work your way up. We're growing—soon enough, that'll rise to a buck sixty-five, easy enough."

Jake did the math fast: sixty dollars a week wasn't bad. Considering his expenses were minimal—gas and the occasional date with Peggy—it suddenly felt like an opportunity, not just a job.

Hurley handed back Jake's ID and diploma. "Got a few minutes? I want to show you the site."

Jake nodded, eager.

Hurley sprang from his chair, snagged a sports coat buried beneath piles of paperwork. "You'll need a uniform," he reminded as they made their way to the reception.

The typist remained lost in her languid typing, oblivious.

Opening the overstuffed closet Hurley asked sizes.

"Thirty-two waist, thirty-four inseam. Medium shirt, long sleeves."

"You're a skinny one," Hurley smiled. "Need to put some meat on those bones, Mr. Hurd."

He rummaged through the clutter, pulling out multiple shirts, pants, a jacket, and a hat with a badge on it. The shirts all bore a patch with a green anvil emblem embroidered beneath 'Security Information Systems.'

"You'll need the pants hemmed but length's good for cuffs," Hurley said, placing the cap on Jake's head. It fit perfectly.

"Hey, Stan!" Hurley called out.

A flushed, balding man appeared from the only other door. "Yeah, Dan?"

"This is Jake Hurd. I'm taking him to BT&T Research to meet the captain. Can you handle applicants while I'm out?"

Stan extended a lazy handshake. "Stan Hanover. Partner. Glad to have you aboard."

He shifted his tone low and led Hurley away from the secretary. "So, Dan, what are we going to do about Miss Trilby?"

Hurley smirked, nodding at the oblivious woman. "Do?"

"She's a terrible secretary," Stan murmured.

"Oh, she's not that bad," Hurley said, voice dripping with amusement. "And she's easy on the eyes, Stan."

Miss Trilby glanced up, smiled, and shrugged, unaware—or unwilling—to admit the exchange.

"I'll be back in an hour," Hurley said breezily and stepped outside. Jake followed to his car to stash the uniform.

"Is that your car, Mr. Hurd?"

"Yes, sir."

"Good choice. Dependable. We'll take mine," Hurley said, striding ahead and sliding open the passenger door.

Jake's breath caught.

"Like it?" Hurley's pride was obvious.

"That's a fifty-nine Caddy!" Jake exclaimed, staring wide-eyed at the gleaming black luxury sedan. It stretched longer than his thoughts, its sharp chrome grille and sweeping rear fins dazzling under the summer sun.

"You know your cars, Mr. Hurd. Get in."

Even in Mendham, new Cadillacs were rare. This one shone with layers of wax, the chrome reflecting every stray ray of sunshine.

The smooth ride swallowed potholes with ease as they cruised down South Street.

Suddenly, Jake's eyes locked on a man walking nearby. Suit and tie, but his coat slipped from one shoulder, swung carelessly by a finger. His dark brown skin and tight black curls made him stand out sharply in Jake's world.

It was the first time Jake had seen a black person in real life—a presence far more vivid than the flickering grayish shadows on his television screen. The man's skin glowed like rich chocolate, so unlike anything Jake had imagined.

Hurley snorted beside him, misreading Jake's gaze. "The coloreds," he said dismissively. "They should stay in Newark, but some are moving into Morristown now. Guess it's inevitable. I would never hire one. They'd be sleeping on duty."

Jake felt a knot tighten in his stomach but said nothing.

The ride continued, Jake's eyes tracing the gleaming dashboard as they drove.

Twenty minutes later they pulled up at a sprawling compound guarded by iron gates and marked by a large sign proclaiming: Bell Telephone and Telegraph Research.

"Take a good look, Mr. Hurd," Hurley said as they approached the small guardhouse. "This place has won more Nobel Prizes than any other company in the world."

A uniformed guard recognized Hurley, stepping aside with respect. They parked near a large brick building, one of at least five on the campus.

"This is very advanced technology," Hurley boasted. "You interested in science, Jake?"

"I like to tinker," Jake admitted, "You know, build stuff."

"You'll fit right in."

Inside the main entrance, the atmosphere shifted. A mix of urgency and quiet brilliance hung thick. Behind a grand, polished desk, uniformed guards stood alert.

An older man with a crown of white hair approached and shook Hurley's hand.

"What have you got for me, Dan?" he asked.

"The last man for your midnight crew, Jim. Jake Hurd, our newest employee."

Jim scrutinized Jake carefully, eyes sharp.

"He'll do. Can he start tonight?"

"Whoa, Jim! He's got to get his pants hemmed first."

Jim's voice dimmed. "Dan, you know we're short-handed."

"Tomorrow, I promise, right Jake?"

Jake nodded.

"Fine, that'll have to do," Jim sighed. "Show him around. I'll get badges."

They signed in, clipped paper badges to their jackets, and set off.

Down cluttered hallways, Jake absorbed a chaotic symphony of sounds: brisk conversations, chemical scents, whispered discoveries.

Two men in lab coats passed, debating the contents of a delicate glass beaker. Green light glowed behind a small door; Jake peered through and saw an oscilloscope humming softly.

Further along, a lone mathematician stared at a blackboard dense with cryptic equations.

Once they stepped outside, Hurley gestured at the massive buildings.

"Bell Labs employs thousands. BT&T Research spends twelve percent of its budget on new projects. Every call helps science advance. Your job is to keep it safe."

Jake swallowed hard, the weight of responsibility heavy. "I'll do my best, sir."

"That's what I like to hear." Hurley pointed to a small, plain door at the back. "The night crew enters through there. That's your HQ."

Back in the Cadillac, they headed toward Morristown.

On the drive, Jake felt a growing sense that this was no ordinary job. This was the start of something bigger.

9. JAKE'S FIRST NIGHT

J ake gripped the wheel of his car as he drove home, a strange tightness gnawing at him.

After cruising in the spacious Cadillac, the interior of his own car felt cramped, like the walls were closing in. The contrast unsettled him, making him keenly aware of the narrow confines around him.

When he reached home, his mom practically bounced with excitement at the news of his new job.

She hurried up the stairs, returning almost immediately with her sewing kit—a large, battered metal cookie tin filled with threads and needles. She proceeded to hem his pants carefully, beaming at him like he'd just brought home a trophy.

That evening at dinner, Jake told his father about the job. The man was usually taciturn, but something softened in his eyes as he listened to Jake's plan: going to college during the day and working nights to pay his way.

Alan Hurd nodded slowly. "That's good thinking, son. Planning it all out smartly."

Jake shrugged. "It was Peggy's idea, actually."

"She's a clever girl, that one—reminds me of your mother back in the day." Alan winked at his wife, who returned the gesture with a shy smile.

After dinner, Jake's father—reserved and distant most of the time—surprised him by patting his back gently before retreating to his pipe and newspaper.

Jake couldn't remember the last time his father had said something kind to him. The moment lingered with a quiet but powerful warmth.

As twilight draped itself over the town, Jake slipped into his full guard uniform and headed to Peggy's house.

The little farmhouse was always noisy and busy, with a family of eight children of varying ages, Peggy being the oldest.

The younger children spotted Jake and burst out, "Jake's a policeman! Jake's a policeman!" Their shrill cries filled the evening air as Peggy's mother, a stout woman in a simple homemade dress, peeked out and gasped softly, "My stars."

Peggy's father, thin and unshaven, shook Jake's hand with something like newfound respect.

Peggy came bounding down the stairs, eyes sparkling with pride and excitement. For a moment she stood behind her parents, cheeks flushed and dreamy.

"You did it! You got the job! When do you start?" she asked breathlessly.

"Tomorrow at midnight," Jake said, his smile wide. "One-fifty an hour at Bell's research lab over in Murray Hill."

Her father nodded approvingly. "That's a fine place—I've driven by it myself."

"Big place," Peggy's mom chimed in, "lots of important folks work there."

"We have to celebrate!" Peggy said suddenly, grabbing his hand. "Mom, Dad, we're going out for ice cream!"

The pair piled into Jake's Lincoln, the car gliding smoothly through the quiet streets. Peggy reached out and rubbed his leg, a touch light and electric. Jake felt warmth rush up the back of his neck.

"Oh, Jake, you look so handsome in that uniform," she sighed. "I think Daddy's impressed."

"So, where to?" Jake asked, grinning. "Dairy Queen?"

"No, silly," Peggy whispered, her voice dropping as her eyes grew dreamy again. "Bernard's Mountain."

The mountain air was sharp and cool when they arrived, the world muted beneath a blanket of stars. Peggy slipped off her bra and practically pounced on Jake, yanking off his hat and pressing a kiss so fierce it stole his breath.

His hands touched her, and she gave no resistance. He moved from her breasts down lower to bring his hand up under her skirt.

As Jake caressed her silken underwear, she pushed herself back with her arms fully extended, gasping for breath.

"No, Jake, we have to control ourselves," she whispered, cheeks flushed and hair wild in the twilight. Her blouse disheveled, bra shifting awkwardly, but her eyes held a fierce resolve.

"I just want to do for you—like you did for me on my birthday," Jake panted, aroused to the point of pain.

Peggy laughed softly, shaking her head.

"What?" Jake demanded, bewildered.

"That's sweet, Jake," she said, pressing a gentle kiss to his lips as she smoothed her clothes. "But girls don't do that like boys do."

"You don't?" His voice cracked with uncertainty.

"No, silly. We just get... excited. That's all." She reddened, embarrassed. "Momma told me. She said sex is fun for boys, but for girls it just gets you in trouble."

"That makes no sense!"

"Well, then blame the Lord," Peggy shrugged. "He made it that way. We have to stop—for tonight."

"Can you at least touch me again?" Jake pleaded.

"That was your birthday! If I did that every time, you wouldn't respect me," she whispered.

"I would."

She slapped his knee playfully. "I know you're worked up—I shouldn't have let things go this far. Seeing you... in that uniform, it just did something to me." She reached forward to adjust his tie, her fingers brushing his skin. "When I saw you walk downstairs, I just wanted—I don't know..." She giggled nervously. "I'm so bad."

"We love each other, Peggy. That's all that matters," Jake whispered.

"That's fine, but it's a sin. We have to be married for... those things." Her eyes darkened with anger. "I don't want to be like my momma—she had me when she was nineteen. If Daddy hadn't inherited the farm, we'd have nothing."

She turned away quickly, wiping a tear before Jake could reach for her hand.

"We can be something," she insisted. "You're going to college. I know you don't want to be a pharmacist, no matter what your dad thinks."

"I know," Jake mumbled.

"But I've got just one more year at beauty school, then I'm done waitressing at the luncheonette. You go to college, I'll work at a hairdresser's and maybe when we're twenty-one we can get married. I've got it all figured out."

Jake pulled her close. "I love you, Peggy."

"And I love you." She hesitated, voice cracking slightly. "And I understand... about men. I know you need... things. But it's got to be special. If I did that every night, soon you'd want more. Then we'd *have* to get married, and you'd be stuck working for your dad."

Jake sighed and thought back to his summers behind the pharmacy counter—bored, restless, his dreams elsewhere.

"I guess you're right."

"Of course I am." She leaned in, kissing him fully and tenderly. "Now, come on. Let's go get that ice cream."

The next night, precisely at eleven-thirty, Jake eased his car down the long, winding driveway toward the stark, imposing complex of Bell Telephone and Telegraph Research.

That morning he'd told Old Man Benson the news—he'd landed another job. Benson didn't show an ounce of anger; if anything, he just nodded knowingly. He understood Jake's ambition and knew the money would be better elsewhere.

But that day Jake hadn't rested.

Attempting to nap was futile—his mind refused to quiet. Peggy's plans haunted him, her grand design for their lives like a cage tightening around his own ambitions.

She had everything mapped out: marriage, a future, stability. But what if his dreams didn't fit into her blueprint?

The thought twisted something deep inside him.

He already knew how disappointed his father would be to hear he wasn't interested in the pharmacy business.

Finally at ten-thirty, he pulled on his blue uniform and stepped out into the chill night. He'd found a shortcut—back roads sliced his commute to just thirty minutes.

Driving past the empty guard booth, he slowed near the door Hurley had pointed to, nestled right beside the loading dock.

A guard's watchful eye made sense here—someone had to oversee the flow of goods into the facility.

Jake climbed the short flight of concrete steps to a solid metal door and rapped firm knuckles. Silence hung thick for a moment until a voice hissed sharply from beyond.

"What's the password?" the voice demanded.

Caught off guard, Jake muttered, "Huh?"

Suddenly the door swung open with a bark. "That's right! Enter!"

Stepping tentatively inside, Jake saw the dim glow of the shipping area. A nearby office jutted into the unpainted hallway, its lower wooden panels blocking half the corridor, the upper third revealing a man behind glass walls seated at one of two desks. His uniform matched Jake's own.

Next to the office door, a blond man stood tall and straight-backed, the very picture of military strength—like a poster recruit.

Extending a firm hand, he said with crisp authority, "Lieutenant Larsen. I run the four-to-twelve shift."

Before Jake could respond, another voice chimed from behind, smooth but edged with an undercurrent of irreverence."Hey there, the new guy!"

Jake turned to face the third man: barely five-five, rail-thin, with wild black curls tumbling untamed, a neatly trimmed mustache and goatee framing his sharp face. His blue uniform hung loose, a stark contrast to Larsen's taut frame, adorned with three stripes below the company patch on his right shoulder.

"John Madder," he introduced himself, shaking Jake's hand firmly. "Sergeant on the midnight shift."

Jake blinked, surprised. The man looked like a beatnik, not a sergeant. The contrast unsettled him.

From the office, a man with dirty blonde, thinning hair rose. He was no more than twenty-five, six feet tall, with distant blue eyes that seemed half-lost in thought.

"I'm Lou Schmidt," he stated curtly.

"Hi," Jake replied, voice a touch too eager. An awkward silence followed, and Jake hastened to fill it. "So... who else is on this shift?"

Larsen stepped forward, commanding again. "You three, that's it. I've got two men finishing up my shift, but since you arrived early, I'll let them go. I've got to punch them out—and myself."

"Let me do that for you, Lieutenant," Madder offered smoothly.

"No, I like to stay until the end—make sure everything's squared away," Larsen said. "Johnny, since you're training the rookie, why don't you start early?"

"Makes sense," John agreed, moving to a desk cluttered with a thick, cylindrical device, its clock face worn and a large keyhole front and center. "Let me get set up."

He sat down, expertly unlocking the mechanism.

"First rule," Larsen said, eyes locking on Jake's. "Never be late. People count on you. This facility counts on us."

Jake nodded solemnly. "Yes, sir."

"Second, no drinking whatsoever. I mean it—one beer on your breath and you're out. Got it?"

"Of course, sir."

"Keep your hair short and your face clean-shaven. Only one guy gets to slack on that one, right Madder?"

John smirked, closing the device and sliding it into a leather cover. "Thanks, Lieutenant."

Larsen continued, voice hardening. "Other than that, stay awake, stay alert, and don't screw up." He glanced at his watch. "You heading out, Madder?"

"Sure am," John replied, slinging the watch clock over his shoulder. "I'll take it this time."

The lieutenant nodded. "I'll be gone by the time you return."

John extracted a large ring of keys from a wooden box inside the booth. "Grab these before your round—and always pass them to the next guy, understood?"

Jake took the jangling keys, eyes wide. "What exactly are these for?"

A hearty laugh from Larsen. "For everything. You carry them to investigate noises or check locked rooms."

John lifted the keys, the metal clinking loudly. "Master keys. I'll explain how each works on the tour."

"Alright, Sergeant," Larsen said, motioning toward the exit.

John glanced at Lou. "You set?"

Lou grinned. "Made in the shade, Sarge."

John strode through heavy swinging doors, Jake close behind. At a cement wall near a roll-up door, John opened a small metal box and removed a large key chained inside. He inserted it into the watch clock, turned it, then removed it and returned it to the holder.

"This is where you start each tour," John said.

The dim hallways stretched ahead, shadows deepening under sparse lighting. Jake noticed how different the place felt at night —empty, subdued, eerily silent.

John kept up a steady chatter, explaining the schedule as they walked.

"You'll work with me two nights a week, Lou two nights, and one day when all three of us are here. Then two nights off for you," John said. "Lou hasn't had a day off in weeks."

Jake frowned. "That rough, huh?"

John nodded grimly. "Yeah. Here's how it rolls: one of us does the first tour starting at midnight—ending just before one. Then the second takes the second tour. We rotate like that until six, when the cleaners arrive. We let them in since we have the keys."

Jake repeated, "And you carry the keys during rounds?"

"Right. Then the Captain arrives at seven-thirty and we're out by eight, trying to avoid the traffic jam of people coming in around eight-thirty."

Jake swallowed, anxiety knotting his stomach.

John looked at him sharply. "You'll do fine."

They passed closed laboratories, each door sturdy with a small window. Inside blinking lights from machines cast ghostly glows.

John led Jake through multiple buildings, stopping at shadowed metal boxes to pull keys and wind the watch clock repeatedly. Each click echoed oddly in the heavy silence.

Suddenly, a faint light flickered from a window in a dark hallway ahead.

"What's that?" Jake whispered.

John's lips twitched. "Oh, that's Einstein."

Jake's hand shot out, grasping John's arm sharply. His voice dropped to a hiss. "Albert Einstein? Here? Seriously?"

The tension in Jake's grip made John chuckle softly, amused by the young guard's reaction.

"No, no," John replied with a grin. "His name's Doctor Goldstein. But around here we call him 'Einstein'—and sometimes, if he's really deep into his experiments, 'Franken-einstein.'"

Jake relaxed his hold, eyeing John warily. "Why the 'Franken-' part?"

John shrugged, a sly smile curling his lips. "Well, you'll have to figure that one out for yourself. Come on."

Without waiting for a reply, he strode toward the heavy, worn door and tapped it lightly.

From inside the lights flickered and then faded, plunging the room into near darkness. A muffled curse echoed from within, followed by the creak of footsteps.

Moments later, the door rattled loose in its frame and burst open. Standing there was a man of average height, his black hair disheveled, a thin pencil mustache twitching beneath a pair of strange goggles. The lenses were dark and bulbous, giving him the uncanny appearance of a giant insect. Welder's gloves shielded his hands as he pulled the goggles aside and bellowed, "You better not be disturbing me all night!"

John raised his hands placatingly in a mock surrender. "Sorry, Doctor G. Thought you should know there's an additional guard.

I wanted him to meet you so you're not surprised if you catch him lurking around."

Goldstein's glare softened slightly, his irritation ebbing. He turned to Jake. "Alright—who are you?"

"Jake. Jake Hurd—sir, uh, Doctor." Jake stumbled over the words trying to mask his nervousness.

"I'm here late most nights—two or three in the morning sometimes. I'm expanding knowledge that will change the world." His voice swelled with pride and a flicker of defiance. "I work days, come home for a few hours, then return to tinker undisturbed. No one around to steal my ideas."

Jake smiled, the tension easing. "That's what I do too, sir. Fix things. Right now mostly radios—shortwave."

Goldstein's interest sparked instantly. "Really? Where do you get your gear?"

"Mail order, mostly. I build what I can from parts."

"You built your own setup?" The scientist's eyes gleamed.

"Yes, sir. My father has a tube tester, so I've made do with what I could scavenge."

Goldstein grinned, the first flicker of warmth breaking through his stern demeanor. "I built my own shortwave rig before the war. Come in—I want to show you something."

John hesitated. "Doctor Goldstein, we still have rounds to finish."

"This will only take a minute," Goldstein waved him off, leading them to a cluttered workbench piled with curious devices. "Now, Jake, do you own a transistor radio?"

"My friends do," Jake said cautiously, intrigued. "The reception's really poor."

Goldstein picked up a tiny brown cylinder about the size of a thumb, with colored stripes circling it. "Transistors! The very first were invented right here at B.T.&T. But this one… this is new."

John squinted. "What is it?"

Jake leaned in. "Is that a transistor?"

"Correct!" Goldstein's voice was triumphant. "But this transistor has more power in a smaller package than anything I've seen."

"What does it do?" Jake asked, turning the tiny device over in his gloved hand.

"For starters, it can replace the type 30 vacuum tube in a shortwave set." Goldstein smiled. "And you can run it off a single D-cell battery."

Jake's mouth fell open. "I thought transistors only worked in the AM band. Shortwave is way harder—"

Goldstein chuckled. "Exactly. This one changes everything."

Jake's eyes gleamed with excitement. "Is this what you're working on? Transistors?"

Goldstein laughed, shaking his head. "No, this is just a tool. I'm working on something far bigger. As I said, my work will change the world."

"Wow," Jake breathed.

John cleared his throat. "We should get back, Jake, but I have to show you this while we're here."

He pulled a jangling ring of keys from his pocket and pointed to the lock cylinder above Goldstein's door. "This is the security ring—that metal band. That's where you find the code."

Jake approached, eyes narrowing. "The code?"

"That's right," John said. "Three letters then three numbers."

Jake leaned closer, reading the faded letters etched into the ring: PNG-304.

"Don't worry about the numbers, just the letters," John explained as he rifled through his keys. "Here's a key for you."

He held up a key with the same letters engraved on it: PNG.

"This key opens any door with those letters," John said, pride dripping from his voice. "Try it out."

Jake slid the key into the lock and easily turned it. The deadbolt clicked smoothly back and forth.

"I got it." Jake smiled in triumph.

"I knew you would," John said, then glanced back toward Goldstein, who was now absorbed in a coil of copper tubing, twisting it absentmindedly like a captive snake.

John cleared his throat. "Thanks, Doctor G. We won't bother you anymore."

Goldstein waved without looking. "Please don't." Then he called after them, "But Jake, stop by during your next round—I might have something for a fellow ham radio operator."

Jake nodded. "Thank you, sir."

As they closed the rattling door behind them, John shook his head. "Maintenance needs to fix that doorknob."

They continued the round, and John suddenly quickened his pace. He led Jake down a pitch-black basement corridor and flicked on a flashlight. Jake's footsteps echoed in the cavernous space.

"Move through here fast," John said, voice low and tense.

"Why?" Jake asked, shivering slightly.

"Look around. Creepy as hell, isn't it?" John grinned as he slipped a key into a watch clock hanging on the wall.

They ascended a narrow back stairwell and arrived just outside the guard booth. John used the key once more, the final one for the tour.

They went into the office; the hallway lights dim. Lou sat at the desk shuffling cards with a bored scowl.

"'Bout time you showed up," Lou grumbled. "I was supposed to start my tour five minutes ago."

"Sorry," John said tersely. "Franken-Einstein got chatty."

Lou stood and snatched the watch clock from John's shoulder. "Really? He usually just tells me to scram."

John smiled. "Einstein took a liking to young Jake here."

"I have my own problems," Lou said.

"You doing your round now?"

"Ja wohl, mein commandant!" Lou declared in a terrible German accent, clicking his heels theatrically.

John rolled his eyes. "Hilarious. You're the one with the kraut name—Schmidt."

"Careful, don't make me madder," Lou teased back with a smirk. "Oh wait, that's your last name."

"Go on, do your tour," John said.

"My tour and my chore," Lou said, spinning the key in the watch clock and disappearing into the shadowed halls.

John shook his head, chuckling softly. He pulled open a drawer and reached inside. "Ever seen Playboy?"

"What?" Jake blurted, cheeks flushing red. "My mom'd freak if she knew I actually looked at one."

John laughed. "Mine too." He extracted the magazine from a messy stack and tossed it to Jake. "But she ain't here, huh?"

Jake stared down at the glossy cover, a mixture of fascination and guilt etched across his face.

10. Franken-Einstein

J ake learned the first tour that night and the second tour the next. Days blurred into a week before he could confidently manage the tours alone, though the chance to visit Dr. Goldstein again slipped out of reach. The tight schedule, the labyrinthine corridors—they all conspired against him.

It was the second week of August, late at night, and the corridors lay dark and silent. Jake moved through the shadows, methodically performing his first tour, the echo of his footsteps reverberating ominously off the walls.

Then suddenly, strange flickering lights caught his eye through the small window of Dr. Goldstein's lab door.

Curiosity pried at Jake's caution. He approached and peered inside to find the doctor hunched over a sprawling array of metal tubes shaped into an upright half-circle, sparks flying from an arc welder that sent fleeting shadows dancing across the cluttered workshop. The sharp, acrid smell of molten metal filled the air.

A sudden curse cut through the silence as Goldstein abruptly extinguished the torch, peeled off heavy fireproof gloves, and pushed aside his thick goggles.

Jake stepped back, heart hammering—noticing how the doctor's eyes sharpened on the intruder before twisting into an unexpected smile.

"Ah, Jake! Come in, come in."

Jake glanced nervously at the stubbornly loose doorknob and gave it a quick jiggle before slipping inside. "Sorry to bother you, Doctor," he said, trying to keep his voice steady.

"Think nothing of it," Goldstein replied, wiping his hands on a rag. "I needed a break anyway."

He straightened and moved to a drawer, pulling out two tiny, glistening transistors. "Since you and I are both short-wave radio enthusiasts, I have something special for you." He held up the tiny cylinders, each with a wire coming out of both ends. "These will replace your old type-30 tubes. But you'll have to solder them in directly. Can you do that?"

Jake nodded eagerly. "Yes, sir. I built every piece of my setup myself."

Goldstein's smile deepened. "Good man." He handed over the transistors carefully as if passing a precious artifact.

Jake inspected the small semiconductors then allowed his gaze to drift back toward the peculiar metal half-circle still resting on the workbench. "May I ask—what exactly are you building, sir?"

Goldstein's eyes twinkled with mischief. "On one condition," he said softly.

Jake frowned. "Sir?"

"You tell no one," Goldstein declared solemnly. The gravity in his voice silenced Jake instantly.

"You have my word," Jake said without hesitation.

Goldstein nodded approvingly. "Very well. Would you like to see the prototype?"

"Prototype?" Jake almost whispered, leaning in. "Absolutely."

The doctor shuffled some papers off an old, battered desk and opened a large filing drawer. "Have you ever heard of a MASER?"

Jake's brows lifted. "Yes, sir. I read about it in *Popular Science*— microwave amplification by stimulated emission of radiation, right?"

"Yes," he hissed, as he pulled a small square base with a power cord hanging from it. "Exactly. Coherent radiation. It's the next step after radio waves. Right now several researchers here at BT&T are trying to amplify light."

"Like a laser?" Jake asked, excitement creeping into his voice.

Goldstein chuckled, a low, delighted sound. "Good, you know your stuff. Gordon Gould coined the acronym LASER in '57. Two gentlemen here, Schawlow and Townes, have been hammering away at it for years, and just recently, Theodore Maiman built the first functional prototype in California."

Goldstein grabbed the power cord and carefully plugged it into an electrical socket. He then opened a nearby drawer and pulled out a large, intricate ring made up of multiple metal bands fused tightly together.

Jake leaned in for a closer look and noticed several tiny transistors mounted on the outer surface of the rings, along with copper wire meticulously wrapped around a pair of the inner bands. The device looked both complex and delicate, as if designed for some advanced technological purpose.

Jake's eyes glittered. "That's incredible, sir!"

"Perhaps," Goldstein muttered, running a hand over the combined rings again. "But useful? I doubt it. They're thinking too small. We need to merge electromagnetics with coherent microwaves and radio waves."

Jake hesitated. "Is that even possible?"

Goldstein's smile became a cryptic half-grin. "Theoretically, yes. But typical methods won't cut it." He pulled on a heavy glove and held the ring aloft. "This is something else. This will change everything."

"How?" Jake pressed, heart pounding.

Cradling the ring like a fragile treasure Goldstein explained, "Using transistors and electromagnets with light and microwave amplification techniques, I can focus the energies precisely…" He paused. "Here, let me show you."

They crossed the room to a squat metal canister, its surface cold and unyielding.

"What's that, sir?" Jake asked.

"Liquid helium in a non-magnetic container," Goldstein replied proudly. He unscrewed the top, releasing a creeping mist that spilled onto the floor like ghostly smoke.

Jake gaped. "Why do you need that?"

"One of these rings is an electromagnet. Freezing the entire unit brings it to a point of superconductivity," Goldstein said, slipping on another glove as he lifted the ring with tongs and lowered it into the frosty depths. "Since we last spoke, I had a breakthrough—and I owe it all to you."

"To me?" Jake blinked, astonished. "How?"

Goldstein laughed softly. "Shortwaves. I was using radio frequencies from the FM band, but after you told me about your shortwave rig, I realized that's where the magic lies."

Jake struggled for words. "I'm glad I could help…"

"Wait until you see the results," Goldstein said, eyes sparkling with quiet pride. "I succeeded for the first time last night."

With practiced movements Goldstein used the tongs to lift the now frost-covered ring, slipped it into the slot atop the square device he'd plugged in earlier, and flipped a switch. A low hum filled the room, laden with vibrating energy.

"This is fascinating, sir," Jake said, stepping back reluctantly. "But I have to finish my rounds."

"The effect won't last. The superconductivity fades as the ring warms. Still, you'll find this interesting. The base unit pumps out microwaves and radio waves while projecting light through a ruby rod."

Jake's brow furrowed. "Are we safe? That sounds dangerous."

Goldstein smiled reassuringly. "That magnetic field focuses the microwaves. Touching the ring would sear your flesh instantly but a few feet away—no problem. Now, watch."

A humming intensified then suddenly, a vivid red light blossomed at the ring's center.

Jake gasped. "Is that laser light?"

"Here, kneel a little." Goldstein gestured to Jake to kneel and the younger man lowered himself.

Jake peered intently, five feet away. "I… I think I see a hole."

Goldstein's voice dropped to a reverent whisper. "Do you see it? A landscape, like looking through a telescope."

Jake's brow knitted with disbelief. "What does that mean?"

Goldstein chuckled, almost childlike in his wonder. "I believe I've created a quantum tunnel."

Jake blinked. "A what?"

Suddenly the red glow flickered and vanished. Goldstein sprang to the base and flipped the switch—silencing the hum.

"It only lasts until the unit heats," he explained, wiping sweat off his brow. "The magnetic field weakens and the effect collapses."

"But what was that—?"

Goldstein laughed and nodded toward the heavy ring he'd been welding earlier. "I don't know! That's why I'm building a larger prototype. This one will have liquid helium circulating inside the metal tubes to maintain superconductivity. If I'm right, then we'll see things change."

Jake took a breath, awe thick in his chest. "That's incredible, sir."

Goldstein's gaze locked onto Jake's. "Come visit me again, Jake. And remember, tell no one."

Jake kept an unconventional schedule sleeping through the daylight hours to wake precisely at three in the afternoon. He needed to drive over to Garden State University and plan his fall classes.

Taking Peggy's advice seriously he enrolled in business courses, but also in the science and chemistry classes his father insisted on.

At work, Jake watched Sergeant John as he carefully opened the watch clock to replace its round paper disk—the device that recorded their patrol routes with unique imprints punched by each key at every checkpoint.

"That's pretty clever," Jake remarked, leaning in.

John smirked, closing the clock and fastening it back into its leather harness. "Yeah, but you've gotta be careful. The paper can jam up and worse, you need to reset the time every day—it loses about half an hour."

Jake's mind raced. "You know I'm pretty handy. I could bring the tools tomorrow, get here early, fix it. No timed rounds until our shift, right?"

John hesitated a moment, then nodded. "That's right. But I'll check with Larsen first. Make sure you don't break it."

The next night Jake arrived two hours early lugging his canvas bag packed with jeweler's screwdrivers, needle-nosed pliers, tiny tubes of machine oil, various wrenches, tweezers, toothpicks, and cotton swabs.

He spread everything out, his fingers steady and deliberate as he opened the watch clock. Taking his time, he meticulously cleaned each gear, applying just a drop of oil and testing the movement.

He finished with a confident nod—just thirty minutes to spare before the shift began. The clock would stop losing time, he was sure of it.

Word of Jake's skill spread quickly. The daytime captain mentioned it to folks at Security Information Systems.

Jake settled into the routine, embracing the discipline of his new role. Every night before work he polished his shoes meticulously. Appearance mattered.

Every other day Jake made time to visit Dr. Goldstein, but only on his first round—not wanting to disturb the delicate work of the complex apparatus.

During the day, in his waking hours, the college library became his sanctuary where he devoured books about quantum engineering. This gave him enough background to ask insightful questions which delighted Goldstein.

Jake noticed Goldstein rarely left the lab for meals; the vending machines were his only sustenance. So Jake began bringing lunches—homemade sandwiches at first, then thank-you pies from his mother. One evening Goldstein savored a slice, eyes lighting up.

"Did you get those transistors into the radio?" Goldstein asked between bites.

"Yes, sir," Jake replied. "They work great, and power demands have dropped."

Jake's eyes scanned the welded metal circles standing upright on the heavy base. Each ring—three feet across—welded to short tubes connecting them, maintaining their separation.

Goldstein nodded. "They're efficient, but you'll want to add a regulator. Prevent any power surges."

Jake leaned closer. "I did some reading on quantum tunnels."

Goldstein's eyes narrowed in intrigue. "Oh? What did you find?"

"From what I understood the only quantum tunnel ever made was the size of an electron."

Goldstein exploded with laughter—fortunately between bites. "Think bigger, Jake." He pointed at the rings. "I intend to make a quantum tunnel that size."

Jake shifted uneasily. "But... what would it do?"

Goldstein shrugged, a gleam in his eye. "Change everything we know about the universe," he said, swallowing another forkful of pie, "or punch a hole in reality."

The seriousness of this statement made Jake's stomach twist.

Weeks passed and Goldstein carefully added two smaller rings between the larger ones wrapped tightly with copper wire.

Jake immediately recognized them as electromagnets.

His nightly visits grew longer as Goldstein shared bold theories of other dimensions and random existence.

September came and Jake's days filled with classes; evenings reverted to guard duty and study. He slept mornings and afternoons, living by the clock. On days off he tried to reclaim daylight hours, and Fridays meant nights out with Peggy, ending inevitably on Bernard's Mountain.

Peggy was proud of Jake's hard work, but she was still careful to control his wandering hands. "We're both busting our asses for our future, Jake. No distractions," she warned softly. "No S-E-X."

One night his patrol led him past Goldstein's lab to raised voices. He froze near the door, straining to listen.

"This has no commercial application—"

Goldstein snapped back fiercely. "How about the expansion of human knowledge? You've supported laser development here for years only to be beaten by Maiman in California."

"Yes, but lasers have practical uses—"

"Which remain undeveloped! Damn it, Tom, you've created a team to build a gas laser. So what? I'm offering something that could change everything."

"And possibly destroy this lab," came the bitter response.

Goldstein's voice softened. "Look, Tom—"

"Doctor Harding to you. I've tolerated this because you worked on this during your own time. But look at you—you're unshaven, no tie—"

"There's no one here but some damn guards!" Goldstein snapped.

"It's our image! This is impressive but the little model you made? A toy."

"A toy!" Goldstein echoed, bitter.

Harding sighed. "That toy alone drained resources. I gave you a canister of liquid helium. Now you want a whole tank?"

"I need it to create superconductivity—"

"Which is little more than theory!"

"Theory? Meissner and Ochsenfeld proved it back in the thirties, for Christ's sake!"

"Don't take the Lord's name in vain here!"

Goldstein pressed on. "I'm close to making it a breakthrough. The tubing can be super-cooled from within. I need a magnetic field of at least one Tesla—maybe two."

Harding's voice rose. "Are you crazy? If you reach one Tesla, every unsecured piece of metal here will fly—"

"I've removed all unsecured metal," Goldstein cut in.

"You call this science? It's foolishness. I'm shutting you down."

Jake retreated into the shadows just as Harding rattled the doorknob, pushing the door open into the hallway.

Goldstein pleaded, "Give me a chance, Tom... uh, Dr. Harding."

Harding's eyes met the unseen Goldstein's in the dim hallway. "It's for your own good. You're smart, maybe even a genius. But focus on what we need—telecommunications—not this... crackpot idea."

Turning, Harding muttered "liquid helium" as he strode away.

Jake edged closer, peeking inside. Goldstein paced, his hand clutching his head. Unshaven, greasy hair clinging to his forehead he looked every bit the mad scientist Harding described.

Jake knocked softly.

Goldstein shot a glare, wild eyes narrowing then softened at the sight of Jake. He opened the door wider. "Come in, Jake. I guess you heard that."

"I'm sorry. I didn't mean to pry—"

"Pry? The whole place will know by morning. 'Crazy Irving Goldstein.' They'll politely ask me to leave."

He gestured toward his creation—the massive rings perched on the lab table, transistors looping around them, copper wire tightly wound on the inner hoops. The base hummed quietly with valves and electronics clutching the apparatus upright.

Goldstein snorted. "They might ask you to escort me out."

Jake swallowed hard. "Well, sir... we've got three guards on tonight. If there's anything I can do..."

Goldstein's head snapped up. "Three? I thought there were only two."

"One night a week all three of us are here. We split the rounds."

A rare solemnity cast the older man's face. "So you don't have to do the rounds," he mumbled. "The sergeant and the other guy cover for you."

"I suppose..."

Jake saw the battle raging inside this brilliant man—caught between revolutionary ambition and crushing bureaucracy.

"And you have those keys, right?" The scientist's voice filled with barely contained excitement, his eyes glinting with obsession. "The master keys to everything?"

Jake swallowed hard. "I do, but I'm not—"

"Jake, this is monumental!" Goldstein practically vibrated with feverish energy. "You can help me. I can't run this alone; too complex, too dangerous for one man."

"Dr. Goldstein, I'm not allowed to touch the equipment—"

"You won't touch it," Goldstein snapped. "You'll assist me. That's all."

Jake hesitated, the weight of the warning ringing in his ears. "But, sir—"

Goldstein's grin turned predatory. "I take full responsibility. And Jake, if this thing works—we'll witness the greatest breakthrough in human history."

Jake glanced at his watch. Time was slipping away while he stood frozen. "I have to finish my rounds, sir."

Goldstein waved him off dismissively. "Do your round. Ask Sergeant John if he can spare you. He can call me to double-check."

Nodding Jake stepped into the dimly lit corridor.

"Oh, Jake." Goldstein's voice stopped him. "One more thing. Can you open a door for me?"

"A door, sir?"

"Yes. A supply cabinet down the hall. I forgot my keys."

Goldstein led him down the shadowed passage, stopping before a metal door marked simply: 'LHe.' Jake recognized the marking but never thought twice about the door on his many patrols.

He glanced again at his watch—he was already behind schedule. Reluctantly, he pulled the master ring from his pocket. Fingers trembling, he found the etched letters on the lock, and the correct key slid home with a soft click.

The door creaked open and a rush of cold air spilled out, prickling Jake's skin—chilling, unnatural.

Goldstein stepped inside blocking Jake's view. "There you go. Finish your rounds. Come back when you're done."

Jake hurried away, uneasy. That door… something didn't sit right. An icy dread unfurled in the pit of his stomach.

He returned to the guard's office mere minutes before one AM, panting from sprinting through the final corridor.

Lou grunted, snatching the watch clock. "Great, now I have to run through my rounds." He slung the black leather harness over his shoulder and vanished down the hall.

"Sorry," Jake called after him.

Lou's response was an extended middle finger.

Jake faced Sergeant John, slouched at the scarred desk flipping through one of the copies of Playboy.

"Dr. Goldstein's running an experiment tonight."

John didn't look up. "And what's that to me?"

"He asked me to help."

"Franken-einstein's on his way out. They're sick of him being here every damn night."

Jake lowered his voice, pleading. "But this might be my only chance to see what he's actually been working on."

John finally glanced up, eyes sharp and mocking. "So you want us to cover tours while you—what? Animate the dead?"

"It's a unique chance. There are three of us on duty."

John smirked. "And what do I get out of it?"

Jake blinked. "What do you mean?"

John stood, closing the magazine with deliberate slow motion. "Nobody does anything for free, Jake. Time you learned that."

"What do you mean?"

His tone was low. "Since I'm helping you, you'll take both rounds the next night it's just us. All night."

Jake frowned. "That means I walk all night."

"You're young. You can handle it."

The offer was absurd—John barely needed to do anything while Jake risked exhaustion. But curiosity won.

"Fine. I agree."

John dismissed him with a wave. "Good. Go watch the mad scientist's last stab before they finally boot him out."

He sank back into his chair flipping Playboy open again.

Jake returned to the lab unease tightening around his throat.

Goldstein was already preparing—sliding heavy, padded gloves onto his hands, like welder's gloves but even thicker.

Dressed now in a stark white coverall the scientist's horn-rimmed glasses had thick plastic screens on both sides. Next to him stood a large metal cylinder marked 'LHe.'

"Jake, in the room next door you'll find another set of coveralls. Strip down and put it on. No shoes either."

"Wait—why?" Jake asked, dread pooling in his gut.

"We're activating a powerful magnet. Metal is deadly here—no zippers, no eyelets. It's strong enough to turn even the smallest piece of metal into a bullet... or worse."

Jake moved quickly down the hall to an unlocked office. How had Goldstein opened that door if he forgot his keys? He shoved the thought away as he removed his uniform and donned the coverall, feeling vulnerable in just his stocking feet.

Back in the lab, Goldstein nodded to him and said, "Grab the safety glasses and that screwdriver."

Jake slid the plastic lenses over his eyes and picked up the tool. "Is it really safe to bring this in?"

"It's safe. It's made from non-magnetic materials."

They attached a heavy black hose to the helium tank, clamped it tight with a plastic hose clamp, tightened it with the screwdriver. Goldstein tested the connection with a sharp tug.

Jake placed the tool on the desk, as Goldstein turned the valve on the tank with a hiss.

It sounded like a predator's breath and frost formed in seconds over the metal hoops nearby as a sickly cold mist drifted upward.

"Liquid helium," Jake whispered.

"Exactly," Goldstein said. "I need to get the circuits running. Put these on."

He handed Jake a pair of thick cloth gloves.

"Why?"

"If anything metallic gets near the magnet when it's on, it'll fly to the core. You might have to touch hot, frozen metal. These gloves will protect your fingers."

Goldstein flipped a switch; blinking lights hummed to life.

Jake's stomach twisted looking at the coils. "How can the hoses handle this?"

"They're double insulated. Made for this."

Goldstein stepped back, eyes scanning the machine like a man awaiting a verdict.

"Let's fire it up."

He motioned Jake to one end while he took the other.

"See these switches? There are three. When I say flip them one by one, left to right. Understand?"

Jake nodded fingers trembling.

"First switch—now!"

He toggled it up. A low hum filled the room, not just audible but a vibration in his skull. Jake covered his ears, but the sound did not lessen—it echoed inside his head.

"Watch for flying metal!" Goldstein shouted, hair bristling. "Magnet's activated. Now we'll add microwaves, radio waves, and focused light."

Suddenly the stagnant air shifted—like a window opening to a freezing storm. The humming swelled, dragging cold currents through the room.

Jake heard a strange rattle somewhere behind him, but the rising roar swallowed it.

"Second and third switches! Then we move back!" Goldstein's voice was almost lost in the noise.

Jake flipped the remaining toggles. The hum spiraled into a terrifying roar, the coils glowing with unnatural energy.

A tiny, spinning vortex of light materialized in the center, hypnotic in appearance.

"It's working!" Goldstein howled like a man possessed.

The air whipped violently, tendrils of energy clawing at the edges of the room.

The helium tank rocked violently on its base as the swirling light expanded—chilling colors pulsing with power.

Then—flash. A strobing burst hammered every nerve ending in Jake's head..

Suddenly, the wind stopped. The lights dimmed to a sickly glow.

Jake's breath caught, heart pounding with dread.

Something had changed.

"Did the circuit blow?" Jake's voice cracked the heavy silence.

"No." Goldstein gasped, eyes wide with disbelief. "Look!"

At the center of the glowing hoop an image shimmered and stabilized. The low hum around them quieted just enough for Jake to catch a strange rattle—not sure where it came from.

The image wasn't a screen; it was more like a window suspended in midair between the rings, displaying a terrifying, surreal panorama in vivid color.

The ground was a sickening shade of red—dark like coagulated blood. Above an eternal twilight hung heavy, casting grotesque shadows across an alien desert.

The reddish soil wasn't sand but coarse, cracked stone. Scattered sparse trees—or what looked like trees—thrust skeletal branches upward, like desperate claws scratching at an invisible sky. No sun, no moon, no stars; just the blood-red earth and a horizon swallowed by darkness.

It wasn't Earth.

Jake strained, the stale stench of the image's air seeming to invade his nostrils. It reeked—metallic, acrid—like burnt flesh, as if he could taste the dust itself.

He reached toward it.

"No!" Goldstein snapped, grabbing Jake's arm. The ring focuses microwaves inside it. You'll fry your hand."

Goldstein stalked over to a nearby bench and picked up a pencil. "I had to switch to pencils because of the magnets."

Standing beside Jake, pencil poised, he said, "If this makes it through the hoop it'll land on the other side. Either that... or it falls right here."

Jake's heart thundered as Goldstein flipped the pencil. It sailed through the center ring, crossing the barrier without hesitation then hit the red ground beyond—bouncing twice.

"How is this possible?" Jake whispered, eyes fixed on the pencil's unnatural landing.

Goldstein was pale and his lips trembled. "I can't believe it... it's a portal." He circled the helium tank, eyes wide. "But where? Another world? Another reality?"

A sudden shift. Movement flickered in Jake's peripheral vision —not in the lab but within the burning landscape beyond the hoop. Something dark and unnameable, crawling closer.

Jake was sure it moved toward the pencil as he heard that odd rattle again, that sounded like bone scraping stone.

"Doctor, shut it down," Jake urged, voice taut.

"Shut it down? This is a miracle!" Goldstein's grin cracked his face like a mask. "And I have nothing to record it—no camera, no way to prove it."

"Sir, this could prove your theories. You can show Harding, all of them—I'm a witness. But we need to close it down."

"Why?" Goldstein demanded.

"Because of we can throw something and it ends up there. Something could come over here."

Goldstein's excitement wavered, and a serious look came over his face as the realization took hold. "You may have a point..."

He stepped toward the machine.

The rattle grew louder, relentless and unyielding. Jake's eyes snapped to the lab's metal doorknob, which was shaking wildly, its metal trembling and twisting as if about to come loose, buffeted nonstop by the ceaseless magnetic thrumming pulsating through the air.

Jake's brow furrowed deeply, a flicker of unease crossing his face.

In a heartbeat, and with a sickening snap, the knob jerked loose from the door.

The sound echoed sharply in the tense silence, as it hurtled through the air—an iron missile aimed at Jake's face.

He dove aside just in time.

The doorknob careened straight toward the pulsating hoops—where it met the back of Goldstein's head with a sickening crack.

Goldstein pitched sideways, time slowing to a sluggish crawl as the knob sailed through the portal and vanished into that hellish landscape.

Goldstein's flailing body caught the helium hose tethered to the machine and tank. The hose yanked free with a sharp pop, severing the lifeline of the cooling system.

Jake's breath hitched. He knew what would come next.

The rapid boiling of the liquid helium would unleash immense pressure—a volatile, explosive fury.

He sprinted for the door just as the lab erupted behind him with staggering pandemonium.

Air exploded behind him, knocking him straight into the tumbling door, shards of metal and glass raining down.

His lungs burned as choking smoke and acrid dust filled the hallway.

He collapsed, gasping, heart pounding in terror and pain.

He rolled onto his back, lying on the floor, gasping for air.

That was when he saw it.

A shadow on the ceiling. No—not a shadow.

A living darkness, writhing and curling with unnatural movement.

It trembled and slithered, and from the inky folds emerged a grotesque shape.

It slid down the wall with unholy grace, pooling before Jake's wide, terrified eyes—forming a blocky head, hollow eyes like slits piercing the gloom.

A predator's gaze fixed coldly on him.

Hungry.

Relentless.

And utterly *alive.*

Jake tried to scream, but no sound came.

As the grotesque shadow advanced—he squeezed his eyes shut as his consciousness faded.

And then darkness…

11. SHADOWY OCCURRENCES

J ake jolted awake, his heart hammering as if trying to burst free from his chest. His eyes snapped open darting frantically around the unfamiliar room.

Panic clawed at him, the memory of that slithering shadow—the oozing black creature—lifting off the wall, invading his mind like a nightmare come alive.

He flailed his arms attempting to push the dark vision away, to break free from its suffocating grip.

But the scene before him was different—ordinary in the daylight. Sunlight streamed lazily through the window casting warm patterns on the crisp, white sheets tucked snugly around his trembling body.

A cold, sharp prick in his arm drew his attention: there was a needle inserted there. That was what he thought was holding him.

He was lying in a hospital bed.

A soft voice interrupted the heavy silence. "How do you feel, dear?"

Jake's breath hitched and he turned his head toward the sound, eyes wide with alarm.

"Where is it?" he gasped, voice raw and desperate.

The voice belonged to a woman—a tall, slender figure, her hair streaked with silver. The warmth in her hazel eyes struck him immediately.

"Where is what, dear?" she asked, brushing her hand tenderly through his messy hair.

All at once he recognized her, she was his mother.

"The... thing," Jake stammered, his voice cracked and dry, his throat raw. His body trembled as he cast one more searching glance around the sterile room. "The thing that was looking at me."

"Jake, you're safe. You're in the hospital," she said softly, coaxing his clenched fingers open. Her cool hand slipped into his, grounding him. "Listen to me."

He fixed his gaze on her face, on the curls of gray atop her head, on the unmistakable kindness in her eyes.

"You were at one of the labs. Do you remember?"

"But I saw something... it—it was there," Jake insisted, voice barely more than a whisper.

Her mouth tightened and she brushed her palm gently across his cheek. "You almost died, Jake."

His eyes filled with tears he hadn't realized were there. Her own eyes shone wet, red-rimmed from crying.

"Oh, God... you almost died," she whispered desperately, pulling him tight against her. Her hug was fierce, protective.

"Mom, I'm okay now... but I saw something," Jake breathed, voice shaking.

"Not now—don't worry about that," she breathed, reaching into the pocket of her dress for a delicate, embroidered handkerchief that did little to stem the flow of her tears. "You've been unconscious… for a day and a half. Your father and I—we were so scared."

Jake's mind dragged him back. A day and a half? And what happened to Dr. Goldstein?

"There's someone here to see you," Mom said, a faint tremor in her voice. "Why don't I let you talk to Peggy while I call your father? Tell him you're awake." She pressed a kiss to his forehead. "I'm so glad you're all right, son."

After she left Jake's thoughts swirled, tangled between memory and reality. Goldstein's device… the alien landscape… the dark shape gliding silently down the laboratory wall. It felt like a twisted dream.

Suddenly the door burst open with a gust of energy as Peggy charged in like a whirlwind.

"Jake!" she cried, hands reaching for him.

Before he could react she was on him, pressing her warm lips to his with a passion he hadn't felt since his last birthday. The heat stirred through him instantly, a raw mixture of relief and desire.

Her soft murmurs of pleasure punctuated the kiss before she pulled back, her emerald eyes blazing with fierce concern. "Don't you ever do that again!" she shouted, but her voice was laced with unyielding relief.

"Shh! Peggy, it's a hospital," he whispered urgently.

"I don't care!" she snapped, poking him hard in the chest. "Of all the stupid things—you could have been killed!"

"Ow! Peggy, I'm—"

"Scaring your mom like that! And me. I was a wreck," she continued, adding an extra jab to underscore her point.

"I'm sorry, okay?" Jake said, wincing.

"Fine, you're sorry. I'm just so glad you're alive." She kissed him again, pulling her legs up on the bed and lying against him.

Her hips rubbed against his, and she sensed his arousal. Her grin turned mischievous. "Looks like you missed me," she whispered.

"Peggy!" Jake hissed, glancing nervously toward the door. "My mom might come in!"

"But you're awake," she breathed, leaning in to kiss him once more. She jumped up, settling into a chair nearby, giggling as Jake adjusted the sheets to hide the evidence of his excitement.

He sat up slowly, placing a pillow in his lap and leaning on it to seem casual. Peggy chuckled uncontrollably.

Her expression softened, serious and full of love. "I'm so relieved, Jake. When we got here... they thought you might have brain damage."

"Brain damage?" he echoed.

"Your heart stopped," she explained. "The doctors said it's a miracle you didn't die—like the scientist with you."

Jake's blood ran cold. "Dr. Goldstein... he's dead?"

Jake recalled the flying doorknob. Moving through the air at such speed, it must have crushed his skull. Still, he'd hoped Goldstein had survived.

Peggy nodded gravely. "They say that frozen gas he was using suffocated him. When they brought you in, you were struggling to breathe—blue all over."

Jake swallowed hard. "How did I get here? The last thing I remember—"

In his thoughts, he saw the dark creature sliding like ink down the wall, making him shudder violently.

"The other guard heard the explosion while on patrol," Peggy whispered. When he found you, he thought you were dead."

A gentle knock sounded at the door. It cracked open, and his mother peeked in.

"Can I come in, dear?"

"Sure, Mom," Jake replied.

Peggy smiled brightly. "He seems fine, Mrs. Hurd."

"Well, that's a relief," Mom sighed. "You certainly gave us a scare."

"I feel fine," Jake said, trying to convince himself more than them. The memory of the black thing clawed at the edges of his mind again.

"I spoke with the doctor," she continued. "They want to run some more tests but should be able to release you tomorrow."

"I'll read to you for a while," Peggy offered.

Mom added, "The doctor wants to do some neurological tests. Peggy, we can come back after dinner."

"Aww, I'm sorry, Jake."

"It's okay, Peggy," Jake said with a weak smile. "When do I eat here? I'm starving."

"First test passed," Mom said with a smile. "Peggy, dear, why don't you have dinner with us? Then after, we can all come over with Jake's father."

"Okay!" Peggy agreed, blowing Jake a kiss as they left.

Minutes later the hospital staff descended—a whirlwind of nurses checking his blood pressure, drawing blood, testing reflexes with rubber mallets, shining penlights into his eyes. A short-bearded man came in, methodically tapping and poking, jotting notes silently on a clipboard before leaving without a word.

Finally, a matronly nurse brought a tray of tasteless food, which Jake devoured in desperate hunger.

After dinner, his mother, father, and Peggy returned, filling the room with light chatter. His father was quiet but let Peggy fill the pauses with vibrant stories from her family and beauty school adventures.

But Jake barely listened; shadows lengthened as the sun dipped below the horizon, and an unsettling apprehension lay heavy in his chest. He kept glancing out the window, pulled by some indefinable dread.

"What's wrong, Jake?" his mother asked gently.

He startled at her voice. "Nothing... just... it's almost twilight."

"You've looked out that window ten times in the last five minutes, son," his father said, frowning.

Jake hesitated, sensing their expectant eyes on him. He wanted to confess—to tell them about the creature, the darkness—but the words sounded insane even to his own ears.

"I'm just... jumpy," he admitted, his upper lip damp with sweat. "I mean, Dr. Goldstein... dying and all."

"Everyone says you were quite the hero, son," Dad said.

"I was?" Jake said, surprised.

"Yes," Peggy beamed. "They said you tried to save Dr. Goldstein."

"That's why BT&T is covering your hospital bill," his father added. "Is that what happened, son?"

"Yeah, pretty much," Jake said, thinking fast. After all, if BT&T were paying for his healthcare, who was he to argue?

Just then, the matronly nurse reappeared.

"All right, Mr. Hurd," she said gruffly, holding out a paper cup filled with tiny pills. "Time for your pill. Then everyone will have to leave."

"What is it?" Jake asked.

"Sleeping pills. Now, take them," she ordered, her tone brooking no argument.

Jake swallowed them quickly, desperate to quiet the fear thrumming in his veins even if it meant surrendering to sleep.

Sergeant Nurse herded everyone out, leaving Jake alone. The heaviness of the drugs swept over him, his vision darkening.

Unbeknownst to him, that night would mark a turning point —the last time in forty years that Jake would ever sleep through an entire night.

The next morning, Jake awoke to sunlight pouring through the blinds, bathing the room in a warm, golden glow.

His body ached—every muscle a dull throb—and a heavy weariness clung to him like a shadow, but physically he was no worse for wear.

The anxious, knot-tight feeling that squeezed his chest the night before was mysteriously absent, replaced by a tentative calm.

His mother appeared at his door shortly after, clipboard in hand, finalizing the hospital paperwork. Her voice was gentle yet clinical as she signed the forms.

Once the formalities were done, Jake dressed in clothes his mother brought and stepped outside into the crisp, bright autumn light.

Leaves crunched beneath his boots, the familiar scent of pine and wood smoke filling the air. Despite the surrounding serenity, a subtle tension lingered beneath his skin—something unspoken.

They drove home in companionable silence. When they arrived, Jake didn't even wait to drop his things—he headed straight up the stairs toward his room.

"Where are you off to, dear?" Mom asked as they crossed the threshold.

"I'm going to lie down," Jake replied, voice low. "I need to be ready for work tonight."

Mom stopped, concern sharpening her features. "Jake, you're not working tonight."

He frowned. "What do you mean?"

"You're off for the next few days. No school, no work. Doctor's orders."

The realization crawled into him like an unwelcome chill. He was tired—yes—but also oddly liberated. His body screamed for rest, and for once, he felt safe enough to listen.

"I'm still sleepy, Mom. I'm just going to rest." He tried to keep his voice even.

"Oh… I suppose that's all right." Her smile was just a little too bright, too forced. "Peggy's coming for dinner."

Jake's brow furrowed in confusion as he checked the calendar in his mind. It was Friday—date night. "I thought Peggy and I would go out."

"Jake," Mom's tone turned lecturing, hardened by worry, "you were in the hospital last night. If you can't go to work or school, you shouldn't be going out on dates, either."

He nodded numbly and climbed the stairs, ignoring the stubborn knot tightening in his gut. He lay down in his bed and went back to sleep.

Jake woke at six, refreshed for the first time in days.

But an unsettling alertness charged his senses—a preternatural awareness he couldn't explain.

Drawn to the window, he stared out at the setting sun casting dark, twisting shadows across the lawn. His eyes flicked nervously over the shadows as if daring them to move.

Could something have come through from that hideous place he'd seen? The gateway—the quantum portal that Dr. Goldstein had spoken about—had let more than just a pencil cross over.

But that was impossible. The microwave emissions would destroy any living creature. But what if…

The thought chilled him to his bones.

Guilt gnawed at him, relentless and raw. If only he had stopped Dr. Goldstein before the experiment, the older man might still be alive.

He dressed slowly, the smell of food drawing him down the stairs. The kitchen buzzed with life: Mom tossed salad in a bright-orange crockery bowl, Peggy placed plates on the table, laughter carried softly in the warm light.

"Well, Mr. Nixon is the Vice President," Mom was saying in a speculative tone.

Peggy giggled. "I know, Mrs. Hurd, but John F. Kennedy is such a dream—and his wife is so glamorous—"

Their chatter vanished as Jake stepped into the room.

"Jake!" Peggy exclaimed, a quick, proper peck pressed on his cheek.

"How do you feel, son?" his mother asked, eyes full of protective concern.

"Better, I guess. Hungry," Jake muttered.

"Wash your hands, we'll eat soon," Mom said briskly.

Peggy fell into step beside him as he left the room.

"Are you really feeling better?" she asked softly, her eyes bright.

"Yeah," he smiled faintly. "Sleeping helped."

She leaned in, lowering her voice to a conspiratorial whisper. "You're off this weekend. If you're up for it, maybe tomorrow we can go up the mountain."

Jake's brow furrowed. "Thought you didn't like that anymore…"

Peggy glanced around and then whispered fiercely, "You almost died. I need to do everything I can to make you want to live."

They kissed, brief but intense, the fear of being caught only stoking their fervor. She slipped back into the kitchen; he washed his hands at the kitchen sink.

His gaze drifted once more to the darkening yard. The shadows deepened, pooling ominously. His skin prickled, but he forced himself to turn away, deciding what he felt was ridiculous.

Dad arrived at six-thirty sharp, just like always after closing the pharmacy. The scent of chicken and dumplings filled the room, one of Jake's favorite comfort meals.

But tonight, dinner felt different.

As Mom and Dad talked about mundane household chores, Jake's eyes kept darting to the window, searching the shadows outside.

Peggy noticed the change, her brow furrowing over Jake's slow eating—he usually devoured his food like a ravenous wolf.

Jake's parents didn't miss it either.

"Jake," Dad's voice was steady but probing. "What are you looking for?"

Jake blinked, startled. "What?"

"You keep staring out the window. Expecting someone?"

Jake shook his head. "I was just… looking at the lawn."

"Well, we're supposed to be at the table, son. You have a guest."

"Oh," Jake stammered, glancing at Peggy and trying to focus on the present. But every shifting leaf, every sway of the branches, pulled his gaze to the darkness beyond.

Peggy nudged him gently. "So, Jake," she said, brushing away the silence, "how does it feel to be electrocuted?"

Mom quickly interjected, a touch of reprimand in her voice. "Peggy, maybe we shouldn't ask that."

Jake shrugged slightly. "It all happened very fast."

"I don't think you should try to play hero, rescuing people from labs," Dad added, voice low but firm. "You're a security guard, not a firefighter."

Jake frowned. "I was just trying to help."

"We're lucky you're here tonight and not at a funeral," Dad added grimly.

Mom snapped. "I don't want to hear this," she said, standing suddenly. "Jake has been through enough! I won't have you badger the boy!"

Dad's voice rose. "He needs to be more responsible. And don't remind me about the hospital bills, even if BT&T is covering most!"

Mom's face flushed crimson with emotion. "You pick on Jake over every little thing! He could have died!" She looked at Jake and Peggy, trembling. "I—I'm sorry. Excuse me."

She sobbed and ran into the kitchen.

The room fell into heavy silence.

Jake's father sighed, red-faced, and followed her.

"Alone at last," Peggy whispered, grabbing Jake's hand.

Mortified by his parents' parents'outburstoutburst, Jake's anger flared. "I'm sorry you had to hear that."

Peggy shrugged. "It's how it is at my house. Parents yell, kids yell—it's life."

Jake clenched his fists. "I wish my dad wouldn't embarrass me like that. Like I'm some kid."

Peggy's fingers tightened around his hand. "To him, but not to me. You're a man, Jake."

He finally looked at her properly. "You look amazing."

"And I smell good too," she teased, leaning closer.

His cheeks flushed. "Peggy," he whispered, "my parents are in the kitchen."

"I know!" she grinned. "So are you going to stare out the window all night or talk to me?"

He hesitated, then spilled the story. "When Dr. Goldstein's device was on, it opened… a window to another place."

Peggy's frown deepened. "Another place?"

"An alien place. We threw a pencil into it, like tossing it into another world."

"How is that possible?" she asked, eyes narrowing.

"I don't know. But things were there."

"Things?"

"When I was on the floor... I saw something. Looking up at the ceiling, this shadow—it moved. It slid down the wall." He sighed. "Am I making any sense?"

"Kind of," Peggy said cautiously.

"It shaped into a body. And I felt like it was watching me."

"Oh, Jake," Peggy said, then suddenly smacked his hand. "You're just trying to scare me."

"No!" he snapped, too loudly. He glanced at the kitchen door and lowered his voice. "I'm serious. The other place it came from, it was red—like what hell is supposed to be."

"That's crazy," Peggy argued, trying to sound rational. "Maybe you couldn't breathe properly and your mind played tricks."

"I saw it—I felt it, like an... evil presence."

At that moment, Dad returned, halting Jake mid-sentence. He and Peggy exchanged a quick glance, sensing whatever was brewing between his parents was no good.

Well," Dad said, clearing his throat, "let's finish dinner."

Mom entered the room, dabbing her eyes with a dishtowel she held like a handkerchief. She sat quietly, her gaze apologetic.

"You'll have to excuse me," she said softly to Jake and Peggy. "The past few days... have been difficult."

"Yes," Dad said. "We're just grateful you're okay, son."

Jake nodded, eyes flicking to Peggy, who stared past him out the window into the night beyond. Now she was looking at the shifting shadows.

That night Jake lay awake, plagued by restless unease.

The light beside his bed remained lit, its warm glow a fragile shield against the darkness pressing in around him. He picked up a book and read for a time, hoping the words would calm the creeping dread.

But from the corner of his eye, a shadow shifted across the floor—and his heart lurched.

The old bureau loomed near, its dark wood polished but worn. Hesitating only a moment Jake swung his legs out of bed and moved toward it, fumbling in the top drawer for his Boy Scout flashlight.

He gripped the familiar green cylinder, noting the distinctive L-shaped emitter at the top. With a flick, the beam sprang to life, cutting a narrow swath of light through the gloom.

He aimed it at the shadow. But the blackness had lightened, almost seemed less solid now. Had something been lurking there, moving just as he reached the bureau?

The thought set his nerves on edge.

Back in bed, Jake scanned the room with the flashlight, systematically chasing down every dark shape, every ghostly form. Each time his furniture and belongings were all he saw, harmless and still.

He lay back and fixed his eyes on the ceiling but the shadows lingered in his mind like a threat he couldn't dismiss.

At 4:00 AM exhaustion finally overtook him—or maybe it was the hopelessness. He tried to close his eyes, but a primal feeling told him he wasn't alone.

He sat up in the bed and flipped on the flashlight, pointing it where he felt the presence.

Nothing.

Just silence. Just shadows.

When dawn's fragile light poured into his room Jake sank back into his pillows, the oppressive weight that gripped him fading like mist. He breathed out, relief flooding through him as the sense of being watched evaporated. Sleep finally pulled him under.

Jake awoke at four feeling refreshed, the nightmares of the previous night seeming unreal—like a bad dream fading.

He ran a warm bath, relishing the steam and the soothing calm of the water. He slid beneath the surface, relaxing muscles still tense from restless sleep. Suddenly a knock came on the bathroom door.

"Jake, is that you?" his mother called tentatively.

"Who else, Mom?" he called back, amused. The absurd thought of a burglar sneaking in to take a bath made him smile.

"I'm glad you're up. Peggy called," she said through the door.

He finished up and quickly shaved, though his sparse facial hair made the ritual nearly pointless.

At five Jake reassured his mother before heading out. She was worried he'd be driving so soon after the accident but he insisted.

Peggy was waiting at her door, her smile lighting up his mood. He invited her out to dinner.

"Kind of early for dinner, don't you think?" she teased.

"Maybe, but I'm starving," Jake said with a grin.

They drove to the nearby Dairy Queen, sharing hamburgers and milkshakes. Jake ate with the hunger of a man grateful for a second chance.

"I'm glad to see you smiling after last night," Peggy said, picking at her burger.

"Yeah, feels good," Jake replied. "Let's take a drive, see the fall colors."

He steered the car back onto the road, the New Jersey autumn unfolding around them—endless fields framed by mighty oaks and maples blazing gold and red, standing tall against the deep greens of the pines. The sun was a glowing orb low on the horizon, casting orange light on the lazy Saturday afternoon.

As the sun dipped below the horizon, casting long shadows across the empty road, a sudden chill seized Jake. His knuckles whitened as his fingers clamped down on the steering wheel, muscles taut with tension. The steady hum of the engine felt too slow now, and without thinking, he pressed his foot harder against the gas pedal, urging the car forward as if trying to outrun the coming night.

"Jake, slow down!" Peggy urged.

"I have to get you home," he muttered.

"Why the rush?"

Jake's jaw clenched fiercely. The fear rose like bile in his throat. "Before dark. I need to get you home before dark."

Peggy's hand grabbed his arm. "Jake, please—slow down!"

"You don't understand," he snapped. "Like last night—I told you, those things, they come out at night."

The color drained from her face. "Jake, stop the car right now!"

"But I have to protect you—"

"Then stop!" she yelled. "I'll walk, take the bus—just don't risk us both."

Jake stared at her, then himself, his anger giving way to confusion. He eased off the gas and pulled onto the gravel shoulder. Peggy slipped out and started down the roadside path toward home. He stepped out of the car and followed.

"Peggy, I'm sorry. It's just—"

"Jake, you've gone truly crazy," she spat.

Her stride was relentless, jaw locked tight. He kept pace, desperate to explain.

"Look, Peggy—"

"Don't. I don't want to hear about shadows and things hiding in the dark. You drive like a maniac and scare me."

Jake looked up; the last light of day was vanishing. Warm waves of panic seized him, urging flight. Part of his mind screamed, *"Go home! Hide! Time's running out!"*

"Peggy, I saw something," he tried.

"Not again." Her voice was sharp as she walked away.

He called after her. "Peggy!"

She didn't break stride. "Forget it, Jake! Forget everything. I'm going home."

Twilight deepened. Shadows blanketed the fields and edges of the woods, swallowing the world in creeping blackness.

Jake stood alone; the darkness pressing, suffocating.

His legs felt nailed to the earth, but instinct screamed to him to go back—to his car, to safety.

A shape swooped suddenly overhead, and Jake gasped.

"It's just a bat," he whispered to himself.

But as his flashlight flickered on shadowy movements teased at its edges, unseen eyes watching. He bolted, slipping in the gravel. His right knee struck the ground hard, pain shooting through him.

A cry tore from his throat.

He yanked the car door open, scrambling inside, breath ragged. The interior light bathed him in benign yellow warmth. His knee bled freely, grit embedded in torn flesh. He plucked out stones with a trembling hand, wrapping his handkerchief around it tight.

Ignition started the engine's roar. Headlights cut twin beams through the darkness. Safe—for now.

Slow and cautious, Jake eased the car back onto the main road, heartbeat pounding.

Ahead, a thin, stiff figure trod the roadside. Peggy.

He slowed, pulled off twenty feet ahead of her, and grabbed his flashlight.

"Peggy, come on. I'll take you home," he called.

Silence.

His hand shook as he clicked the beam on and swept it toward her.

"Peggy?"

"I'm not talking to you. Go away," came the bitter reply.

"Please. Let me drive you home. I don't want to be alone."

After a long pause, she sighed and appeared at the window.

"No more talking about shadows?" she asked.

"No," Jake promised.

"And no speeding?"

"Slow as an old lady," he said tightly.

She sighed, slid into the seat. "Okay, but I'm still mad at you." Her glare pinned him like a dart.

Inside Jake's eyes darted unsettled in the night, spotting movement just beyond the beam. Shadows danced—but nothing solid. His hand trembled, clenching the flashlight as if for protection.

They drove quietly, tension thick but unspoken.

"Maybe you should see a doctor," Peggy finally said.

"What do you mean?"

"That shock, it must have done something. I read about how the brain's electricity can make you act like a flake."

Jake swallowed hard. "Yeah?"

"You're terrified. You weren't like this before."

He looked ahead. The road stretched like a thin thread through the darkness.

"Maybe you're right," he whispered.

"Good. Get some sleep. On Monday, we'll go to the doctor. I'll be late for beauty school."

At her driveway, Jake pulled in.

She smiled, light flickering in her eyes. But then—a flicker, a mist swirling at the edges of her hair drew his attention.

Jake blinked it away, forcing breath from tight lungs.

On the drive home, a shadow flickered in the headlights ahead of the car.

Jake yanked the wheel, narrowly avoiding a startled groundhog —just inches between calamity and death.

His body shook uncontrollably, breath ragged with each exhale.

"Peggy's right," he muttered. "I'm losing it."

Back home, Jake burst inside, using the flashlight to light his way.

Sitting at the kitchen table, he heard his mother's gentle voice. "What are you doing home so early?... Your knee! What happened?"

He winced as she gently pulled back his bloodied handkerchief. "I fell on some gravel. I thought I should get it cleaned."

She worked quickly, applying iodine and fresh gauze, her calm presence a balm. Her eyes softened. "So, what happened with Peggy?"

Jake hesitated, then confessed, "She thought I was driving too fast."

She smiled wisely. "Sometimes girls are right. Your father had his wild youth, too. But he grew up fast during the war—it changed him. That's why he's hard on you."

Jake absorbed her words, the weight of her faith and practical wisdom grounding him.

She kissed his forehead. "Peggy is a good girl, Jake. Listen to her and you'll have a good life."

When his mother left for the living room, Jake remained seated, thoughts swirling.

"Mom?" he called softly.

She turned, eyes warm.

"If you saw something strange—and nobody believed you— what would you do?"

"Like a flying saucer?" she teased.

"Yeah. Something like that."

She paused, thoughtful.

"I guess I'd try to find proof—evidence. If I were sure."

Jake nodded, a plan forming.

"Thanks, Mom," he said.

"Remember my advice about Peggy too," she teased.

"I know. Thanks."

Alone now, Jake resolved with quiet determination: if the shadows were real, he would find the truth—no matter what it cost him.

12. UNILLUMINATED ASSAULT

J ake didn't close his eyes that night. The darkness seemed to press in on him, heavy and suffocating, every time he tried to rest.

He lay back on the creaking mattress, heart pounding, only to see it in his memory again—the black, oozy creature sliding down the wall, its slick, unnatural form shifting slowly, swallowing the light. His eyes snapped open, staring into the void, breath shallow.

Morning couldn't come soon enough.

When the first pale fingers of sunlight slanted through the curtains it was like a balm to his ragged nerves. The warmth and brightness steadied him, coaxing his rattled mind into a quiet oblivion. At least during the day sleep came easily—like a welcome escape from the long, stretching nightmare of the night.

Monday's sun rose, full and unforgiving. At nine his mother nudged him gently, whispering his name but Jake only mumbled incoherent responses, barely lifting a hand. He drifted in and out, caught between restless consciousness and the pull of sleep.

By ten, Peggy stormed in, frustration etched on her face. "Jake, you have an appointment with the doctor. Come on, get up!" She shook him, impatience thinly veiled beneath her concern.

Jake didn't respond.

Noon passed.

At one in the afternoon, Dr. Hawes finally arrived. The old man's presence filled the room with a curious blend of sternness and goodwill.

He pulled Jake upright with a firm hand, blinking at the dim light in Jake's eyes, clearly used to tougher patients.

"This'll be quick," Doc said, peeling back the blanket and pressing an ice bag against a tender spot—a method that worked like magic. Jake jolted awake nearly jumping off the bed, heart suddenly racing. He nearly lost control of his bladder in shock.

"Well, now that I've got your attention young Master Hurd," declared Dr. Hawes, adjusting his bifocals and sweeping his wild tuft of white hair from his forehead. "I hear you nearly fried yourself last week and haven't had the decency to show up at my office since. You sick, son?"

Jake coughed, wrapping the blanket tighter around himself. "No, sir. I… I just can't fall asleep at night."

"When do you sleep then?" Doc asked, raising a brow.

"When the sun comes up," Jake admitted, voice hoarse.

"Dawn, huh?" The doctor rubbed his chin thoughtfully, tugging his bow tie. "Why's that?"

"I… guess because I'm working nights now as a night guard," Jake said, shrugging.

Doc, with a knowing look on his face, said, "Couldn't be you're afraid of the dark, could it?"

Jake said nothing, only shook his head faintly, eyes down.

"Listen here," Doc said sternly, pulling out his stethoscope and pressing it against Jake's back. "Take a deep breath. In…" Jake complied. "Now out…" The doctor's voice softened. "Ain't nothing wrong with being scared of the dark. Cavemen were terrified of it. That's why they made fires, candles, gas lamps—electric lights even."

He shifted to the front, pressing the stethoscope to Jake's chest. "You took a shock—you scared the pants off yourself. You're not ready to look death straight in the eye yet—not like me, an old coot with a wrinkle or two."

Doc chuckled softly, pulled out a blood pressure cuff, and expertly slid it onto Jake's arm as he spoke.

"A scare like that can mess with your nerves. Plus, Peggy Clune," he nodded toward the door. "She sees you acting out of sorts and gets all riled up. She doesn't know it's just your nerves playing games. Am I right?"

Jake nodded reluctantly.

Doc pumped the cuff and listened carefully. "Women get worried about their fellas." He put away the cuff and grabbed a tongue depressor. "Open up and say—ah."

Jake's mouth fell open as Doc peered inside, pressing the wooden stick deep enough to trigger a gag reflex.

Reaching into his bag again, Doc pulled out a small flashlight with a paper cone. He tilted Jake's head, examining each ear carefully.

"You've had a shock, that's all," Doc said, turning Jake's head side to side. "Things will spook you for a while, but you don't have to let it ruin you."

Next, he looked into Jake's nostrils as he replaced the paper cones.

"Get back to your life as soon as you can. That night watchman job—you fell off the horse, now get back on—it's the best medicine."

He shone the light into Jake's eyes studying the reaction carefully.

"If you want to sleep during the day, fine. Wait on college until you're ready. Mark my words, get back to a routine, give it time, you'll be right as rain."

Doc rummaged in his bag once more and pulled out a small bottle of pills.

"And if you find your brain won't shut up? Take one of these. That's all. I guarantee you'll sleep."

He stood up, fixing Jake with a serious look. "It's hard juggling school and work. I know, I lived it. But listen close—if after a couple of weeks you're still rattled you come talk to me, man-to-man. There's no shame in asking for help. You hear me, son?"

"Yes, sir," Jake murmured, rubbing his tired eyes.

"Good, good. And if you need to talk, my office door's open. But don't bother the ladies—they just fuss and make mountains out of molehills."

Doc shuffled downstairs, leaving Jake staring after him.

He got dressed and headed downstairs to find Peggy and his mother waiting in the living room.

"Jake, you're awake!" Peggy chirped far too bright.

His mother smiled, moving toward him with a plate stacked high with oatmeal raisin cookies—Jake's favorite.

The warm, comforting scent made him momentarily forget the night terrors.

Peggy rushed forward, pressing a quick kiss to his cheek. "We've got the afternoon free now. Want to go somewhere? Anywhere you like."

Jake blinked, caught off guard. "Where?"

"Anywhere."

He grabbed a couple of cookies and headed for the door. "I thought maybe a walk."

Outside the cool breeze was a welcome relief.

"So," Peggy asked, "what did Doc Hawes say?"

Jake shrugged, nibbling a cookie. "Funny, I was just about to ask you the same."

Her cheeks flushed. "He said you had a shock, a scare, and just need time to get your courage back."

"And what did you tell him?" Jake asked, wary.

She sighed, folding her arms. "What could I say? You were talking about creatures... and driving like a maniac. I had to tell him what you said."

"In front of Mom?" Jake's temper flared.

"She needs to know why you're acting weird," Peggy said quietly. "You've been hiding things."

"It's none of your business!" Jake hissed.

Her jaw dropped. "How dare you? Of course it's my business!" Her voice cracked, tears shining in her eyes. "I'm trying to help you even if you won't help yourself."

"I didn't ask for your help," Jake snapped through clenched teeth.

"You can walk by yourself then. I love you—even if I don't know why right now." The word 'why' stretched out as tears spilled down her cheeks. She covered her face and fled down the street.

Damn it. It was supposed to be a secret.

Jake turned inward, back toward the house. In the kitchen he grabbed another cookie, trying to find some comfort in the simple sweetness.

His mother appeared suddenly, carrying a basket of laundry. "You're back! Where's Peggy?"

"She had to go," Jake said, biting into the cookie.

Mom set the basket down, watching him carefully. "She's worried about you."

"I know," Jake said, swallowing hard.

"This whole thing's been hard on her."

He met her gaze. "It's been a damn lot harder on me."

"Jake Hurd!" Her voice sharpened, iron cutting through gentle concern. "Watch your language in this house!"

"Sorry." He looked down.

Her expression softened. "You haven't been yourself since the accident. We're all trying to be patient. But you have to be kinder, especially to Peggy. She's heartsick over this."

"Okay, Mom." Jake shoved the cookie aside and moved to the hall where the phone sat on a small table. "I'm working tonight."

"Is that a good idea?"

"Doc said I should get back to my routine. If I'm going to be awake all night, might as well get paid."

He picked up the receiver and dialed the Security Office at BT&T Research, the weight of the coming night pressing down on him once again.

When Jake pulled up to the BT&T Research facility a cold wind whipped across the parking lot, rattling the leaves like distant whispers.

The building loomed before him, cold and sterile under the flickering security lights. Lieutenant Larson was waiting right at the front door, arms crossed, a faint smirk tugging at his lips.

"Hey, Mr. Fixit! How're you feeling?" Larson's voice was casual but Jake caught an edge of something else beneath it—concern? Doubt?

Jake forced a grin. "Better, thanks." His voice sounded hollow, even to himself.

He stepped inside the security booth where three guards already sat, half-listening to low static from a radio.

Jake spotted an empty chair and sank into it, gripping the time clock fastened to the shelf. As he pulled out the tape to change the paper his eyes drifted upward catching sight of a dark, shifting shadow on the ceiling. It was the same shape, the same unsettling distortion, like the one from that night—the night the impossible slipped through into his world.

A shiver crawled down Jake's spine, involuntarily tightening his grip on the clock. He forced his gaze back to the task but the memory flared at the edge of his mind.

At precisely eleven fifty-five the door creaked open, and John Madder slid in, a wry smile on his face.

"Hey, Jake. Heard you'd be back tonight."

Before Jake could answer, Tony, the guard finishing his shift, held out his timecard to Larson. "Can I head out now?"

Larson glanced up. "Sure, you're covered."

John turned to Larson. "Any updates for us?"

Larson shook his head, irritation creeping in. "Late delivery at 9 PM in building C. It's blocking the hall."

John frowned. "Can we get past it? We actually have to walk through there, y'know."

Larson's jaw tightened. "Yeah, you can squeeze past but the door won't open fully." He shrugged, tired. "Well, night, guys." Punching his card and the others, grabbing his coat, he strode out.

As the door sealed shut John leaned toward Jake, voice dropping to a low murmur. "So, you gonna tell me what really happened?"

Jake blinked. "Happened?"

"You know. That night you and the 'wizard of smarts' nearly blew the place up. You're lucky you didn't end up dead."

Jake laughed softly, uneasy. "It's weird. My parents think I'm some kind of hero."

John nodded toward himself, grin widening. "That's all me. Told the captain you heard something during your shift, called me up about Goldstein collapsing, said you went in to help. Since you knew about the magnets you changed and went into the lab to save him. I spun a good story for the captain."

"How'd you know about the magnets?" Jake asked, surprise sharpening his tone.

John smirked. "Franken-einstein told me on a late shift once. Lucky I was listening. Came up with a pretty convincing tale."

"You should write for a living," Jake said, shaking his head.

John glanced at the clock. "I'm taking first shift."

"I thought I was covering both," Jake said, trying to hide his fatigue.

John chuckled. "Recover first. Then you're up for double duty."

Jake swallowed hard. The thought of being alone in the dark beneath that shifting shadow on the ceiling, sent a ripple of unease through him. "Th—that's fine."

John grinned, clapped him on the shoulder. "Good. No more flying through doors, Peter Pan. And keep your ears open."

Jake's head snapped up. "Why? Did something happen?"

John's expression darkened. "Saturday night some underage drinking in the parking lot. They had a party."

"What'd you do?"

"We called the cops. Cleared them out, notified parents. But Lou didn't hear a thing for an hour."

"That's bad."

"Captain Jim lit a fire under Lou's ass when he found out. Now he wants rounds through the parking lot every couple of hours. Not exactly what we want come January."

Jake shivered. "Brrr."

"So stay sharp," John warned, picking up his watch clock. "If something's off, be ready. Gotta go."

By 4:00 AM, Jake had walked tour two twice over. Confidence trickled back, washing away the initial trembling. The dark corridors seemed less menacing under his flashlight's beam, each shadow shrinking and disappearing when bathed in light.

Maybe Doc Hawes was right—he'd just been shocked. Nothing more.

But at 4:05 AM everything changed.

Back in the guard's office Jake had given John a watered-down version of the accident. He left out the portals, the impossible shadows. He told John that the magnets activated; the doorknob had come loose hitting Goldstein in the head.

"Maintenance cleaned the lab, but never found the doorknob," John said, shaking his head.

"What happened to Goldstein's invention?"

"Dismantled." John shrugged, then added, "What was left of it.'

He headed out to start his tour.

Jake's mind lingered on the brilliant machine—Goldstein's lost marvel—discarded like waste along with the man who created it.

A sudden heaviness filled the room. Jake wasn't alone.

No footsteps. No whispers. Just a crushing silence filled with cold intent—a suffocating presence he was suddenly aware of.

Goosebumps prickled up his arms; every hair on the back of his neck stood erect as a primal fear rooted him to the floor.

He tried to look up, to scan the room slowly. But panic held his head in place.

His breath was shallow and erratic, he told himself to calm down. He forced his eyes upward toward that ever-shifting shadow on the ceiling.

There it was, unchanged—the black mass blending seamlessly with the dull ceiling tiles, but with movements that defied logic.

Slowly Jake stood, turning his head to peer across the room. There was no doubt anymore: it was here, watching him.

His hand trembled as he reached for his flashlight, flicked it on, then swept the beam across corners and walls.

His anger flared, pushing back the fear that threatened to swallow him. This thing had robbed him of peace, stolen his claim to a safe night.

"Come on, you bastard," Jake muttered, face flushed, voice low and fierce. "I know you're there."

The light landed on a corner shadow—a dark shape cast by a chair. Or so he thought.

The shape writhed.

Jake's heart rate spiked. It squirmed like a swarm of bees—tiny, swirling bodies forming an ever-shifting cloud surrounding a mysterious center. Like when he was a boy and witnessed a queen bee surrounded by protector drones.

But something other than insects created this shadow. It was fluid, alive in a way no shadow should be.

Despite the restless movement, its outline stayed an undefined mass—a looming presence like a storm threatening to break.

He found himself edge-to-edge with dread, but eyes locked with the twisting darkness.

"I see you," he growled, jabbing the flashlight beam directly at it.

The shadow jiggled, then streaked—a blur—a sudden shape like a bat on swift wings darted down the wall, across the floor, vanishing beneath the office door.

Jake fumbled toward the door and yanked it open. The floor beyond was awash in minimal light, swallowing most corners in deeper blackness.

"Ha!" he shouted. "Run you bastard!"

A thrill coursed through him. His flashlight was a weapon, his sensory radar against the unknown. He could fight back.

But then a loud crash from outside shattered the moment.

He dashed through the metal door, propping it open with a stone so it wouldn't lock him out.

Near the loading dock an overturned aluminum trash can spilled glass bottles across the concrete. Empty and clattering in the forced silence.

Were the kids still here? Had someone returned?

He swept the flashlight over the parking lot. Nothing.

Yet, out here in the open, the night felt enormous and hostile as if the dark itself was watching him.

Jake hurriedly righted the trash cans and gathered the bottles. One glass bottle was broken—missing a sharp piece.

Intent on ignoring the danger Jake set it back and turned to head inside.

Suddenly, a noise from the building jerked his attention. He bolted up the stairs, yanked the door open, and pointed the light toward the security booth.

The shadows scattered under the beam—but nothing visible lurked.

Jake's skin crawled with unease.

He switched off his flashlight and slumped into a chair, trying to steady his racing heart.

How had the trash can fell? And what—or who—had knocked it over?

As he mulled over the impossible his silver flashlight slipped from the desk's edge, clattering to the floor and rolling under the desk.

Panicked, he dropped to his knees groping blindly beneath the desk for the shaft.

A sudden, sharp pain seared through his hand.

He yanked it free—blood poured from a ragged cut on his wrist.

A startled yelp escaped him.

And then, out of the corner of his eye, he spotted movement— black and quick—fading into shadow.

On the floor lay a jagged piece of glass. Blood—his blood—dotted the sharp edges crimson.

With trembling hands Jake grabbed his handkerchief and wrapped the wound tightly.

He thought about the broken bottle with the missing shard. The bloodied glass on the floor would fit in the missing spot on the bottle. A grim puzzle solved.

How did a shadow move a piece of glass into the office?

One conclusion pulsed in his mind with the weight of a dire premonition:

This was a warning.

If this thing could move that fast in the dark, if it intended harm—

It could've been a lot worse.

Sergeant Madder found Jake slumped on the chair in the guard office, his fingers clutching a blood-soaked handkerchief.

For the second time in less than a week Jake was on his way to the hospital. The wound wasn't deep—only four stitches—but the timing was uncanny.

At the emergency room Jake tried to brush it off with the doctor, explaining how he'd cut his hand when cleaning up a broken bottle from a fallen trash can. It sounded plausible enough, a careless accident.

His parents arrived shortly after; his mother driving the family car with Jake nestled quietly beside her and his father taking Jake's car back home.

When Jake repeated the story once more, his father muttered under his breath, "Clumsy, just like always."

With his stitched hand wrapped tight in gauze and pulsing with a dull, persistent throb, Jake staggered through his front door just after sunrise. He hadn't even made it out of his shoes before collapsing into bed. Pain, exhaustion, and a lingering sense of dread weighed him down.

He slept like the dead.

13. GLOOMY PORTENDS

T he next thing he knew his mother's knock echoed like a rifle shot through the fog of his dreams.

"Jake?" she called, her voice strained and urgent. "You need to get up. Peggy's here. And... she seems really upset."

Jake blinked at the ceiling, momentarily confused by the afternoon light slanting through his curtains. *Peggy?*

"Thanks, Mom," he called groggily but she was already gone—retreating down the hallway.

Jake sat up slowly, his hand a bundle of raw nerves beneath the bandage. The incident from the previous night still played on repeat in his head. Not just pain, not just fear—a warning.

He pulled on jeans and a clean shirt, ran a comb through his tangled hair, and descended the stairs with his heart already tightening in his chest.

Peggy stood in the living room, arms folded tightly across her body. Her complexion was pale, almost gray under the eyes, and she kept flicking nervous glances at the windows and door like something might burst through them at any moment.

"Hey," Jake said gently, stepping close enough to kiss her cheek. "What's going on?"

She tried to smile but it barely lifted the corners of her mouth. "Hi, Jake. I was hoping we could take another walk. Just talk. No arguing this time."

Jake nodded. "Of course. Just let me grab a coat."

The sun was deceptively warm as they stepped outside but a breeze carried the sharp bite of coming cold. Peggy kept close to him, not speaking, her steps brisk and her posture tense. When he reached for her hand she gripped his like a lifeline—tight, trembling, and urgent.

"I need to tell you something," she said finally, eyes still locked on the sidewalk. "But first... I'm sorry. For not believing you. For going to your parents."

Jake raised an eyebrow trying to mask his surprise. "That's... a change."

Her laugh was brittle, more a sound of nerves than humor. "Yeah. Well. A lot can happen in a night."

They turned a corner, cutting across the edge of a quiet neighborhood park—empty swings creaked gently in the wind and the seesaw stood still like a held breath. Peggy walked faster, then paused at a lonely bench under the bare branches of a maple tree.

She sat, curling her hands into her lap. Jake followed, lowering himself beside her, eyes never leaving her pale face.

"Okay," he said softly. "Tell me."

She swallowed hard. "You remember what you said, Jake? About a shadow that moved?"

Jake nodded, watching her closely. "Yeah. You said I was scaring you."

"Well, last night… I think I saw it too." She looked away at the shade under the trees and then back again. "It started with this dream. Something was following me, something I couldn't see. It blended into the night perfectly—like it was part of it. When I woke up I thought it was just the dream getting to me."

Jake's heart skipped a beat.

"You were home?" Jake asked.

"In bed," Peggy said, nodding tightly. "The room was dead quiet—just the sound of my sisters' breathing. Karen and Julie were out cold on their mattresses, and I couldn't shake this feeling like something wasn't right."

Jake leaned forward. "What happened?"

"I looked up at the ceiling. The moonlight comes through the torn curtain just right, throws this bright rectangle up there. And in the middle of it I saw a shadow." She swallowed, her voice trembling slightly now. "It wasn't from anything in the room. It was just… there, in the middle of the light."

Jake said nothing, letting her speak.

"At first I thought it was just a branch or something outside. But then it moved." She rubbed her arms like the memory still chilled her. "It didn't shift like something being blown around. It pulled back. Like it knew I was watching."

"Did you see it clearly?" Jake asked.

Peggy shook her head. "Not clearly. Just the way it blocked the light. But I got this feeling—like it was looking back at me. Like it knew me."

Jake nodded slowly.

"I tried to tell myself it was nothing," she said, voice cracking. "But the fear—it was the same kind you described. That… sick-in-your-stomach kind. Like something ancient just noticed me."

Jake's brow furrowed. "Then what?"

"It vanished. Gone in a blink. I turned on the lamp as fast as I could. Woke Karen up. Julie stirred but didn't really wake."

"What did you tell them?"

"That it was just a bad dream." Peggy laughed bitterly. "I didn't want to scare them. I threw on my robe and went downstairs. Couldn't sit still. I kept thinking about what you said—and Jake —" she looked at him, eyes wide, haunted, "you were right. Something's out there. Something real."

Jake stared at her for a long moment. "And it saw you too."

"Yes." Peggy reached up to brush back her hair, but her hand trembled slightly. "It saw me."

"I think it's only just starting," he said, and held up his bandaged hand. "They can be dangerous."

Peggy's lip trembled. "They did that?"

"Yes."

"Then we need to figure out what it wants. Because it's not just watching anymore."

Jake grabbed the watch clock and the cumbersome dry-cell lantern from the desk without hesitation. The lantern was one of those unwieldy beasts—a bulky square battery nearly half the size of a car battery powering a furious, blinding beam of light. Its glow cut through darkness like a knife.

"I'd better take the first tour," Jake said to Lou, slinging the weight of the watch clock over his shoulder.

Lou raised an eyebrow looking at the big flashlight in Jake's hand.. "What do you need that thing for? It's a beast to carry."

Jake shrugged, his fingers tightening around the lantern's handle. "For the dark rooms," he replied simply.

"Suit yourself. That thing's gonna kill your arm." Lou shook his head but let it go.

Jake stepped toward the door, ready to face the creeping shadows ahead.

"Oh—hey, Hurd!" Lou called out just as Jake's hand touched the doorknob.

Jake turned back. "Yeah?"

Lou's grin was half-serious. "Don't hurt yourself out there tonight, okay? Wouldn't want to cart you off in pieces."

Jake's lips curled into a small, wry smile. "I hope not."

He stepped into the night's silence, the heavy lantern casting harsh light ahead.

Every corner seemed pregnant with danger, every shadow a possible beast waiting to pounce.

Heart pounding Jake moved carefully, the giant battery thudding against his side as he searched for any sign of the dark creature.

But the night was quiet—too quiet. He completed the first tour faster than ever before, no creatures in sight. A hollow victory, maybe.

When Lou returned from his second tour, he found Jake strangely out of character—lounging back in a chair, a tattered copy of Playboy open in his hands. Lou's eyebrows shot up. "Studying, huh?" He pulled an apple from his bag lunch, biting into it lazily.

Jake let out a bitter chuckle. "Looks like I'm dropping out."

"Seriously?" Lou's eyes narrowed in disbelief. "You? Mister Big-Time College Guy? Thought you had your entire future mapped out."

Jake's gaze darkened. "Plans change."

Lou smirked and pulled a fresh Playboy from a paper bag. "Well, I don't need whatever crap you're reading. I got the latest issue." He plopped down chewing thoughtfully, flipping with exaggerated lethargy through the glossy pages. "You can see it when I'm done. Sloppy seconds, kid."

Jake grunted but didn't ask what he meant. Instead he heaved the lantern again, preparing for the next patrol. The heavy weight reminded him of the stakes—he needed to stay alert.

Moving carefully, with the dull hum of the surrounding building, Jake tried to pierce the darkness, every shadow seeming just a breath away from becoming alive.

At four o'clock his lantern's beam caught a pile of refuse slumped in a corridor. For one horrible instant the heap resembled a crouched man. Jake leapt back with a startled grunt, flicking the light in wide arcs. His heart hammered furiously as he stood frozen, trying to will the trembling in his limbs to ease.

The final stretch was the basement storage chamber. An immense space jammed with relics from the past: desks, chairs, and tables wrapped meticulously in brown paper and held together by brittle tape and rusty staples. Like mummified trophies of some ancient, forgotten pharaoh. The air was stale, thick with dust, and the darkness here pressed heavier than before.

No matter how Jake moved the lantern, its light didn't reach far into the vast gloom.. Countless places lay hidden beyond the beam, perfect places for shadows to hide.

He felt it immediately: something watching, lurking just beyond the edge of light. Sweat beaded on his forehead—cold, clammy, unwelcome.

His voice shattered the silence, raw and desperate. "I know you're here! Coward! Show yourself!" The echo rolled back, hollow and mocking.

Step by trembling step, Jake advanced, dread coiling tighter in his gut like a descending serpent. The darkness thickened around him, almost suffocating.

The hairs on the back of his neck prickled, his breath shallow and ragged. He fought the rising panic clawing at his mind.

Suddenly he fumbled the staircase door, fingers slick with sweat. Relief flooded through him as he pushed open the exit and climbed rapidly, the basement's icy grip loosening with every step upward.

Yet even as fresh air kissed his face the shadows seemed to cling still—to linger just at the corner of his vision, promising they were far from finished.

At the top Jake leaned heavily against the doorway, gasping for breath, heart hammering like a war drum in his chest.

"I will find you!" he shouted into the hollow hall, voice raw with rage and fear.

His voice echoed back, cold and empty.

He whispered to himself, eyes blazing with determination, "I will find a way."

14. Shadows Step In

J ake was being shaken roughly, pulled from his sleep suddenly.

Groggy and disoriented, he mumbled, "Wuzza?" His eyes fluttered open, struggling against his fatigue.

"It's me," his father said in a low, firm voice. "Get dressed. We have to go—now."

Jake blinked twice, still unsure of the hour. "What time is it?"

"Four o'clock," came the sharp reply. "No time to waste. Come on."

A strange mixture of childhood obedience and confusion clouded Jake's mind. It felt like the nerve-wracking mornings before school when haste ruled every movement.

He threw on his underwear, a shirt, and his worn dungarees—his father referred to as 'farmer pants'—though surprisingly, Alan made no comment this time.

His dad waited just outside the door, pacing with restless energy. Jake noticed an absence of his usual teasing and the knot in his stomach tightened.

"You ready?" Alan asked, eyes sharp.

Jake swallowed hard. "Where are we going?"

"There's someone you need to meet. An appointment," Alan said without elaboration. "Get in the car."

Too hazy to protest, Jake followed his father out to the dusty driveway and climbed into the worn leather seat of Dad's 1956 Buick. The afternoon air was crisp as they rumbled over the back roads of Randolph; the sun scraped the horizon.

Still clouded in sleep but growing curious, Jake piped up, "Seriously, Dad, who are we going to see?"

Alan glanced at him with a rare softness. "A man I know. He might give you advice better than your mom, me, or even Doc Hawes."

Jake frowned. What could this be about?

The Buick turned onto a gravel driveway leading to a cluster of somber stone buildings. One bore a large, rusted plaque:

GREYSTORM

A cold chill traced Jake's spine. Greystorm. The place whispered of madness, the sort of place families sent the 'lost' and the 'broken.'

Suddenly, Jake felt every shadow sharpen, every breath tighten in his chest.

"Why are we here?" His voice cracked.

Dad pulled into a small, grim parking lot and killed the engine.

"I want you to talk to someone," Alan said carefully, "someone I know."

"Why here?" Jake demanded, but the tremor in his voice betrayed his fear. Was his father having him committed?

Alan's hand landed on Jake's arm—steady but unyielding. "Because sometimes, to understand where you might be headed, you need to see where losing touch with reality gets you."

Jake recoiled from the touch like it burned. "I'm not going in."

"Son, I will not commit you. I just want you to look around, talk to a guy I know."

His anger flickered bright. "You think I'm crazy."

Alan exhaled deeply and leaned back in his seat, eyes like flames. "If you let what you're experiencing get to you—believe me—you'll end up in a place like this."

A tense silence hung between them, then Alan's voice hardened. "Now either you come in willingly or I'll carry you there myself."

Jake locked eyes with his father, weighing pride against fear. The choice wasn't truly his, but this was no time to fight.

"All right… just to talk," he conceded, climbing out of the car. Alan followed, gesturing for him to stay close.

The inside of Greystorm was a world Jake had only glimpsed in nightmares. It smelled stale and sick; the linoleum cracked and stained; yellowed walls bore marks of neglect.

"Alan! Over here!" a bright voice called.

From down the hall emerged a short, thin man with dark hair slicked back to a shining sheen, his canvas shoes tapping sharply on the floor. He wore standard green hospital pants and a tunic.

"Bill, this is my son, Jake," Alan said, stepping aside.

The man sized Jake up with an amused grin. "Whoa. Thought you were tall, Alan. Jake, you're at least six-foot-four."

Jake barely registered the comment. His attention was drawn to a small room behind a glass window where two nurses struggled to restrain a woman in a wheelchair. She fought fiercely, nails scraping the nurse's face and Jake saw the marks and the blood.

Bill followed Jake's glance and sighed. "That's Rose. Delusional. They have to tie her down to keep her from hurting herself."

Jake didn't look away.

"Mental illness is strange," Bill said quietly. "She started with obsessive compulsion—washing her hands over and over, never stopping. Then it spiraled down. Her family had no choice but to bring her here."

The woman's cries echoed hollowly through the hall, raw and haunting.

Bill led them on. "This isn't even the worst of it. Come on."

Jake froze. "Can't you help her?"

Bill shook his head with bitter acceptance. "Too far gone. If therapy worked she'd be somewhere else."

Hallways stretched dark and oppressive as they trudged through Greystorm's corridors. Padded wheelchairs sat silent, patients' eyes vacant or wild. The sharp tang of antiseptic barely masked the underlying stench of despair.

A man with a misshapen skull stared at Jake, forehead wrinkled, drool streaming down like a sick river. Jake swallowed hard.

Bill broke the suffocating silence. "Your dad told me you had a shock recently."

Jake nodded.

"He tried to be a hero and got hurt badly," Alan said grimly. "An electric shock threw him through a door."

"You're damn lucky," Bill said with a terse smile. "Here, look at this."

They stopped at a window peering into a sterilized room. A man was strapped to a table, electrodes affixed; a buzzer of electricity surged through and the man convulsed violently.

Jake gasped. "What's that?"

"Electroconvulsive therapy," Bill said. "There are studies that back using it, but I'm not a fan."

Jake's eyes couldn't leave the twitching figure.

Bill continued, "It's funny: they say it helps the delusional become rational. But it might just as well do the opposite." He glanced at Jake. "Your dad said you saw strange things after your shock."

Jake shot a glare at Alan. "What if I did?"

Bill's eyes softened slightly. "I wouldn't trust what you saw. Dreams feel real, but they're just that—dreams."

"Yeah?" Jake muttered skeptically.

"There's an experimental drug out there. Lysergic acid. Changes brain chemistry so much you see things that aren't real. Makes hallucinations so vivid you can't tell the difference."

Jake nodded slowly.

Bill's voice lowered: "You got a shock, lost oxygen, and passed out. My advice? Don't believe a thing you saw."

"That's good advice," Alan agreed, visibly relieved.

Bill's tone sharpened. "Now, come on—the serious cases are last."

They made their way down stairwells into a windowless basement. Cold concrete walls lined the halls, heavy barred doors locked tight. Armed guards stood watch, shadows looming.

"This is the criminally insane ward," Bill said, greeting one guard by name.

Jake surveyed the scene: men confined in stark cells, faces vacant or twisted with madness, some pacing like caged predators.

Bill stopped at a door where a man lay half on the floor, matted hair and unshaven face stark against the padded room.

"Bill! I need a shave!" the man called out, voice jarring in its everyday tone.

Jake tensed as Bill replied, "Sure, George, I'll bring you an electric shaver tomorrow."

"No," George muttered, eyes burning with fierce pain. "I need a straight razor."

"You know we can't do that," Bill mumbled.

George's face crumbled with despair as Bill moved on.

"What did he do?" Jake asked, voice hushed.

Bill answered with cold finality, "Killed three girls with a straight razor."

At the next cell, a bald man paced wildly. Someone had shaved his head, face, and even his eyebrows.

When they neared he lunged at the open panel, voice sharp and manic. "You here for the freak show? I'm the number-one freak!" he sneered.

A guard readied his nightstick, but Bill waved him away.

The man laughed and paced again.

"Frank," Bill said, "We've got an appointment Wednesday."

The pacing ceased, a bitter laugh escaping him. "Like I have a choice."

They stepped away, Jake's skin crawling.

"Murderer, too. Electric chair or here—he got lucky."

Bill's words lingered as they ascended back into daylight.

Jake exhaled deeply, relief washing over him as the oppressive weight of Greystorm lifted.

Alan turned to Bill. "Thanks for showing us around."

Bill grinned, "No problem. I'll probably be in your store Thursday to pick up supplies."

His father nudged Jake's arm, shaking him from his reverie.

Jake fumbled for words. "Uh, thanks, sir."

Bill handed Jake a slip of paper. "If you ever want to talk, call me. I'm still in residency—no cards yet."

The slip of paper had the name 'Bill Benning' and a phone number with a Morristown exchange.

"T-thank you," Jake stammered, voice tight and brittle. "I'll... keep that in mind." He tucked the paper away, the afternoon sun warm against his skin, but the shadows inside Greystorm clung tightly to his mind.

Bill Benning's gaze flicked toward the looming stone building behind them, its ancient, unforgiving facade cutting through the gloomy afternoon sky.

"Yeah," Bill murmured, voice low, almost a whisper. "It's a scary place. Believe me, the first thought in my head every day is how to get out of here."

Alan Hurd raised an eyebrow, skepticism threading his tone. "Really, Bill? I always thought this was a good place to learn."

Bill let out a bitter snort. "Learn? Maybe, if your lesson is how deep the hole goes. I've learned this isn't the answer. We fix nothing here—we just throw people in cells, pump them full of drugs, and suppress what's inside them. I don't know what the actual solution is, but there has to be one." He spun back to Alan, eyes fiery. "I want to help them. I have to."

Alan's hand closed around Bill's in a firm shake. "A noble goal. I'll see you Thursday."

Bill waved tiredly, the weight of his words lingering in the space between them as they climbed into the car and pulled away.

The drive home stretched out quietly. Fifteen minutes of pressing silence, the hum of tires against asphalt the only sound inside the car. Jake's father never seemed to want distractions—no radio murmuring in the background, just the road ahead and the stillness inside.

"So," Dad finally broke the silence, voice steady but probing, "what did you think of that place?"

Jake's jaw tightened. "They caged those people like animals," he said flatly.

"That's where they put folks who get carried away by their imaginations, son." Dad's voice was softer now, almost distant. "I hope you learned something… valuable."

Jake's grip on the edge of the seat tightened. Yes, he had learned—a lesson far darker than anyone had warned him about: if you started seeing things the best thing you could do was keep your mouth shut. Otherwise you might someday find yourself trapped inside a place like Greystorm.

As the darkened landscape sped past outside the window the night no longer seemed menacing. Whatever awaited in those shadows couldn't possibly be worse than the suffocating cold stone and whispered despair of that place.

They pulled into the driveway just as the clock neared 6:30 PM. Inside, the table was set, a warm glow spilling out from the kitchen. The smell of dinner wrapped around the house like a fragile promise of normalcy.

"Where have you two been?" Mom's voice was genuine, but edged with worry as they stepped through the door.

"It's alright, Jane," Dad said with a quick wink towards Jake, a message begging silence. "We ran some errands."

"Yeah, errands," Jake echoed, unease curling in his stomach.

"Well… Peggy stopped by looking for you after beauty school."

"Where is she?" Jake asked.

"I sent her up to your room to look for you. You appeared to have left in a hurry, which puzzled her. She went back up because she had left her soda up there."

"In my room?" Jake's voice cracked with surprise.

"I guess she is waiting until you got home," Mrs. Hurd said. "No doubt playing some of your records or something. Go find her and come down for dinner."

Jake nodded, swallowing down the knot of dread. He moved up the stairs, flicking on the stairwell lights as he went. Each step echoed in the quiet house.

On the second floor, then the third. Then, standing just outside his door, Jake froze.

The door was open, the darkness inside twisting into a familiar shape—a presence he could feel, cold and slow creeping.

The shadow waited.

His body stiffened, trembling from the inside out. Sweat slicked his palms as he reached cautiously beyond the doorframe, fingers searching the wall for the light switch. The surface beneath his touch felt unnervingly clammy, as though something oily clung to it.

With a small, shaky breath, Jake flipped the switch.

Suddenly the room flooded with bright, clangorous light— sharp, intrusive, yet fiercely protective, dazzling enough to chase away the shadows and let Jake breathe again.

His eyes fell to the floor.

A figure lay sprawled, motionless.

Jake stumbled back.

The shadow wasn't just a shape; it had taken form.

It was Peggy.

Her skin was ghostly pale, eyes dull and unseeing. No breath, no twitch, no pulse.

Jake's throat clogged, panic closing in like a vice. The room tilted, the air tightening as if the walls themselves suffocated him. Fear thundered in his heartbeat—this was the first time he'd ever stood so close to death.

"DAD! MOM!" Jake screamed, voice raw with terror.

He spun and dashed down the stairs, the world a blur. His foot caught on the first step, and he tumbled awkwardly down the stairs, pain flaring sharply in his ankle as he reached the bottom of the staircase.

"MOM! DAD!" he shrieked again, clutching his throbbing leg.

Suddenly the stairwell light blinked once—and died.

Darkness swallowed him whole.

Blind, panicked, Jake flailed his arms, desperate to fend off the unseen terror pressing in. His ankle pulsed violently, and the black void around him seemed alive with menace.

Then—light.

The door at the bottom of the stairs burst open; a sudden flash felt like salvation.

"What is it? What's wrong?" Dad's voice boomed, frustrated as he flicked the light switch in vain.

"The light burnt out," Mom said hurriedly. "Jake, are you hurt? Did you fall?"

"Get a flashlight, Jane," Dad ordered sharply.

Jake sucked in a ragged breath. "It's Peggy—in my—room."

His father hurried up the stairs, leaving the door open, fingers fumbling nervously for the light switch in the darkened doorway.

"Oh, my God," came his whispered gasp.

Jake's heart dropped. The light he'd left on inside the room had gone dark. Not only the stairwell—something had turned off the light inside his own room.

Mom appeared at the top of the stairs, flashlight and a fresh bulb in hand.

Suddenly, his father's booming voice echoed from the room: "Jane? Is that you? Call an ambulance… right away!"

His mother's voice was trembling as she shoved the flashlight into Jake's hand and rushed downstairs to the phone.

Jake's legs faltered as he struggled to stand, agony flashing through his ankle. Clutching the handrail, he limped back up to the doorway of his room.

Peggy lay there, face pale and still.

His father knelt beside her, pressing down rhythmically on her chest with a desperate urgency.

An empty bottle of soda lay dripping on the floor.

Peeking out from under the dresser in the darkest corner was a small, discarded pill bottle—empty, its cap missing.

FOR OCCASIONAL SLEEPLESSNESS

TAKE ONE CAPSULE AT BEDTIME

DO NOT EXCEED RECOMMENDED DOSAGE

The sleeping pills Dr. Hawes had given him.

Peggy would never have taken them.

Then where did the pills go?

Jake looked over at the bottle of soda lying on the floor and saw some white particles in a brown droplet of the soda that hung from the bottle.

If the shadow creatures could cut his hand with broken glass, could it put pills into a bottle of soda?

Jake's breath caught as he stared at the grim scene. The shadow's presence whispered in the dark corners of the room, a cold warning lingering in the air.

The funeral day dawned cold but clear, sunlight slicing through a pale blue sky. A hint of winter's chill bit at exposed skin.

Jake wore his best suit, balanced carefully on crutches. His ankle still throbbed fiercely, tightly wrapped, a reminder of his fall.

The Clunes had done what they could—arranging the service with limited means. Mrs. Clune's secret savings for Peggy's wedding paid for the coffin; the church collection covered the plot and headstone; the preacher donated his time and the use of the chapel. Jake's mother and father provided their home for the gathering and hired a caterer.

When Jake's mother offered help, tears overflowed from Mrs. Clune's eyes once more.

Neighbors, family, classmates, beauty school friends—many came to say goodbye.

The police classified the death as a suicide because tests revealed over ten sleeping pills in the soda. Their conclusion: Peggy poured the pills into the soda.

Jake's father pressed them to reconsider. Reluctantly, they changed it to 'accidental death.'

But Jake knew the truth.

Peggy never had a chance. Her admitting she saw the creature doomed her.

As the preacher's voice droned on beside the fresh grave, Jake's heart burned—but not with sorrow. Beneath the numbness, a fierce, icy rage simmered.

It wasn't the wild fury that shouts at the heavens. No—it was cold, methodical, a blaze of wrath that demanded justice.

Goldstein's experiment tore open a gateway to a darker world. A creature or creatures from there—unknown, intelligent—had slipped through the barrier and now moved unseen in the shadows.

This thing, this visitor, was no mindless phantom. It knew. It learned. It hunted.

How else could it have known the pills were lethal?

His brief struggle with the creature, shining his flashlight at it, had enraged the intruder.

It protected its secret with deadly precision.

And now Jake understood.

If he told anyone what he'd seen, he would end up in that place—Greystorm.

He vowed silently with cold resolve to hunt down whatever this was.

He would uncover their weaknesses.

He would make them pay in time.

But he would never tell.

Not a soul.

THANKSGIVING

15. FAMILY GATHERING

"**W**hy the hell didn't you tell me?" I demanded, my voice sharp, eyes locking onto Bill Benning as his face flushed dark red. The blood rushing to his cheeks betrayed his discomfort.

"It had absolutely nothing to do with here and now," Bill spat defensively, avoiding my gaze.

"Nothing to do—" I began, struggling to keep control. "You meet this young man, scare him half to death, and then just keep it to yourself?"

Bill's jaw tightened. "It's what his father wanted," he said, his voice rising. Then, as if wrangling with his conscience, he softened. "A father desperate enough to think his son was imagining things, afraid talking openly would make it worse."

I let the words sink in. "So you break every ethical boundary for a paranoid parent?"

"Oh, spare me, *Doctor* Lucas," Bill shot back, his frustration bubbling over. "You've never made a mistake? I was just a resident then—full of ego, hating every minute here, dreaming of being the next Freud, thinking I knew everything."

"You should have told me about it," I insisted, refusing to let it drop.

Bill exhaled, slumping behind his desk. "A half-hour meeting forty years ago? It didn't seem relevant."

"It explains how you knew what was wrong with him," I muttered, flipping through my notes. "Seeing creatures in the dark."

Bill leaned forward, eyes narrowing. "He told you?"

"In vivid detail," I said. "Once he started, he amazed me with the intricacies of his obsession—how real it feels to him."

"Good for you. I got nowhere," Bill said bitterly.

"You made a bad first impression," I snapped, driving the point home before relenting.

A week and a half had passed since Jake began unraveling his life-story. His words spilled out like a torrent, precise and relentless. My notes rivaled War and Peace in volume—with the timeline only inching through the 1960s.

Bill nodded as if oblivious to my fatigue. "Where will you spend Thanksgiving?"

"With Marcie's mother," I sighed, "but I'm hoping to work with Jake in the morning."

Bill raised an eyebrow. "You rarely work holidays."

"I don't want to miss a day. Besides, Jake's always here."

"You know Mr. Hurd's obsession," Bill said, watching me with a mixture of concern and warning. "I hope he's not becoming yours."

Ignoring Bill's comment, I left Greystorm in a hurry as rushing had become a habit. Anne adjusted my appointments to carve out time for Jake in the mornings, cutting back my schedule. But our sessions always ran late. No matter how I tried to organize I was late more often than not.

Jake fascinated me. I constantly reminded myself the interest was purely professional, but the truth tangled up my thoughts.

He had dragged me through most of the sixties already. It didn't surprise me that the chaotic world outside seemed unreal to him—his mind locked tight on the shadows only he could see. It was typical of his disorder: self-absorption, blinding focus.

A wise man once said life would be easier if we didn't take things so personally. Jake clearly lived in his own private war.

He moved out of his parents' house in '61, renting his first apartment—a tiny space that somehow thrived as his sanctuary for nine years. The basement held special significance. A locked door, a private key, a workshop. His refuge.

Jake could describe every inch of his workbench—the tools, the clutter, the worn manuals—but could not remember where he was when Kennedy was shot. That gap screamed his reality: he'd pulled back from the world, obsessed with the dark creatures he believed were bound to him.

In Jake's apartment, technical manuals replaced newspapers; scientific journals took the place of television.

He still sensed the creatures nightly. They favored the dark corners of BT&T Research, but now Jake didn't yell or chase. He observed quietly, took notes, studied their habits—like a scientist scrutinizing a wild animal.

The draft board called him in '63. He showed up in his guard uniform and claimed he was a member of Civil Defense, which was big back then. They passed him over without contest.

His membership wasn't patriotism—it was a chance to learn about Geiger counters, tracking tech, and any way to hunt his shadows.

When his Civil Defense unit disbanded in '65, Jake didn't mind; it meant more library time and building devices to fight what no one else could see.

While civil rights protests, war demonstrations, and cultural shifts grew louder outside, Jake's concerns remained small and focused. He thought about work, guards, research, and getting enough sleep.

Sundays brought trips home. His father's heart attack in '68 injected the first genuine emotion Jake felt in years—a crack in the armor of detachment. His mother fretted over his bachelor status years after Peggy's death.

Jake listened, tight-lipped, nodding patiently to their worries that meant nothing to him. His parents' frustration was static background noise to his singular obsession.

He recounted 1968—the Summer of Love—differently from the rest of the world. Hippies, protests, peace signs—all distractions he ignored.

Just as Jake finished his story of that year, there came a knock at the door. Big Carl appeared looming in the doorframe, silently signaling our time was up.

"Well, that's our time for today," I said gently.

Jake shrugged, masking his anxiety with detachment. "I guess so."

"Would tomorrow work for another session?"

"Why not?" His voice was flat. "It's Thursday."

"Thanksgiving."

He paused. "I guess that means we'll have turkey."

"Eat all you want. But I think we're making progress. I want to hear more about your father."

"Will your family mind?"

The question caught me off guard. Mind? My kids barely saw me, Marcie was openly furious, and I sacrificed patients for these sessions.

"No, it's fine," I assured him.

Jake nodded, a rare flicker of sincerity. "Then I'll see you tomorrow. The earlier, the better."

"I can't believe it!" Marcie snapped, tugging the soft flannel nightgown over her head with a frustrated jerk. "You're working all the damn time. You get home after the kids are asleep, and then the one day you have off—"

"Marcie," I interrupted, trying to stay calm as I watched her twisting and turning under the dim bedroom light, her fingers awkwardly fumbling to unhook the bra beneath the flannel. The movement, so familiar and yet so intimate, caught me off guard.

My irritation softened, replaced by something warmer, something urgent. "It's just for an hour or two. I'll be back by eleven at the latest."

Her eyebrows shot up, eyes flashing with all-too-familiar stubbornness. "We won't even get to my mother's until two!"

She slipped off her flannel nightgown just enough to peel away her pants and panties, the bare skin glimpsed beneath the worn fabric suddenly igniting a long-dormant desire in me.

Weeks of exhaustion and obligations had kept us apart, our lovemaking reduced to occasional distracted moments.

I swallowed the frustration bubbling inside and focused on her words. "It depends on traffic."

"We're supposed to be there early—to help cook."

I nodded, remembering the chaos of my mother-in-law's kosher kitchen. As Marcie called it, 'a real Jewish kitchen'— separate refrigerators, different stoves for meat and dairy, double dishwashers. The rules weren't just dietary; they were a minefield of etiquette and tradition enforced with unrelenting scrutiny.

I'd learned to dread these visits. Her mother always showed displeasure. Arrive late, she'd grumble. Early? She'd complain. And even arriving precisely on time didn't spare us from her endless nitpicking.

"Two is plenty early for dinner around there."

Marcie let out a tone I both hated and somehow loved—it was that whiny, you-should-know-better voice, the one that made me want to roll my eyes and pull her closer at the same time. "Not when dinner's at four!"

I sighed, feeling the weight of our unspoken tension. "I'll go early and get back as soon as I can."

She grabbed a brush, moving it through her hair as she stared at me in the mirror. "You're getting too wrapped up in this case."

"Obsessed," I corrected gently.

"That too."

I moved toward her, hands coming to her shoulders where knots of stress had gathered.

"Relax," I murmured, kneading the tight muscles until she sighed softly. "When was the last time we made love?"

She shook her head, tired but playful. "Almost three weeks. You passed out at eight on Friday."

"A good bottle of wine and a long day." I leaned down, kissing the pale curve of her neck, the only skin not hidden beneath the nightgown.

Her brush dropped onto the dresser. "Interested?"

"Are you?"

Marcie laughed, exasperated. "You have all the passion of a bored accountant. Some soft words, flowers, a little attention… could go a long way."

"Does that work on patients?"

She smirked. "Might be worth trying with your wife. Make me feel more like your partner and less like a coworker."

I continued to massage, shifting my hands lower, tracing the tension in her back.

She moaned and said, "Your chances would improve if you came home early sometimes."

"You know how important this case is to Bill."

"And you." Marcie's eyes caught mine in the mirror, her gaze sharp as a blade. "Can we spend the night at my mother's?"

"Oh, brother," I growled, pressing harder into her lower back. "I hate your mother's house. The beds are rocks, the rooms sweltering, and the cats trigger my allergies."

"Easy," she said, and I lightened my grip. "I understand, but I like it. She showers the kids with attention and I get a break."

"I hate that traffic on Friday."

My hands rose to her scalp, running gently through her hair, trying to soothe both her and myself.

A sly smile crept over her face. "How about a compromise?"

"What?"

She turned, eyes gleaming mischievously. "We go away for the weekend."

"W-What?" I stammered.

"I thought about it," she said, a small grin on her face. "I decided you were right."

"I was right?" The words tumbled out, tinged with disbelief.

"Beginner's luck." she shot back as I continued to rub her body. "We could go to that kosher place in the Catskills. We drive home Thursday night. You see your patient Friday morning. Then —just us—until Sunday."

"What about the kids?"

"We leave them at grandma's house," she said, grinning wickedly in the mirror.

I paused, hands still in her hair, considering.

"Say it, Doctor," she teased. "Go 'Eureka! What a great idea!'"

"Eureka, what a great idea," I repeated dully.

"Could you fake enthusiasm a little better?"

"I'm thinking," I said, as I considered the possibilities. "It is a splendid idea, since it was mine to begin with."

"That's a trifle better."

"It sounds great," I effused with some life.

"You're learning," Marcie gloated. "It's a universal truth: women fake orgasms when their men are making love, and men fake enthusiasm when their women are talking."

"If that's so, I shouldn't be required to fake enthusiasm."

"Oh, how unkind! I enjoy sex even when I don't orgasm." She moved my hands to her breasts. "However, if you put in a little effort, I guarantee I won't have to pretend."

The weeks apart kindled something raw between us. That night it was electric—slow touches, lingering kisses, rediscovery.

For the first time in months we moved in sync, passion and tenderness intersecting as we climaxed together. Afterwards we lay wrapped in each other's arms, skin slick with sweat and hearts beating in tandem.

"What brought all that on?" she asked softly.

"What do you mean?"

"I saw how you looked at me when I undressed. I know that look."

"You looked sexy."

She laughed. "Really? With my sagging breasts, stretch marks, and cellulite?"

I pulled her closer. "Stop. You're a psychiatrist—haven't you had enough therapy to stop dwelling on negatives?"

"And I'm also a woman."

"And if I made a dumb stereotype about that you'd bite my head off," I whispered, kissing the curve of her jaw. "You're beautiful. Sure, maybe the breasts sag a bit…"

"That's not helping."

"When you were pregnant…"

"They were huge!"

"So, that's why they hang lower now. The stretch marks are from giving birth to our lovely children. And every woman has cellulite. Men don't notice it."

"Really?"

"Honestly. If I were your therapist, I'd work with you on that poor body image." I ended the sentence with a yawn. Sleep tugged at me like an undertow.

"Sam? You asleep?"

"No," I muttered, barely conscious.

"Why isn't it like this anymore?"

"What do you mean?"

"Like this—us. We haven't made love like that in months."

"Marcie, every marriage goes through ups and downs."

"Not like this. Lately, there's so much anger between us."

I sighed. "I don't want to pick apart our marriage for the five-hundredth time."

"See? Like that," she said, exasperated.

We lay there, silence stretching between us. Her body warmed mine, yet even that closeness felt foreign. We had drifted apart, becoming strangers in the same bed.

"Maybe a weekend away," I suggested. "No kids, no careers—just us."

She smiled and nestled close. "What about sleeping naked?"

"Fine, if you keep your cold feet off me."

"Always ruining the mood."

"I promise romance all weekend," I vowed. "This is the least I can do to avoid staying at your mother's house."

"I'll hold you to that."

We drifted to sleep entwined—until 7 AM when Rueben crashed onto the bed, yanking blankets and pleading for breakfast. Embarrassed, we scrambled to cover our naked bodies before sending him out to pick a cereal.

Marcie leapt from the bed like a nymph, took the flannel nightgown and threw it over her head, pulling it on rapidly. I grabbed my robe en route to the shower but paused at the doorway. I pulled her close, planting a kiss on her cheek and squeezing her ass.

"Oh my," she gasped, adjusting her glasses.

"Just getting warmed up for the weekend," I teased.

She shuffled off with a grin, and for a moment, I believed things would really change.

Of course, it didn't happen that way.

I arrived at Greystorm just after eight, clutching a thermos of strong coffee from home in one hand and a warm, slightly squished bagel in the other.

The building was unnervingly quiet for a hospital—especially on a holiday. The staff was a skeleton crew, stretched so thin every whispered request echoed down the sterile halls.

Patients were restless, their frustration bubbling under the surface. The ones coherent enough were painfully aware they'd be spending their holidays trapped here, far from family and any semblance of normalcy.

I headed toward Jake's ward—the section where they kept the so-called 'nervous breakdown' patients. It was a term long out of favor in medical circles even then, but the orderlies and nurses still quietly used it as if that label somehow made things simpler.

The entire wing had been gutted and rebuilt to resemble a boutique hotel rather than a hospital: soft lighting, muted earth tones, even thick carpets that deadened footsteps.

It was a far cry from the grim, state-run asylum Greystorm had been just a decade before.

By 1999, Greystorm had reinvented itself completely. No more criminally insane, no more indigent patients shuffled into forgotten corners. They boasted live-in condos for chronic patients, and the grounds—once neglected—were now manicured to perfection with walking paths and flowerbeds bursting with color.

It was Bill Benning's stroke of genius in the late 80s that saved Greystorm from oblivion—turning it into a teaching hospital and bringing in tuition-paying students who learned the sanitized, triumphant side of its history. Workers refurbished the old buildings, making their new facades gleam with promise.

I approached the nurse's station, spotting Althea Winters buried under a mountain of paperwork. "Althea, is Carl bringing Jake down today?" I asked, trying to keep my tone light.

She looked up, eyes tired but sharp. "Carl? He's off today." Her voice was flat, almost clipped.

"Anyone else available? I need to get Jake to the office," I pressed, forcing a smile despite the knot tightening in my chest.

She let out a frustrated sigh, irritation beginning to rise. "Available? I've barely got enough hands to feed these patients, let alone change their bedpans. If you want him, you're signing him out yourself. Don't forget to sign him back in when you're done."

I nodded, suppressing a growl of frustration, and made my way down the hall to Jake's room. I knocked softly against the doorframe; inside, Jake lay propped against the pillows, absorbed in the New England Medical Review.

"Trying to be smarter than me?" I teased.

Jake tossed the magazine onto the bedside table and swung his legs over the edge. He glanced at the clock, eyebrows raised. "You're early."

"Needed you fresh. We've got a lot to cover about '68." My voice held a quiet urgency.

He stood, pulling on one of those drab hospital jumpsuits, slipping on his shoes with practiced ease, his long stride effortless as he headed for the door. "Then let's get to work."

Ten minutes later, we sat face-to-face in my office; the blinds cast thin striped shadows across the room. My legal pad was open on my lap, pen poised.

"Your father had a heart attack," I stated, breaking the silence.

Jake nodded slowly. "That's where we left off. He was lucky—even then, heart attacks were brutal. Survival rates were... well, not great."

"But how did you feel about it?" I pressed, sensing deeper turmoil beneath his calm exterior.

Jake's eyes darkened, voice lowering. "It was a shock. Everything I'd known—suddenly became fragile. Like a dam cracked, and I wasn't sure if I could hold back what was rushing in."

The past hadn't finished with Jake—and neither, it seemed, had the darkness lurking just beneath Greystorm's polished surface.

16. SARA

J ake told me how his father, Alan Hurd, had collapsed
unexpectedly in the pharmacy. Jake hadn't been there, but
the image haunted him.

His mother drove Jake to Morristown Memorial Hospital,
where they waited endlessly in the sterile waiting rooms.

The doctor met them solemnly in a quiet hallway. "Your
father's in surgery," the man said, voice steady yet grave. "He's
having a bypass."

A week later, Jake visited his father in the hospital. Alan Hurd
was sitting up, pale-faced but lucid. The fatigue in his eyes was
overwhelming. Then Alan dropped a bombshell: he was selling
the pharmacy. "I wanted to leave it to you, Jake," he said, voice
barely a whisper, "but I know that won't happen."

Jake's gaze locked onto mine with a mix of defiance and
resignation. "I told him it's better to sell it while it's still making
money than risk me ruining it and selling for a loss." He looked
away, eyes glazing with regret. "In my father's eyes, I did nothing
to live up to his expectations."

Since 1960, Jake worked the same midnight shift at BT&T. The familiar faces who once shared the night—Lou, Sergeant John—had long since moved on. They were gone, replaced by strangers who lasted just a few months before leaving themselves.

Now Jake was the midnight shift sergeant.

"At first I loved it," Jake admitted. "Being in charge was everything."

"And then?"

He lowered his head, shoving his hands deeper into his pockets. "The shadows. They were always there, just beyond sight. But over time, they got smarter... quieter. Or maybe I was just growing blind to them."

"Which led to?"

"A theory," Jake said, voice tight with determination. "If they were real, maybe I could detect them another way. Not by sight, but by sound. I started building traps."

"Traps? For... shadows?"

He shot me a look as if I'd asked the stupidest question in the world. "Yes. That's exactly it. They killed Peggy Clune. And who's to say they didn't cause Dad's heart attack?"

I frowned. "You really believe that?"

"I thought about it every day." His hands curled into fists. "Peggy wasn't unstable... not like some people said. It was the shadows. They killed her."

I hesitated. "But isn't it possible she... took her own life? I mean, you've spent years chasing ghosts, Jake."

His voice dropped to a cold growl. "I thought you were here to listen."

I stayed silent, backpedaling carefully.

Jake exhaled sharply, his anger simmering down. "I built my first trap. Around this time, my parents sold the store. I stopped visiting them on Sundays. Dad was still angry; he thought I was wasting my life, especially after the heart attack. I didn't want to upset him."

I scribbled a note: 'disassociation'—his retreat from the world into his obsession.

"I'd been reading *Popular Science*," he continued, eyes lighting up. "Something about ultrasound—high-frequency sound humans can't hear. I thought it might annoy the shadows."

Jake described his device in painstaking detail—the circuits, the transistors, the delicate tuning—a motion detector at its core but smarter.

He installed his invention in a shadow-filled subbasement at BT&T, a place so dark and silent it felt almost like a tomb. The device emitted an ultrasonic pitch meant to chase the shadows away.

"The week I finished it," he said, voice bitter, "my parents moved away. I helped Mom pack. Dad... was a ghost of himself. The heart attack stole more than a part of his heart—he'd lost his will."

"How long after the surgery?" I asked.

"Four months. Maybe five." Jake's voice faltered. "He survived only a couple more years. He was barely fifty but looked seventy."

"Ever heard you look older than your years?" I asked lightly.

Jake snorted. "Yeah—if I were a hundred, I'd look good."

We both laughed, but then he plunged back into his story.

He climbed down into that subbasement alone, carrying his device, surrounded by darkness and silence broken only by his own breathing.

He switched on the device—the sharp, inaudible whistle sliced through the stale air. Suddenly he felt it—a fluttering, like leaves caught in a breeze. Shadows moving, disturbed.

He secured the device on top of a large electrical panel.

Jake would be the only guard doing tour one the next night and therefore the only person in this part of the building. He wandered off, excited about how his device might keep the shadows away.

"Did it work?" I asked.

"Not the way I planned."

The next night, he went to the subbasement to check on his machine and to replace the batteries. He opened the door to the room and flicked the light switch.

The lights didn't come on.

Jake used the flashlight from his belt. "I descended the steps slowly, senses sharpened. The shadows weren't there. In fact, they were suspiciously absent., but then I stepped on something. A small piece of black plastic—the remains of my creation."

"What happened?"

"They smashed the box to pieces. Wires torn out. Screws ripped loose. One of them had dismantled it with ruthless precision. Then I hear a 'swish'—and pain exploded at my temple."

"What was it?" I asked, enthralled.

"My vision danced with flashing lights, and I fell to the floor. The flashlight rolled out of my grasp, its beam shown on a D cell battery."

"A battery?" I repeated.

"That's what hit me," Jake explained. "There I was, staggering on my hands and knees, reaching for the flashlight but it rolled further away, like something I couldn't see was pushing it." His eyes met mine. "Then the flashlight went out."

"What did you do?"

"I shouted, 'Help me', as if that would do anything. And that's when I felt them…"

"Them?" I repeated.

"One of them brushed against my legs like a swarm of wings, like moths flapping against my skin. Then I reached up to touch my head, and it came away wet. I was bleeding."

He shook his head, the memory burning bright in his mind. "I stood with my hands raised, you see, because it was totally dark, no light of any kind. But my hand brushed something overhead. I knew what it was, a light fixture. I felt the bulb, and it was intact, just loose in the socket. So as quickly as I could, I tightened it, and light—blessed light—flooded into the space."

"That saved you," I said.

"So I thought. But as I made my way to the door, there was another 'Swish!' and another flying battery caught me in the shoulder and knocked me down. I got up and headed for the door and they kept throwing those damn batteries at me, and harder than you can imagine."

"But you got away," I said.

"I got through the door, clutching my bleeding head. As the door slammed shut behind me I swear I heard them laughing."

"Laughing?" I asked, leaning forward.

"I felt it more than actually heard it." Jake whispered. "Climbing those stairs was like scaling a mountain, but I made it. The other guards got me to the hospital." He pointed to a scar near his hairline. "Five stitches."

I nodded sympathetically. "But, Jake—" I stopped talking as I glanced at my watch. The tiny digital screen read 11:35.

"What is it?" Jake asked, confused by my sudden silence.

"We've been talking for three hours. I lost track of time. I have to go."

He nodded wordlessly and we stood.

I hesitated. "I want to see you again tomorrow."

He chuckled darkly. "I don't think you'll make it."

I stopped and stared hard at him. "What does that mean?"

"Call me if you can come," he said. "Less pressure on you."

Together, we walked down the corridor in heavy silence. I felt the weight of those words pressing me down.

At the desk, I signed him back in.

I sprinted out to my car, heart pounding, and grabbed my cell phone sitting on the passenger seat. My fingers fumbled over the memory dial, desperate.

"Hello?" Marcie's voice crackled through the speaker—icy, tense.

"It's Sam. Sorry... I got held up," I said, trying to keep my voice even.

"A little held up? Dammit, Sam, we should have left an hour ago," she snapped, frustration sharp enough to cut through steel.

I swallowed hard. "I know. I lost track of time."

"Lost track of time?" she repeated, her voice dipped into something darker.. "And I tried to beep you—but you left the stupid thing here."

My hand twitched toward my belt out of habit. The small plastic box wasn't there. A cold rush of panic followed.

"Oh, jeez," I muttered, feeling the weight of my mistake settle like a stone in my gut. "I guess I ran out without it."

Marcie's tone sharpened—cutting, accusing. "Sounds like classic passive-aggressive behavior. You don't want to come to my mother's so you just forget the time—and your beeper."

I bristled. "C'mon, Marcie… Save the psychoanalysis for your patients."

"You've got ten minutes to get home—or we're leaving without you." She hung up, a harsh mutter, "Son of a—" lingering before the line went dead.

I shoved the phone into my pocket and gritted my teeth, focusing hard on the drive home. Great. After all the progress I'd made with her last night, Marcie would be sour for the entire trip.

But maybe—just maybe—a weekend away, some attention and a little romance could turn things around.

Pulling into the driveway, I spotted Marcie loading Rueben into the minivan. The rear door yawned open, revealing mountains of luggage spilling out. Rachel's overpacked bags threatened to burst at the seams and Rueben's toys looked enough to fill a toy store.

Marcie slammed the door shut and shot me a look so cold it could kill. I swallowed my dread and crossed to the driver's side.

"Marcie, I'm sorry—"

"I don't want to hear it," she hissed, eyes flashing dangerously.

"I got caught up with a patient. You know how that goes. When the session's really intense, you lose track of time—"

"Lose track of time?" She stepped closer so the kids inside wouldn't hear, voice low and sharp. "You bill by the hour—fifty minutes. You've done this long enough to know exactly when to end a session, Sam. And suddenly you 'lose track'?"

I rubbed the back of my neck, trying to explain. "Jake's case is complex. The layers of his delusion—"

"Just get in the car and drive. You knew how important this was to me!" She spun away. "I don't want to talk anymore."

I felt like a fool—small, helpless. Marcie climbed into the van, closing the door behind her.

Rueben's cheerful shout broke the silence. "Whee! We're going to Grandma's!"

"Shut up, Rueben!" Rachel snapped.

Marcie's voice cracked with authority. "Rachel, leave your brother alone." Then, facing both of them, she said firmly, "I want you two to get along on this trip."

Rage bubbled up in Rachel's voice. "It's not my fault you and Daddy are fighting!"

Marcie's eyes hardened—they were sharp daggers of contained anger. She wagged a finger at Rachel. "Young lady, if you want to set foot in the mall again this millennium you'll keep *your* mouth shut."

Rachel's angry retort died as quickly as it flared. She clenched her jaw, swallowed the hurt, retreating into pre-teen sulkiness. Rueben, oblivious to the tension, stayed cheerfully indifferent, humming a little tune as we pulled out of the driveway.

"Grandma!" Rueben yelled and ran to her as Sara appeared at the front door of her house.

He bolted forward, his small feet pounding against the porch steps, and without hesitation he threw his arms around her waist. The force nearly toppled the older woman backward, but she caught him effortlessly, a soft chuckle escaping her lips.

Sara was diminutive, her stature betraying none of the strength she carried within. Her black-and-gray hair swept high atop her head in a deliberate coil. She wore barely any makeup yet the lipstick she chose exaggerated her lips just enough to give her face a permanent flutter of warmth and charm. She was slender and still striking, her dress remarkably stylish—far too elegant for a day spent in the kitchen, and Marcie's subtle frown didn't go unnoticed.

"Hi, Grandma," Rachel chimed softly, stepping forward and pressing a quick kiss to Sara's cheek. It was a gesture that brightened the older woman's face.

"My darling, you look radiant," Sara said, her eyes flashing briefly toward Rachel before turning back to Marcie. "Where have you been? I was worried."

Marcie exhaled wearily, her voice almost apologetic. "Sorry, Mother. Something delayed us."

I carried Rachel's suitcase up the creaking porch steps, glancing at Sara with a mixture of unease and fatigue. Her lips pressed into that familiar, thin line, and she nodded slowly. "Sam," she said, her voice tight with unspoken judgment.

I've been with Marcie for nearly seventeen years, including the years we dated. I've worked hard, shared the joy of our children's births, and tried to be a good husband and father.

So why did her mother's eyes always pierce through me with silent disdain? I knew one reason: Marcie's daily phone calls to her mom inevitably included me—my flaws, my failures, my every misstep unwittingly dissected by someone who perhaps knew too much.

As a therapist, Marcie's habits weren't surprising—an only child, a daughter—an endless stream of dialogue and analysis that left little room for smooth boundaries. I sometimes wished we had more children, more distractions for Sara, so she wouldn't notice me.

I'd grown up with three siblings; my mother's attention had to stretch thin, tangled in the chaos of many lives—not just one.

Marcie and Sara drifted into simple conversation cloaked with a thin veneer of civility, and I slipped into the living room for a moment's respite. Rueben dashed down the stairs eagerly to watch his favorite shows while Rachel busied herself in the kitchen, offering to help somewhat awkwardly.

I settled onto the couch with my shoulder bag and laptop, flipping through my notes about Jake. It astonished me how Jake managed—how he functioned despite the mounting accidents and injuries that should have raised red flags to his fragile state of mind. That unsettling thought clung to me.

Despite our late arrival, Sara was determined to serve dinner promptly at four. The centerpiece was a massive kosher turkey, overcooked to the point of dryness, its scant juices pooled beneath what she called "gravy." Sara had a cook and a maid yet only deigned to cook for the family on holidays—as if it elevated the act into something special, something sacred. She was out of practice and ate like people did in her generation—everything cooked to death.

Or maybe it was just her and me, tangled in years of silent rivalry that made her food taste worse.

Marcie offered a Jewish blessing—a customary grace, something familiar and grounding. "We all have much to be thankful for," she said, her voice steady but strained. The rest echoed it, lips moving out of habit, and then we ate.

The table groaned with Thanksgiving staples: turkey, stuffing, cranberry sauce. But there were also dishes foreign to me— tzimmes, a slow-cooked sweetness of carrots and other root vegetables, and potato kugel in place of mashed potatoes, golden and crusted atop.

The kids didn't seem to notice Grandma's culinary quirks; Rachel eagerly sampled everything, and Rueben found excitement in the meal's novelty. I picked at the offerings, sipping the White Zinfandel Sara had chosen. Predictably, it tasted more like soda than wine, but no one seemed to mind.

We gathered around that enormous dining table, toasting quietly amidst the uneasy truce. I swallowed my critique of Sara's cooking. She held back any barbs about me and for a brief, fragile moment we were just family.

Marcie and Sara whispered about overnight plans. Rachel's eyes sparkled as she dreamed aloud about what shopping excursions awaited while Rueben jabbered nonstop about where they might eat at the mall.

It all promised a peaceful weekend, one that finally seemed to soothe Marcie's worries. I took care to moderate my wine intake —driving home demanded full attention.

Dessert was better, a secret recipe plum crunch that was moist and golden followed by pumpkin pie. This was Sara's nod to me, a rare gesture of recognition of something I enjoyed, although pumpkin was Rueben's favorite, too.

With the meal finished, Rueben slid away, heading downstairs to claim his spot for evening TV. Rachel eagerly made plans with Sara while Marcie and I settled into the living room. For the first time that day, Marcie seemed visibly more at ease.

"Feeling better?" I asked gently.

"Yes," she sighed, deflating slightly. "Family events always stress me out."

"I know. I'll try to be better about time next time."

She nodded, eyes thoughtful. "Especially tomorrow. We need to leave early if we want to get to the Catskills before sundown."

I smiled, trying to lighten the mood. "I'll park myself across from a clock."

Her smile was soft, grateful. "That might just work."

I reached out, taking her hand in mine, drawing strength from the simple contact.

Then came the sound.

At first it was faint and indistinct—a soft wail that blended with the murmur of the television or maybe the distant howl of sirens in the city. I blinked, puzzled. Marcie's brow furrowed in confusion as she listened too. Then, like a cruel trick, the crying swelled—piercing, desperate.

Our eyes met. Instant understanding.

Rueben.

We leapt from the couch, barely noticing the chaotic echoes in our own hearts.

We thundered to the basement steps, yanking open the door. The sound seemed to explode in the cramped stairwell—sobs turning to piercing screams. I raced down two stairs at a time, adrenaline pushing my legs, heart hammering against my ribs. At the bottom Rueben sat on the floor clutching his small hand, blood slipping like crimson rivers between his fingers.

I lunged forward instinctively. But a movement caught at the edge of my vision.

A shadow.

Not cast by any light source, but a presence—a dark shape that seemed to slip and pulse independently, drifting silently from the room's edge.

I froze.

Marcie dashed past me kneeling beside Rueben, panic tightening her voice. "Oh God, oh God…" She turned sharply to me. "Sam! Call an ambulance!"

The command shattered the trance. I scrambled back up the stairs, heart racing, and shouted down, "I'm on it."

Marcie ripped at the hem of her dress, fashioning the fabric into a makeshift tourniquet against the gushing wound.

At the top of the stairs Sara appeared, her hands fluttering nervously. "What's going on?"

"Call 911—Rueben's hurt," I gasped. Sara nodded frantically, fumbling toward the phone.

I darted into the bathroom, yanked open a cabinet, and grabbed gauze pads and adhesive tape. Returning, I found Marcie holding Rueben steady, the makeshift bandage tight against the bleeding arm.

Glass littered the surrounding floor, and a large glass sculpture of Sara's lay in fragments. Even shattered, the broken pieces made sharp shards, jagged edges gleaming menacingly in the dim light.

"Calm down, honey," Marcie whispered fiercely, voice breaking with fear. Tears streamed down Rueben's cheeks, mixing with whimpers almost too raw to hear as his little body shook and he breathed raggedly.

He coughed once, then tried to speak.

"It wa—wa—" Rueben stammered, "It was… a black thing."

My breath caught in my throat. I stared, disbelief battering my thoughts.

"It was a black thing," he repeated, voice trembling. "It w-went that way." His good hand pointed shakily toward the darkest corner of the basement where I had seen the shadow retreat.

"Like a shadow?" I asked, swallowing hard.

"Hush, Sam," Marcie hissed. "The child's in shock."

"L-like a sh-shadow," Rueben sobbed, "a b-bad shadow…"

Marcie rocked him gently, keeping the pressure on his arm steady. I stood frozen, staring at the oppressive darkness in the corner, my mind racing, heart pounding in a rhythm I barely recognized.

Hours later with ten stitches sewn into his small arm, we carried Rueben out of Bayshore Medical Center. He lay in the back seat, head in Marcie's lap, drifting in and out of haunted sleep, quiet sobs escaping between his breaths.

I drove through the ominous blackness of the night, eyes darting to the ghostly outlines of trees and streetlights that blurred past.

"Sorry about the weekend," Marcie murmured, her voice soft, a mix of regret and exhaustion.

"It's okay," I said, voice low but firm. "Rueben belongs in his own bed. We'll head home first thing in the morning."

Sleep eluded me that night. That distant, impossible shadow haunted my every thought. Jake's grim prediction echoed: *I don't think you'll make it.*

I slept with the light on.

17. Night Falling

I strode briskly down the sterile hallway of Greystorm and nodded curtly to Althea as I signed Jake out. Her bright smile was almost painfully normal, a stark contrast to the chaos still echoing in my mind.

"How was your Thanksgiving, Dr. Lucas?" she asked cheerfully.

My thoughts were anything but cheerful. I rushed my son to the hospital because of some nightmarish creature my patient conjured. The drive home was a nightmare in itself—a two-and-a-half-hour slog through Black Friday traffic trapped with my angry wife, my surly teenager, and Rueben, half-doped and whining.

"Fine," I lied, forcing a tight smile. "Very nice. How about you?"

"Oh, just fine. The whole family was at my sister's," Althea said, patting her stomach. "She's a really good cook."

I returned the smile but my eyes flickered to the clock. Five past four in the afternoon.

Althea's expression shifted suddenly, the warmth draining away. "Dr. Lucas, it's the wrong time to come by. Jake's asleep."

"I'll wake him," I said sharply.

She shrugged, unfazed by my tone, and I pushed open Jake's door. His thin frame was curled beneath the covers, a pillow drawn over his eyes, mouth and nose just visible. He looked fragile, vulnerable.

"Jake?" I called softly, reaching over to shake his shoulder.

The pillow flew off like a missile. Jake bolted upright, eyes wide and unblinking, legs tucking beneath him in a frantic, protective crouch.

"Sorry, didn't mean to startle you," I said, though I wasn't sorry. Let him lose some sleep like I did the previous night.

Jake's eyes darted around the room, skeptical, before settling on me. He sucked in a breath, visibly relaxing.

"Sam, what time is it?"

"Seven after four," I replied, checking my watch.

He nodded, rubbed his eyes, his voice barely above a whisper. "I thought you'd want to talk to me."

His words felt like a challenge. "What does that mean, exactly?" I snapped.

"About yesterday," he said quietly.

"Do you know what happened?"

"I'm not sure."

I felt my temper rise. "That's a hell of a convenient answer."

He looked down, voice small. "It's the only one I have."

"That's not good enough." I barked, the edge in my voice betraying my professional calm. "My kid got cut badly—from a glass statue, and you come to me with uncertainty?"

"They like glass," he murmured, distant.

"And then he says some 'shadow things' did it to him."

Jake's gaze locked on mine, pale and serious. My heart twisted, but I went on. "You knew something was coming, didn't you? You know more than you're telling me."

"I—had a feeling," he stammered.

"Right now, I don't give a damn what you felt." I was beyond anger now—I was terrified. "My son's seeing what you see. That's worse than any physical wound."

Jake's eyes searched mine, seeing past the fury. "What did you see, Sam?"

I scoffed. "What difference does that make?"

"A big one," Jake insisted, unwavering. "If you saw something, even out of the corner of your eye... that's how people can see them."

I sank into the chair beside his bed, tracing a circle on the scratched plastic armrest.

"I... might have seen something," I admitted in a low voice. "But it could've been the power of suggestion. You've filled my head with these 'shadow things' for weeks. It was probably just a trick of the light."

Jake smiled faintly, nodding solemnly. "Logical. But now, tell me what you really believe."

I felt the words bite back. "I think you're playing me. You spin these wild stories, then fold when it's time to be honest."said

"Sam," Jake cut in, raising a hand to stop me, "I'm trying. But without context it all sounds crazy."

"Context?" I echoed, brow furrowed.

"Everything will make sense when you know what I know."

"That sounds ominous."

Jake's sly grin returned. "Yeah. But you're in it now. You need to learn how to protect yourself."

"Protect myself—from someone else's imagination?"

"Or to protect your son," Jake countered, eyes darkening.

Emotion twisted inside me—a mix of anger, fear, and helplessness. "What do I do?"

"Let him sleep with the light on," Jake said. "If you can, bring a cot into his room. Sleep in his room for a week. That helps."

I looked at that tall, scrawny man and hated him. Hated him for giving me advice on how to help my son. Hated him for coming into my life and taking away my stability.

But what if it was true?

What if the shadows were real?

A sudden chill ran down my spine. No matter—if these things existed the only thing I wanted was for them to leave us alone.

"Those are some good suggestions, Jake," I said, slipping back into my therapist's voice, masking the turmoil inside.

"Hear the rest, Sam. Then you'll understand."

His words echoed with the cry of the self-obsessed, the desperate plea of a fractured mind: if only you knew my suffering you'd be just as crazy.

Why was he different?

I glanced at my watch. "Not today."

"When?"

"Sunday. I'll give you a couple of hours."

Jake nodded solemnly. "Come early. Days are getting shorter; I get little sleep."

"When?"

"Six AM. That way, we have time."

I nodded, another thread pulling me deeper into his story, into his dark world. I was no longer just a doctor—I was a man teetering on the edge of a nightmare he couldn't yet understand.

"I'll be here."

1970

18. TERESA

I n 1970, Jake kept his distance from personal relationships, aloof as a cat on a ledge, careful never to reveal too much.

However, he thought back to 1968, the year of the sound machine experiment—a desperate attempt to repel the creatures that haunted the edges of his world. It seemed promising, but the sound only irritated them.

The shadows only recoiled from light, not from noise.

Worse, nothing in his research could explain the eerie, almost psychic way he sensed their presence lurking behind doors and in empty corners.

His genuine passion, however, was technology—anything new, anything that could help him fight back.

Computers thrilled him. In the late sixties, these machines were beasts of punch cards and tangled switches, but at BT&T, he'd glimpsed something magical, talking to technicians, watching them breathe life into cold circuitry.

Lost in thought, Jake barely noticed Tony's teasing voice cut through the hum of the security booth.

"Hey, Jake, you gonna sleep with your eyes open? Setting a bad example, Lieutenant."

Jake blinked, turning to see Tony—a dark-haired Italian with a slick pompadour and an always-present pleasant aftershave—smiling with mischief.

"Just thinking about that tour you're supposed to make," Jake said, tucking the corner of his science magazine beneath his arm.

Tony grinned. "On my way. After the tour I'm relieving Malcolm at Main Reception, right?"

"That's the plan. His lunch break's due."

Jangling keys, Tony drifted away, ready to make his rounds.

Expansion at BT&T had transformed the night shift. Five guards patrolled now, no longer lugging antique watch clocks but wielding one special key that fit into wall-mounted slots, a different form of electronic tracking.

The Command Center monitored their every move with banks of closed-circuit televisions and a maze of telephone lines.

From his station near the loading dock, Jake felt a kinship with the glowing screens, watching every entrance and corridor, the pulsating heart of security. After hours, employees could signal the booth with a red push-button by the door; the guard would verify identities from a printed list and buzz them in remotely.

It was a comfort, having some control in a world dimmed by the shadows.

"Hey, Jake!" a cheerful voice sliced through the quiet. His coffee-colored skin contrasted with his crisp blue uniform as he marched into the office.

Winston, the first African-American guard Hurley had hired in these changing times, grinned like a kid caught sneaking candy.

"Did you see the new magazine? Penthouse. Unbelievable what they show."

Jake shook his head, voice firm but fair. "You know we're not supposed to have magazines like that here. Put it in your locker."

"Man, you're no fun."

"It's not work-appropriate."

"Okay, Mr. Lieutenant, but can I sneak a peek at lunch?"

Jake sighed but nodded. "Fine. Just don't leave it out."

Winston grinned. "You're a fair man, Jake."

Chuckling, Jake said, "I probably should have just told you to leave it at home."

Winston shrugged. "Are you nuts? My wife wouldn't let me have that in the house—too many white women. Makes her jealous."

Jake smiled wryly. "Why buy it then?"

"Lieutenant, a man needs stimulation now and then."

"Just don't get overstimulated."

Winston shrugged. "I'm dedicated, no worries."

Ed, short and broad behind the glass window, arrived fresh from tour one. He snorted from the corner of the room.

"Sure you are."

"I am," Winston insisted, grinning. "I just like good-looking women."

"We all do," Ed agreed.

"Speaking of fine women," Winston leaned in, "how about Teresa Quinga?"

"She's hot," Ed said, eyes gleaming.

"Yeah," Winston agreed, shaking his hand like he'd touched fire. "One hot tamale."

Jake snorted, half-amused and half-annoyed. "That's pretty derogatory."

"She's Mexican."

"Ecuadorian," Jake corrected softly.

"How do you know that?"

"She told me."

"Oh!" Ed crowed. "You've been talking to her."

"See? Told you," Winston said smugly.

"What?" Jake frowned.

"She's got the hots for you," Winston claimed. "Yeah, but she's awful short—"

"You must be a foot taller than her," Ed teased.

"She's got a wide caboose," Winston added, smirking. "Gives a man something to hold on to."

"And bounce off of," Ed laughed.

Jake glared, not saying anything to encourage the other guards.. "Winston, don't you have a tour?"

"Just leaving, lieutenant," Winston said with a smile.

Jake's eyes pinned Ed. "You got something to do?"

"Not exactly," Ed admitted, settling back in his chair, ready for whatever.

"Fine. Take the outside tour."

Ed grabbed a walkie-talkie and strolled out to the small pickup parked behind the office. Jake returned to the window, one eye sharp on the bank of TVs.

He thought about Teresa Quinga. She'd sent signals, clear as day. But since Peggy's death Jake buried those desires deep.

He recalled a strange night in '68—not long after his parents moved away—when loneliness nudged him out into the dark.

He was restless. The repair job that evening had driven him mad without an answer. Jake drove aimlessly in the hills he and Peggy used to travel. He fought his fear and focused only on the streetlights and headlights. He noticed a hand-painted sign bathed in floodlights that pointed with a large black arrow. It read:

Brethren Coffee House
Music and Java

His '65 Volkswagen Beetle felt spacious under his long legs as he drove it up a driveway where an old chapel stood.

Haze filled the chapel, which consisted of marijuana smoke and cigarettes that pressed thick against the low ceiling. Jake's short haircut made him stand out amid the long-haired, free-spirited crowd.

He attempted to blend in, awkward yet unrepentant.

On stage a bearded man strummed a guitar. Across the room a blonde girl with a headband danced—or rather swayed—with a gentle grace, her eyes glassy, stoned.

Jake bought a cup of coffee and sat sipping it, watching the tiny pinpoints of light from a spinning mirror ball—a kaleidoscope of blue and red circles drifting eerily across the old nave.

He tried almost instinctively to sense the shadows here. Nothing. Perhaps the chapel, formerly a place of sanctity, repelled them.

A voice startled him—soft, inviting.

"Hey, want to dance?"

He looked up—it was the blonde girl with a headband, a tie-dyed shirt hanging loosely over bell-bottoms.

"Sure."

They moved together, swaying to the music, the haze blurring the edges of the room and of time. Her eyes glossed over but Jake felt calm.

Suddenly, a hand gripped his shoulder, spinning him around. Two tall black men loomed; one wore a fringed leather vest over a bare chest, the other silent, imposing.

"What are you doing here?" the one who held him demanded.

"Dancing," Jake stammered.

"We don't want no fuzz here."

"Fuzz?" Jake frowned, confusion flashing. "You think I'm a cop?"

"That's right, man. Get lost, narc."

Jake caught an almost imperceptible shimmering around the man's head like a halo—and something darker beneath.

"Sure," Jake said, forcing a calm smile. He had no desire to spark violence tonight.

The girl ran to the man, pleading in hushed tones as he ignored her.

Jake stepped out into the crisp night, lungs inhaling the clear, cold air. Jake still felt safe, though he couldn't figure out what the cloud around the man's head meant. He'd seen nothing like it before.

The girl soon followed him out. "Sorry. That's Mack. He's quick to anger."

"It's okay. I guess I didn't fit in."

"Yeah, but man, we're supposed to see people for who they are, not by their hair or clothes."

Jake nodded, swallowing the awkward silence between them.

"Are you a cop?" she asked.

Jake laughed, a dry, surprised sound. "No. Night guard."

"Like a cop?"

"I wear a uniform but no gun. And I don't bust people."

"Cool."

"Thanks for the dance."

"Where now?" she asked, falling into step beside him.

"Home, I guess."

"Near here?"

"Fifteen minutes."

"Need company? I came with friends but it's getting to be a drag, y'know."

They arrived at his Beetle and she lit up. "That's yours? Man, I love Beetles! Now I gotta ride with you."

"That'd be fine," Jake said, but he was nervous. He hadn't been alone with a woman since Peggy died.

"Great! By the way, my name is Sally."

"Jake. Jake Hurd."

Inside the VW they drove off—stopping at a grimy package goods store to pick up Boone's Farm Apple Wine at Sally's insistence.

They talked casually on the way to Jake's apartment, the conversation light, but the air between them felt charged with energy..

Sally sipped the cheap wine as Jake drove. At a red stoplight she held out the bottle, teasing, "Try it."

Jake hesitated but took a small sip—it fizzed on his tongue like soda, cloyingly sweet. Still, the lingering haze from the coffeehouse's intoxicating vapors already had lifted his spirits.

When they arrived Sally's eyes scanned Jake's apartment with mild wonder. It was immaculate—every book aligned, every surface spotless—as if he'd scrubbed the place just for her.

She giggled softly, the wine loosening her tongue and inhibitions. "It looks like you were expecting company," she said, half-mocking, half-admiring.

Jake shrugged, grabbing a plate with some cheese and cold cuts, slicing them deftly, his movements casual but precise.

They settled in, glasses clinking, conversation flowing. Jake smiled politely asking questions that kept Sally talking, her voice growing warmer and slower. The room seemed to shrink as the wine—and something more intoxicating—loosened the tension.

Gradually, Sally edged closer on the sofa, her shoulder brushing Jake's. "Hey, you ever give back rubs?" she asked, eyes sparkling under dim light. "I just loooove back rubs."

Jake hesitated, then reached out, pressing his fingers firmly into her shoulders, easing into softer strokes along her spine.

Sally sighed, a soft sound of pleasure, her body relaxing into his hands. Jake's breath caught as he realized she wasn't wearing a bra under her thin shirt. The warmth beneath his fingers was unmistakable.

Without breaking the rhythm of his hands, Sally slid her shirt off over her head, hair tumbling free. Jake's touch became gentler, feather-like, his fingers tracing paths that sent goose bumps trailing across her skin.

She turned to face him, eyes darkened with desire, nipples erect against the soft curves of her chest.

"You have a great touch," she moaned, before leaning in to kiss him.

Desire ignited between them—his fingers finding the swell of her breasts, her lips deepening the kiss, breath hitching against his.

Suddenly she took his hand, pulling him to his feet. "Come on," she whispered, her voice a mixture of command and invitation leading him toward the bedroom and the queen-sized bed.

Jake froze as they reached the door, his cheeks flushing. "It's my... I mean... I haven't—"

Sally's grin was mischievous, almost feline. "Really?" she purred. "That's cool. Guess I'll have to take charge."

That night their bodies tangled and explored each other's desires repeatedly. Sally was eager, inventive, guiding Jake with patient whispers and gentle corrections.

He wanted desperately to prove himself, making up for his awkwardness with earnest passion. She showed him ways that made her shiver and sigh; he listened, eager and attentive.

As dawn painted the sky with pale hues they finally collapsed, exhaustion and contentment sinking into the mattress. Jake drifted into a restless sleep, half-aware of the shower running, half-feeling a gentle kiss lingering on his lips.

But the morning brought solitude. Sally was gone.

Weeks later Jake returned to the coffeehouse. He never got inside.

At the door Mack blocked his way, his expression hard, unyielding. "You don't belong here," Mack said flatly, his voice low but unmistakably threatening.

Jake blinked. The fog around the man's head was thicker. Yet no one else seemed to notice. The strange gray mist swirling faintly around Mack unsettled Jake and he couldn't understand why.

He left and didn't go back.

Days passed—three, then four—until a headline caught Jake's eye: a car accident on a dark highway. A driver lost control, barreling across lanes before meeting oncoming traffic head-on. The victim was Mack Brown. The paper ran an old photo—younger, smiling, unaware of the fate that awaited him.

It was the Mack from the coffeehouse.

The fog around his head and his untimely death. Something about it nagged at Jake, a connection he couldn't yet grasp.

But it was another shock that slammed him: a week later a burning sting whenever he urinated.

Reluctant but desperate, Jake sought his family doctor's office. The verdict was quick: gonorrhea. Without delay, the doctor administered two large antibiotic shots deep in Jake's backside—painful injections that left Jake nursing bruised muscles for days.

His brief dalliance with free love had left far more than bittersweet memories.

That was almost two years earlier and now, as Ed finished his tour and Jake moved back to the seat that faced the console, he thought of Teresa Quinga. The way her voice rose when she saw him, the furtive glances, the suggestive jokes.

Was she interested? And what was the right way to respond?

19. JAKE'S DATE

"Hi, Jake."

Jake jumped as a warm female voice sliced through the early-morning hum of Building One's reception area.

He turned, heart unexpectedly quickening. Teresa stood there, casually leaning against the wall, a teasing smile playing on her lips.

Building One—'One F,' as everyone called it—was the nerve center where employees streamed in, badges clutched in hand.

Jake didn't mind manning the reception; after all, it was infinitely better than being stuck alone in the guard shack by the gates where silence gnawed at him.

"Oh, hi, Teresa," Jake said, feeling his face flush. He cursed himself silently—did she know he'd been thinking about her all night?

She waved him aside with a knowing glance. Jake caught Tony's eye behind him and nodded—Tony would cover reception while he slipped away. Tony grinned back, already immersed in greeting the incoming employees.

Leaning in closer Teresa's voice dropped to a hush, thick with urgency. "Jake, I need your help."

A flicker of tension hit Jake's gut. "Sure. Forgot your keys or something?"

Her eyes scanned the bustling lobby before she whispered, "When's your shift over?"

Jake hesitated, tongue unexpectedly heavy. "Uh, seven-thirty."

"Great," she breathed, a spark lighting her eyes. "Can you come to my office after? You know the way—1C-214?"

"Sure," Jake answered, heart thumping.

She nodded quickly, then, barely audible, added, "See you soon."

The clock in the guard's locker room ticked closer to 7:40. After swapping his uniform for a jacket and slacks, Jake found himself standing in front of Teresa's small office door, nerves on edge.

"Oh, Jake, come in!" Teresa greeted him warmly, peeling off her stenographer earphones and powering down the machine in front of her. The fluorescent lights softened as she closed the door behind him.

"What's going on?" Jake asked, instinctively stepping closer.

Teresa twirled a strand of her dark hair, her accent tinting her words like a melody. "Jake, I need a big favor... What are you doing Saturday night?"

Jake blinked, surprised. "Saturday? The weekend crew's on."

A sigh escaped her lips. "Good. I have a family gathering—my parents' thirty-fifth wedding anniversary."

Jake offered a polite smile. "How nice."

Her eyes rolled upward, a mix of dread and frustration. "Nice? For my two married sisters and my brother and his wife. For me? Hell." She paused, anxiety threading through her voice. "All night long, it'll be the same questions—'Teresa, why aren't you married?' 'Teresa, why are you alone?' I'm the only single one, and they won't let it go."

Jake studied her face— the vulnerability, the resignation.

She took a hesitant step closer. "That's why I need your help. As a friend."

"What do you need me to do?"

Her lips curled into a hopeful smile. "I hope this isn't too forward, but… if you could come with me—to the party—it would change everything. Everyone would stop the questions. Could you do that?"

Jake felt a flicker of excitement laced with caution. Going out with Teresa was tempting beyond words, but the night held unknown risks—dark, unfamiliar places.

"If you'd like," Jake whispered, surprised by his own words.

Her smile blossomed, relief flooding her eyes. "You don't know what this means. You're a lifesaver."

"Just give me your address and number."

"With pleasure." Teresa pulled a neatly folded slip of paper from her pocket, her handwriting neat.

Jake returned her smile. "Sounds like fun."

"And there'll be food—like you wouldn't believe. So come hungry." She jabbed him playfully in the ribs. "You look like you should eat more."

Jake chuckled, eyes flicking down to the note.

Her expression softened, vulnerability surfacing again. "Jake, I hope you don't think I'm, y'know… asking you out or anything."

"No," Jake said quickly, looking up. "Not at all. I'm… flattered. Anyone would be. I mean… with you."

Warmth spread through him as he stepped toward the door. "I should… get some sleep."

Teresa giggled softly. "Thanks, Jake. See you Saturday night."

"I'll call if I need directions." Jake took a breath, then—curse his clumsiness—banged his hip against the doorknob.

That night, Jake phoned Theresa at exactly seven o'clock. She answered, her voice flowing easily from an apartment somewhere in Orange that she shared with a roommate.

For the next hour, they spun laughter and jokes through the receiver. Jake felt lighter as her giggles spilled across the line, the sound a balm to his often weary soul.

When the call ended, Jake leaned back, chest swelling with a rare confidence. In a few days, he would step out of the quiet shadows of his life and into the glowing spotlight of a social event —a world he'd avoided for years.

Feeling almost ten feet tall, he danced his way down the creaky stairs to the basement workshop that served as his sanctuary.

The double neon tube desk lamp flared on over his latest electronic project, and he hummed a cheerful tune, hands coaxing the parts together like a master artist.

But then—a chill ran down his spine. The air shifted; a weight fell over the room.

He froze.

One of them was here.

His foot groped the floor instinctively, finding the small foot switch beneath his bench. In a practiced reflex, he covered his eyes with trembling hands and stomped down.

Blinding light flooded the cramped space, six powerful photographic lamps igniting the darkness with merciless glare. He pressed the switch again; the bright light winked out.

Slowly lowering his hands, Jake exhaled. The presence vanished —for now. A flicker of a smile played on his lips. He wasn't alone, but he could handle it.

He bent back to the workbench, scrutinized a circuit, and soldered it into place with steady hands.

Friday morning dawned gray but buzzing with anticipation. Jake met Teresa at the One-F entrance, flanked by a second guard as if escorting royalty. She glowed beside him, her excitement bubbling over as she praised his gallantry with a radiant grin, blowing him a kiss that sent a thrilling jolt through his chest.

A thought struck him—a corsage—an emblem of charm and old-fashioned romance. He jotted a reminder to buy one, determined to make this night unforgettable.

Friday night yielded to dawn, but Jake remained awake, nerves and excitement churning. At four in the afternoon, he slipped out and drove through the chaotic city streets to a florist's shop.

The corsage, delicate and perfect in its clear case, felt like a talisman in his sweaty palms.

That night, Teresa emerged at her apartment doorway, transformed. Her lilac dress clung and flowed just right, soft curls framing her face, makeup subtle but striking.

"You look great," he whispered.

She smiled up at him. "So do you."

Blurted words and shy gestures followed. "Oh! This is for you." The corsage extended, trembling slightly in his hand.

"A corsage! I haven't worn one since prom!" she breathed, pulling him inside.

Her cluttered living room—piled magazines, dishes from forgotten meals—felt almost inviting in its chaotic honesty. Apologies spilled from Teresa's lips.

Jake shrugged. "It's fine. It looks lived in."

A delicate dance began as Teresa handed him the pin. His hands, clumsy and awkward, brushed against soft skin, and a spark crackled between them.

"Don't linger too long, Jake," she warned with a teasing smirk.

Beet red, he moved quickly, hoping the warmth flooding his face wasn't too obvious. Her laughter needed no translation—it was the sweetest sound he'd ever known. She touched his cheek with a tender gesture that lingered longer than necessary.

"You're shy. I like that."

The fragrance of the flower wrapped around him as they left, arms linked. She adored the diminutive Beetle, marveling at how someone so tall could fit inside.

The restaurant was a muted facade—a home hastily converted —its dim interior bristling with whispered shadows that seemed to crawl along every surface.

Jake's skin prickled in the stifling darkness; clammy sweat gathered as he fought the rising sense of dread. Teresa, radiant and oblivious, laughed beside him.

They were swallowed by the throng.

Voices mingled, rapid-fire Spanish crashing over Jake's limited understanding. He watched Teresa shift effortlessly between languages, a chameleon in the social jungle.

Faces emerged, smiles and inquiries, each gaze piercing Jake's unsteady confidence. He felt exposed, vulnerable—a fish thrashing against unseen wires in a sea of humanity.

Teresa introduced, laughed, danced seamlessly through her world. Her cousin Marianitta approached them, and Jake caught hints of laughter and blushes. Words flew in rapid Spanish. Marianitta laughed again and headed up the stairs.

"What did she say?" Jake asked.

"Oh, I can't tell you. It was vulgar," Teresa chuckled. Apparently, speaking with her relative affected her, because more of an accent had crept into her speech.

"It can't be that bad," Jake said.

Teresa smiled and whispered, "She said you were very tall, so you must be… big… in other places." She covered her mouth. "Oh, what you must think."

"I guess it's a compliment."

Theresa shook her head. "That Marianitta, the mouth on her."

They walked up the stairs, and Teresa stopped on a step above Jake and turned around to face him eye to eye. "This is nice."

"We should carry steps with us wherever we go," Jake remarked and broke into a smile. She was so close, and he caught the intoxicating scent of her perfume—lilac, like her dress. He forgot the shadows as he suddenly felt the urge to kiss her; so close, so exciting.

Teresa broke the spell. "We'd better go up. We don't want to start tongues wagging."

"I guess it wouldn't be good for us to be necking on the stairway."

"Maybe later." Teresa gave Jake a quick, but full, kiss. Jake felt the touch of her lips down to his toes.

Upstairs, there was a dance floor and tables for guests to sit.

The air thick was with music and whispered secrets, Jake's heart pounded as Teresa's intoxicating scent drew him dangerously close, almost tasting the moment that might change everything.

"Come meet my relatives!" Teresa announced and pulled Jake along.

The room was alive with movement and the noise of people chattering. They couldn't go two feet without someone yelling 'Teresa!' and clapping her into a hug and a kiss. Each new person looked at Jake questioningly.

Jake felt as if he was being assessed with each step. It was like swimming through a sea of humanity, and Jake felt nervous. So many dark places, the noise and the crowd. He couldn't focus his attention to feel if the creatures were there. Or was he just afraid to try? He wanted to grab Teresa and run out into the street. Get under a bright lamp and be safe again.

Jake felt a tug at his arm as Teresa propelled him toward the dance floor.

"I don't dance!" he hissed.

"Neither do I. Just move!" Teresa screamed at him, and shook her hips.

There is a moment at the beginning of every relationship when the man sees a woman do something: a feeling of inevitability strikes him from a gesture or a certain word.

Men don't control sex, but they can read the signals of interest and passion and know when they're selected.

Jake, watching Teresa's hips shake and her body undulate to the music, felt that inevitability. He didn't know the road or the path it would take. But there was knowledge that she and he would eventually become a we. It was a feeling that both aroused and frightened and was as genuine as a toothache.

It was at that moment of insight as Jake moved his own hips in response to the hypnotic sway of Teresa's, that he saw it. A woman who stood near the record player. A light flashed behind her, probably a cheap strobe from a local head shop. There was enough light, so Jake saw the mist floating around her head like a living thing.

The sight froze him in his spot. Jake's blood ran cold. His breath caught.

"What is it?" Teresa shouted over the music.

Jake could barely speak. "Who is that?"

Teresa shaded her eyes with her hand and peered over. "That's Carmen, another cousin. Why?"

Jake bent closer to Teresa's ear. "I have to talk to her. It's very important—"

"What?" Teresa yelled back, not hearing him.

Jake worked his way through the crowd, his eye on the swaying body.

They're here, a voice shouted in his brain.

He weaved through the dancers, worked his way to Carmen. He gently took her arm to get her attention.

"Carmen?" Jake shouted.

"Si?" the tall, thin girl responded, and turned to face him. Her hair was wild and curly and fell halfway down her back. She was pretty, her skin a darker shade than Teresa's.

"I need to talk to you," Jake yelled.

"Qué?" she yelled back.

Oh, great! Jake thought. *She doesn't speak English.*

"*Senorita, muy importante.*" Jake attempted, with a gesture to make his point clear, "Have you seen—shadows?"

"*Qué?*" she yelled back and frowned.

Jake wanted to say the Spanish word for head. "*Cucuy,*" he attempted.

"*El Cucuy?*" Her mouth fell open and her eyes grew wide. "*Diablo!*"

"*No, sombra, tú sabes?*" Jake yelled back, trying to think of the Spanish words.

Carmen turned away from Jake, and suddenly, like magic, several large male relatives came between them. The men yelled at Jake in their clipped Spanish. He felt them push him back, so the message was clear. They forced him back, and Carmen fled toward the door, glancing fearfully behind.

Jake stumbled, crashing into dancers, falling hard onto the floor. Suddenly, someone stood over him and shouted back at the group. From the floor, Jake recognized the lilac dress. Teresa moved to the side as two of the men pulled Jake up to his feet.

"You okay?" her voice was fierce, protective.

"I tried to—warn her."

Teresa grabbed Jake's arm, not gently, and pulled him away from the group, who pointed and laughed. She escorted him down the stairs and out of the restaurant.

"What the hell happened?" Teresa demanded, her accent thickening with frustration.

Jake swallowed, the truth raw on his tongue. "I saw something. Around her head… shadows. I tried to warn her."

"What're you talking about? That was her crazy hair."

"No, Teresa, something else. I wanted to warn her—"

"All you did was scare her!"

"I didn't know she didn't speak any English."

Teresa exhaled with a disapproving hiss. "Half of them don't."

"I tried some of my high school Spanish, but she thought I said 'cucuy'."

"*El Cucuy?*" She stood silent for a moment. "Jake, never talk about *El Cucuy* to an Ecuadorian."

"I don't understand," Jake said.

"*El Cucuy* is like your American boogeyman. It's the big, bad shadow of death."

"I'm sorry—I—"

"You just embarrassed me in front of my entire family! Now they'll all say Teresa brought a 'loco gringo' to the party." She sighed heavily, a blade cutting through his hope. "Take me home."

He drove Teresa home in heavy silence, the night pressing in like a shroud around them.

Every so often, Jake caught her wiping at her eyes discreetly, her fingers trembling as they lifted at the delicate corsage pinned to her dress.

Each time, her vulnerability stabbed at him, but he couldn't find the right words to bridge the growing distance. Every phrase that formed in his mind felt hollow, weaker than the last, as if the shadows clinging to the night had stolen his voice.

When they pulled up outside her apartment, she slipped out of the car, her steps light yet hesitant.

"I can get to the door on my own, Jake," she said, her voice fragile but firm. "See you at work."

Her door slammed shut behind her with a somber thunk, the sound echoing into the quiet street. She didn't look back.

Jake drove home, and parked in his usual parking space, the engine ticking as it cooled, doubt gnawing at him.

Dating again felt like walking straight into a trap—the past pulling him under, dragging him down, taking him deeper into his own storm of regret.

At his place, he descended into the basement sanctuary of his workbench. The soft hum of circuits and the faint glow of the soldering iron were familiar comforts.

Lately, he'd been obsessed with a motion sensor he'd read about in *Popular Science*, something he hoped to perfect—a device that could detect movement at a much more sensitive level than what currently existed. A machine that could detect the shadows as they slipped into a room.

But no amount of tinkering quieted the storm in his mind.

His fingers paused over the components, eyes glazing as memories washed over him—Teresa's sharp, unexpected kiss on the stairs; the hypnotic sway of her hips under the dance floor lights. Those images crawled into his thoughts unbidden, refusing to fade.

By the time the first blush of dawn seeped through the basement window, Jake dragged himself upstairs, peeled off his suit, and collapsed into bed, the weight of the night pressing down on his chest.

Hours later at three in the afternoon, the phone's shrill ring shattered the fragile silence, jolting Jake awake. Probably work— another frantic call about a missing coworker or an extra shift.

He groaned, reaching groggily for the receiver. "Hello?"

A woman's voice broke through the haze, calm but heavy. "Jake?"

His heart lurched. "Teresa?"

Her voice trembled, raw under the weight of grief. "You said you tried to warn Carmen last night… What exactly were you warning her about?"

Jake sat bolt upright, the images snapping into sharper focus. "I told you… there was a shadow around her. Something dark—dangerous. I felt she was in danger." His voice cracked. "I shouldn't have said anything. I—"

"Jake," Teresa's tone sliced through his rambling like a blade, stopping him cold. "Carmen was in a car accident last night."

He felt his throat tighten. "God…"

"She crashed into another car. She was thrown through the windshield. She bled out before help could arrive."

Jake's breath caught in his chest. "I'm so sorry, Teresa."

"You knew. Somehow, you knew. You tried to warn her, and everyone thought you were crazy—even me."

"I should've talked to you, had you translate."

Teresa hesitated, voice nearly breaking. "You said, El Cucuy. Is that what you saw? The shadow of death? When Carmen left the party, she told Antonio you frightened her."

"Why is it so—"

"In my parents' culture, there are stories—horrible stories—about El Cucuy. A dark creature no one's ever seen, that shifts shape to hunt those it targets." She swallowed hard, gathering courage like a shield. "Maybe you really saw something. Something real."

Jake clenched his fists. "There was nothing we could do."

"I want to come over," Teresa said quietly, "I'm shaken. Do you have to go to work?"

"Not tonight. Come by. I'll make you dinner—it won't be fancy, but…"

She sighed on the other end. "Thank you."

After he hung up, Jake leapt from bed, heart pounding.

Later, he watched nervously through the window as her car pulled up, headlights piercing the gathering dusk. When Teresa stepped out, hesitating a moment before crossing the street, he rushed out to meet her.

She threw herself into his arms in a tight, desperate hug—a lifeline in the storm. They stood locked together for long minutes before Jake led her inside.

"This is your place?" Teresa's voice was soft, almost breathless as she looked around. "So neat."

Jake shrugged. "I like to know where things are."

"What's that smell?"

"Dinner. If we ever get around to eating it," he teased.

She grinned, eyes shining with something warmer. "Why, what else do you have in mind?"

Jake smiled, relieved to see her smile again.

"I feel like an idiot," she admitted. "I was so hard on you last night."

"I should've handled it better," he said gently. "Want to sit down?"

She shook her head. "You cook. I'm impressed. You clean better than I do."

Jake's eyes lit up. "Want to see something fun?"

"Okay," Teresa said, caught in his excitement.

He sat beside her on the sofa and waved his hand over the table. Instantly, a soft light flickered on.

"How'd you do that?" she gasped, eyes wide like a child watching a magic show.

He gestured again, and smooth jazz spilled from the speakers.

"Jake, that's amazing!"

"Just a couple of photoelectric cells connected to an electric switch," he explained. "Like an alarm that trips when a beam's broken, but I improved it so it doesn't need the beam."

"Wow! Did you patent it?"

"Patent it?"

"When you invent things, you've got to patent them."

"But these things already exist. I just put them together differently."

"Thomas Edison did that. And he died rich." She nudged him playfully. "People would buy it."

Jake shifted awkwardly. "I don't know…"

"That's your problem. You're too shy—you never give yourself a chance."

He hung his head. "I made a fool of myself last night."

"You tried to save someone's life. That's a good reason to embarrass yourself." She reached out, gently turning his face to hers. "That's why I'm here. To make up for not listening. I was so worried about what people thought… but you saw the truth."

"I sounded crazy."

She smiled softly. "If it happens again, I'm giving you the benefit of the doubt."

Her lips met his, slow and electric, tongues brushing with aching familiarity. Her hand drifted from his cheek down his chest, fingers curling possessively. A sharp heat surged through him.

"This is what I had in mind last night," Teresa whispered, smiling. She stood, fingers entwined with his. "Show me the rest of your place."

"The rest?" Jake raised an eyebrow, heart racing.

"You have a bedroom, right?"

He led her past the kitchen to a closed door.

"This the bathroom?"

Jake nodded.

She slipped inside. "Excuse me—and close the drapes in your bedroom."

Jake stood frozen, mouth tingling from their kiss. He moved to the bedroom and lowered the curtains, then he lit a few candles from a drawer to set the mood.

To his ears, the flush and running water trembled like distant thunder.

When she emerged, wearing only her bra and panties, the flickering candlelight painted shadows over her amber skin. Her breasts strained against the fabric, her curving legs and whisper of dark hair beneath silk inviting him closer.

"You're beautiful," Jake murmured, eyes drinking in every curve.

She smiled, pushing him gently onto the bed. "And you know exactly what to say."

Their lips met fiercely, hands exploring, desire crackling between them like static. Jake's fingers roamed up her legs, touching in places that made her shiver.

She sighed and deftly unbuttoned his shirt, pulling him deeper into the flickering heat of the moment—oblivious to the darkness lurking just beyond the candlelight.

Later, they lay side by side on the bed, tangled beneath a thin blanket, their breath still heavy, the room thick with the scent of sweat and candle wax.

"That was... incredible," Jake sighed, his voice low, almost reverent.

Teresa chuckled softly, her fingers tracing lazy patterns on his chest. "So, what they say about tall men is true."

Jake grinned, eyes sparkling. "You didn't seem to mind."

"Not in the slightest, my stallion."

He raised an eyebrow. "Burro? Isn't that a stallion in Spanish?"

Her laughter bubbled up again. "No, that's donkey."

Their laughter faded into the warm quiet, but a flicker of tension stabbed through the softness. When Teresa told him she didn't have any birth control, Jake's heart tightened—fear clutching cold in his gut.

But he'd remembered an old box of condoms tucked away.

"We probably scared the neighbors," Jake said, breaking the stillness.

Teresa smirked, eyes gleaming. "I've always been on the loud side."

They lay in the flicker of candlelight, shadows dancing eerily on the walls. Suddenly, a strange unease swept over the room.

"Jake," Teresa murmured, voice barely above a whisper.

"Yeah?"

"You made dinner?" The question was innocent, but carried a subtle edge, as if searching for reassurance.

His smile faltered. "Oh—yeah, sorry." He leapt from the bed, bare skin glowing faintly in the candlelight. "Let me get that going."

"Careful—no clothes. Don't burn anything important," Teresa teased, but the tremor in her words betrayed her.

As Jake moved toward the kitchen, she added, *"Buéno."*

"What?"

"It means 'good'." She grinned. "You've got the best ass I've ever seen on a white man. And you are a *very* white man.."

Jake laughed softly. "I don't get much sun."

The kitchen was dim, with the pan of eggplant parmigiana neatly nestled in the oven, needing only a quick reheat. He pulled two bowls from the fridge, mixing oil, vinegar, fresh garlic, and spices into a thick, tangy dressing. Carrying the tray back, he stepped quietly into the bedroom.

Teresa was sitting up, her silhouette framed by candlelight, hair tangled and wild.

"Now that's service," she said, eyes sparkling. "And I see several things I'd happily eat."

She reached out, hand hovering.

"No—don't—" Jake's warning came just seconds before the entire room exploded in blinding, searing light.

Teresa screamed, hands scrambling to shield her eyes as the white glare poured from the ceiling, walls, seeming to flood the room from everywhere at once. The harshness of the light pressed on them, suffocating, unrelenting.

Jake, eyes screwed shut against the sudden assault, set the tray down with trembling hands and batted wildly at the nightstand. With a sharp click, the light snapped off, plunging them back into shadows heavy and thick.

Teresa gasped for breath, blinking tears away. "What the hell was that? I thought my eyes would burn out."

Jake winced. "Sorry, stupid photoelectric switch—you triggered it without meaning to."

Her smile was shaky, but forgiving. "I guess it's alright then."

He stood and pulled on his pants and shirt, shoes scraping across the floor. "Wine? White or red?"

"You gonna go buy some now?" she asked.

"No, I have bottles down in the basement."

"Okay, I'd like white—and sweet, if you have it."

"Chablis?" He reached for his shoes. "I'll only have one glass—I have to work on one of my projects later.."

She smiled, settling back against the pillows. "I'm driving, but a glass would be nice."

As Jake moved through the house fetching wine, the atmosphere shifted—the earlier warmth now undercut by a crawling undercurrent of unease. He heard her footsteps dart toward the bathroom, the echo of the toilet flushing, then rapid footsteps back to the bedroom.

He emerged, bottle in hand, to find her standing naked, a fragile figure poised at the doorway to the bedroom.

"Hi, good-looking," he said softly.

She spun around, startled. "Jake! You move so quiet. You scared me!"

Concern etched deeply across his face. "What's wrong?"

"Nothing," she forced a smile. "Just the afterimage of that light. My eyes haven't quite recovered."

He crossed the room, wrapped her in his arms, kissing her. "I'll open the wine. And honestly, I love what you're wearing."

"If you want me to have dinner like this, you'd better take your clothes off, too," she teased.

They laughed, and Jake popped the cork, pouring generous glasses as he shed his clothes and climbed back onto the bed.

"Seriously, this dressing is amazing. Don't tell me you made it."

"Okay, I won't tell you—but I did," Jake said, offering her a glass.

They talked in low voices, wine loosening their tongues, until the eggplant came out—steaming, fragrant, devoured with hungry mouths.

Jake swallowed and grinned. "I've never had a meal with a naked woman before. Or naked myself for that matter."

Teresa smiled wistfully. "You're long and thin—wish I could be like you."

He reached for her hand. "You're beautiful," he said. "Every inch."

She frowned. "You don't think my hips are…?"

"Beautiful," he repeated firmly. "I wouldn't change a thing."

Their kisses grew deeper, more urgent.

"I think I know what's for dessert," Teresa whispered, a mischievous grin playing across her lips as she felt Jake's body press against her thigh.

They pushed dishes aside, hands exploring, breath hitching.

"Jake," Teresa's voice caught. She stopped, eyes searching his.

"Yeah?"

"Where are the rubbers?"

He froze, searching under the nightstand. "Under here."

She pulled out the small box, selecting one and tearing it open. Jake fumbled it on clumsily, slipping back beside her as she lay down, her breath shallow.

"Show me what you can do," she whispered.

For half an hour time blurred—skin against skin, breaths tangled, moans soft and desperate.

Finally, Jake shifted, moving on top of her so hard and fast she gasped, her body arching beneath him.

Afterward, they lay tangled, a heap of sweat and whispers.

"That was absolutely the best—"

"My stallion—you nearly split me in two."

"Did I hurt you?"

She smirked. "I can take it."

Jake reached down to pull off the condom—and froze. "Uh-oh," he muttered.

Her eyes narrowed. "What?"

"The condom... it's not on me."

"What?!"

"Probably inside you."

Her breath caught sharply. "How did you let that happen?"

"I didn't know."

Teresa's face hardened. "What kind of stupid excuse is that?"

"I was making love to you—that's all I was thinking about."

Madre de Dios," she said, voice trembling. "Reach inside me... Check if it's there."

She lay back, tension coiling in her muscles as he carefully slid two fingers inside her, grappling for the condom. The silence stretched like tangled wires before his grip found the smooth latex.

He pulled it out.

"Jake, is there anything inside?"

"No... it's empty."

She bolted upright, trembling like she'd been shocked. "Oh my God. You came inside me," she whispered, panicked.

Jake moved closer, voice soothing. "It's okay, really. I'm sure—"

"Sure? When was my last period? I shouldn't have—" Tears gathered in her eyes. "I'm being punished for giving myself to you like this—for being so brazen!"

"Teresa." He took her hands, steadying her. "If you're pregnant, we'll face it. Together. It's not your fault. It was us."

Her eyes searched his, searching for a lifeline, then she leaned into him, hugging him fiercely.

"You're a good man, Jake Hurd."

The next week slipped by with an eerie swiftness for Jake, each day weighed down by a creeping unease he dared not voice.

He kept seeing Teresa—Tuesday, Wednesday, then again Friday and Saturday nights—each encounter charged with something electric but unspoken, like a storm gathering just beyond the horizon.

His coworkers noticed the change, the lift in his spirits, but Jake clammed up tighter than ever, guarding his secrets with a rueful smile.

Although they didn't quite forget the lost condom incident, it faded as their nights together became more intimate.

Tuesday they shared a quiet dinner at Teresa's favorite bistro, the dim lighting casting shadows that worried Jake.

Wednesday night was a rush: an early movie right after her shift, then back to Jake's for dinner and more. Years of packing elaborate cold meals for his solo lunches now transformed into cooking for Teresa, the act somehow grounding him.

He found himself more open, more willing to talk—or at least listen—as Teresa did most of the talking. Her words spilled out like warm honey, and Jake soaked them in, grateful for her voice.

Friday and Saturday arrived with a swell of anticipation. Teresa came prepared for the night, a hanging bag slung casually with a silky negligee peeking out.

When she changed in the bathroom, the sight of her in the nightie ignited Jake's desire like wildfire—he kissed her from head to toe, savoring every inch with a hunger he hadn't felt in years.

But beneath the sweet moments lay a restless tension.

At midnight Saturday, while Teresa drifted into a heavy sleep, Jake slipped silently into his basement workshop.

The machine he'd been painstakingly building stood nearly complete, but the quiet of the apartment gnawed at him. He hated leaving her alone, hated the shadows that might creep closer whenever he was separated from her.

Large, heavy-glass candles flickered downstairs, their flames stubborn amid the faint drafts.

Jake toyed with the idea of a monitoring system, a device to hear any sound from the apartment above as he worked in the basement. He vowed to build it next week.

Tonight, he soldered circuits and transistors inside a metal box he'd scavenged from the electronics store. No music. No distractions. Only the scratch of tools and the pulse of his own apprehension.

Around two in the morning, a sound sliced through the silence. Movement upstairs. He froze, senses sharpening like a predator stalking prey. Footsteps—deliberate, calm—reassured him at first. Maybe Teresa simply needed the bathroom.

He returned to his work, heart thudding with a faint hope.

A sharp bang—a door slamming hard—shattered the fragile calm.

His skin prickled as a gut-wrenching cry pierced the air.

"Jake! Help me!"

Panic crashed over him like a wave. "Teresa!" he bellowed, scrambling up the stairs two at a time.

Breath ragged, he flipped the emergency switch by the basement door. Brilliant, searing light exploded through every room—an all-encompassing blaze designed to banish shadows from the corners.

Blinded by the gleam, he rushed through the apartment to the bedroom—empty. Then to the bathroom—door shut tight.

The bathroom was the one place lacking his protective lights.

He threw the door open and found her sprawled on the cold tile floor. Relief and terror collided in his chest.

She wasn't fragile; she was strong. Yet he lifted her as if she weighed nothing, the silk negligee torn and hanging loosely, dark streaks beneath her eyes from tears and fear.

Kneeling beside her, he whispered, "It's okay, you're safe now."

Cuts marred the delicate fabric, jagged slashes that didn't belong. Her right breast peeked through a jagged tear—skin unbroken, but vulnerability raw.

"My butt... it hurts," she whimpered, voice trembling. "And my head... God, the pain..."

"I'm here," Jake soothed. "You're hurt, but not seriously, I think. Tell me what happened."

The words tumbled out in a shattered whisper: "The candles… they went out. The lights… the door slammed shut. I tried to move, but it was like the floor shifted beneath me. Someone… was there. I could feel it. I fell."

Jake's gaze flicked to the candles in their glass tubes. They stood extinguished. An icy shiver raced down his spine.

"There's no one here now," he said, trying to sound confident.

Tears welled in Teresa's eyes, smearing mascara into dark rivers as she shook, reliving the nightmare.

"What was that, Jake?" she asked.

His throat tightened. "Who? What—"

She clutched his hand, trembling. "I don't know. But it was something."

The room grew colder despite the flickering candles he relit. Shadows clung to corners lurking just beyond sight.

Jake held a penlight to her eyes, tracing slow, steady arcs— checking for concussion as he had learned to do long ago.

"Stop," Teresa murmured, breath shallow.

"Hold still," he urged gently. "You're going to be okay."

But the terror in her gaze refused to fade.

"What's happening here?" she demanded, voice cracking. "Don't tell me you don't know."

He swallowed the truth he had buried deep down: of the machine, of the shadows, of the things that haunted his nights and whispered threats in the dark.

"We'll talk in the morning," he promised, "right now just rest. I won't leave you again."

Reluctantly, she obeyed, the exhaustion finally dragging her into the fragile safety of sleep.

Jake lay in the bed beside her, watching the flickering candlelight dance across her face, haunted by the unspoken threat lurking in their midst.

Because whatever had come for her that night—it was only the beginning.

And soon, he would have no choice but to tell her the awful truth.

20 LIGHTLESS FOREBODING

Jake stood by the stove, the aroma of sizzling bacon and eggs filling the kitchen as soft sunlight streamed through the window.

Suddenly, a low groan drifted from the bedroom. He stiffened, turning toward the sound just as Teresa's voice, hoarse and weary, called out.

"Ugh... *Madre de Dios,* I hurt everywhere," she moaned, her voice thick with exhaustion.

Jake wiped his hands on his apron and leaned against the doorframe. "You all right?" he asked gently.

"What's that... smell?" She sniffed the air, curiosity replacing some of the pain in her tone.

Without a word, Jake smiled and stepped into the bedroom, his eyes lingering on her tangled hair and the way she clenched the blanket tightly around her shoulders. "I made breakfast."

Teresa blinked, pulling the blanket closer. "Breakfast? Like, a proper one? That only happens when I'm at my parents' house."

"Come see for yourself." Jake took her hand, tugging gently.

Wrapped in the soft fabric, Teresa shuffled into the kitchen, her bare feet silent against the cool floor. Her eyes widened at the sight: a small table draped with a cheerful yellow cloth, plates neatly arranged, silverware gleaming, and the morning sun casting a golden glow over it all.

She moved toward the table, her fingers running through her messy hair as if trying to tame the chaos. "I would've dressed—"

Jake cut her off with a grin. "You look great. Sit down and relax."

The scent of cheese omelet, crisp bacon, warm toast, and fresh coffee filled the room as Jake plated the food and placed it before her.

Teresa stabbed a forkful of egg, pausing thoughtfully. "So… what the hell happened last night?" she asked, voice low but insistent. "Is this place haunted?"

Jake set the cast-iron skillet in the sink with a clatter, rubbing his face tiredly. "I spent most of the night thinking it through. It all makes sense, logically."

Teresa's fork dropped to the plate with a clink. "Logically? Candles blowing out on their own, doors slamming shut—every damn minute? That's supposed to be 'normal'?"

Jake moved closer, leaning on a nearby chair. "Here's what I think. I heard you in the bathroom so I came upstairs. When I opened the cellar door a gust of wind must have rushed in and blew the candles out. The door slammed behind me. You probably got startled and slipped on the rug."

Her mouth fell open in disbelief. "That is the biggest pile of bullshit I've ever heard. Jake, you heard me fall. That was after the candles went out and the door slammed."

He rubbed his chin. "Maybe we're wrong about the order. Or maybe the wind hit the door differently than we thought."

Her glare turned sharp, edged with frustration. "Okay, what about my negligee?" She whipped the blanket aside, revealing the torn fabric clinging to her. "Explain this!"

Jake looked sheepish. "I don't know. We were rough last night. Maybe it caught on something. Maybe the fabric is just fragile."

Her voice rose. "Or maybe you're seriously suggesting I imagined the whole damn thing!"

"I just want to keep you safe," Jake said quietly, trying to calm the storm brewing in her eyes.

She shot him an incredulous look. "You promised you'd tell me everything this morning—when it was safe."

"We've both calmed down since then," he tried to reason.

"Calmed down?" she snapped, the words dripping with bitterness as she pushed back her chair and stormed around the table. Her brown eyes flashed dangerously. "Calmed down?!"

Jake sighed. "Maybe that was a poor choice of words."

"You bet it was," she hissed. "So now I'm the hysterical girl? Fine." She pushed past him and slammed the bathroom door behind her.

Jake stood frozen for a moment, the echo of the door slam ringing in his ears. The sound of running water filled the silence.

He hated lying to her, hated pretending it was just coincidence. But if the shadows—the things lurking in the dark —didn't see her as a threat she might be safe. He'd rather have her angry than dead, like Peggy.

His lights and devices kept him protected but the shadows weren't bound by the rules of the physical world. They could appear anywhere at any time, slipping through space like ghosts. They didn't need cars or keys; they simply manifested.

He didn't want to escalate the fight until he had more weapons in his arsenal.

Later, Teresa stepped out of the bathroom, wrapped in a towel, her hair dripping wet. She shivered slightly as she walked into the bedroom, clutching her bag with intent.

Jake leaned against the doorway. "Teresa—"

She cut him off, her voice cold but fragile. "I don't want to hear it. I'm going home."

"I'm sorry. I just... I don't want you to be afraid."

She paused, her hands fumbling as she slipped on a bra. "You don't want me to be afraid?" Her voice cracked, surprised.

"Exactly."

She fastened the clasp and turned, a flicker of vulnerability crossing her face. "Then tell me what's really going on."

Jake swallowed hard. "I really think it was just a series of coincidences."

She shot him a skeptical glance and tried the word herself, her tone teasing but rough. "Coin-kiden-ses..."

He fought to not smile, but failed. "Coincidences."

"Coin-SEE-daynses!" she corrected, a smile tugging at her lips despite herself.

Jake could not suppress a chuckle. "You're cute when you say it wrong."

Teresa fought back the laughter that bubbled up, but a giggle escaped despite her best efforts. Jake stepped forward, wrapping her in a warm embrace, peppering small kisses under her laughing eyes.

"No," she murmured, pulling away, though her fingers lingered on his chest.

He stood there in pajamas watching her just in bra and panties, feeling a yearning he couldn't shake. "Can we just chalk last night up to a bad dream?"

She exhaled sharply but her gaze softened at his earnest expression.

"Okay," she relented, "we'll 'chalk it up' to… unexplained circumstances."

"Coincidences?" Jake prodded with a hopeful smile.

Those dark eyes sparkled with mischief. "Those things." Her expression hardened slightly. "But if I stay…" She stepped closer, voice low, serious. "You never leave me alone. Got that?"

"No problem," he promised.

"It better be. Or this is the last overnight."

Jake leaned in, brushing his lips against hers. "You have my word."

She laughed softly, tilting her head up. "Why'd you have to be so tall?"

"I dunno," he teased. "Why'd you have to be so short?"

They kissed with a fierce passion, her breath hitching softly. She pulled back, eyes bright.

"Oh! What time is it? I have to meet my parents at church."

Jake glanced at the clock. "Eight."

She smiled slyly and let her hand rest on his waistband. "Well, I guess there's time… but I'm going to need another shower. I can't show up smelling like sex."

Jake laughed. "It just gives you more to confess."

Two weeks crawled by since that ominous night, and Friday morning found Jake posted at the One F entrance, scanning badges with a restless eye, waiting for Teresa.

She hadn't been to work on Wednesday or Thursday, and every call he made to her went unanswered. The silence gnawed at him, a silent alarm shrieking just beneath the surface.

Still, it was Friday—Jake's favorite day of the week. Unlike everyone else, his weekend felt stretched out, beginning at 8:00 AM Friday and dragging lazily to midnight Sunday night.

This weekend held promise: a gathering of his computer club where the newest gadgets and breakthroughs would be on display, followed by dinner with Teresa near her place so he could drop her off ahead of eleven and be safely tucked in by midnight.

It was a trade-off, sacrificing sleep—his routine usually meant rising late Sunday afternoon—but he could make up the rest with a full day of rest. He needed the rest, desperately.

The memory of that frightening night at his apartment still worried him. Teresa's reluctance to stay over wasn't surprising, and he spent nights trying to rationalize her experience, trying to convince both her and himself there had to be a logical explanation.

But Jake's life had grown smaller over the years, confined to places he deemed safe. Blinding lights at home and in the workshop. Carefully rerouted security tours, forcing other guards to navigate the dark subbasements alone. His schedule was a cage, precise and uniform—a fortress against the dark corners that whispered threats in the darkness.

Inviting Teresa into his world meant opening a door to a more adversarial dance with those shadows.

He remembered how warning Carmen had cracked that door wide open. This violent episode against Teresa—he saw it clearly now—was a test. They wanted to see if he'd reveal their secrets to her as he had to Peggy before.

And he hadn't forgotten what happened to Peggy.

His relationship with Teresa needed structure—a schedule that would lull the shadows into complacency.

Meanwhile, he would keep developing weapons, traps, or whatever it took to incapacitate even one of these things. That would put them in fear—of him.

Jake nodded politely to employees flashing plastic badges as they streamed past him.

Then Teresa arrived.

Relief surged hot in Jake's chest, though she looked pale, worn. No wonder she missed work. She moved deliberately toward him.

"We need to talk," she whispered, voice tense like a taut wire ready to snap.

Jake blinked. Four words a man never wants to hear.

"Sure," he said, his smile coming too easily, too bright. "I get off at—"

"No. Now," she cut in, jaw clenched, eyes sharp like knives.

He wanted to remind her he was on duty, the lieutenant who set the example, but the fire smoldering behind her eyes told him compliance was the smarter path.

"Okay," he said, attempting to keep his voice light as she turned and began walking down the hall.

Jake glanced at Tony, who was still scanning badges nearby.

"I'm going to—uh—I'll be right back," Jake mumbled.

Tony smirked, flashing that "you're so whipped" look that made Jake want to punch a wall.

Jake quickened his stride, his long legs swallowing the distance between him and Teresa, who—though smaller—moved forward with the determined energy of a freight train.

She suddenly stopped, and Jake nearly collided with her.

"Go into my office. I'll be there in a minute," she commanded, then spun on her heel and disappeared into the ladies' room.

Jake unlocked the door to her office with his keys, slipped inside, and quietly closed the door behind him. The last thing he needed was for prying eyes or gossip to leak this meeting to the site supervisor.

Sitting on the corner of her desk, Jake felt calmer—but his mind was racing. What had she discovered? Was this about the strange events at his apartment? Or something new entirely? Why was she angry?

Teresa reappeared, slipping inside quietly. Jake rose, concern knotting his brow. She shut the door behind her with a quiet click.

"What's up, honey?" he asked, soft and tentative.

She gawked at him. "Don't 'honey' me, you bastard."

Not... good.

"Okay," he said cautiously. "You wanna talk?"

"Talk?" She scoffed bitterly. "If we'd talked all night instead of... other things, I wouldn't be in this mess now."

"Teresa," Jake said gently, "you're not making sense."

She circled the desk and collapsed into her chair, hands shaking as she pressed them to her face, surrendering to shuddering sobs.

Jake was unmoored. He knew he should comfort her—but he was terrified his words might make things worse. "What is it, Teresa? Please. Tell me."

Slowly, she pulled a tissue from the box and wiped her nose. The fight seemed to drain from her bones.

"I missed Wednesday and yesterday because... I was throwing up," she confessed, voice cracking, "Like I just did a minute ago."

Jake frowned. "Are you sick? What's wrong?"

After a deep breath, she whispered, "I've got morning sickness. I'm... I mean, I'm pregnant."

A heavy silence dropped over the room.

"Are you sure?" Jake asked, disbelief threading his words.

"I find out today. I got tested Wednesday when the vomiting started."

"If you are... isn't it too soon? Could be the flu, or—"

"My sister? She was puking the day after she conceived," Teresa said between tears. "My breasts—they feel different, funny."

Jake fought the rising panic clawing at his throat. "Maybe it's just your mind playing tricks. The night the rubber slipped—"

"Fell off, Jake!" she snapped sharply, then whispered brokenly, "Put two and two together."

The word 'fatherhood' hammered inside his skull like a fist against glass.

"I find out today," she said. "Supposedly they have to... I don't know, kill a rabbit or something to test properly."

"We shouldn't get upset," Jake said firmly, trying to steady his breath. "Until we know for sure."

"What're we gonna do, Jake?" Her accent blanketed her question in uneven syllables, 'gonna,' 'do' twisting oddly on her tongue.

"We wait. We have months—"

"My roommate said she'd take me to a clinic in New York."

Jake's throat tightened. "Why? You're healthy, right?"

"To get an—an abortion," she confessed, her voice cracking under fresh sobs. "It's not even legal in New Jersey."

He swallowed hard. The weight in his chest was crushing.

"Teresa, please. Don't get ahead of yourself. Let's get the results first, okay?"

The tears still flowed freely. "But, Jake—"

"No. You can sit here miserable, or you can wait. When we know, we'll sit down and decide what comes next."

She nodded, wiping her nose in defeat.

"Call me after five this afternoon," Jake said.

"Yeah." Her nod was resolute. Then shyly, "You still… like me, don't you?"

Jake looked into her searching eyes, a swirl of fear and need tightening his chest.

For once, he let himself feel.   "Teresa, I love you."

Her face lit with sudden hope. She sprang from her chair and pulled him into a fierce embrace, squeezing with desperate warmth.

"I… love… you, too," she stammered amid tears.

Jake held her tight, whispering into her hair. "We'll work it out."

He glanced at her face, kissed away the tears, and said softly, "Now, you better wash up if you're going to get anything done today."

"I don't know if I can. The nausea won't quit."

"Eat something. Crackers help."

"Really?"

"Couldn't hurt."

She kissed him gently. "I feel so stupid."

"Hush. Go wash your face." Jake glanced at his watch. "I gotta get back."

"Sure, Jake." Her voice quiet, submissive. She stepped back, letting him go. "I'll call you later." One last tissue, a forced crooked smile.

Jake walked back to the One F entrance feeling hollow—like a ghost passing through his own body—while outside life continued unaware, as unforgiving and relentless as a ticking clock.

On the drive home Jake's mind was a wild storm of 'what ifs' and 'what thens,' each scenario piling on top of the last like an avalanche threatening to bury him.

His heart hammered a chaotic drumbeat against the silence of the car's interior. The tension built so sharply that he knew he couldn't just face it all head-on.

He needed a pause, a moment to catch his breath.

Pulling into a small, nondescript store, Jake completed his quick errand with trembling hands and a restless spirit.

Yet, unexpectedly, the task worked like a balm, soothing the tempest inside him and slowing the pounding of his heart. By the time he returned home and lay down, a fragile calm had settled over him, coaxing him toward sleep.

But sleep wouldn't claim him for long.

At five sharp, the phone shattered the evening's quiet making his nerves tighten in his chest until he snatched up the receiver.

"H-hello?" His voice was rough, the words barely tethered to consciousness.

"It's me," Teresa's voice came low, firm. "And it's yes."

His stomach dropped, as if someone had sucker-punched him in the gut. The weight of her affirmation crushed him, but beneath it stirred an urgent hope. "You'd better come over."

"I'll be there soon."

Almost an hour later, amid the chaos of Friday's rush-hour traffic, she arrived. When Jake opened the door, Teresa stepped inside like a warrior entering a battlefield—her back straight, jaw clenched, her entire being radiating fierce resolve.

She crossed her arms, and the air felt thick, charged with unspoken questions and simmering tension.

"So," she said finally, voice steady but tight with emotion, her eyes fixed on the floor. "What are we gonna do?"

Jake leaned forward, forcing a smile to bridge the distance, then raised her head to let her eyes meet his. "Hey! I'm up here."

Teresa's gaze flickered upward but held firm. "Now is when the nice words stop, Jake. Don't try to be sweet or understanding. I don't need that. I just need to know where I stand."

He nodded, the gravity of her demand settling on his chest like a stone. Wordlessly he led her to the kitchen table and they sat opposite each other, the space between them filled with raw uncertainty.

"Jake," she began, eyes fixed ahead, a tremor in her voice. "You don't have to spare my feelings. I'm not a child." Her words hung in the air, then cracked under the weight of irony. "I know men say things they don't mean."

Jake swallowed hard, feeling years of silence press down on him. For a decade, he'd locked away his fears and truths, letting nothing show on the surface. Now, faced with this fragile, difficult moment, he struggled to be honest.

"You're right," he admitted slowly. "Sometimes I say things just to be polite. But when you mentioned abortion…"

Her words slipped out, tightly clenched and bitter: "It might be the best choice."

Jake frowned deeply. "I don't think so." He rose and paced the small room, voice tense with raw fear. "There are things I've seen… things that terrify me. The thought of being a parent… scares the hell out of me."

"Me, too," Teresa whispered, a sudden sniffle breaking through her armor.

He sank back into the chair, hands stuffed deep into his pockets as if rooting for courage. "But the idea of losing this child —or you—scares me even more." He placed a small jewelry box on the table between them. "Open it."

Her hands trembled violently as she lifted the lid. Inside, nestled in velvet, lay a modest diamond ring, its single stone shimmering with gentle fire. Teresa's breath caught sharply in her throat.

Jake locked eyes with her, voice steady but vulnerable. "Teresa, will you marry me?"

Tears welled and spilled freely down their faces as they dissolved into an embrace. She whispered a hoarse, broken "Yes" while he slid the ring onto her finger—a perfect fit, a fragile promise.

They didn't leave the apartment that night. Instead, they lay together, stripped bare physically and emotionally, sharing food, making love, and weaving fragile dreams from hope and fear.

"I think I can reserve time at the church," Teresa said, her voice soft with excitement. "My friends will make beautiful bridesmaids."

Jake shook his head with a tired smile. "All that expense… and we're on a deadline. You'll show in two months, tops."

Teresa laughed softly. "My sister started showing even earlier."

"And there's only so long to say the baby was premature," Jake added with a touch of humor but deadly earnestness. "I don't want anyone calling my kid a bastard."

"Bastardo!" Teresa shot back. "You're right. All we need is a blood test and a Justice of the Peace—"

"Better choice."

She hung her head, voice dropping. "What about people wondering why we rushed?"

"Let them think what they want. It's the seventies—nobody cares like that anymore. Besides, we need to save money."

"You're right!" Teresa's smile brightened with hope. "We have to find a place to live. Especially with the baby."

Jake's mind flicked to his workshop, the anchor he might have to lose. "We've got months for that."

"This place scares me, Jake. And moving means money—baby things cost so much. I don't have a penny saved."

He shrugged, trying to keep his voice light. "Well… I have twenty thousand."

Her mouth fell open, disbelief shining in her eyes. "Twenty thousand *dollars*? No way!"

Jake gestured toward his modest apartment. "I'm thrifty. This place is a hundred bucks a month. I don't eat out—"

"Until recently," Teresa teased.

"Last decade's been just work for me. Repairs mostly, bringing in extra cash. No social life except my computer club." He paused, meeting her excited gaze. "We could even buy a house."

"Oh, Jake…" Teresa's voice trembled with joy. "That's wonderful. I don't need a fancy wedding if our baby can grow up in a home. We could move to a nice neighborhood." She sprang to her feet, her movements bursting with newfound life and hope. "Twenty thousand dollars—we're practically rich!"

Jake laughed softly, eyes tracing the curves of her naked body dancing around the room. "Don't get carried away. We have to be careful."

She pinned him with a grin. "We could have a party after the wedding. That would bring in wedding presents as well! Jake, I'm so happy. I don't even feel nauseous!"

She threw herself back onto the bed, kissing him fiercely. "Love me, Daddy," she whispered, eyes closing in bliss.

Later, as Teresa slept peacefully, Jake brought his latest tinkering project upstairs to the kitchen. Working quietly, cautiously, he kept a watchful, protective eye over her—and the fragile life growing inside her.

A house. The idea always lingered in the corners of his mind. Now it wasn't just idle thought. It had to become real. A sanctuary, a castle of safety—not just for him and Teresa, but for the child.

His child.

21. BACHELOR PARTY

··

The next few weeks swept Jake and Teresa into a relentless storm of preparations that left little room for anything else.

They moved quickly, getting blood tests done, selecting and ordering invitations, and setting the wedding date just a month away.

After some debate, they settled on the restaurant where Teresa's parents celebrated their anniversary—a place rich with memories and meaning. Finding a Justice of the Peace who would perform the ceremony on the cheap was another tick on their rapidly growing list.

Amid this flurry of organization and Teresa's tentative, exhausting attempts at house hunting, their time together shrank. Long weekends and sleepovers became scarce.

Teresa, wanting to deepen the anticipation and make their honeymoon something they both truly desired, made a difficult decision.

"No sex until the wedding night," she told Jake, locking the promise between them. It was a test of patience neither took lightly.

They agreed on a Saturday afternoon—Jake's choice—believing even if exhaustion pressed down on him, at least there would be no lingering shadows or whispered doubts.

Jake phoned to request a week off—his first vacation in ten years of working for Security Information Systems. The phone rang and rang before finally connecting to yet another one of the revolving door of pretty but incompetent secretaries. Jake explained he needed the time off for his honeymoon and was met with silence before being abruptly put on hold.

A booming voice exploded through the receiver. "Mr. Hurd! Dan Hurley here. You're getting married, you son of a— Wait—you're only what—twenty-two?

"Twenty-nine, sir."

"How in the hell did you do that, getting older while I hardly age at all? All kidding aside, Jake, I had to congratulate you. You've been an incredible asset to this company and the best damn midnight lieutenant I've ever seen."

"That's very kind of you, Mr. Hurley."

"Dan, come on. And listen—the paycheck this week is going to have a little something extra. From me and Stan Hanover. Though I know Stan's going to lose his mind when he sees how much I give you."

"Wow, that's really amazing. Thank you, sir."

"It's the least I can do, son. Now listen, kiss the bride for me—and while you're at it, bang the hell out of her."

Jake laughed, a little embarrassed but grateful. "I'll do my best, Dan."

Dan's laughter boomed louder, mostly at his own irreverent joke. "Take care, lieutenant. Mark my words, you're going to be a site supervisor before long."

"As long as I can keep the midnight shift," Jake shot back.

"Thrilled to hear it! You're a rare gem, Mr. Hurd."

As the phone clicked off, Jake sat back, a mixture of nerves and excitement tightening in his chest. The countdown had truly begun.

Jake's coworkers insisted on taking him out the Friday night before the wedding, especially when they found out he didn't have a best man, insisting on dragging him out.

The implication was clear: Jake needed a bachelor party.

"Come on, Jake," Winston grinned, sliding behind the wheel of his '66 GTO as the others piled in. "You gotta loosen up a little."

Tony smirked from the backseat. "Yeah, lieutenant, it's your bachelor party. Only once, right?"

Jake shifted uncomfortably. "I honestly didn't think I needed one," he muttered, already questioning why he'd agreed.

Ed leaned forward, a twinkle of mischief in his eyes. "It's not really for you, Jake. This night's for us old married guys to have an excuse to... look at undressed ladies."

Winston slapped the steering wheel hard. "You gotta do it for us, man. I told you how my old lady feels about me looking at white women. The only thing worse is me looking at any women at all."

Jake groaned. "I'm here, aren't I?"

Tony laughed. "Boy, you'd think he was picking up the tab."

Winston glanced around the dimly lit street as he pulled into a grimy parking lot. Neon flickered above a battered building—a faded sign flashed, 'GoGo Dancers,' alongside another barely legible one: 'The Dive.'

Jake raised an eyebrow. "Truth in advertising, huh?"

Tony grinned, ever the salesman. "Don't worry. You're about to see girls you've never even dreamed of. All within the legal limits of the State of New Jersey, of course."

Winston was first out of the car, cracking his knuckles with a sly grin. "How much do they take off in there?"

Tony whispered conspiratorially, "They have to keep their tops on because they serve booze, but they push every limit."

Inside, the club was heavy with cigarette smoke and cheap perfume. Shadows clung to the low ceiling. A long bar ran along one wall, behind which two small stages flickered weakly under pale spotlights, barely cutting through the gloom.

Two dancers commanded each stage. One was a blonde—thin but curvaceous, her black bikini top barely containing her ample chest. The other was a waif-like Asian with delicate features, clad only in a two-inch spandex band covering her nipples and a G-string.

"Holy damn," Winston muttered with reverence as he slumped into a chair near the bar. "I'm in heaven."

The bartender, Carmine, nodded in greeting. "Evenin', Tony."

Tony smiled. "Hey, Carmine. This guy," he said, pointing at Jake, "needs to get drunk. Like, right now."

Carmine grinned. "I got just the thing."

Jake felt the blonde dancer's eyes on him. She winked, flashing a perfect smile. Heat rose to his cheeks despite himself.

Ed nudged Tony. "How often you come here, Tony? The bartender knows you."

Tony shrugged. "When I need to avoid my old lady—couple nights a week. Cheap cover, cute girls, overpriced drinks. Best deal in town."

Carmine set down a dark, muddy-looking concoction in front of Jake.

"What's this?" Jake asked cautiously.

"New York special," Carmine said. "I call it an East River, 'cause it looks like the water there."

Jake eyed it skeptically but took a tentative sip. Rich coffee liqueur coated his tongue. It was like a White Russian with a twist.

"Good?" Carmine asked.

Jake nodded. "Yeah. It's good."

"Drink it slow," Carmine warned, moving away. "It's got Kahlua and Bailey's, but I added a shot of Everclear."

"Everclear?" Jake asked.

"It's like moonshine, almost pure alcohol," Carmen explained.

The music pulsed, a Top 40 beat crackling through cheap speakers. The blonde dancer pushed up onto the bar and swayed close to eye level, crouching low with a teasing smile.

Tony slipped bills into her G-string with a wink. With a cheeky grin, she slipped away to the other stage, then turned, grinding provocatively, her hips moving like a machine. The group howled in approval.

"Oh, Lord," Winston breathed, raising his glass. "My dreams have come true."

Jake forced a laugh, still uneasy. There was something familiar about the blonde. He tried to place her face but couldn't quite do it.

The blonde walked off and a brunette stepped up to the empty stage and began dancing, shedding a corset as she moved. Underneath was a top that consisted of only two black stars covering her nipples.

After a moment, the blonde approached their table, her costume covered by a thin robe draped over her shoulders.

"Enjoying the show?" she asked, voice light.

Jake straightened, heart pounding. The voice stirred something in him, memories he hadn't expected to surface tonight. He also noticed he felt drunk. Carmine had been right, that one drink was powerful.

Tony flirted shamelessly. "You sure look beautiful up there."

Winston leaned in. "How do you do that thing with your butt?"

The blonde laughed and said, "Well, buy a girl a drink and I'll tell you."

Carmine instantly appeared with an unrecognizable beverage, which the blonde picked right up.

"Actually," she admitted, the men in rapt attention, "you see Terry there?" She nodded toward the dancing brunette. "Now, she's gorgeous."

"Not as beautiful as you," Ed said.

"Oh, but I would love to look like Terry. I could just eat her up."

"Hoo," Winston hooted, "I would love to see that."

The men all laughed along with the blonde girl. Except for Jake. The connection clicked in his mind.

"Sally?" he said.

The girl turned to Jake, surprised. "No, I'm Candy."

"Yeah," Tony agreed, "I bet you're twice as sweet."

The men laughed but the blonde looked at Jake, tried to place his face.

"You used to be Sally," Jake drawled. "I met you at the Brethren. It was a coffee house out in the woods."

"I don't remember—"

"The black guy threw me out, Mack? You went with me? I'm the night guard?"

"With the VW bug!" Sally shrieked, eyes wide. She smiled and hugged Jake.

"Hey, wait, Jake. You know this girl?" Ed gasped, his fantasies crushed.

"I know him, too," Sally or Candy said, and then gave Jake a wicked grin. "Repeatedly, to be honest."

Jake cleared his throat. "What happened? I tried to look for you—"

"Oh, I was pretty free in those days. But did I hear right? You're getting married?"

"Tomorrow."

"That's really great. She's getting a good guy."

"Hey," Tony interjected into the conversation, "being it's his last night as a free man, and since you're already, y'know, familiar with him, perhaps you could give him one last thrill."

"Oh, guys, come on!" Candy demurred and slapped Tony playfully on the arm. "He's off-limits now!"

"Don't listen to Tony," Jake said, uncomfortable with Tony's attempt. "He's just a big talker."

Jake pulled her aside for a minute. She followed with suspicion.

"Don't take her too far, Jake," Ed warned.

Jake waved at the guys and brought his mouth close to her ear. "I had a problem after we—well, I got the… uh… clap."

"Oh, geez," she said, her hand at her mouth. "Did I have that then? I'm so sorry. I got it taken care of, and I've been a lot more careful."

"I just wanted to make sure you knew—I mean, for your own sake."

"That's sweet." She sipped her drink. "Yeah, I was stoned most of the time back then. I'm a lot more stable now."

"That's good."

She brought her mouth close to Jake's ear. "I've got a little boy."

"That's wonderful!" Jake said, surprised. "Who watches him when you work? His father?"

"No, his grandma. I—well—kinda don't know who his father is. I told you, I was pretty free back then."

Jake's mouth fell open; the idea of parenthood with Teresa was overwhelming enough, but he had to ask…

"How old is he?"

"Sixteen months," she lowered her voice and gazed around the room. "Don't tell the customers. It's not good for business if they find out they're ogling someone's mom."

"Sure, of course." Jake nodded. He was drunk, but he could still do the math. Sixteen months old and their encounter was over two years ago. The timing was very suspicious.

"I gotta get back to work."

"I understand," Jake said as his mind raced.

Sally assumed her 'Candy' persona, yelled to Jake's group, "See you guys! Remember, when you're here, just ask for Candy."

"Good enough to eat!" bellowed Winston as Ed and Tony hooted and clapped.

Instead of dancing on her stage, Candy leapt up on the stage where Terry, the brunette, capered. Candy threw off her robe. They moved close, kissing under the dim lights. The room erupted in cheers.

Suddenly, Jake's breath hitched. He saw a shadow slipping through the crowd. Panic flared in his chest. He stumbled backward, crashing into a table.

His friends rushed to steady him.

"You okay?" Candy asked, concern softening her features.

"Never seen two girls kiss before," Tony quipped, helping Jake up.

"His loss." Terry laughed, blew a kiss to Candy and walked to a door next to the bar, the dressing room for the dancers.

The guards sat Jake down and put a fresh drink in front of him. He took a strong slug and tried to stop his hands from shaking.

"Whew, slow down, Jake," Winston warned.

"I don't blame him," Ed said. "Those two could knock anyone off his feet."

"Yeah," added Tony, "but don't worry, Jake, we'll tell Teresa you kept it in your shorts."

Jake looked around the room. The shadow was gone; had it been there at all? He glanced at Sally who had gone back to dancing. "I need a piece of paper."

He pulled a small notepad out of his pocket he kept on him in case he got design ideas. He hastily wrote his name, phone number, and work number, then ripped the page out and folded it.

"He's gonna give her his number," Ed hissed.

"You got cojones, Jake," Tony said.

"The blonde really is an old friend," Jake responded, and forced himself to sound coherent. He would have to wait until her next break.

He watched Sally/Candy come off stage and wander over to his group.

"You okay?" she yelled to Jake over the music which was louder now. "I saw you fall."

"Yeah," Tony chuckled, "I guess you can say your act knocked him out."

The men laughed and Candy did, too.

Jake, struggling to focus through the haze of the alcohol, waved Candy to join him a few feet away. She shrugged at the men and walked over to Jake again.

"I gotta change outfits—" she began.

"Sally, I have to go," Jake said, "but I want you to have my number—"

Her expression darkened. "Hey! You're getting married."

"It's not a come-on." Jake tried to keep his words from slurring. "It's just if you need anything—for your boy."

Her smile dimmed. "I take care of him just fine."

"I'm sure you do," Jake attempted to sound supportive and more sober than he was. "But I can't help but wonder, y'know, the timing and everything."

She met his eyes, stunned. "Oh, God, you were that summer!" She glanced over at the bartender, as if for reassurance. "You don't have to worry. I mean, I must've slept with twenty guys."

"It's not anything like that. Look, I'm handy. I fix things. Toasters, TVs, that kind of stuff. And maybe you need a friend to help you with your boy. I don't know, just call me if I can be of some help."

She looked at the piece of paper in her hand. "That's really sweet. I mean it. I'll remember that." She peered over at Carmine who nodded. "I gotta go change. Good night—uh—"

"Jake."

"Right, Jake."

"Good night, Sally."

Jake told the others it was time to leave. Tony slipped Carmine an extra few bills.

As they drove Jake home, his head swam—his grip on reality slipping like the shadows he'd glimpsed. He stumbled through the door of his apartment and collapsed into a restless, alcohol-fueled sleep.

At 10:00 AM his alarm rang. He woke disoriented, and incredibly hung over—a problem he tried to alleviate with coffee, aspirin, and by throwing up for a good five minutes.

Showering and shaving with shaky hands, Jake cursed his fellow guards. He dressed while sipping Pepto-Bismol and jumped in his car to drive to his wedding. He swore he would never drink again.

The wedding went smoothly. He and Teresa exchanged vows amid smiles and champagne, but Jake's mind was elsewhere—haunted by ghosts in the dark and his past crashing into his future.

Teresa was oblivious to Jake's condition, happy to be a bride and the center of attention. It was not the big church service she wanted, but she knew she and Jake would be the first in her family to buy their own house.

Jake hoped it would all work out.

22. A Visit With Sally

In her seventh month, Teresa's relentless morning sickness finally eased—a long-awaited mercy. It was a help as her belly had swelled so large that bending over the toilet was a struggle.

Jake exhaled deeply, relieved not only for her but for himself. Teresa's constant queasiness had overshadowed their brief honeymoon near the Delaware River at the Stockton Inn.

In the days that followed, Jake had thrown himself into researching every conceivable remedy—adjusting diet, meal timing, even switching vitamins.

Nothing worked.

The pungent scent of cleaners, the sight of food, even normal household smells triggered waves of nausea. Ice cream became their sanctuary, with Jake frequently venturing out to fetch tubs of vanilla or chocolate to soothe her stomach.

Amid the turmoil of her pregnancy, Teresa found hope in the idea of purchasing a house. And she found one she loved. It was an old, sprawling Victorian house on an acre of land in Basking Ridge.

But at eighty thousand dollars, it was a financial stretch that made Jake's stomach twist with worry.

"We should be more realistic," Jake argued softly, running a hand through his dark hair. "There are places in Millburn you can get for fifty thousand—less in Irvington."

Teresa's eyes sparkled with an almost desperate hope. "But, my stallion, this place has room—an acre! And the schools, Jake… you don't understand what they mean to me."

Jake shook his head, frustration creeping in. "I just hate us going over our heads. What if it's too much?"

"We'll both work," she said, shutting down the conversation with a stubborn finality.

He studied her carefully, seeing the weight of the impending responsibility settle on her shoulders. "Who'll raise the baby, Teresa? We'll barely have time for ourselves."

"You work nights, I work days. We'll manage. She'll always have a parent home."

Jake wasn't convinced. "And what if she has needs we don't know about? What if…"

"You liked the house, Jake," Teresa interrupted, her voice a mix of hope and challenge.

That was the turning point. Jake relented, telling himself the feeling of safety the house gave him was worth the risk. Though the mortgage made his nerves raw—they had little credit history and only his money as a down payment—it was a future to build on.

One afternoon, Teresa arrived at Jake's small apartment, casual but with an edge in her voice. "Wake up. I'm home."

Jake rolled out of bed, rubbing sleep from his eyes. "I'm awake."

"Some girl called you last night. Said she knew you."

Jake frowned, confusion tightening his chest. "Probably a repair."

"She said you knew her, an old friend?" Teresa's voice sharpened, suspicion creeping into her tone.

Jake tried to stall, his mind racing. "I can't think of anyone... What's her name?"

Teresa lifted a scrap of paper near the toaster. "Sally O'Brien."

Jake felt his pulse quicken. "Sally?" He forced calm into his voice. "Yeah, I knew her about two and a half years ago."

"She said she knew you from the Brethren, that you fix things. Said her TV broke down."Teresa's temper flared instantly, her eyes darkening. "Anything your wife should know?"

"No, it's a repair job," Jake insisted.

Suddenly, Teresa's lip trembled, her face twisted as her eyes grew wet. She spun away, fleeing into the bedroom.

Jake followed swiftly. "What's wrong?"

She collapsed onto the bed, voice breaking, "I'm... fat..."

"Teresa, no. You're beautiful," Jake murmured, wrapping his arms around her from behind, caressing the swell of her pregnant belly.

Tears spilled over. "You think I'm ugly. You're seeing another woman, aren't you? Someone younger."

Jake's breath stalled. A reluctant chuckle escaped. The thought was laughable—painfully so. Teresa's desire had waned with the pregnancy, and their encounters were infrequent. He accepted it without complaint.

"Honey, the last six months are the happiest I've ever known," he said softly.

"You mean it?" she sniffled.

"Yes. Before you, I was preoccupied with myself. But you... our life... it changed everything."

She bit her lip, still uncertain. "But we only see each other at night... for such a little while."

"That's how most marriages are," Jake said with a smile.

She hesitated, then softened. "Look... you said Sally O'Brien just wants her TV fixed?"

Jake nodded, tracing gentle circles on her belly. "I'll call her and see if I can help. Friday or Saturday."

Teresa's brow furrowed. "You alone with a woman?"

"She's got a son," Jake said offhandedly, bringing up a detail he thought would help..

"How do you know?"

"My mom knows hers," he lied, offering a small, reassuring smile. "I'll leave the door open if her husband's not home."

Teresa glanced down, her pride bruised and her insecurities raw. "I just feel so... ugly."

Jake pressed a tender kiss to her temple, drawing her close.

When Jake called Sally, Teresa stood nearby, watching as he spoke with calm professionalism on the phone.

"Hi, Sally? It's Jake Hurd. You called last night?"

"Jake! Wow, you actually called back! Your old lady sounded funny."

Jake laughed, trying to downplay the awkwardness. "She was worried. I don't get many calls from women."

"I need help with my TV—it's acting up. You said you could fix it?"

"Sure thing. When's good for you?"

They agreed on Friday at 3:00 p.m. The call ended smoothly but Teresa's mood darkened.

"You made me sound like a jealous bitch," she said, pouting.

Jake shrugged. "She just wanted to make sure you were okay."

Teresa sulked the rest of the week, and Jake tried to ease her worries with gentle touches and reassuring words. But inside, he too was restless.

Friday arrived with a knot in his stomach. For once, the shadows that haunted him for years stayed silent. Maybe because he had Teresa, a reason to fight, a reason to hope.

That morning, Jake reminded himself of the life they were building—the new house, Teresa's quirks, the baby growing inside her. Love softened him in ways he never imagined.

But now, on the way to Sally's house, his mind tumbled with questions and uncertainty. Angry ghosts of jealousy, doubts about trust, and a desperate need to protect the fragile happiness he had found—all wrestled for dominance.

He took a deep breath, gripping the steering wheel tightly. Whatever waited behind that door with Sally and her son, Jake vowed he would face it head-on.

"Sally! Hey, it's me," Jake called, knocking firmly but not too loudly.

The house before him was a tall, sprawling Victorian with peeling white paint and a sagging porch swing that creaked ominously in the steady breeze.

Evergreen Avenue in Plainfield was a quiet, middle-class street —kids riding bikes, neighbors watering lawns—but none of them would guess a go-go dancer lived behind those lace-curtained windows.

The door opened and there she was—Sally, looking nothing like the glittering silhouette he'd seen under the dim, flickering lights of The Dive.

At home, she was frumpy in loose pants and a worn sweater, her face clean but bare of makeup, her hair pulled back carelessly.

"Hey, Jake," she greeted, her voice softer, worn around the edges. "Come on in."

Jake stepped over the threshold, the scent of stale smoke and household disinfectant blending oddly in the air.

Despite the stately exterior, the interior told a similar story to the neglect on the outside. Water stains spotted the wood floor near the radiator, curling the edges of the boards. The once-white walls bore smudges, cracks, spider-webbing toward the ceiling, and doors hung unevenly on their hinges.

"Thanks for comin', really," Sally said, leading him into the living room.

There, amid the faded floral wallpaper and a battered armchair sat a wooden playpen. Inside it, a blond-haired toddler—small but sturdy—rolled to his knees and looked toward the door.

"Mama! Mama!" the boy cried out, arms flailing for attention.

Sally bent and scooped him up, a grunt under her breath as the boy clung to her tightly. The child turned his head toward Jake, flashing a wide grin that revealed a perfect set of small teeth.

"Well, hello there," Jake said, smiling gently. The boy's bright blue eyes caught his—an uncanny mirror.

"This is Shawn," Sally said, turning the boy's face toward Jake.

"So how old's this little guy?" Jake asked, loosening up.

"Twenty-two months. He's big for his age," Sally replied, her voice steady but tired.

Shawn grinned again.

"Man, those are some serious chompers," Jake laughed, looking at the boy's teeth.

The boy's eyes flicked toward the bulky television on its wheeled stand. "Dat?" he demanded, pointing with a stubby finger.

"That's a television," Jake said. Shawn studied him carefully, his gaze sharp and restless.

"Mama!" Shawn called again, holding tight to his mother.

"Right here," Sally said, shifting Shawn to her other hip with practiced ease.

Jake headed out to his car to fetch his toolbox. Sally lingered on the porch, eyes tracing the peeling paint on the bannister.

"It's a nice place," Jake ventured.

Sally's eyes narrowed. "I own it."

"That's impressive," he replied, adjusting the straps of his bag.

"Yeah, well… places like The Dive pay well, and the tips help. Terry and I, we make the most when we do that kissing thing," she said with a bitter laugh, brushing hair out of Shawn's reach. "But why am I telling you all this crap?"

Jake shrugged, heading back inside. "Most folks talk about what they do."

Back in the living room, Jake sank to the floor beside the TV, prying off its back panel. The wires and tubes familiar.

"So, how's married life?" Sally asked, perching on the armchair and watching him work.

Jake smiled faintly. "It's good. Teresa's pregnant."

Sally's eyebrows shot up. "Whoa, that was quick! Or did you two have to get hitched?"

Jake's smile faltered. "I don't think that matters."

For a moment, silence hung heavy before she grinned. "Then that's a 'yes,' huh?"

"Yes," Jake said quietly..

Sally returned Shawn to his playpen. "How long did you know each other?"

"Not long. But we're figuring it out. The pregnancy's been rough on Teresa, though."

"Oh man, I get it," Sally said, voice hitching. "I didn't even realize I was pregnant for months. I was stoned half the time, taking antibiotics for the clap."

Jake looked up sharply.

"Yeah," she said, catching his gaze. "I'm sorry I didn't tell you about that. I barely remembered your name back then, and I thought I picked it up after you. Must've been rough—especially since you said it was your first time."

"It was," Jake admitted, fingers fiddling with the TV tubes.

Sally sighed. "I thought I was taking the pill every day, but I was so out of it that maybe I was just taking vitamins or something. Damn lucky Shawn turned out okay, considering I was high, drinking, and sick."

Jake smiled again at the boy. "He really is something."

Shawn pulled himself upright in the playpen, soaking in the attention with wide-eyed delight.

"When I found out I was pregnant, I had to get my act together fast," Sally said, lighting a cigarette with a shaky hand.

She inhaled deeply as Jake unplugged the TV, and one at a time pulled tubes from the back and inserting them into a small machine. "You've done okay, then."

"This all happened in the last year. I lived with my mom until Shawn was born. Then we bought this place. I snapped back—dancing helped. Honestly, my boobs were so huge then, got me work easy enough."

"You could do better than The Dive," Jake suggested.

"I dunno. It's close. Carmine, the bartender, he looks out for us."

Jake held up a small tube. "Found your problem here. I can get you a new one."

"Oh, please? That'd be amazing—I don't know the first thing about electronics. I'd probably screw it up."

"Happy to. I'll bring it by tomorrow."

"Is it out of your way?"

"Nope."

Jake fastened the TV's back panel as Shawn sat cross-legged, absorbed in his toys.

"So… do you know who Shawn's father is?" Jake asked cautiously.

"Jake—"

"It's just… you should have some kind of support, you know? Financial help at least."

"I'm fine, Jake. Really." Her voice sharpened. "It's nice you care now, after I gave you VD and all. But you have a kid on the way —you should worry about that."

He nodded slowly. "You're right."

Shawn wobbled to his feet and reached toward Jake.

"Up-ee!" he squealed.

Jake lifted him, surprised by the boy's easy trust.

"God, he's never done this with anyone but me—not even my mom," Sally marveled.

The toddler bounced happily in Jake's arms. Jake shifted him for comfort, feeling a protective instinct rise.

"Look, you've got a lot going on here—repairs, paint, pipes. I can help. Maybe even babysit."

Sally hesitated. "He likes you. But how would your wife feel about that?"

Jake shook his head. "I just want to help."

Sally took a last drag of her cigarette, crushed it in the ashtray. "Just as long as it doesn't mess up your marriage. I'm doing fine raising him on my own—without some guy telling me how."

"Fair enough. I'll bring the part tomorrow."

"Okay, before five. I work early on Saturdays."

Handing Shawn back to her, Jake stood. "I'll see you then."

"Yeah."

On the quiet drive home, Jake stopped to pick up the replacement tube.

At home, cooking dinner for Teresa, Jake felt uneasy.—he hoped the help he'd offered Sally would be enough to make a difference.

23. Birth Day

J ake returned to Sally's the next day, the late afternoon sun casting long shadows as he stepped across the threshold.

This time, he stayed for dinner—a rare invitation that seemed to hang heavy with unspoken meaning.

That evening, he met Sally's mother: an older woman with a sharp wit and a wicked grin that never quite reached her eyes, her humor edged with a mischief that unsettled Jake more than it amused him.

He worked quickly, fixing the television and then moving on to a stubborn leaky pipe that had plagued the old house for weeks.

As he tightened the plumbing fixture with a wrench, Sally's mother leaned in close, whispering, "Don't be a stranger, Jake. We might find more things for you to fix."

Jake smiled and promised to return.

Jake finally arrived home at eight o'clock, the door swung open before he could knock. Teresa stood there, her short, pregnant frame filling the doorway like a barricade, her eyes wide with worry and anger.

The air inside the cramped apartment felt thick, suffocating.

"Where have you been?" she demanded, voice tight with panic.

Jake looked into the eyes of his pregnant wife—the woman he was supposed to protect—and felt his options closing in on him like a noose tightening with every passing second.

"I finished that repair, remember?" he said, hesitant.

"Trying to come up with a good story?" she said, her voice rising.

"Teresa—"

"No. I don't want to hear it," she snapped, cutting him off. "You always do this. You start with a half-truth and twist it just enough to fool yourself. But I see through you, Jake."

The words stung, and anger flared in Jake before he could stop it. "I went to Sally O'Brien's and fixed her television, just like I said I would."

Teresa blinked, as if surprised.

"And they invited me to stay for dinner." The anger boiled hotter, coming from deep inside Jake, from a place he barely recognized. "So I spent one damn night with a woman, her son, and her mother instead of staying home, picking up after you like I do all day."

Teresa's face crumpled, anger mixing with hurt until tears ran freely down her cheeks. "Oh, fine!" she yelled. "I sleep alone in this damn postage-stamp apartment—"

"I'm buying you a house!" Jake interrupted, feeling his own frustration build.

Her voice broke. "And every night, I'm alone here while you work. My only time with you is weekends, but then you sleep all day."

"That's how I've always been! That's who I was when you married me!" Jake shot back defensively.

"Then why did you marry me if you didn't want to spend time with me?" she shouted, voice trembling with rage.

Jake's temper snapped. "We both know why I married you!"

The moment the words left his mouth, Jake wished he could take them back.

Teresa's eyes widened, her mouth opening in disbelief. Then, from deep inside her, a primal, painful howl rose shattering the fragile night. She spun on her heel and fled to the bedroom, slamming the door with a finality that echoed in his chest.

Jake rushed after her, yanking at the doorknob. Locked.

"Teresa," he said softly, pounding on the wood, "I'm sorry. I didn't mean it."

The door flew open abruptly, and a cascade of his clothes went flying as Teresa pushed him back.

"Get out," she sobbed, tears streaming down her face. "Go be with your girlfriend."

"Teresa," Jake said, gathering his scattered clothes. "I didn't mean it—"

"So I forced you to marry me?" she screamed, eyes wild. "I won't let you say that to me, you bastard!"

He moved toward her instinctively and grabbed her arms as she flailed out clumsily.

"Honey—"

"Don't 'honey' me!" she shrieked, struggling in his grasp. "Let me go!"

"I love you," Jake said, voice softer now.

She threw back her head and spat, the wet glob landing sharply just below his eye. "You only love yourself. I'm going home to my mama."

Jake clenched his jaw, forcing the fury down. "I didn't mean it. I love you."

Then, a sudden sharp cry cut through the argument. Teresa bent over, clutching her belly, her face drained of color. "Ah!" she moaned, eyes wide with fear.

"What is it?" Jake's heart slamming in his chest.

"It's the baby... I think it's labor."

"No, it can't be. It's too early—"

"Tell that to the baby!" she exclaimed, gasping in pain.

He helped her to a chair, her body trembling as waves of discomfort washed over her.

"Are they contractions? Do they come and go?"

"I just hurt," she said, focused on the searing pain. Jake swung into action, phoning the doctor, who instructed him to take her to the hospital immediately.

Helping her up, Jake steadied her. "We have to go now."

"I... I have to throw up..." she moaned, staggering toward the bathroom.

He followed closely, cradling her head as she emptied her stomach into the toilet, soft moans punctuating the silence.

When she finished, she waved him away. "I have to pee. Get out."

"I'll be right outside," Jake promised, heart pounding, ear pressed to the door.

My fault, he thought bitterly. *I shouldn't have gone to Sally's. I can sense the shadows—they're close. They're watching. They want to hurt her.*

"Teresa?" he called softly. After a moment, the toilet flushed. He opened the door to find her leaning against the sink, pale but resolute.

"We have to get to the hospital," he said, helping her gather strength.

"Okay," she whispered, gripping her belly, each step heavy.

Outside the night pressed down on them with cold fingers. Jake looked around nervously, the darkness thick with menace. Shapes flickered just beyond his vision, shadows he felt without fully seeing.

"Do you want me to carry you?"

She laughed weakly. "That would be a sight... Ah!" She stopped, clutching her stomach and muttering in Spanish.

"We're almost there," he reassured, opening the car door and helping her into the passenger seat. She settled back as he reclined the seat for her comfort.

Jake slid behind the wheel, his grip white-knuckled as the car hummed through the night. His eyes darted nervously toward the darkness beyond the headlights.

Teresa's soft gasps and small cries filled the cramped space, growing more urgent as they neared the hospital. Suddenly, her water broke.

An orderly rushed over instantly, firm and businesslike, and wheeled Teresa inside, straight to maternity.

The bright hospital lights at least offered some comfort to Jake whose mind raced with dread and anticipation.

A doctor soon appeared, his voice brisk but not unkind.

"It's better if you wait here," he said.

"Wait? What do you mean?"

"Nowadays they let fathers in during delivery, but I'm old-fashioned. Another person can just get in the way. Besides, your wife has a complication—we suspect partial placental detachment. It's going to be touch and go."

Jake's face flushed. "But it's too early."

"I know. The baby's past thirty weeks, but preemies come with no guarantees. We'll do everything we can."

The doctor hurried away leaving Jake alone in the sterile waiting room. He dropped his head in his hands, stifling sobs with a trembling handkerchief.

They are here, screamed the terror deep inside his mind.

He wiped his eyes, grasping at logic. Seeing Sally didn't cause this, nor did the shadows. It's just medical. That's all.

But when he rose, he found himself drawn toward the nursery down the hall. Behind glass windows tiny babies lay in plastic bassinets bathed in subdued light—fragile lives hanging by a thread.

One bin at the end drew his attention. Around the infant's tiny head hovered a faint, darker haze—a shadow he knew all too well.

"No," he whispered.

Hurriedly he sought the nurse station. A tired, gray-haired woman peered through oversized glasses.

"Excuse me," Jake said urgently.

"Yes? Your wife is in the ward. I don't know anything yet."

"No, it's about the babies. One seems… off."

She frowned but followed him down the hall. Together they looked through the glass.

"That one," he said, pointing to the bassinet with the hazy aura.

The nurse sighed and flicked on the light.

In that instant, before the room lit, Jake saw it—a small, black, blocky figure only two feet tall, perched atop the bassinet. Its rectangular eyes locked with his, boring into his soul with cold emptiness.

The light flashed on, and the creature vanished like a flicker at the edge of vision.

The nurse gasped, her face paling. "Oh my God!" she whispered, wheeling the bassinet away hurriedly. "Doctor! Doctor!"

Jake stood frozen, heart racing, the residual adrenaline from confronting the shadow mixing with dread.

Then Jake's doctor approached. "Mr. Hurd? Are you alright?"

"Y-yes. How is Teresa?"

"She's in Intensive Care. She nearly died. You got her here just in time." The doctor's words hit like a punch to Jake's gut.

"And the baby?"

"She's stable but tiny. We had to perform an emergency Caesarean but she made it."

Jake grasped the doctor's arm, eyes wide. "Thank you."

"It's alright. Come, I'll show you."

Dressed in gown, mask, and gloves, Jake followed into the bright intensive care unit. Teresa lay pale, tubes running from her arms and mouth, her olive skin nearly translucent.

"Is she awake?"

"Not yet. It will be hours."

Jake's breath caught as the doctor led him to another small room filled with incubators holding delicate little lives.

His daughter lay wrapped in cloth, her tiny chest rising and falling with shallow breaths, fists clenched tight as if already fighting the world.

In that moment, every fear, every shadow, faded into nothingness.

There she was—his daughter. And Jake vowed in his heart to protect her from everything… no matter the cost.

No matter what.

FESTIVAL

OF LIGHTS

24. JAKE'S TINKERS

I wandered through the crowded mall Rueben trudging silently beside me.

Gigantic Christmas ornaments—gleaming red and gold spheres—hung from enormous bows draped from the ceiling, their shiny surfaces reflecting the holiday chaos below.

The corridors thrummed with a tidal wave of shoppers all squeezed into the narrow evening hours, hunting desperately for that 'perfect' gift, the trinket or toy that would capture this season's magic.

Maybe I'd made a mistake coming here on December second in the heart of the Christmas storm. Glittering Christmastime glory swathed every store, relentlessly reminding Rueben and me, as Jews, that we were outsiders to the party.

But Rueben hadn't been himself since Thanksgiving.

Marcie insisted he needed more time with me. After the scare he'd had—the stitches, the panic—it made sense. Some solid, everyday 'guy time' might pull him back from whatever dark place he was falling into.

I knew I felt guilty. I'd been losing myself in Jake's story to avoid dealing with Rueben's quiet withdrawal.

Anne, my assistant, was fraying at the edges from juggling client cancellations every time I postponed meetings just to spend another hour at Greystorm with Jake. Anne was famously unflappable—patience personified—but even she had complained.

When Anne complains, it means I'm in trouble.

But Rueben came first. Hanukkah was barely a day away, and he showed no spark, no excitement.

Since Thanksgiving at his grandmother's house, he'd been quieter, withdrawn. He demanded a brighter nightlight in his room now—"to keep the bad thing away."

Every time he said it, a cold shudder ran down my spine. I wanted to dismiss it as childish fancy, a lingering effect of the stitches and the trauma.

But inside me, a memory remained; the flash in the corner of my eye that night. I'd told myself it was autosuggestion, a trick my mind played because of Jake.

So how do I explain Rueben seeing this… 'shadow thing'?

Rueben didn't know about Jake. Hell, I hadn't even spoken of Jake to Marcie in any detail. There wasn't much chance of Rueben overhearing anything.

Jake's story was driving me mad. He insisted on recounting events piece by piece in the order it happened—dragging me through the entire nightmare instead of letting me focus on one part of his delusion..

But was it really a delusion? If Rueben had seen that shadow, too, what did that mean?

"Want to grab a Cinnabon?" I asked Rueben as he hopped up onto one of the raised ledges lining the hallway.

"Okay," he muttered, indifferent.

This was the same boy who used to spin around with laughter at the simplest things, radiant joy spilling from him like light. Now suspicion clung to his every gesture, as though the world shifted beneath his feet and he no longer trusted it.

Oh, my beautiful boy. The world isn't safe. Mothers snuff out their newborns, thirteen-year-olds haul guns into schools, and strange, gaunt men spend nights chasing shadows no one else sees.

And doctors like me clutch at words to explain the madness, labels to contain the chaos, hoping it helps anything make sense.

We stood in line for our cinnamon rolls.

"So, how're you doing, buddy?" I pressed gently as we took a red plastic tray and found a seat.

"Okay," he muttered again, the same hollow tone.

"Just okay? We're at the mall! Isn't there something you want to see? KB Toys? The museum store? You always liked the things they have."

"They're okay," he said again, stabbing at the cinnamon roll with his fork, clumsy and distracted.

I saw it plain—the same distant look Marcie worried about. The blankness I'd glimpsed in Jake's eyes so many times. And I hated that vacancy I saw in both of them.

"Perhaps a specialist in children can help," Marcie whispered, the softness of her voice barely cutting through the darkness between us as we lay tangled beneath the sheets. "I mean it's not our field of expertise."

I stared up at the cracked ceiling, shadows dancing just out of sight.

"We're too involved," I admitted, voice low, weighed down by exhaustion.

She turned her head slightly, a faint half-smile ghosting her lips. "I pushed him out of my body, Sam. That's about as involved as anyone can get."

I swallowed, trying to keep the bitter knot from rising in my throat. "I'm not against getting help. He's not himself. Then again, it's only been a week. Injuries frequently result in psychological trauma."

Marcie exhaled slowly, a sigh filled with frustration and worry. "But he won't talk about it. Not with me, not with you. That's new. Rueben's always been the loudest one in the room."

I shifted, hesitating. "Maybe he thinks someone's listening. Watching. Not people—but something else."

Marcie's laugh was brief, almost a scoff. "The shadow things you mean? Really, Sam?"

"Yeah, the shadow things," I said, reluctant but firm.

"Oh, Sam… you're no help." She rolled over facing me, her eyes sharp in the muted glow from the hallway. "You're indulging him. Feeding into his fears."

"They're real to him. That means something. We can't just write it off."

"By leaving every light on in the house?"

"If it helps him."

"I can understand his bedroom light and the hall light. But why our bathroom light?"

"He... uh... well, in case he comes here during the night."

Marcie's wasn't buying it.

"Nice try," she said. "It's not about the bathroom. It's about Jake. The things he's been telling you... it makes you wonder, doesn't it?"

"Wonder what?" I asked, but my voice trembled, betraying a secret fear.

"Maybe he isn't crazy. That the dark things he talks about... maybe they aren't just nightmares from the 1960s. Maybe he really opened a doorway to something out there."

The silence stretched thick between us. I said, "What if he did?"

Marcie sighed, a deep, weary sound filled with years of hard-earned skepticism. "Sam, it's supposed to be the patient who gets attached to the psychiatrist. Not the other way around. You're letting yourself get sucked into his fantasy."

"I'm not," I said, trying to keep the defensiveness out of my voice but failing. "It's just... strange things have been happening since I started working with him."

"Sam, if you can't keep your professional demeanor, you should be off the case."

I bit back a retort. "I'm the only one he trusts. No one else."

"That's because he's insane. By any clinical definition, Jake's lost it. He sees shadows where there are none. He belongs in a secure institution. Your job is to help him get back to reality."

"But the coincidences—"

"Nothing more than coincidences," she interrupted firmly.

We stayed silent, the tension thick enough to choke on. Then, slowly, Marcie reached out and gripped my hand, a small gesture that steadied me.

"You know," she said softly, "it's kind of refreshing to talk about a case with you again."

I smiled despite the heaviness pressing on my chest. "Even when it's our own son?"

"Especially then," she replied with a nostalgic warmth. "Feels like old times. Like when we were partners."

That night, sleep evaded me. With the bathroom light casting a pale glow I lay awake, haunted by an unshakable sensation—something unseen, watching just beyond the edge of the light.

"Jake, you were talking about the hospital—" I started, my voice tentative.

He shifted in his chair, the faintest flicker of discomfort crossing his eyes. "Oh, yeah," he said, his voice flat as he adjusted his sleeve. "They kept Teresa for over a week, and the doctor told us we couldn't have any more children."

For a heartbeat, the room hung heavy with unspoken weight.

"And how did you feel about that?" I pressed gently, watching him closely.

Jake shrugged, a brittle gesture. "What I felt didn't matter. That was just how it was."

I caught the trace of avoidance, like a wall rising between us.

"Come on, Jake," I said, leaning forward. "You're suppressing again. You can't just brush it off like it's nothing. This had to affect you—good, bad—whatever. You felt something, and you shoved it away."

His eyes narrowed slightly, brows knitting. "Okay, fine. I wasn't happy about it. Is that what you wanted to hear?"

"I'm just trying to point out this technique you have of avoiding things," I challenged, forcing a steadiness in my voice.

Jake exhaled slowly, his shoulders falling. "I'm just saying, you're the one twisting this into some big deal. You always have to pull something out of me."

"That's my job," I said, feeling my temper rise. "To help you face things you don't want to look at."

"Sam, you're not yourself," he said suddenly, eyes narrowing with concern. "Did you sleep at all last night?"

I hesitated, then lied, "Yeah. Slept fine."

But Jake's gaze dropped to the dark circles shadowing my eyes. He sensed something deeper. "It's the boy, isn't it?"

I sighed, more exhausted than I let on. "He's not sleeping well."

Jake reached into the pocket of his jumpsuit and pulled out a small disk, no bigger than the palm of my hand. He held it out to me. "Let him have this."

I took it cautiously. The disk was flat, maybe two inches across, studded with dozens of tiny bulbs on its surface.

"What is it?" I asked, turning it over in my fingers.

"Something to help," Jake said, taking it from me and setting it on the table with care. "Clap twice."

I raised my hands skeptically and clapped. I half-expected a light to flick off somewhere, but instead—

A blinding light exploded across the room, intense and overwhelming. I slammed my hands over my eyes, my breath hitching. Even through my fingers, a pink glow pressed against my vision, as if the light was seeping into my brain.

Jake clapped twice more, and the dazzling brightness faded, leaving afterimages dancing stubbornly in my sight.

"What... the hell?" I whispered, pulling my hands away to blink repeatedly.

Jake shrugged, a rare smile cracking his face. "This'll take care of whatever the boy's afraid of."

I rubbed my eyes, still dazed, and reached to pick the device back up. "As long as it doesn't blind him," I muttered.

"Well, he should cover his eyes. Better if he also looks away."

I clutched the disk like it was a ticking bomb. "Is it safe? Could it go off unexpectedly?"

Jake chuckled, seeing my hesitation. "It only activates with sound. Clap twice, just like you did."

The smile lingered—a real, teeth-baring smile—not the drugged-out blank stare I'd seen on him in the first chaotic days.

I turned the device over again, marveling at how something so small could generate so much light. "Impressive," I admitted. "How the hell does it work?"

Jake leaned forward, enthusiasm brightening his features. "Without getting too technical... those bulbs are special LEDs— my prototype. I had them custom made."

"LEDs?" I echoed, confused.

"Light-Emitting Diodes. Like the tiny lights on a computer. But this? It's about a thousand times brighter."

"That bright? From such a small device?"

He nodded. "I amplified the output digitally. Think of it as controlling the light's coherence and wavelength."

I furrowed my brow. "You lost me."

Jake grinned, undeterred. "Do you remember what a laser is?"

"Yeah… light focused into a beam strong enough to cut steel."

"Exactly. It's coherent radiation—light with all its waves synchronized on the same wavelength. This device amplifies visible light into a focused, intense frequency."

"How did you even learn this stuff?" I asked, genuinely impressed.

Jake shrugged. "Had some theories. Lots of trial and error."

"But the technical knowledge?" I persisted.

"Edison had little technical knowledge. He just kept trying things—ten thousand attempts before he got the light bulb right."

I regarded the little disk again. "And you?"

"Maybe five hundred experiments. Plus research. My advantage? I don't know what's impossible."

I blinked. "Excuse me?"

Jake leaned back, calm and sure. "Alexander Graham Bell made the telephone because he didn't believe sending a voice through a wire was impossible. Everyone else did. That's why he succeeded."

I considered that for a moment. "You really like that, don't you? Inventing what others can't even imagine."

He scowled playfully as if I'd exposed a secret. "There you go with feelings again."

"You're brilliant with your mind, but you bury your emotions. You're happiest when you're impressing someone."

"What's wrong with that?" he replied, crossing his arms.

"It's your escape. You'd rather dazzle people with inventions than face emotions head-on." I placed the disk gently on the table between us. "Even with me. Every time I get close to what you feel, you change the subject—stories, gadgets… you pull back."

Jake's jaw tightened, then he suddenly stood, voice sharp. "This is all crap. We're done."

Without another word he stormed out, slamming the door behind him.

I sat there for a moment, heart pounding. I'd hit a nerve— maybe the core of his struggle. Part of me felt a quiet triumph.

I slipped the disk into my pocket, hope sparking. Maybe this device could help Rueben feel safe.

But first... I needed to talk with someone else.

Bill's footsteps echoed sharply across his cluttered office as he paced in agitation. "So what if we let him tinker in his room? Big deal. Why not?" he snapped. "He won't blow the place up or anything."

I folded my arms, observing him. "It was the security company's idea, wasn't it?"

He stopped and shot me a quick glance, irritation simmering under his calm facade. "They're pouring a lot of money into having him here. He's functional, and besides, it's good therapy. Both sides benefit."

"So you just signed off on that," I said, my voice low but sharp.

"Yes."

"Without consulting me."

"I am the head of the facility," Bill said bluntly.

Leaning in, I kept my voice steady but firm. "I told you, Bill— I run this show. You should have brought it to my attention!"

"Look, this Hurley fellow—"

"Wanted Jake producing," I finished, cutting him off. "How does he get the equipment? The tools?"

Bill ran a hand through his hair. "He makes a list. The security company sends a guy who delivers whatever he needs."

"And you check these lists?"

"I have—once or twice. Look, Sam, I have a lot on my plate. Can you at least understand that?"

"I understand. What I can't understand is why you think that's okay."

Bill's brow furrowed. "What do you mean?"

"Stop pacing. Sit down." I let the words fall with command. "I want to show you something."

From my pocket, I pulled out a small disk and placed it deliberately on his desk.

Bill stared at it like it might explode. "What's that?"

I met his gaze steadily. "A sample of what Jake invents. Brace yourself."

"For what?" he asked, frowning.

Before he could react further, I clapped my hands twice just like Jake did, shielding my eyes this time. In an instant, the room burst into an intense, blinding light.

Bill yelped, scrambling back from the desk. "What the hell? Turn it off, Sam!"

I clapped twice again. The glow dimmed, retreating until the room returned to its dull, normal lighting.

"Jee-zus," Bill groaned, rubbing his eyes. "I'm seeing spots."

I blinked rapidly, my own vision swimming with afterimages.

"What the hell is that for?" Bill said, returning to his chair.

"This," I said quietly, "is what Jake made for Rueben."

Bill scowled. "Happy Hanukah, huh? Does he want to blind the kid?"

"No," I said, voice softer now. "Jake wants Rueben to feel safe."

Bill shook his head, the skepticism stubborn. "I can almost see you through the spots." He shook it off. "Do you think it'll help?"

"Help with what?"

"Your son." Bill's tone softened. "Marcie told me she's already looking for a specialist for him."

"We talked about that," I said. "But this—this device is like a magic amulet, something to ward off evil. If I introduce it to Rueben, maybe it comforts him. Maybe it makes him believe he's protected."

Bill raised an eyebrow. "Is that sound psychiatric theory, Sammy?"

I shrugged. "If it works, that's enough for me."

He nodded slowly. "Fair enough."

"But," I pressed, "don't you see the bigger picture? Jake can build this kind of technology—"

"That's why no expense is too great for the company," Bill said, picking up the disk with unusual care. "You understand what you're holding? This disk? This is the future of loss prevention."

I frowned. "Future of what?"

"Think about it. Thieves break into a warehouse, set off the alarm, and then—bam—they're hit with a light like this." He held the disk up triumphantly. "They're temporarily blinded. They might try to run, but they risk hurting themselves. The police just have to pick them up."

I raised a skeptical eyebrow. "Unless they're wearing welding goggles. Come on, Bill. No matter what someone comes up with, there's always a way to beat it."

He smiled thinly. "Exactly. And that's why Jake's value is so high. He keeps his company ahead of the curve."

I folded my hands on the desk, feeling the weight of the conversation settle hard in my chest, "But what if I succeed? What if we get him cured, release him? Will he still want to build things that mirror his paranoia?"

Bill shrugged with a hint of disdain. "Well, he does like to tinker."

That was it. Without another word, Bill practically shoved me toward the door.

The entire case was spiraling beyond my control.

25. LIGHTING THE CANDLES

Things were no better at the office—in fact, tension seemed to thicken the air.

So it surprised me when I stepped into the waiting area and found Mr. Simmons pacing nervously, his face pale and his breaths coming rapid and shallow.

Anne caught my eye, relief washing over her features as if I were a lifeline.

"Dr. Lucas, thank God you're here—" Mr. Simmons blurted before I could even step fully inside the room.

I glanced at my watch. I wasn't late. In fact, he was at least half an hour early. His agitation seemed disproportionate, like something urgent bothered him.

"George, please—calm down," I said gently, voice steady, hoping to ease the quickening panic in his chest.

"But, Dr. Lucas, I have to tell you about—" He was speaking faster now, words tumbling over one another. His eyes darted, failing to settle.

I raised a hand gently yet firmly. "George. Take a breath. Go into my office and try to relax a moment. I just got here, and I need a minute to talk to Anne first."

His mouth opened then closed. "But I—"

"Now, please," I said softly, touching his arm, steering him toward my office door. "And take deep breaths."

He hesitated, the desperation still flickering in his eyes, but finally nodded and went inside, shutting the door behind him.

Turning back to Anne, I lowered my voice. "What happened?"

"He came storming in, demanding to see you immediately," Anne whispered, glancing toward the closed door. "I was about to call building security."

"I can manage him," I said, trying to steady the knot forming in my stomach. "Anything else I should know?"

Anne nodded. "You got a call from Dr. Franklin."

This was a surprise. Why was my therapist calling me?

"Janice?"

"She said you're to return the call as soon as possible," Anne said, then gestured toward the closed door behind me: "Now see what you can do with Mr. Simmons."

I forced a reassuring smile and stepped inside.

George collapsed on the couch, gripping its edges as if they'd keep him anchored when the panic threatened to swallow him whole. He breathed raggedly, struggling to find a rhythm.

Pulling a chair close, I settled beside him. "George, you're clearly upset."

His eyes were wide, haunted by sleepless fear. "I didn't sleep. No more than two hours. Dr. Lucas... tell me what this means."

I reached out, gently placing a hand on his arm. "Tell me everything. Whatever's on your mind."

He ran a trembling hand through his untidy hair, his voice barely above a whisper. "I had… a dream. It was terrible."

"A dream?"

"But it felt real. There was a place—I've seen nothing like it. Everything was red… like blood in color, the ground, the dirt. But the sky—it was as black as ink with no stars."

I scribbled something about blood symbolism in the margin of my notebook, then paused.

"It had to be what Hell looks like," George continued, voice catching. "But with no fire. Just endless red dirt and that choking black sky."

I nodded sympathetically.

"Dr. Lucas… there were things there," his voice cracked. "I couldn't look directly at them. Only out of the corner of my eye —but they were alive, watching." His breaths hitched, hands shaking.

"Things?" I echoed, my pen halted mid-air, curiosity mingled with concern.

"Shadows. They were all around me, creeping closer, with teeth and claws. They wanted to hurt me," George babbled. "Everywhere, closing in…"

"Calm down, George. It was just a nightmare," I soothed, trying to infuse calm into the storm raging inside him.

"But it wasn't," he insisted, eyes suddenly wide and fixed on the ceiling. "When I woke up—in my bed—I saw it. A shadow. On the ceiling. It moved, Dr. Lucas. The goddamn thing moved."

It took the full fifty minutes—and every ounce of patience I had —to calm George Simmons down.

When he left my office, clutching a prescription for a powerful sleep aid, his trembling had lessened but the unease still lingered in the way he shuffled out, shoulders hunched as if bracing against some unseen weight.

Anne watched him disappear down the hall, eyes bright with admiration. "Sometimes, Doctor," she said, practically beaming, "you really are a miracle worker."

I forced a smile but inside, a knot was tightening. "Maybe more of a miracle than I bargained for," I muttered, glancing after Simmons. "My patients are catching each other's delusions."

Anne cocked her head, brow furrowed in confusion. "What do you mean?"

I waved off the concern. "Never mind—that's a private joke," I said, trying to sound lighter than I felt. "Can you patch me through to Janice Franklin?"

Back at my desk the phone clicked as Anne connected the line. "Janice! Sam here. How's it going?"

There was a sharp intake of breath. "Sam, you did all those sleep deprivation studies, right?"

I rubbed my tired eyes. "Yeah. What's going on?"

She sounded tense. "A lot of my patients have been… nervous at night lately. Like seriously on edge. Remember your dream about that black, oily shape lurking in the dark?"

I let out a dry chuckle. "I try to keep my nightmares to myself."

"Don't be flip with me," Janice snapped. "One of my patients believes something is watching her from the shadows. We were finally making progress before this started. And it's worse than that!"

"How do you mean?"

"All of my patients are anxious about things in the dark—if this were a physical illness, it'd be an epidemic."

I frowned, suddenly cold. "Janice, is this some kind of joke?"

"No joke," she blurted. "I swear."

I took a deep breath. "Remember that case I told you about at Greystorm? That patient is terrified of shadow creatures lurking just out of sight."

There was a long silence on the other end. Then Janice's voice, quieter, more uncertain: "Sam… what the hell is happening?"

I didn't have an answer for her—and the question churned in my gut like ice. "I don't know. Look, I have to see someone now and then get home for Hanukkah."

"Mazel tov," she offered, the warmth in her voice at odds with the tension between us.

"Janice, can you check around? You've got contacts with a lot of other psychiatrists. See if they're hearing anything about this— patients afraid of shadows, paranoia out of nowhere."

"I'll try," she promised.

As the line went dead I sat back, dread pooling heavy in my chest. Whatever this was… it was spreading.

We locked up the office at two o'clock sharp.

Anne smiled, waving goodbye as she slipped out the door to savor her Friday half-day, leaving me alone with the hum of an empty building.

I slid into my car and drove home, the familiar anticipation settling in my chest. Hanukah's first night was special and there was only one dish worthy of it: latkes.

Not just any latkes mind you. Those frozen, mix-made potato pancakes could sink you like a leaden weight. But freshly grated potatoes and onions, fried to golden perfection in hot olive oil—now, those were miracles on a plate. The sizzling, the faint aroma of crisped edges, it all stirred memories deeper than any ritual.

I set about making them; peeling the potatoes, mixing them with onions and matzah meal in the food processor, and heating the oil.

By four sharp Marcie and the kids arrived home, their cheeks flushed from wherever they'd been between school and dinner—some mysterious detour only she knew. This arrival was its own ceremony, part of our Hanukah rhythm, unwritten but unwavering.

The children scurried to set the table with the good china. Tonight was not only Hanukah but Shabbos as well, doubling the gravitas. But before settling we moved room to room, lighting every menorah we had scattered through the house.

Our collection was a patchwork of stories and personalities: a ceramic sculpture of Israelite figures with upraised hands, their fingers framing the candles; a tiny porcelain train with candleholders on the top of each car was in Rueben's room; the cuddly teddy bears with candle tummies nestled in Rachel's; an electric menorah glowing in the front window; and finally, our pride and joy—the oil menorah above the fireplace. We bought it just after Rachel was born. Getting its flames to dance without flickering or guttering took years of trial and error—perfecting the delicate balance of oil and wick, a meditation in patience and love.

We ignited the candles individually and chanted the blessings, our voices blending harmoniously like only family can. I took the final blessing, the shehecheyanu, letting gratitude pour through me—the quiet thankfulness for life, for these seasons that had shaped us.

Outside, Christmas spilled into the world with its frenzy and chaos. But inside, our Hanukah was its own sanctuary. No frantic crowds—just calm, candlelight, and the soft shimmer in my family's eyes.

We gathered around the table, the kids practically vibrating with excitement, forced to wait until we finished the meal before the first gift appeared.

That was tradition: small presents on early nights, building up to the grander ones after they'd seen five or six nights of little surprises.

I was in a rare good mood as I carried the steaming plate of latkes to the table. The same meal every year, but no less expected, no less thrilling.

Marcie lit two Shabbos candles and offered the blessing. We took turns joining in the prayers, the kids full of bubbling energy, their anticipation almost tangible.

After the blessing over bread I served the salad, watching as Rueben was more sedate than I preferred. But then, a faint, genuine smile crept onto his face, and that minor victory was enough.

From near the fireplace, a pile of vibrantly wrapped presents called to me. I chose three and placed them deliberately before each family member trying to suppress my grin.

The clatter of forks ceased instantly. The kids' eyes widened, surprise sparking in their faces—because we never did gifts before dinner. I nodded once. That was all the invitation they needed.

They tore into the wrapping with unrestrained enthusiasm.

"I got a Game Boy!" Rueben's shout filled the room.

"Me, too!" Rachel yelped, clearly peeved she hadn't called it first.

Marcie lingered over hers, delicately peeling layers as if preparing to re-wrap a fragile artifact.

"Just rip it open, Marcie," I urged, trying not to laugh.

"Yeah! Tear it good!" Rueben echoed, his booming voice filling the space between us.

We exchanged a smile—good to hear him come back to himself, better than the last few weeks had allowed.

"She can manage it, squirt," Rachel teased, cheeks flushed.

"Okay, squirrel breath," Rueben shot back, a playful gleam in his eye.

Marcie tried to intervene. "Alright, you two—"

But their bickering was a balm. To me, their quarrels were a choir of cherubs' laughter, proof that Rueben was rebounding, reclaiming his spark.

Finally, Marcie peeled back her wrapping to reveal a long black box. She opened the lid, and the spring-loaded top snapped back with a satisfying click.

"Oh my," she murmured, eyes widening as she looked at me.

"What is it?" Rachel asked, sliding forward to peer.

Rueben leaned closer, curiosity overcoming disinterest.

Marcie turned the box slowly: inside lay a bracelet, a delicate chain studded with gleaming gems. The stones danced through the spectrum—deep purple, shifting to fiery reds, warm oranges, golden yellows, fresh greens, and finally a serene blue.

"I admired this at the jewelry store—when?" she asked, eyes searching mine.

"About six months ago," I said proudly. "Lucky it was still there. All the stones are sapphires."

"Sapphires come in colors?" Rachel asked, astonished.

"They do," I said with a smile. "Your mother admired it."

"I haven't worn a bracelet in ten years!" Marcie said softly as I slipped it over her wrist. "I know how much this must've cost. We can't afford it."

"Tut tut," I rebuffed gently.

"Did you really say 'tut tut?'" Marcie teased.

"Daddy's turning into Auntie Anne," Rueben suggested with a grin, referring to my assistant.

"This is for you—to make up for all I've missed because of Jake Hurd," I explained, then grinned wide. "So, what do I get?"

The kids and Marcie closed in, showering me with hugs and kisses as we settled around the table to eat latkes, laughter threading through the flickering candlelight.

Marcie's eyes glowed, and not from the extravagance of the gift. It was because I'd paid attention and remembered.

That night was perfect in its simplicity: warm, glowing candles, the quiet happiness of my wife and children. I felt the joy of it deep in my chest—precious and fragile.

But a whisper of unease lingered beneath the surface. This fleeting moment, this warmth—it would not last.

26. HOLIDAY GIFT

The next day an orderly brought Jake to my office. There was a smile playing on my patient's lips.

"So, how'd your boy like his present?" he asked.

"The light disk?" I glanced at him, smiling myself. "He thought it was neato."

Jake chuckled, shaking his head. "Neato?"

"I swear those were his exact words," I said, sinking into the chair across from him. "He slept through the night for the first time in weeks. I appreciate it, Jake."

Jake ran a hand through his short hair, the tension in his jaw cutting through his casual demeanor. "I thought it might help."

"And that's from personal experience?" I asked, raising an eyebrow.

He grunted, jaw clenched tight. "Yeah."

I flipped open my yellow notepad and scribbled quickly. "Now, as far as your story, you mentioned your child, a girl, right?"

"Amanda," he mumbled, his entire face shifting as a flicker of warmth replaced the hard edges. "That was Teresa's choice. She wanted a name that sounded… American."

"How were things with Teresa after? I mean, a baby is a hell of a lot of work."

Jake sighed deeply. "I had to do most of it. Teresa was out of commission for months—complications. Thank God I had weeks of vacation saved up. Otherwise, I don't know how we would've gotten through it."

"Did you try to sleep at night during that time?" I jotted down the question, observing him.

"Absolutely not," Jake said, sitting straighter as if the words weighed on him. "I needed to watch her in the crib."

"You just sat there staring all night?"

"No," he said, voice low but steady. "I brought my tools up with me, tinkering until dawn. Then I packed them away and tried to function during the day. Sleep was a luxury I couldn't afford, but someone had to keep things running."

"That's a lot to carry. Did you ever get angry?"

"Teresa was sick," he said flatly.

I exhaled slowly, pushing a little harder. "Jake, your brain might know that, but it's okay to let your frustration out."

He hesitated. "I don't know…"

"Yes, you do!" I snapped. My voice surprised me, rougher than I had intended. I paused, tapping my pencil sharply against the pad. "You bottle it up. Bury it so deep you don't even realize it's there."

"Do you want to hear the story or not?" Jake challenged, unfazed.

I looked into his clear-blue eyes—a flicker of something vulnerable hiding behind the guarded facade. Like a child holding back a secret, afraid to share.

"Only if you promise to be honest with me," I mumbled.

"I've been honest, Sam!" His voice cracked but remained firm.

"You've given me facts," I said, leaning forward. "But the moment I pry beneath the surface you shut me out or make excuses."

"You'll understand when the time's right," he said.

"That's another excuse," I shot back. "Look, Jake, I know you're making those little toys again. The company's thrilled, but I want to help you—really help."

"They want me back on the job. Plain and simple."

"They want you tinkering because you've made them rich," I persisted, making sure he understood.

He shrugged nonchalantly. "They made me rich too."

I blinked in surprise. "What?"

"Over a million dollars over the years," he said like it was nothing.

I couldn't help but ask the obvious. "Then why are you working as a night guard?"

Jake's shoulders sagged. "What else would I do? Look, Sam, I'm getting there."

I nodded, reluctant but curious. "Okay, so talk."

"We bought too much house back then. Teresa had to go back to work once she was well enough. I stayed home with Amanda during the day while Teresa worked. When Teresa came home, I'd sleep, then head to work."

"Sounds like there wasn't much time for intimacy with your wife."

Jake shrugged, with a hint of bitterness in the gesture. "Teresa had internal injuries after the birth. We had to see doctors for years before anything got better. By then, we weren't very close as far as intimacy."

"A pity," I said softly.

"But Amanda was amazing," he smiled, the memory brightening his features. "When she started kindergarten, I slept while she was at school. She was happy. That's what mattered."

"So, what happened?" I asked, sensing the shift.

His smile vanished; darkness clouded his eyes. "The shadows wouldn't leave us alone."

1980

27. AMANDA & SHAWN

J ake ascended from the basement, his hands grimy from a night spent tinkering in his workshop.

He grabbed an old, ragged towel and rubbed at his palms until they were as clean as he could make them. Dirty hands were the last thing he wanted to carry upstairs, especially in a house he had painstakingly restored.

The soft click of the solid wood door closing behind him echoed faintly in the quiet morning.

Thanksgiving was just days away, yet the house remained bare— no garlands, no wreaths, no hint of Christmas cheer.

In the recent election, the voters swept out Jimmy Carter, with Ronald Reagan soon to be sworn in.

But Jake didn't give it much thought.

Outside the windows, a pale winter light filtered in, casting long shadows across the orderly living room. His eyes roamed over the furniture: the sofa with its fine upholstery, a lucky find he'd painstakingly reupholstered; the coffee table and side tables he'd bought at a garage sale for fifteen dollars and brought back to life with stain and varnish; the fireplace, tidy and waiting. His fingers brushed the fake logs, pausing on a hidden switch embedded deep within—a secret line of defense.

Saturday mornings like this were routine but never easy.

He'd stayed up all night in the basement, fighting a buzzing fluorescent light and the constant drone of his tools. The Basking Ridge house was a far cry from his cramped old apartment; it took relentless weekends to keep it spotless.

Yet the order, the subtle hum of security devices hidden behind the walls, gave him a sense of control in a world that often felt fragile. Light sensors, ultrasonic alarms—small machines whispering protection for himself and Teresa, and most of all, Amanda.

Jake's hand slid along the glossy oak banister of the stairs, the varnish a testament to hours of patient sanding and polishing. The previous owners had painted over the wood, leaving it cold and lifeless, but Jake restored it to its former glory—a reflection of the care he poured into everything.

Upstairs, he reached a large gray metal panel inset into the hallway wall. His fingers moved deftly, flipping switches that silenced security systems scattered throughout the house.

From there, he slipped into the hall closet, opening the door cautiously. A small contraption sat bolted inside, its single lens peering out to monitor hallway movement. A thin roll of adding machine paper fed through its belly, printing a detailed log of every living thing that passed in the dead of night.

Jake ripped off the last segment, scanning the recorded times. Everything checked out. The last entry was at 12:01 a.m. when he'd checked on Teresa and Amanda before retreating to the workshop.

The installed clock glinted in the morning light: 6:00 a.m. Perfect. The batteries were fresh, and the systems were functional. Closing the closet, Jake padded down the hall to Amanda's room. The child lay beneath tangled sheets, serene in sleep.

Through tiny, motorized closed-circuit cameras tucked away in the basement, Jake could watch her—her gentle rise and fall, soft breaths, a half-grown girl—five feet tall, no longer a child but not yet a teenager.

His wife, Teresa, often teased, "She's a weed like you," at their daughter's lanky frame, but pride softened her words.

Blonde hair, piercing blue eyes, skin kissed by a perpetual tan —the product of an odd but perfect blend of his Scandinavian roots and Teresa's Hispanic heritage.

Amanda was their beautiful inheritance.

Jake moved back to the hall, pulling on rubber gloves and hefting a plastic bucket filled with soapy water.

Quiet as a mouse he tiptoed through the kitchen, sliding chairs and mopping floors with a meticulousness born of habit. Teresa helped where she could, and he admired the transformation from her single days—she'd come a long way.

As he scrubbed, memories curtained over his thoughts.

Since Amanda's birth, his life shifted. He'd risen to captain in the guard, steady and reliable. Teresa advanced up the corporate ladder at BT&T, recently promoted to executive assistant—a role crafted just for her. She worked under a manager who was full of ideas but scattered, with Teresa being the glue turning his concepts into reality.

Money was still tight. The oil embargo drove prices sky-high, inflation gnawed at their savings.

Jake's sideline—repairing electronics for neighbors and friends —added crucial dollars. Part of that income flowed quietly to Sally and Shawn, without Teresa knowing.

He made weekly visits, seeing Sally, still beautiful—her dark eyes bright and fierce. Every week he would slip cash into Sally's hand discreetly. At first she refused, but now took it without question.

Teresa was no longer intimate with him, yet he did his best to remain faithful. He only had one lapse—with Sally—on a night that still haunted him.

His mind drifted to Christmas Eve in 1975—snow falling softly over the New Jersey landscape, turning it white and clean.

He'd trimmed the tree with Teresa and Amanda, then slipped away at 7:30 AM, claiming an early shift covering for a guard so he could be with his family.

"What about *your* family?" Teresa demanded.

Jake shrugged, put on his uniform and headed out.

But he didn't go to work. Instead, he drove through icy streets to Plainfield, carrying a bag heavy with presents for Sally's family.

"Uncle Jake!" shouted Shawn, nearly seven, launching himself into his arms. The warm glow of the tree and candlelight illuminated the house.

Jake settled onto the sofa, sharing cookies and eggnog, watching Shawn tear into a handcrafted wooden control panel Jake made—switches that lit up, buzzers that sang. The boy's eyes sparkled as he pretended to pilot a spaceship, escaping from cosmic villains.

Later, after he and Sally tucked Shawn in with threats of Santa's wrath if he stayed awake, Jake washed the dishes in the candlelit kitchen. Sally's smile was weary but grateful as she watched him, sipping a glass of eggnog.

"You've done so much—you really didn't have to," she whispered.

Jake shrugged. "Things are tough since your mom died."

She twirled a strand of hair. "We lost her social security income... life insurance helped, but not nearly enough. Babysitters are expensive."

"Off tonight?" he asked.

"The Dive is open," she said with a shrug. "Japanese tourists bring in the money. I can't understand a word, but their money is green. No, I wanted to take the night off."

They sipped drinks by the fireplace—the glow warming the room.

Sally added a shot of amber liquor to her eggnog, and Jake knew it wasn't her first. He could tell by the way her eyes danced in the firelight. Jake dug into his bag for more presents—one for Shawn, labeled from Santa, and a slim box for Sally.

Her fingers trembled as she revealed a delicate wristwatch, rhinestones glittering in a circle.

"It's beautiful," she whispered.

"I knew you broke your old one. Thought you could use something nice for work."

She fastened it around her wrist. "Perfect... and just rhinestones, right?"

Jake smiled. "Just rhinestones."

She leaned in, pressing a kiss to his cheek, smelling of whiskey and spices. "Thanks, Jake... for everything."

Jake stumbled over carefully rehearsed words. "Sally, have you thought more about the blood test?"

Her face twisted in frustration.

"Jake, it's Christmas Eve! I don't want to talk about it."

"But with your mom gone, you need the test. You're entitled to child support. I won't fight you. Then you get the financial help. Teresa could know... Amanda's two years younger. She'd understand."

"No," Sally shook her head, voice breaking. "I was... reckless that summer."

"You've never been reckless," Jake said firmly.

Her bitterness rose. "I was. What if the test shows Shawn isn't yours? What then?"

"Then I do what I've always done."

She laughed bitterly, tears in her eyes. "Jake, if you knew—*for a fact*—that Shawn wasn't yours, you'd stop coming around. Not at first, but eventually."

She lit a cigarette, the orange glow flickering in her delicate hands. "Who would Shawn look up to? Me? The losers I date? That last one was a drunk, a hitter. You know what happened."

Jake clenched his jaw, recalling the moment he'd confronted the man in full uniform, to leave or face ruin. The man fled town, stealing cash from Sally when he did.

"Sally, I'll always be there—for Shawn and you."

"Don't say it," she whispered, smoke curling. "Let's keep it how it is."

He reached out, brushing her arm gently. "I don't want to upset you on Christmas."

Tears threatened again. "Meeting you was the luckiest thing. I want to believe you gave me Shawn. I want him to have your goodness."

Jake scoffed. "I'm not good."

"Yes, you are," she said firmly, drawing close to press a slow, soulful kiss to his lips—warm, intoxicating, bittersweet.

His body responded instinctively, as though the years of abstinence had been only a cruel dream. Their hands explored, hesitated, then yearned, shedding barriers both physical and emotional. Her blouse spilled open; his shirt rose, revealing skin stirred by desire.

They clung to one another, moving apart only to remove another obstacle, caught in a rhythm both new and achingly familiar.

At last she lay back on the sofa, pulling him close.

"I don't have any rubbers," he whispered, voice thick.

"I'm on the pill," she murmured, half-closed eyes burning. "Please, Jake." The words were more command than plea.

He entered her feverishly, their bodies rocking in sync—moans soft, urgent. He bit into a pillow, muffling cries as his passion poured out.

When the storm passed, they lay entwined—breathless, flushed, fragile in each other's arms.

Guilt crashed over Jake like a crashing wave, fierce and unrelenting. The weight of what he'd done settled deep in his chest, squeezing the breath from him.

He and Sally agreed—settled, really—on a simple friendship, a mutual understanding for the sake of their boy.

What had he just allowed himself? This wasn't friendship or kindness. It was raw, selfish desire masked as something else entirely—a reckless, devastating betrayal of everything he'd promised himself.

But it was Christmas. And she lay there, breathtaking in a way that stabbed him right through the heart. Her hair spilled messily over the worn couch cushions, her clothes a tangled mess around her, the faint scent of cinnamon and something more intoxicating drifting between them.

Her smile, slow and satisfied, was so achingly familiar—like a melody he thought he'd forgotten but hummed instinctively. He felt an ache for her, a deep, old ache that neither time nor circumstance could dull.

"Ohhhh," she breathed softly, a sigh that wrapped around his name like silk. She reached to a nearby box of tissues, carefully folding several and sliding them between her legs. With a simple motion, she pulled her skirt down, straightened her blouse, and sat up, the movement drawing his eyes unwillingly. "Jake, my dear, dear Jake."

She moved closer, slipping her arms around him as if anchoring herself. He stiffened, hesitating, the past and the present tangling in his thoughts.

Sensing the lingering tension, she drew back just enough to meet his eyes with a knowing look. "It's been... a while, hasn't it?"

Jake nodded, shame burning in his cheeks. He glanced away, embarrassed by the vulnerability in his own admission.

"Amanda's birth... it did a lot of internal damage. Teresa... she can't have any more children. It's changed her—changed what she wants." His voice broke as he pulled his underwear back on, avoiding her gaze.

Sally was gentle, her fingers threading through his short hair in calm reassurance.

"It's okay," she murmured, her voice soft and unyielding. "Don't beat yourself up over it. It's been a while for me too." She lifted her glass of spiked eggnog, sipping slowly, eyes locked on the flicker of the firelight. "Sure, I get offers every night, but the only lips I've felt recently? Terry's—just for show, nothing real."

Jake let out a long sigh. "Guess it's the same for both of us, Candy?"

Her expression turned suddenly fierce as she leaned in close, whispering in his ear. "Don't you call me that. I'm Sally to you—Sally, nothing else."

He swallowed hard, the words catching in his throat. "I should try to see you only as Shawn's mom," he muttered.

She pulled away sharply, the hurt flashing in her eyes like a slap.

"Yeah," she said, voice cold and steady. "We both probably should."

She picked up a cigarette burnt down to a stub in the ashtray, took a slow, deliberate drag, and let the smoke curl between them before speaking again—quiet, almost a whisper. "Jake, I'll play whatever role you need me to. You gave me the most precious thing in my life. And here you are, the only man who showed up for me on Christmas Eve." Her gaze drifted to the fire, moisture blurring the edges of her eyes. "You know, a girl finds that... damn sexy. And, honestly? You're still one hell of a man."

For the first time that night, a genuine smile cracked through Jake's guilt. "You always have a way with words, Sally."

"Damn straight," she said, a spark of her old defiance lighting her eyes.

They sat there, wrapped in each other's arms—two children clinging to a fragile safety as the fire popped and hissed, the tension between them thick yet somehow comforting.

When the moment finally broke, Jake got up quietly and left for work, the weight of the night settling behind him like a shadow.

The next day, guilt gnawed at him cruelly. Teresa's kindness toward him felt like both balm and blade. She smiled, played the part perfectly—rubbing his back after dinner, admiring the gifts he'd chosen with quiet affection.

She even took Amanda to her mother's so she could surprise him later that evening.

When he woke, it was to gentle caresses and the warm feel of her skin beneath his hands.

They made love, soft and familiar, but he couldn't shake the ache of what slipped away between them over the years.

That was five years ago. Since then, even as the distance in their bed grew and Teresa's desire faded like a dying ember,

But Jake had honored his vow—never crossing the line with Sally again.

Jake finished mopping the kitchen floor, the rhythmic swipes grounding him.

For a while, the ghosts of the past haunted his thoughts, but now he pushed them aside.

He had tasks to complete—and he intended to see them through.

The bathrooms were next on his list. If he could have them spotless before the house stirred awake, perhaps he could keep the fragile peace a little longer.

Amanda would be up soon, bleary-eyed and smelling faintly of sleep, shuffling down the stairs for her cereal. She was only ten, still innocent to the complexities that weighed on Jake's heart.

Shawn was nearly twelve, a towering presence with restless energy, yet like Amanda, a stranger in his own family. The siblings had never met, each living in separate orbits, ignorant of the other's existence. But Jake saw himself in both—fine-boned, blond-haired. Amanda's skin was darker, but the family resemblance was undeniable. Both children wore his features like masks, each one an echo of the man who longed to hold them close but remained distant.

Jake's visits with Shawn and Sally had to be stolen moments, fragments of time snatched away from a relentless schedule.

Shawn had shot up to nearly five-foot-ten, already marking himself a star on his school basketball team. Jake saw the boy's potential in every graceful leap and sprint.

Yet Teresa—the mother of Amanda—never understood Jake's sudden investment in middle school sports, though she didn't argue about him going to games. Too many walls separated them: Jake's nocturnal addiction, the alarms rigged throughout the house, and the silent resentments simmering beneath their fractured family life.

Teresa's nighttime solitude felt like imprisonment. Each quiet moment locked away behind her bedroom door while Jake moved like a shadow elsewhere.

In contrast, Jake and Sally frequented Shawn's games, cheering in the wooden bleachers as the gym echoed with the screech of rubber soles and the sting of bouncing basketballs beneath bright, unforgiving lights.

It was at one of these games that the long-awaited subject came up again—a blood test had become a source of undercurrents and tension.

"I don't want to talk about it!" Sally hissed, her voice sharp as she leaned close to Jake's ear on the cramped car ride home. Shawn went out with friends to celebrate the victory and would be home later.

"You never want to talk about it," Jake snapped back, his patience fraying.

The silence that followed was thick with frustration.

Sally once confided she wanted a college degree—something real, a way out of "waving her tits in front of a bunch of lowlifes." His shoulders tensed at her blunt words.

But he pressed on. "It's the solution. You take the test, I'm financially responsible. You get the money for school."

"If, if, if! And what if you're not the father?" She shot back, the familiar argument etched in her tone.

Jake braced himself. "Wouldn't it be better for him to really know? Amanda and Shawn look like brother and sister. In a few years, they'll both be dating. Isn't it better if they know the truth?"

Sally's sarcasm cut through the car. "Afraid they'll date?"

Despite her sharp tongue, Jake's affection for her was fierce—but her attitude often tested his resolve.

Slowly, her anger ebbed.

"All right," Sally whispered, almost inaudibly.

Jake turned toward her. "What?"

"We should get the test—not for me or you, but for him. Shawn deserves to know if you're his father." She shifted uncomfortably on the seat, then leaned close, voice barely a breath. "He's been asking… about his dad. What he was like. Why he didn't stay. I guess if he knew it was you—"

Jake felt his chest tighten with something like hope. "I understand. This is the best thing. You won't regret it."

Sally's face twisted with a mix of worry and fierceness. "I already regret it," she said with a bitter laugh, then hugged his arm tightly. "Jake Hurd, you're the only man who can get to me where I live."

"I want to do what's right by you, Sally."

She sighed, her resistance melting away. "I know. That'll have to do."

After finishing the last bathroom, Jake pulled out a carpet sweeper —a quieter alternative to the vacuum that wouldn't risk waking the household.

His Saturday ritual was unchanging: clean the house, sleep until late afternoon, and then slip away to see Sally and Shawn before Sally went to work.

In the daytime world, he claimed he was out "with the boys," a harmless excuse no one questioned anymore.

Teresa stopped asking long ago.

Routine was his shield, a silent truce with the shadows that stalked the edges of his life. His habits kept him less exposed to the invisible threats—night creatures that still lurked, their menace steady and unyielding.

He felt their presence more acutely every day but wore indifference like armor to protect those he loved.

They killed Peggy. That memory burned deep, a brutal warning he never forgot.

As his daughter and his unacknowledged son grew, Jake carefully avoided the perilous subbasements at BT&T where his enemies lingered.

Instead, he patrolled safer zones—classified government projects where his vigilance was less tested. His job had become easier, but his paycheck hadn't kept pace. Inflation soared twenty percent, courtesy of President Jimmy Carter's assurances that it was all just an economic cycle.

They bought their house in better days, low-interest rates securing their foothold. But everything else rose in cost, forcing belt-tightening and sacrifice.

Offering Sally money for college was a silent act of penance, a way to give back after years of quiet struggles. Sally asked so little and never used Shawn as leverage.

Jake wished Teresa had the same fairness, often irritated by her using Amanda as a weapon to get her way. In arguments, Teresa's voice could frighten a tomcat six blocks away, while Jake stayed calm beneath her fury, listening to the repeated threat—that she would take Amanda away and find a man who would be a better father.

That threat poisoned whatever passion remained in their marriage.

Despite the domestic discord, Jake kept tinkering and made an appointment with Dan Hurley to show him his inventions, hoping it might bring some financial relief.

That night, during his weekly visit, he could repeat the request for the blood test, as Sally had finally agreed. If she tried to delay, Jake would repeat that it was what was best for the boy.

He was sure she would make him swear not to abandon them.

That vow hung between them, fragile and heavy, as Jake prepared himself for what was to come.

28. A New Beginning

···

The Saturday night after Thanksgiving hung heavy with a brittle calm. Jake, Shawn, and Sally sat around the dinner table, sharing an early meal that felt more like ritual than celebration: spaghetti drenched in thick, red meat sauce—a welcome if modest departure from the ever-creeping leftover turkey that seemed to take over the fridge each November.

The clatter of forks on plates mixed with Shawn's animated chatter as he proudly waved his report card.

"I got straight A's," Shawn beamed, eyes shining as he shoved another forkful into his mouth. It was the unfiltered pride only a kid could possess, and watching him, even Jake felt a flicker of warmth.

"Nice work, Shawn," Jake said, dipping into the sauce with deliberate slowness, savoring the moment.

Sally smiled softly but said little.

Without warning, Shawn pushed back his chair and bolted toward the door. "I'm heading to James' place," he said over his shoulder, barely stopping to zip his jacket. "We're gonna play Space Invaders on the Atari."

Sally's voice followed him, stern but caring. "Make sure you have your key. I'm leaving for work at ten. Be back before that."

Shawn grinned with the mischievous flicker of youth still intact and flashed her a carefree smile before disappearing into the chilly night.

Jake watched Sally gather the dishes in near silence, marveling at her efficiency. "He's a good kid," Jake said, breaking the quiet.

She nodded but didn't meet his eyes. "I got lucky."

Jake washed the dishes mechanically, droplets of soapy water sliding off the plates like unspoken words stuck between them. Sally set the coffeepot on the burner and sighed.

"Are we all set for the tests?" Jake asked, trying to sound casual.

"Yeah," she muttered, flicking ash from her cigarette, refusing to meet his gaze.

Jake detected the tension coiling in her voice. "You're not changing your mind again?" He forced a smile, deliberately attempting to lighten the moment.

"No," she said, exhaling smoke slowly. "Did I tell you it's going to cost five hundred dollars?" The words came out hard, full of something close to bitterness.

"I know." Jake's voice was steady, rehearsed. "I've been saving up for it. Got it all planned." The money was there—set aside from his repair gigs—but the weight of the cost gnawed at him more than he let on. "Does it bother you?"

Her silence stretched, suffocating, and Jake realized this had become one of those unspoken battles they fought—waiting for one of them to speak first.

"We have to change Saturday nights," she said simply, the cigarette trembling between her fingers. Her gaze locked onto his with a sharpness that could cut glass. It was a warning more than a request.

Jake dried his hands, facing her squarely, swallowing the growing knot in his chest. "We've been doing Saturday nights for a long time."

Her lips pressed into a hard line. "Yeah, well… things change."

Jake tried to keep the calm he desperately needed, the balm that used to smooth over their cracks. "Sally, we've always been able to talk—"

"Talk!" she spat, the word tasting of bitterness and betrayal. "You don't want to talk. You just want to be around Shawn—to prove that he's yours. That's the only reason you've been coming around all these years: to be a part-time father when it suits you." Her voice rose, flames licking at the edges. "Maybe it's not convenient for me anymore!"

Jake took a step closer. "Sally, you're upset—"

"No, I'm not!" she snapped, extinguishing her cigarette with a violence that made the ashtray jump. "I'm being a realist."

He reached for her, but she recoiled, hard edges sharpening. "I'm seeing someone. He's going to want Saturday nights from now on."

The words landed like a punch in Jake's gut. "Why are you doing this?"

Her mouth fell open, anger radiating from every pore. "Because you're fucking married!" she hissed.

Jake's voice dropped, the strain clear. "There's no need for that —"

"What? Fuck? Well, fuck you." She jabbed a finger at his chest, trembling with rage. "Who asked you to come back into my life? To complicate it?"

"I only wanted—"

"I don't care what you wanted." Her voice cracked on the edge of fury and hurt. "I didn't want to dance through these years alone, but I did what I had to do. Now I'm older. I need a degree or, hell, some fool who can support me—because you won't."

With a flick, her palm slapped Jake's cheek—a gesture more desperate than violent. The sting woke every nerve, but Jake didn't flinch.

She turned away, picking up her last cigarette like a lifeline. "And what the hell are you going to do about it? He's my son. Only mine. You have no say."

Jake's voice hardened. "Why are you acting like this?"

She pivoted, close enough to feel the heat of his breath. "Like what?"

"Like a bitch!" The word slipped out, sharper than intended.

Her hand shot up, ready to strike again, but Jake was quicker —grabbing her wrists gently but firmly until she stopped struggling.

Against his strength, she yelped, and he scooped her into his arms—unstoppable. He carried her to the living room, to the couch where, years ago, they had shared a different intimacy. He set her down with a soft thump.

She stared up at him, eyes blazing with fury and heartbreak. For a moment, a primal sound escaped her throat—the raw cry of a wounded animal.

Jake knelt beside her, voice softening. "What is it?"

"I'm… losing you," she whispered, pressing her face into his shoulder, tears soaking through his shirt. "Then I realized… maybe I never really had you."

His heart wrenched. "You always had me. I'm here when you need me."

"No, you're not." She shook her head, her voice breaking. "Not for the little things… not when I'm alone or… when I'm h-horny."

The blunt admission broke through Jake's defenses. A small, involuntary smile tugged at his lip, which he tried to suppress, but it was too late.

She jumped on it, her fury flaring but empty now. "It's funny to you!" she bawled. "I've been alone for years."

Jake's eyes searched hers. "Why?"

"You're with Teresa, your wife." Her voice thickened, bitter. "And all I have are lonely nights, a once-a-week visit, and the rare Christmas bang."

"It's what you said you wanted." His voice dropped, vulnerable. "I told you to date."

Her voice fell to a near whisper. "I didn't know… I didn't know I'd fall in love with you."

He reached for her, desperate to confess, but she pulled away, sitting up stiffly. "I know you don't love me." Her words sliced through the warm space between them. "I finally realized that at the basketball game." Her jaw clenched, a fortress of pain. "But I need someone. I need a man."

Jake's chest tightened. He wanted to reach out, to kiss her, to tell her everything he'd buried inside for years—but a ghost stood between them: Amanda, with her blonde hair and soft smile, etched on his mind.

She wiped her tears with the back of her hand and whispered, "Say something, Jake."

"No," he blurted, his voice louder than intended. His hand brushed her shoulder, and confusion flickered in her eyes. "It's not true. I am in love with you. I have always been."

Pulling her close, Jake's heart thundered wildly. "I don't want to lose you."

Their lips met in a deep, urgent kiss that fired through them both, erasing the years and pain. In one fluid motion, he lifted her bodily, ignoring the protest in her gasp.

"Jake, you'll hurt yourself," she warned breathlessly, but he silenced her with another kiss.

He carried her up the stairs, down the hall, and flung open her bedroom door. The glow of the overhead light illuminated the disorder: an unmade bed, piles of books, faded walls marred by time, and laundry spilling over a battered desk.

Sally's voice broke through. "No, no, it's a mess!"

But Jake didn't care—not that night. He laid her down and kissed her again—deep, open-mouthed, driven by all the need and regret simmering beneath the surface.

Sally surrendered with a soft sigh.

Monday morning came too soon. Leaving BT&T earlier than usual, Jake deliberately veered from his regular route, clutching a folded slip of paper Sally had written—a doctor's address in Morristown. He pulled into the parking lot of a towering medical building, its architecture designed to convey expertise and reassurance to nervous patients.

But Jake's mind wandered back to Saturday night: the curve of Sally's smile, the warmth of her skin under his hands, the way their bodies folded into each other like they never had been apart —the night they'd made Shawn.

He pushed the door open, heart pounding with a new certainty. Teresa had been a mistake. He'd spent years fighting monsters in the dark when all he needed to do was fight for this —the woman who had held his heart all along. Lightness bloomed inside him like a fragile dawn.

Jake found the doctor's office behind a heavy wooden door, filled out the paperwork, and waited until a nurse appeared. The needle broke his skin, blood pooling silently into a vial.

"Two weeks," the nurse said. "You'll get the results in two weeks".

Jake decided that when the proof that Shawn was his son arrived, he would ask Teresa for a divorce and tell Sally.

Tell her he was all in.

For the first time in what felt like forever, Jake was taking control of his life.

As December 1980 crept in with its biting chill, Jake found himself trapped in a limbo of plans unfulfilled.

Though his interview with Dan Hurley in November had exceeded his own uncertain expectations, nothing had yet crystallized into action.

He recalled that afternoon vividly: unveiling his latest tinkers, each finished prototype a fragment of his dreams laid bare upon the table. At first, Dan's posture was lukewarm, almost as if he humored Jake's enthusiasm out of simple politeness.

But as the devices reacted to movement, or sensed someone nearby and lit up, something changed—the owner's gaze sharpened, his skepticism replaced by keen interest.

"Leave these here," Dan had finally said, taking the prototypes into his care. "I'll get back to you in a few days."

Those few days stretched into weeks, a tantalizing pause filled with slim hope. If the company bought his designs, Jake could finally carve a path to freedom—from his life with Teresa, from the suffocating routine that held him captive.

One gray December afternoon around two-thirty, Jake busied himself in the kitchen, preparing a snack in anticipation of Amanda's arrival at three. Their interactions were simple rituals—chatting about her day, easing her into homework, then cooking dinner. It was all familiar, a shallow routine that disguised his personal turmoil beneath.

At two-fifty, the shrill ring of the phone broke through the quiet. Jake's heart leapt. Sally, he thought—after their confession of love and the secret meetings they'd shared, it had to be her reaching out again, calling to arrange their next stolen moment away from curious eyes.

Instead, the voice on the other end was smaller, more uncertain. "Uncle Jake?"

"Shawn?" Jake blurted out, concern flooding him. "Is everything alright? Your mother?"

"Mom's fine," came the reply, soft but wary. "We got our blood taken today—she was a trooper. But me? I got dizzy… had to sit for a minute."

Jake chuckled quietly, trying to lighten the mood. "Nothing to be ashamed of. Bigger men than you have passed out at the sight of their own blood."

There was a pause and then Shawn asked in a trembling voice, "Can I talk to you? Without Mom around? Could you meet me at the Plainfield library at eight?"

Jake swallowed hard, surprised but grateful, and quickly agreed.

They said their goodbyes just as Amanda's footsteps echoed on the porch. The timing felt like a small mercy, and he offered a silent thanks.

Dinner passed with little conversation. When asked about his plans, Jake vaguely mentioned errands. With Christmas looming, secrecy seemed easier to swallow.

Teresa, immersed in the remains of a pumpkin pie, hardly noticed his absence. They felt less like a couple sharing a home than strangers cohabiting a space.

In the quiet of the approaching evening, a part of Jake felt a flicker of hope. If Shawn was reaching out, man to man, it could mean he might accept the truth about his lineage.

Maybe even the complicated reality of Jake's relationship with his mother.

The Plainfield library was a relic of the '70s—one story, walls of amber glass framed by sweeping metal struts that curved like iron vines. From the street in the daylight, it looked like a monolithic black granite box. But at night it was almost transparent, its quiet readers and wandering patrons illuminated in the soft glow.

Jake arrived five minutes early, scanning the familiar space for Shawn. He found the boy seated at a long table, his lanky frame sprawling awkwardly.

Sitting opposite him, Jake took in the in-between nature of this boy—not quite a child, not yet a man. His face was still soft and round; his voice had yet to drop, and his limbs arranged themselves with the gracelessness of adolescence, except on the basketball court where he moved with practiced ease.

But the Shawn Jake faced now was anything but confident. There was fear etched deeply in the boy's eyes.

"Uncle Jake!" Shawn's voice was urgent as he stood. "Thanks for coming."

Jake nodded. "What's going on?"

Shawn hesitated, his fingers tangled nervously together. "Some things," he said finally.

"Want to tell me about it?" Jake's voice softened, remembering his own difficult talks with his father when he'd felt stupid and small.

Shawn began, then faltered. "Did you know my father?"

Jake's mind caught a flicker of caution. "Shouldn't you talk to your mom about that?"

Shawn's shoulders slumped. "She won't tell me a thing. I keep asking, but—" His voice cracked, frustration and confusion clashing in his gaze. "I don't see what the big deal is."

Jake seized the moment with gentle wisdom. "The memory might be painful for her."

That changed something. Shawn's eyes darkened with a mix of anger and sorrow. "How?"

"They aren't together," Jake shrugged. "Usually that means something happened. Maybe he had to leave."

A shadow passed over Shawn's features as he studied his hands again. "You're just not telling," he said accusingly.

"What do you mean?"

"You and Mom talk all the time. She must have told you about my father. And you've been around as long as I can remember. You must 'know him."

Jake stared at him. "What I know is that your father loved you and your mother very much. That I'm sure of."

Shawn's lip curled bitterly. "Yeah, real nice of him to stick around."

Jake sighed, cutting through the tension. "Shawn, I don't think that's why you asked me here tonight."

The boy shifted in his chair; his voice dropped to a whisper. "Uncle Jake... do you think there might be—people—in the dark?"

An icy shiver ran through Jake, eyes scanning the shadowed corners of the library. "People?"

"No. Not people. Something that lives in the dark places—in the shadows of a room."

"Shadows," Jake breathed, a grim understanding settling like a stone in his gut.

Shawn nodded eagerly. "Yeah, shadows that are alive."

Jake's fear swelled, yet beneath it stirred an unexpected kinship. "What makes you say that?"

"You probably think I'm crazy."

"No, I don't," Jake urged. "Tell me, where did you see it?"

Something in Jake's calm voice seemed to uncoil the boy's tight fear. Shawn's eyes flicked upward as if summoning the vision. "At

James's house, in the hall. I thought it was just light playing tricks. But then in my own room… it moved around the room. When I flipped the light on, it vanished." His voice lowered, conspiratorial. "Pretty weird, right?"

Jake's throat tightened. "What did it look like?"

"Flat, with two slits for eyes." Shawn's gaze darted around, wary of listeners. "It felt like it was watching me. Like it was smart."

"Are you sure it wasn't just moonlight or shadows cast by trees?"

Shawn glanced toward the cloudy glass, shadowed patches lurking near the street lamps outside. "I thought so too. But then it—they—spoke."

Jake's brow furrowed, voice a harsh whisper. "Spoke?"

Shawn nodded, eyes locked on Jake's. "Whispers—just beyond hearing, like the rustle of leaves or the wind. Not one voice, but at least two. At first, I didn't understand. But now I can make out words."

Jake felt dizzy, the room tilting slightly. He caught himself before his jaw sagged. "What do they say?"

Shawn leaned forward, wildness sparking in his eyes. "Terrible things." He leaned back, releasing a breath heavy with despair. "They say I should hurt people."

Tears brimmed in the boy's eyes. Despite his height and bravado, the frightened child beneath was raw and exposed. "Uncle Jake… I'm scared."

Jake gripped Shawn's hand tightly, voice steady despite the whirlwind inside. "I know you are, son."

The word slipped out before he could stop it—but Shawn didn't notice.

"There are ways you can protect yourself."

"Protect? How?" Shawn's voice barely rose above a whisper.

"They hate light. Even a lamp left on helps. I'll bring you some special lights—ones I've made—that do even more."

Shawn's skepticism surfaced. "But how—?"

Jake met the boy's eyes. "I'm very familiar with what you're talking about. Do you understand? I can help keep you safe."

The boy nodded slowly. For the first time that evening, a fragile hope flickered through the fear.

Jake explained his inventions—his special lights that acted as a shield against the dark, a beacon strong enough to push back the shadows.

And as the library's dim amber glow enveloped them, two souls —one boy, one man—bonded over lurking fears and whispered secrets, standing together against the darkness.

29. Income & Death

....

Dan Hurley turned the small device over in his hand, a slow smile spreading across his face. "These gadgets of yours are brilliant, Jake. I've seen nothing like them. And—wait—what makes them work?" He shook his head in amazement, the weight of the technology tangible between his fingers.

"Computer chips," Jake corrected, his voice low but steady.

"Whatever. People are going to love that. Our clients will have computerized security at their fingertips. It's revolutionary—mind-blowing, really."

Jake's pulse quickened. "So you think there's a market for this?"

Hurley's grin grew wider. "Reagan didn't just win the election promising tax cuts. No—the country is hungering for security. Protection. We're tired of feeling vulnerable like a spineless, third-world nation where anyone can take us hostage. There's going to be a security revolution, Jake. And you—you've handed me the ammunition."

Jake swallowed hard, a flush creeping up his neck. The unspoken question pressed at him: would there be any money for his designs?

"I wanted to ask," he began hesitantly, eyes fixed on the device in Hurley's grasp, "if there would be... any money for my work."

Hurley leaned back, eyes boring into Jake's like a hawk sizing up its prey. Then, slipping smoothly into salesman mode he said, "I'll be upfront with you. I can give you some cash—maybe five grand, perhaps more."

Five thousand dollars. Suddenly the air seemed thick with possibility. He could pay for Sally's semester at college—or an excellent lawyer for the divorce.

"You're a longtime employee, Jake. More than that—we're old friends. But this is a risk. We might not make a damn dime."

Jake frowned. "I'm not sure I understand."

Holding up the box again Hurley explained, "I could sell one of these to a big security company. We both make a little money and move on. Or we can build them ourselves—mass produce them, break into that market."

"And that means—?"

"I couldn't offer any money upfront," Hurley said, leaning forward, he steepled his fingers. "We'd have to invest in catalogs, a sales force, marketing. But I'm willing to front the costs."

Jake bristled at the 'we.' He had never been a partner before—always the hired hand.

Hurley pressed on. "I'd like to offer you a percentage of the profits. If it takes off, you could do much better than selling the rights."

Jake's mind raced, the weight of his financial needs pressing down like a vise. "I kind of need money right now."

Hurley nodded slowly, eyes sharp and understanding. "I get it. It's your choice: a small payday now or the whole enchilada if it succeeds. Do you want to be a night guard for the rest of your life?"

Jake stiffened, the jab hitting close to home.

"Well, I—"

"No judgment," Hurley said quickly, waving a hand. "I mean you're great for us. But listen. There's no risk for you. I'm not asking you to invest a dime. Just keep making these doohickeys of yours—and I'll need specs."

"Specs?"

"Blueprints, technical sketches. We need to patent them. Protect your work."

Jake nodded thoughtfully. He remembered an old book on technical drawing he had tucked away at home.

Hurley leaned back again, voice firm. "The risk is all mine. If your gadgets flop, I'm the one out big bucks. I'll create a whole new division around these security systems. If it works—well, the money will be like nothing you've ever seen. But if it fails, I eat the losses. What I need to know is if you're willing to put your doohickeys on the line."

Jake hesitated for only a moment before nodding. What did he have to lose?

"That's what I like to hear!" Hurley exclaimed, standing and grabbing Jake's hand in a firm shake. "I'll get Stan to draft up the paperwork first thing tomorrow."

Jake exhaled, heart hammering. The future had just shifted— and with it, everything he thought he knew about security, success, and risk.

With Christmas just a week away, Jake spent the day calling many of his regular repair customers, angling for work to get extra money.

But beneath the steady stream of phone calls simmered a nagging frustration. He cursed himself for agreeing to Hurley's scheme—the plan to launch a new side business under the banner of Security Information Systems.

They'd sell the gadgets Jake painstakingly engineered—'doohickeys,' as Hurley liked to call them—but for Jake, the payoff felt distant and vague. Worse, all the added labor to draft plans and oversee production pulled him away from creating new ones.

He kept the whole thing to himself—didn't even mention it to Teresa. She didn't need any extra worries especially not with the holidays approaching.

Still, Jake attempted to brighten the season at home. He dutifully hung Christmas lights outside and bought a fresh evergreen for the living room. Amanda, now ten, was practically bubbling with excitement. She'd long outgrown belief in Santa Claus, but the magical pull of sights, smells, and sounds of the holidays still thrilled her in a pure, innocent way.

By late afternoon, Jake swung by Sally's place carrying several of his latest devices for Shawn. Nothing extravagant—just a couple of his sound-activated lights which Shawn could keep by his bed.

He'd even fashioned a special eye mask so Shawn could sleep with his lamp on without distraction.

Afterward, a routine trip to Watchung to pick up a repair led Jake to cross the bridge over Highway 22, steering into Plainfield's shopping district.

On a whim, he headed for Sally's house and realized with a sudden pang that he should have called Sally first.

The storefronts glittered with lights, open late to catch last-minute shoppers. He passed beneath the rows of street lamps hung with green wreaths, and as he pulled onto her street, a heavy unease crawled up Jake's spine.

The neighborhood was unusually dark. Street lamps flickered along every block—except one.

Her block.

His pulse quickened; a cold tingle danced down the back of his neck, a familiar dread from days past.

He sensed them, a lot of them.

Jake scanned the shadows lining the unlit street. Shapes moved —how many? One? Ten? Or was it an entire nightmare army, shifting like a herd of spectral demons, fluid and yet tangible?

He told himself no—there could only be one or two, right?

But the dark swallowed certainty.

He parked in her driveway, heart hammering, afraid to look left or right lest unseen phantoms filled the surrounding air. His hands shook as he drew his high-powered flashlight from the glove compartment and bolted toward the house, the chill slicing into his skin.

A shape darted near the side of Sally's house. Jake trained his beam on it—only to watch it vanish like smoke.

Darkness swallowed the house. Not a single light glimmered— not the porch light, not the floodlight he'd installed himself with a photoelectric sensor to burn bright after dusk.

He climbed the steps quietly, slowing so as not to bang against the heavy front door. To his shock, the door creaked open in his grasp. Sally never left it unlocked.

Going inside, Jake's flashlight slashed through the oppressive blackness of the living room. The darkness felt suffocating—like swimming through thick oil, stealing his breath.

A Christmas tree sat near the couch, its tinsel glinting dimly. Without its glowing bulbs it was mournful, like a wreath atop a freshly dug grave.

"S-Sally?" he whispered, voice breaking in the cold, silent house. The temperature dropped; heat fled the rooms like a frightened animal.

A shadow flickered across the wall. Jake whirled, ready to fight, falling to one knee as he fished a battery-powered device from his pocket. A press triggered blinding white light flooding the room. Jake shielded his eyes, counting slowly to thirty before slamming the device off with a shuddering breath.

"Sally?" His voice echoed strangely in the tomb-like quiet. Outside, the street lamps blinked back to life sending a dim light through the curtained windows.

Moving cautiously, Jake flicked on switches in the dining room and throughout the house until every lamp blazed. Still, no answer came. No movement. No warmth.

He climbed the stairs toward her bedroom—the room where just days ago they'd shared a tender night.

He stepped into the bedroom as a foul stench hit him, acrid and rancid, souring his mouth. He slammed on the switch.

There she was.

Sally lay on the bed, sheets stained from snowy white to a deep, viscous crimson. Her flannel nightgown—lavender once, now soaked in blood—draped chaste and haunting over her frame. Jagged tears rent the fabric, brightest where fresh blood seeped: a brutal slash across her throat.

Her eyes stared, unblinking—empty, yet strangely filled with disbelief, as if surprised Jake should witness her like this.

Jake staggered back, breaking into the bathroom. He vomited violently; bile and last night's meal spilling out in a torrent that felt elemental. He coughed, sobs breaking free uncontrollably.

But another terror seared his mind—Shawn.

Steeling himself Jake stepped into the hallway, desperate to avoid Sally's corpse, fearful that her dead gaze would shatter what remained of his reason.

"He's upstairs," Jake muttered, voice low but steady.

Near the bathroom door was another, barely noticeable. Jake pulled it open to reveal a narrow, dark staircase descending into a pitch-black corridor.

He tried the light switch. Nothing.

An awful memory played across his mind—the night Peggy died, trapped in such blackness.

His grip quivered on the doorknob but he forced his flashlight beam upward.

"Bastards," he growled under his breath. "You'd better not have hurt him!"

Fueled by anger and dread Jake climbed the stairs, tracing the light's beam as he rose.

He reached the door at the top and kicked it open. Visions of Shawn, hurt or worse, went through his mind.

He flicked the light switch, and the room flooded with a pale light from twin wall sconces.

There on the bed sat Shawn—alive, blinking against the sudden brightness. But blood stained his hands, thick and dark.

"Shawn?" Jake's voice caught as he crouched beside the boy, searching for the source of the blood dripping from trembling fingers.

The boy's glazed eyes met his, lips slack as he whispered, "Uncle Jake?"

"Are you hurt?" Jake asked, heart pounding.

"No. I'm fine," came the flat, monotone reply.

Jake's eyes caught the glint of metal—a hunting knife clenched between Shawn's fingers.

His heart sank. The blade was the same size as the wounds on Sally's body.

"Shawn, your mother is dead," Jake said, voice barely above a whisper, watching for any   spark of recognition.

"I know," Shawn replied, still hollow and numb. "I killed her."

Jake grabbed his son's shoulders, shaking gently yet urgently, "Why, Shawn? Why?"

Shawn's gaze sharpened slightly. "They wouldn't leave me alone."

"They—?"

"The shadows," Shawn whispered brokenly. "They shut off the lights… I stumbled in the dark. They told me to kill—"

He pressed his bloodied hands to his ears, voice rising in torment. "I grabbed the knife to fight them, but I—I—"

"It's okay," Jake soothed, pulling him back onto the bed and removing his hands carefully. Tears spilled down Shawn's blood-streaked face. "It's okay."

"Oh my God," the boy sobbed, lost and broken.

Jake looked into those wounded eyes and felt a surge of helplessness—his son, a shattered child caught in a nightmare not his own.

He wanted to wash the blood away, bundle Shawn up, and flee —to vanish where none of the horrors could reach them.

But he knew he couldn't—his daughter Amanda still needed him. The shadows had already taken too much.

"I'm going downstairs to call the police," Jake said firmly.

"Don't leave me," Shawn wept, voice cracking, sounding smaller than his years.

"I'll be right back," Jake promised, pushing the flashlight into Shawn's hands. "Keep the lights on. Stay here."

Downstairs, Jake stared at his own blood-covered hands in shock. Then he realized he'd touched Shawn's hands and he went to the kitchen sink, scrubbing them clean until the water ran clear.

He made two calls: one to the police—local number—and another to work, letting them know he wouldn't be coming in.

The night stretched ahead of him: long, cold, and merciless.

30. ENDLESS QUESTIONS

At the first hint of dawn, the heavy door of the Plainfield Police Station opened, releasing Jake.

He felt like a man emerging from a nightmare.

The old stone building loomed ominously behind him, its grim facade a stark reminder of the long night he endured.

Across the hours he was grilled relentlessly, the bright fluorescent lights in the interrogation room burning into his eyes, the unyielding bars on the windows both a physical and psychological cage—yet oddly comforting.

Isolation under bright light had been his only solace, as there were no shadows there.

Detective Walden—a mountain of a man with a neck as thick as an oak branch and the menacing intensity of a pit bull—had made Jake repeat his story again and again.

His deep-set eyes never wavered, drilling into Jake, searching for cracks, lies, anything. Each question landed like a jab, especially the ones that insinuated darker motives.

"How do you know Sally and that boy, Shawn?" Walden pressed, fingers steepled thoughtfully.

Jake's voice was steady, measured, a practiced calm gained from years of writing reports. "Sally and I—we were lovers years ago. Shawn might be my son. We recently took blood tests to find out."

At this, Walden's tone sharpened, suspicion coiling in his voice. "So you set the whole thing up? Killed her, staged it with the boy's blood? To avoid child support?"

Jake met the detective's gaze, firm yet tired. "That blood test was my idea. Sally didn't come to it easily. I helped financially where I could..."

He stuck to the facts, layering his account with small but honest details: meeting Shawn at the library, the boy's crippling fear of the dark, the carefully planned delivery of special lights to ease that fear. He described the streetlights that had gone out— simple, logical explanations woven tightly into his narrative to make it undeniable.

Walden's fatigue showed long before Jake's did, as Jake was used to being up all night. The detective's eyes glazed, shoulders slumping, while Jake's mind remained razor sharp, his composure strong. The night stretched on, but Jake held firm.

Finally, as pale light crept through the barred window, Walden's voice softened with reluctant acceptance. "You're free to go," he said, though the edge of a warning lingered. "Stay accessible. Don't leave town."

Jake's throat tightened as he pressed the one question on his mind. "What about Shawn?"

"That's not your concern," Walden snapped.

Jake's patience cracked. "Detective, I might be his father. I deserve to know."

Walden's sneer was cold. "You want mercy for the kid who killed his mother? Why? Because he's an orphan?"

Jake shoved closer until their faces were inches apart, anger burning in his chest. "I'm all he has." He paused, voice low but fierce. "I respect law enforcement—I'm a guard myself."

"A guard?" Walden scoffed. "Big deal."

"I agreed to talk without a lawyer," Jake said carefully.

"And I think you're hiding something."

The accusation stung, but Jake expected it. "I'll get a lawyer for Shawn. Make sure he's protected."

"Easy, Daddy," Walden said with a cruel grin. "The kid's in for a psych evaluation. Looks like he's nuts—unless you want to convince me otherwise."

"Me?" Jake's voice cracked with disbelief.

Walden's gaze sliced into him. "He talks about… shadows. Strange things. You know more than you're saying. Are you going to tell me?"

"I've told you everything," Jake said.

"Then, get outta here."

Jake stepped into the icy bite of the December morning feeling raw as if stripped bare. The grip of suppressed emotion unclenched suddenly—grief rolled over him like a tidal wave.

"She's dead," he whispered into the cold air, a hollow ache twisting inside him. "My last chance at happiness is gone."

But no. One life remained—Amanda, his beautiful daughter. His priority now was her safety.

He stopped by BT&T to check the reports and meet his men before they left. He needed the distraction—to replace the haunting vision of Sally's blood-soaked body with purposeful action. Beneath his steely calm, grief simmered dangerously close.

Pulling up to his driveway at home, Jake spotted Teresa already at the car, impatience in her swift movements. Amanda was in school, so Jake typically slipped inside to rest, but today was different. He caught Teresa just before she slid behind the wheel.

"I'm gonna be late," she muttered, irritation sharpening her tone.

"Teresa, we need to talk," Jake said, weariness thick in his voice.

Her stern brow softened for a heartbeat. "You look like shit," she said, her slight accent softening the harsh word.

Jake exhaled, raw truth spilling out. "I've been with the police."

A gasp escaped her, eyes wide. "Ohmigod! What did you do?"

"Nothing—I did nothing. But we need to make plans. To protect ourselves."

"Should I talk to my boss? Get a lawyer?"

Jake nodded, the weight of exhaustion hanging over him. At thirty-nine he felt decades older.

"What is it? I can't go through my day worried sick," she said, voice hardening. "You always drop big things on me right before work."

He wanted to scream that this wasn't about her—that if they didn't act, she or Amanda could be next, left bleeding in a pool of their own blood like Sally.

"There was a murder," he said carefully. "People I know… knew. I found the body."

"Oh God," Teresa whispered, shrinking away.

Quickly, he grasped her shoulders, forced her face back to his. "I'm not a suspect. But we have to be ready. You find out about a lawyer. I'll sleep. We'll talk at dinner."

She nodded, eyes falling. As she turned away, there was a look of aching compassion in her gaze—one Jake would carry with him forever.

Inside, Jake slipped off his shoes and collapsed into bed, exhausted but unable to escape the nightmares. Blood, knives, those haunting shadow creatures—they stalked his mind even as exhaustion claimed him.

He awoke abruptly at two-thirty in the afternoon—his usual hour —but this day felt different.

Sweat soaked his shirt and soaked through the bedsheets, and he'd twisted them into a chaotic mess as if he'd fought a brutal battle, the kind fought in nightmares. His muscles screamed with stiffness, each joint rebelling as he pushed himself upright.

With aching limbs, Jake slid out of bed and tiptoed downstairs. The stillness of the house pressed against him, thick and suffocating.

He put the kettle on to boil for tea, the faint hiss of steam a minor comfort. Without waiting he headed straight to his sanctuary: the basement workroom. Here, amid tools and tangled wires, he wrestled with uncertainty, the night's dread echoing in every breath.

His current project was especially delicate. The new sodium lights he was developing held promise—but came with peril.

They ignited quickly and burned fiercely, but with that brilliance came dangerous heat.

His mind churned restlessly. The creatures—they struck Shawn and Sally like an unstoppable army. How had their numbers multiplied so fast? Had Dr. Goldstein's device ripped open portals that let hordes of the creatures flood through? Or was there an even deadlier force at work, one creating fractures into our world, allowing them in?

Jake knew he needed a weapon capable of repelling such an assault. For now these sodium lights were all he had.

He pulled out the three prototypes, slim and flat to fit standard sockets but unlike any bulb. Two were stable, gleaming faintly in the dim light. The third thrummed unpredictably and stayed behind on the workbench. He gripped the other two carefully and climbed the stairs, mindful of every creak.

As he reached the top step, a sudden, cheerful voice sliced through his focus.

"Hi, Daddy!"

The shock was physical. Jake jerked so sharply the lamps nearly slipped from his hands. His heart slammed against his ribs.

"H-hi, honey," he stammered, tightening his grip.

Amanda stood by the kitchen table, her golden hair catching the late afternoon light, olive skin glowing softly. Clutching a cup of tea, she beamed with innocent pride.

"I made this for you," she said, holding out the porcelain mug. She watched the kettle steam and quietly brewed the tea herself—an act small but brimming with love and routine.

"Just put it down, sweetheart," Jake said, forcing calm into his voice.

She cocked her head, concern tugging at her features. "Are you all right, Daddy?"

"Sure, honey," he reassured, setting the lamps down and planting a kiss on her cheek. Leaning against the table, he forced himself to smile, masking the storm inside.

"How was your day?" he asked, as if the previous night's horrors were only faded images on a screen.

Amanda launched into the typical recounting of a ten-year-old's life: beloved teachers, annoying classmates, minor triumphs and frustrations.

Jake listened with practiced patience, feeling no need to correct or intervene. In this moment she needed him to hear her.

As she spoke, Jake fetched snacks and involved her in the small task of choosing—a peanut butter and apple butter sandwich on toasted wheat bread, made with the care of a ritual. She ate eagerly, each bite reminding him of her innocence that he longed to protect.

When Amanda retreated to her homework Jake cleaned the kitchen quietly, every motion mechanical—yet heavy with unspoken grief.

Then the sobs broke from his throat, unbidden and raw, shattering the silence. Doubling over with spasms of pain and sorrow he sank to the floor, muffling his cries into damp paper towels. The weight of fear and loss pressed down on him, crushing and relentless.

Crawling to the small half-bathroom near the kitchen, Jake locked the door behind him. He couldn't bear Amanda seeing him like this—in the grip of despair.

Minutes passed. The waves of grief receded slowly leaving behind a hollow calm. Splashing cold water on his face he caught his reflection in the mirror. The man staring back was familiar yet haggard, haunted. Most terrifying were his own eyes: twin blue orbs flickering on the edge of madness.

No wonder the detective suspected me Jake thought bitterly. *That look—like I'm hiding something darker.*

He straightened, wiped the last tear from his cheek, and headed back to the kitchen. Suppressing his pain by burying himself in work had long become second nature.

Jake placed one sodium lamp in the second-floor hallway where the motion detectors could saturate the area with the blinding light. The installation was simple—like changing a bulb —but measured carefully to balance safety and efficacy. The fixture hung high enough to avoid anyone touching it and low enough to be effective.

Downstairs the task was grimmer. He rigged the second lamp into the contraption concealed within the artificial fireplace logs —a temporary measure borne of necessity. Mounting it properly on the wall would require more time than he had before nightfall.

The motion detector itself was a masterpiece, one of Jake's proudest creations. Using sound, movement, or shifts in light, it triggered alarms or light bursts instantly. He also left a sonic alarm in place. Together, the system was their best shot at standing against the dark creatures.

Finishing his work, Jake glanced at the clock. It was past four and December's short days promised sunset soon. As he moved heavy logs aside, activating the device's 'watch mode'—ready to flare to life at the slightest disturbance—he left it unplugged for safety.

Dinner preparations began, but Jake's mind hovered over the disturbances at Sally's place, the mysterious power outages that left unanswered questions. He made a silent vow to double-check all of his own battery backups after the meal.

At half-past six Teresa arrived home, calm and composed. She walked inside with the ease of a woman who'd long mastered her household's chaos. The tension between her and Jake was taut yet unspoken.

Teresa asked Amanda about her day, eliciting terse grunts and curt answers. The girl, bright and warm with her father, grew cautious and withdrawn around her mother—guarding herself against words that might backfire.

Amanda finished eating quickly and asked to be excused.

"Of course, honey," Teresa replied, her voice polite but cool. Jake noted with surprise how little Amanda had eaten—and that Teresa herself had barely touched her food.

Amanda skipped off to watch television, and Teresa reclaimed the girl's plate, her eyes locking on Jake's with an unreadable expression.

"So?" she demanded, voice sharp as a blade.

Jake braced, going over what he wanted to say in his mind.

But Teresa was having none of it. "I'm waiting. And don't make shit up," she added, her stare icy.

Jake glanced toward Amanda's retreating back. "Teresa!"

"She can't hear. Now, tell me what happened. How did you find a dead body?"

He sighed, defeat settling deep in his bones. The truth spilled out—his first meeting with Sally, the later discovery of Shawn, his secret visits and quiet support. He cast it all as concern for the boy.

Teresa's lips pressed thin. For the first time in their marriage she said nothing.

When he finished, Teresa rose sharply. Jake stood as well, tension crackling between them.

"Sit!" Her bark stopped him cold.

She moved to the kitchen, started the kettle, then ascended the back stairs to Amanda's room. Voices carried faintly down the hall.

"I don't care what time it is—you get your pajamas on and get in bed. If you're not ready when I come back, there's gonna be trouble."

A muffled whine. Amanda scurried to comply.

Teresa returned tea in hand, sat at the table, and silently slid a slip of paper across to Jake.

"What's this?"

"The lawyer's number. Criminal law. If I wanted a divorce I'd be calling him myself." She stirred sugar with calm menace. "If I had a brain, I'd open the front door and put you—and your clothes—out on the lawn."

"You're angry."

"Angry? Amanda mouthing off to me when I tell her to go to bed pisses me off. You lying to me all these years—that's a whole other level of bullshit."

"I thought if you knew about Shawn—"

"Oh, shove it up your ass, Jake," she spat, voice rising. "You're only telling me now because you want to get the kid a lawyer."

Jake's mouth went dry.

"You think I'm stupid? You think I don't see what's going on? Were you banging that slut?"

Rage flared in him at the slur. "No."

"Don't lie!"

She stood, the hot tea trembling in her hand like a weapon.

"We have to help the boy," Jake whispered, watching the cup like a hawk.

"Why? Because he sees things? Like you?"

Again, Jake was speechless.

Teresa's eyes glittered triumphantly. "See? You think I'm stupid. Ten years of marriage, and you think I don't know you're scared at night? This house rigged with alarms, the lights left on, the endless nights tinkering? How dense do you think I am?"

The flood of realization hit Jake. His fear, his obsession—she'd known about it all the time.

"Your stupid Ecuadorian wife can't figure out what you do, huh? You ignore me, lie to me; you're one cold, unfeeling bastard."

"Well, you ought to know cold," Jake snapped bitterly. "Or is frigid the correct word?"

Her glare sharpened. "You know why you never screwed her? You don't have the balls—"

"Teresa, stop!"

"Make me, you pussy!"

There was something unsettling in her eyes—not just fury, but something darker. Longing, fierce and wild.

Jake straightened, towering over her. "Actually, I did screw her."

"I knew it!" she hissed, turning away.

"You knew nothing."

"You haven't touched me in months. What else was I supposed to think?"

"You don't even sleep in the same bed with me!"

"So it's my fault you screw around?"

"I work, I cook, I run this house—and get nothing but cold shoulders."

"Don't forget your late nights sneaking downstairs to tinker. If you wanted affection, come and get it."

"And be turned down again?"

"If you were a real man you'd take it!"

They stood, furious and breathless, and in that moment, Jake felt an overwhelming, desperate desire for her—the woman beside him who sparked his rage and lust in equal measure.

He closed the gap, his arms around her.

"Leave me alone, you bastard," she warned breathlessly.

He pressed his lips to hers. To his shock she pulled him closer, grabbing the back of his head and drawing him fiercely into a battle of tongues.

Jake let her go, surprised by this response. She glared at him as she made a decision. Grabbing Jake's arm, she pulled him into the kitchen, then opened the small half-bathroom and guided him in. She stepped in and turned the lock on the door.

"What are you doing?" Jake blurted.

"You want some affection?" Teresa growled, then turned away from him and pulled her dress up. She pulled down her panties and wiggled her hindquarters under his gaze. "Then take it."

Jake dropped his pants without hesitation, moved behind her, and entered her with such force she squealed.

As they moved together and he pushed into her like never before, his anger and fear focused on the place their anatomies intertwined, as he sought more than pleasure, but redemption.

She grabbed a hand towel, put it over her mouth, and screamed unabashedly into it. This pushed Jake over the edge, and they both moaned and whimpered as their bodies twitched from the onslaught.

They stayed linked, Teresa supporting herself on the sink. Jake slid free and sat on the closed toilet, reeling from the intensity of the experience. He sat there and tried to make sense of it all.

Teresa finally composed herself, took a washcloth, dampened it and delicately washed herself between her legs. Even this mundane cleanup seemed unbelievably sexy.

Dressing swiftly, she glared. "Put your pants on."

She unlocked the door, grabbing her underwear as she left, slamming it behind her.

Jake sat alone on the cold seat, stunned by the woman who had reclaimed him in tempest and fire.

He cleaned up quietly, dressed, and emerged to find Teresa poised with tea, the faintest smile playing on her lips.

He opened his mouth; no words came.

She laughed, a soft, triumphant sound that made Jake laugh too, though unsure whether the joke was on him.

He pulled her into his arms, kissing the delicate skin of her neck.

"What was that about?" he murmured.

"I don't know," she smiled, freeing herself gently. "Claiming territory? I always wanted a nice man, but when we met you had that dangerous edge. I saw it again tonight... and I wanted you."

He kissed her again, awed.

"That was the most intense—I mean—I never—"

"Me, too," she giggled, then added seriously, "But if you ever cheat again, I'll cut your dick off."

They let the weight of secrets fall away. That night, they went upstairs together, stripped bare in every way, and lay tangled in sheets and each other's arms.

For the first time in years, Teresa slept in Jake's bed, and for once, Jake didn't have to face the night alone.

31. HELPING SHAWN

T he next morning, Jake's fingers tightened around the steering wheel as he navigated the slow crawl of traffic toward Plainfield.

The sky hung heavy with gray, matching the weight in his chest.

Pulling into the cracked asphalt lot of the police station he sat for a moment gathering himself, before sliding from the car.

Dressed in full uniform, Jake looked every bit the cop—more so than some of the jaded men inside these walls. The badge on his chest felt heavier today.

He waited, pacing nervously just outside the main entrance, his boots echoing on the concrete. Hours ago, the world had shifted beneath his feet—Shawn, his boy, drawn into a system that felt cold and unyielding.

When Detective Walden finally emerged, his shoulders hunched and tie askew, staring at the cracked pavement as if hoping the day might somehow right itself, Jake approached him cautiously.

"Detective Walden?" Jake's voice was steady though his throat was dry.

Walden glanced up, his eyes tired but alert. "Yeah? What now?"

Jake swallowed his apprehension. "Detective, it's Jake Hurd. I'm trying to find out about Shawn O'Brien."

Walden's eyes narrowed, recognition flickering grudgingly. "Hurd, huh?"

Jake nodded, trying not to sound desperate. "I just want to know what happened to my boy."

The detective sighed, rubbing the stubble on his face as if trying to scrape off the weight of the entire case. "Look, Mr. Hurd... I'm not obligated to tell you anything," he said gruffly. Then, as if convincing himself, he leaned in. "What the hell? They sent O'Brien to Biscayne, but you didn't hear it from me."

Jake blinked, surprised. "Biscayne? Isn't that... in Louisiana?"

Walden shook his head sharply. "No, Biscayne's the state psych ward for juveniles. Here in New Jersey. It's south, down the Garden State Parkway."

"Where exactly?" Jake pressed.

"Farmingdale. Near Exit 98."

Jake felt an icy knot tighten in his stomach. "Couldn't they put him somewhere closer? Somewhere better?"

Walden lifted an eyebrow. "You want him to end up in Greystorm?"

Jake shuddered visibly. "No, not that place."

"Biscayne's no palace," Walden admitted, "but it's better than lockup." He placed a rough hand on Jake's shoulder. "Look, I didn't want the kid to suffer, you know?"

Jake forced a small smile, uneasy but grateful for Walden's rare softness. "You seem a lot friendlier than the other night."

Walden shrugged, half amused. "Forensic evidence backs up your story. And I checked you out—everyone says you're a stand-up guy. Hell, you don't even have an overdue parking ticket."

"Thanks… I guess." Changing tack, Jake asked, "Did you find out why the streetlights were out on that street when I arrived?"

Walden shook his head. "No. One of the many puzzles here. You say the entire block blacked out, but no one's backing you up. Not a single witness."

"What? Nobody else saw the lights were out?" Jake's voice cracked with disbelief.

"Not one," Walden confirmed and walked off.

"Thanks," Jake murmured into the heavy silence, turning back to his car.

Behind the wheel Jake pulled the New Jersey state road map from his glove compartment, thumb hovering over Farmingdale on the index. The town sat alone halfway down the coast near Exit 98.

The round trip would be at least three hours, longer than Jake wanted to spend away from home. But he had to see Shawn.

He stopped at a nearby 7-11 off Route 22, the smell of stale coffee and warm butter filling the air as he grabbed a roll and a steaming cup.

On the rack by the door newspapers screamed the grim headline: *Local Woman Found Dead in Gruesome Scene.*

The papers plastered Sally's death across every front page, a morbid feast of graphic detail. They kept Shawn's name hidden citing his age, but the story made Jake's stomach churn.

They mentioned an 'Unnamed Good Samaritan' who discovered her.

Behind the counter, a gruff voice broke his reverie. "Are you buyin' that? This ain't no damn library."

Jake replaced the paper gently as if it might shatter and forced a polite, "No, thanks."

Outside, he used the payphone to call the medical lab handling the blood tests. A receptionist answered, her tone clipped but polite.

"Mr. Hurd? We can't give medical records over the phone without proper ID."

"It's urgent. The boy and his mother were in an accident." Jake's voice softened, trying to convey the gravity.

"Oh—that's concerning," she said, shuffling papers. "According to the tests, there's an eighty-five percent chance you're the boy's father."

Jake's breath caught. The truth he had silently hoped for was real.

"Thank you," he whispered, hanging up, heart pounding.

His watch read 9:15. Time was slipping through his fingers. Amanda would be home at three and he still had to meet with the lawyer. Planning, moving forward—it all felt like walking through fog.

He called the attorney, securing a mid-afternoon appointment, then bolted toward the Parkway, knuckles white on the wheel.

A nervous energy buzzed beneath his skin—a mix of hope and dread.

They'd locked Shawn up in a juvenile psych ward. If it was anything like Greystorm—the stories whispered in the shadows—his boy wouldn't last long without breaking.

Jake's mind spun with images: Shawn surrounded by troubled kids, cut off from light, haunted by voices only he could hear, spiraling into despair.

As he drew closer, battered signs greeted him:

DR. ALFRED BISCAYNE
PSYCHIATRIC CENTER FOR MINORS
NEXT LEFT

The road curved up a hill past leafless trees casting naked shadows on brown grass. A rusted chain-link fence, crowned with barbed wire glinting wickedly even in the weak sunlight, reared up.

It was a prison disguised as a care facility.

Jake followed signs for 'Admissions,' approaching a vast stone mansion, Gothic arches clawing at the sky. The grandeur betrayed cracks—fallen cornices, warped doors, and shattered windows left unrepaired. The air smelled musty, heavy with neglect.

An elderly woman behind the admissions desk barely looked up.

"Can I help you?" she intoned, voice flat as peeling paint.

"I'm here to see Shawn O'Brien," Jake said, steady but expectant.

She scrutinized him in his uniform, as if he were a stain on a white shirt. "Is he going to trial today?"

"No. I'm a visitor. His uncle."

The woman's face hardened. "O'Brien, you say?" She thumbed through a worn folder. "It says here he has no relatives."

"That must be a mistake." Jake smiled, trying to inject warmth.

"Not the first time," she muttered, closing the file. "An orderly will escort you."

Moments later a mountain of a man in green scrubs appeared. He was over seven feet tall with a shaved head and a thick mustache that looked like he'd trapped a caterpillar beneath his nose.

"Harold, this man's here to see O'Brien," the woman said, nodding to big man.

"Yeah?" Harold grunted, sizing Jake up. "That kid's trouble."

Jake held up his hands in apology. "Sorry to hear that."

"He needs the light on all night," Harold muttered. "Keeps the others awake. We moved him to a cottage—isolated. More work with him on suicide watch."

Harold shook his massive head as if the weight of Shawn's troubles rested squarely on him.

"Can you take him?" the woman suggested.

Harold led Jake down shadowed halls—majestic woodwork now scarred, once glossy oak floors worn thin with dirt. Doors and ceilings loomed with old-world grandeur but decay whispered in every corner.

Suddenly, they stepped into the biting chill of the outside air. Jake shivered; Harold merely shrugged.

They approached a two-story cottage in much better repair: windows intact, the doors dead-bolted tight on both sides. Harold used his keys to unlock the door with a heavy click.

The cottage was modest—a living room doubled as a kitchen, cramped but functional. At the end of a short hall, stairs led up.

"He's up there," Harold said, collapsing onto a battered couch and flipping on a flickering television.

Jake ascended the stairs, the harsh glow of a 200-watt bulb glaring like an interrogation light. No door at the top barred his path—just a transom beyond which lay a small bedroom.

Inside, Shawn lay tangled in twisted sheets, asleep with the serene face of a cherub. His pale, almost translucent skin and tousled blonde hair made him look fragile—like he might shatter at any moment.

Jake knelt beside him, softly shaking his shoulder and whispering, "Shawn."

The boy's eyes fluttered open, panic flashing. He recoiled into a corner, eyes wide and untrusting.

"It's me, Shawn. Uncle Jake."

Recognition dawned slowly, the tension in Shawn's body melting as he flung himself across the bed and wrapped Jake in a fierce embrace.

"Uncle Jake! I knew you'd come!" The words spilled in a jumble as Jake stroked his hair, soothing him.

"Shh, it's okay. It'll be all right." Jake held him until the boy relaxed. "I'm going to see a lawyer today."

Shawn seemed smaller now—no longer the confident twelve-year-old from days ago but a child hollowed by fear and confinement.

Jake asked. "How is it here? Are they treating you okay?"

"They put me in the main house," Shawn explained, voice low, "but I wanted the light on, and the other kids got mad."

"Really?"

"So I came here. It's alright. I eat in the main building, but gotta wear with a coat to go."

"I met Harold."

"Yeah, he's something, ain't he?" Shawn smiled slyly. "Complains all the time, but I think he likes me. He's teaching me checkers."

Jake pulled out the little notebook always in his pocket and scribbled a number on a page. "I haven't forgotten about you. Here's my number—have them call me if you need me."

Half an hour passed before a small, gentle nurse appeared carrying pills. Shawn took them grudgingly, complaining, "All I do is sleep."

"It's okay, Shawn. I have to go meet the lawyer." Jake watched the nurse leave, then whispered, "Have you had any trouble with the shadows?"

"No. Whatever they give me keeps me from hearing them. And the lights keep them away." Tears welled up in Shawn's eyes. His voice trembled. "I'm so sorry about M-M—" He choked and shook violently.

Jake pulled him into a tight hug. "It's okay. It was terrible, but we'll get through this."

"You're all I have left, Uncle Jake."

"That's going to have to be enough, son." Jake gently lifted Shawn's chin, locking eyes "Your mother is gone, but you still have your father."

Shawn stared back, eyes wide.

"Remember the blood test? It was to prove it." Jake took a breath. "I'm your father."

"Why didn't you tell me? Why'd you make me think—"

"I wanted to for the longest time. But your mother didn't want you to get hurt."

Jake's anger flared. "I don't see how it would hurt to know who my dad is."

"I have another family," he admitted quietly, "and I didn't know about you until years after you were born. 'Uncle Jake' was a compromise."

Shawn's eyelids drooped, exhaustion overtaking his anger.

"Get some rest. I'll visit soon."

"Okay, Uncle Jake." Shawn pulled the blankets over his shoulders like a weary old man.

Jake descended the stairs where Harold waited, his towering frame filling the room.

"You done?"

Jake nodded.

"Goin' back to sleep?"

Another nod. Harold locked the door behind them, escorting Jake back through the main building to admissions.

Before leaving Jake asked about visiting hours and phone numbers. The woman at the desk gave him curt, bare-bones information.

Sliding into his '76 Mustang Stallion, Jake gripped the wheel as the engine roared to life. He felt heavier than when he'd arrived —shaken by his fears and the harsh truth.

But at least now his boy knew who he really was.

Jake's eyelids felt heavy with exhaustion but his hands gripped the steering wheel firmly. The long drive to the lawyer's office drained him, yet he knew this couldn't wait.

Despite the fatigue gnawing at him Jake arrived at Arthur Prentis' building with time to spare. He sat in the car for a moment, taking deep breaths, steadying himself before finally stepping inside.

The secretary greeted him briefly before showing him into the inner sanctum—a glass-paneled office that held an air of seriousness.

Arthur Prentis himself was nothing like the imposing figure Jake imagined. Instead, he was a compact man with graying hair and a trim beard, his eyes sharp and a touch inquisitive. Despite his size, an energetic presence filled the room as Arthur rose and extended his hand with a firm grip.

As Jake launched into the story of the slain Sally O'Brien, Arthur's attention never wavered.

But barely a minute into Jake's account of discovering Sally's body, the lawyer raised a hand to halt him. With practiced efficiency, Arthur pulled out a folded newspaper and pointed to the headline on page one. The bold print detailed the case.

"That's it," Jake confirmed, voice low.

"'Unnamed Good Samaritan', huh?" Prentis's brow furrowed skeptically. "And what are they charging you with?"

Jake shook his head. "Me? Nothing. But the boy—the one accused—Shawn O'Brien? He needs a lawyer."

Arthur arched an eyebrow, leaning forward. "Why would you take on his defense? What's your stake in this?"

Jake swallowed hard, voice catching. "He's my son."

The words hung in the air, thick with unspoken history. Arthur leaned back, measuring the weight of the confession. "And where is he now?"

"In Biscayne, locked up tight."

For the next hour Arthur peppered Jake with detailed questions, jotting notes furiously on a legal pad. He scrutinized everything: the paternity test, minute discrepancies, motives, and timelines.

"After all," he noted, "you didn't see Shawn kill his mother. You only found him holding a bloody knife, babbling incoherently."

Jake nodded, then confided Detective Walden's suspicions—that Jake himself might be involved.

Prentis tapped his pen thoughtfully. "Wrong target. We need to prove someone else was there before you arrived. You knew Sally well?"

"Yes."

"Did she ever have violent friends? Men who might want to harm her?"

Jake mentioned the one who fled town after leaving Sally bruised and empty-handed. Arthur wrote the name with a grim nod.

By mid-afternoon the interrogation eased. Jake signed a retainer check for a thousand dollars but more importantly, he felt a flicker of hope. Arthur Prentis, Esquire, appeared more than capable.

Driving home, Jake was a bundle of conflicting emotions—exhaustion mingled with cautious optimism. Amanda would be home from school soon. He braced himself for the familiar warmth of family life after the legal chaos.

Back at the house Jake brewed another pot of coffee, though the caffeine churned in his stomach like a storm.

Amanda arrived, eager for her snack and their usual after-school chatter before retreating to her homework.

Jake set the alarm clock for five, climbed into bed, but sleep eluded him. The caffeine and anxiety warred inside him, pushing him into a fevered dream. He ran across a dusky plain chased by shadowy riders atop fiery black steeds, their burning nostrils blazing as they closed in.

The alarm gnawed at his senses. He woke tense and uneasy, the nightmare's echo lingering.

That evening, Jake was determined to restore some normalcy. After the turmoil of the previous night and the fragile truce with Teresa he wanted to make the night special. He cooked dinner, deciding to uncork a bottle of red wine from the basement's dusty collection.

But when he flipped on the basement lights and stepped down the stairs, the sight that greeted him froze him in place. On his workbench lay one of his latest inventions—a delicate sound detector—shattered into jagged pieces.

His mind raced. Was it a warning? A threat? Or something more sinister?

With a growing knot in his gut Jake retreated upstairs to finish preparing dinner. The earlier buoyancy dissolved, replaced by a creeping dread.

The icy darkness of Sally's house—the sudden loss of power— pulled at him, and he debated whether to keep vigil through the night.

Dinner was a hollow exercise, routine and mechanical, though Teresa and Amanda smiled appreciatively. Jake opened the wine; Teresa savored her glass but Jake sipped nervously, fingers twitching with unease.

Amanda soon scampered upstairs to watch TV leaving Jake to clear the table while Teresa slipped into pajamas and settled on the couch. He joined her, the soft glow from the Christmas tree casting multicolored patches across the room, oddly comforting amid unresolved tensions.

She smiled, breaking the silence. "Why so quiet tonight?"

Jake forced a smile. He appreciated her effort to bridge the gap between them. "It's nice to see you like this."

"Like what?"

"Being nice. We used to be a lot nicer to each other."

Theresa shrugged. "Can we light a fire?"

Jake agreed, setting about the task. He unplugged the Christmas lights briefly, replaced the sodium lamp and fake logs with real ones, and carefully ignited a crackling fire. Teresa nestled close on the sofa, sighing contentedly, and they spoke quietly of Christmas cards and presents yet to be bought.

Later, Jake sent Amanda to bed, cuddling her close before she disappeared upstairs. As he and Teresa settled back on the sofa, she turned seriously to him.

"Jake?" she began.

"Yeah?"

"I have one thing I must insist on—all of this," she gestured vaguely.

"What's that?"

"That Amanda knows nothing—about any of it."

Jake studied her face, earnest and protective. "I wouldn't want her to. She needs to be protected."

Teresa leaned into him, voice soft but firm. "That's why I never threw you out."

He sighed, relieved yet burdened by past wounds.

"One 'roll in the hay' will not fix everything," she added, half-smiling.

"We've both got to change," he acknowledged, caressing her dark hair.

They peeled back layers of old resentment—Teresa confessed her anger at him during Amanda's birth, the months of separation —and Jake admitted his regrets.

"I'm done running," he vowed. "I want us to work."

"Do you think we can?"

Without hesitation Jake suggested, "We could… sleep together tonight."

She turned in surprise. "Sleep?"

"Well, share the bed, anyway."

A playful smile crossed her face. "Has that ever happened?"

"Obviously," Jake teased, "or we wouldn't have Amanda."

They laughed softly, watching the fire. Teresa asked, sheepishly, "Can we turn the lights down upstairs? I'm… not as skinny as I used to be."

Jake grinned. "You weren't skinny when I married you."

"It helps me relax," she said.

"Alright. Tell you what. I'll bank back the fire, check the doors and come up in about ten minutes."

"See you up there," she said, heading upstairs.

Still uneasy—haunted by the broken device in the basement— Jake checked the house's security systems, locking the doors and putting the metal cover in front of the logs that had burned down to ash.

Finally, he went upstairs and stopped at the hall closet to activate his nighttime protections.

Going into the dimly lit bedroom, he found Teresa lying on the bed, naked, her strong, full figure glowing warmly in the candlelight.

He retrieved baby oil from the nightstand, warming it in his hands, and massaged her.

Her gentle moans and relaxed sighs drowned out the worries in his mind. The sturdy, comforting weight of her body beneath his fingertips was a balm after the past harrowing days.

"Oh, that's good," she sighed, arching into his touch.

Playfully, he smacked her rear end gently, earning a mock protest.

For nearly an hour, Jake worked every muscle, his own exhaustion fading in the moment's warmth. They made love slowly, tenderly, a silent promise of fresh start.

When they finally rested Teresa nestled close. Jake closed his eyes, feeling something fragile and new sparking between them—a fragile hope amid the dark storm swirling just beyond their walls.

It's a new beginning, Jake thought as exhaustion overwhelmed him and he fell asleep.

32. The Attack

Jake sank into a sleep deeper than he had known for years—perhaps decades.

The crushing weight of the day and exhaustion from sleepless nights long past finally wore him down.

The wine he'd shared with Teresa, the warmth of their embrace, the lingering touch of her skin—all conspired to ease him into what felt like a precious peace.

For the first time in a long time, Jake slept at night.

His dreams carried him to a place bathed in warm light, glowing softly with countless Christmas trees twinkling in festive splendor.

There, Peggy, Sally, and Teresa waited, each dressed in rich red velvet, perched inside an old-fashioned sleigh that seemed pulled straight from the jingling melodies of a child's Christmas song.

The three women rose, smiling gently and holding out brightly wrapped gifts. Among them stood Shawn.

Jake smiled, convinced that Santa Claus himself could not be far behind in this idyllic snow globe.

"Daddy," a small voice whispered—barely audible, seeming to drift from a great distance.

Jake turned, a sudden chill rippling beneath the warm gloss of the dream. Someone was missing.

The voice came again, a little louder, filled with raw fear: "Daddy."

He scanned the scene once more. Something was terribly wrong.

Where was Amanda?

Peggy remained where she was, but now her radiant, crimson velvet transformed into something grotesque. Her skin had dried and tightened, clinging to her skull like brittle parchment. Her eye sockets were empty voids. The hands that had held the gift now resembled dead, brown skeletal claws with blackened, jagged nails.

Jake froze, cold terror ripping through his chest.

Yet Teresa and Sally stood as though untouched, their smiles unbroken and serene. Or so it seemed.

His focus shifted to Sally—her dress no longer crimson velvet but stark white, stained and soaked in dark, coagulated blood. Her lifeless eyes unmoving, the jagged cut across her throat and multiple stab wounds painted a scene of unspeakable violence.

And lurking just beyond the sleigh's ornate frame, behind the flickering lights and evergreens, shadows crept—they waited, hunched and hungry. Silent predators with nightmare forms, ready to pounce, to drag him down into their suffocating darkness.

"DADDY!" the voice screamed now, raw with desperation.

Jake fought to break free of the dream, clawing at the night's thick veil.

He bolted upright, heart pounding, sweat icy cold against his skin. His feet hit the floor with a sharp tingle. Around him, candlelight flickered, half of the candles burnt to stubbed shadows.

"Mmmph?" Teresa murmured, her voice a soft tether pulling him back from the edge.

Jake's mind raced. The dream, the voice—it wasn't gone. His ears strained into the empty night.

A distant, muffled cry echoed in the silence.

"Amanda," he croaked, voice hoarse and unsteady.

He flung open the hallway door, and stepped out into suffocating blackness, denser than any night he'd ever known— like an endless void at the end of a blind alley—swallowed him.

But there should have been light.

His emergency system was foolproof: backup lamps powered by a car battery in the attic, designed to cast powerful illumination even if the main power failed. Optical sensors were supposed to trigger them.

Yet here in the oppressive dark, there was only the total absence of light. Even the windows facing the street which should have been lit by streetlights were dark.

Jake clapped his hands desperately, trying to activate his devices, but the sound stirred only Teresa who shifted uneasily.

"What is it?" she whispered, sleep thick in her voice as she drew herself upright, strands of hair shadowing her face, one breast slipping free beneath the sheet.

Jake hastily pulled on his pajamas and reached for the heavy flashlight wedged beneath his bedside table. The beam cut through the black with bold defiance, slicing open the hallway shadows.

"It's Amanda!" he urged, voice thin and brittle.

Teresa's eyes snapped open. She bolted from the bed. "Where is she? And where's the damn light?"

"I don't know!" Jake whispered.

"I'm naked!" she shot back, as if this accusation alone could explain the chaos.

"Get dressed!" he hissed and tossed her a pajama top from his closet and they moved into the hall together. His pajama top hung loose on Teresa. She rolled up the sleeves, clinging to Jake like a lifeline.

"Amanda!" Jake called again, voice breaking.

Suddenly a scream echoed—frantically desperate, fragmenting the darkness.

A fierce voice tore through his mind: *They are here! Everywhere! All around you!*

And then, piercing in its clarity: "Daddy!" Amanda's wail reverberated, chilling and echoed by unseen walls.

"Ah!" Teresa shrieked in terror. "Something just brushed past me!"

"We have to find her. Now!" Jake snapped. He felt things— wet and scaly—whip past his legs like rat tails or leathery bat wings.

"OW!" Teresa cried out, faltering. Jake turned and caught her making the flashlight's beam swing wildly.

"Something cut me, Jake!" she gasped.

Jake shone the beam to the floor. A shard of glass, thin and cruel, glistened faintly—lay on the wooden floor.

A single drop of blood trickled down Teresa's ankle.

"What is happening?" she demanded, voice rising in panic.

"Keep moving," Jake urged. They reached Amanda's bedroom door. He flung it open, aiming the flashlight in.

Teresa pulled close under his arm, trembling.

"Amanda!" he shouted, dread clawing his throat.

"Daddy!" the voice screamed again, but this time Jake recognized it echoing from the bathroom.

Teresa gasped. "Oh God, my baby!"

He charged down the hall, Teresa clutching him. Jake heard whispers slithering through the air—hissing, a sound like knives rasping flesh from bone.

Jake yanked open the bathroom door, flashlight pitching wildly. Shapes writhed and tumbled fleeing the searing beam.

There—on top of the closed toilet—sat Amanda, legs pulled tight, screaming with raw terror. Cuts marred her face as she shrieked uncontrollably.

With Herculean effort, Jake scooped her up, brandishing the beam like a shield against the darkness.

Teresa remained close, sobbing quietly.

"I have to get to the panel," Jake barked. "Teresa, hold Amanda!"

"I can't!" she choked out, clutching their daughter desperately.

The darkness pressed in, invisible fingers sliding over Jake's skin, choking him with cold and pressure. His limbs burned as if caught in a vise of shadow.

He pushed his way out of the bathroom and fought his way to the cold metal box embedded in the wall.

The steel door groaned as he yanked it open and Jake felt invisible fingers clawing at his hands to stop him.

His finger found the small red button—his final emergency switch he installed years ago but never dared to use.

Jake held the button for five seconds, a precaution in case he ever brushed it accidentally. He felt tentacles of darkness pull at his hand to disengage it but Jake held on tight and moved his lips as he counted the passing seconds.

He released the button and turned his back to the wall, feeling invisible hands slide against his face and body. Jake knew that slivers of glass could replace the soft touches but there was nothing he could do.

If the shadows could shut off the household electricity and all of his battery units, then the system reactivation button might not help.

Teresa and Amanda had the flashlight, but he could hear them screaming. Jake prayed they weren't being ripped apart.

"Oh, God!" Jake yelled.

His terror needed release. He couldn't see the light he'd left with Teresa, the darkness so thick that it was impassable even for the bright beam. It might have been for nothing. Without electricity the system couldn't reset the alarms, wouldn't go active.

The three of them would die here in the dark, in this ocean of blackness, suffocated by the hundreds—maybe thousands—of invisible hands.

Jake felt the weight crushing down on him. He couldn't fathom how things with no physical form could do it, but he heard a sound above his own screams.

A high-pitched whine.

There was something pulsing in the darkness, becoming clearer with each flash.

The hall came into focus and cleared around him. Two huge lights were throbbing rhythmically at both ends of the hall. One of them, the sodium light, flashed with a reddish tint, the illumination so bright that it was like a miniature sun. He felt the heat it gave off with each pulse.

Finally, the hall brightened. The harsh pulses turned the darkness to burning light and the invisible presences recoiled.

Jake flipped switches, stabilizing the illumination. The sonic alarm—a piercing, mind-shredding whine—stopped, clearing the ringing in his head.

He carefully peeked around the corner, half afraid he would find his wife and child with their throats slit, their lifeblood puddled in a red lake around them.

In the bathroom, he found Teresa huddled on top of their daughter, protecting her with her own body as a shield. Jake's breath caught in his throat, but he saw Teresa's breathing.

Jake touched Teresa's shoulder. She flinched, recoiling fiercely.

"Don't touch me!" she hissed, clutching Amanda tighter, the pajama top torn with small cuts, like made with a razor..

Amanda released a shrill scream, a wail that echoed through Jake's bones.

"It's okay," Jake whispered, brushing Teresa's hair back. She looked at him with eyes wide and frightened, scratches marking her face and hands.

Jake's gaze dropped to shards of glass scattered on the floor.

The bathroom light flickered weakly and came on.

"We need a doctor," Jake insisted, gently taking Teresa's hand.

"No!" she snapped fiercely, barely letting go of their daughter. "I'm not leaving this house."

"It's safe now," Jake reassured her softly.

"That's why I'm not leaving," she said as she freed her hand from his grip and clutched Amanda as her shrieks quieted into sobs. "What happened?"

Jake knew, but if he told her, would that increase the danger for her?

"I need to check everything," Jake said firmly. "But I can't leave you alone. Come with me."

Teresa nodded, reluctant but resolute.

He bent down and picked up Amanda. The child clung tightly to him, unwilling to be separated.

Together, the small family moved down the staircase bathed in the bright floodlight.

Jake reached the living room and put Amanda on the sofa. She was loath to let go.

"No, Daddy, no!" she pleaded.

"It's okay. It's only for a minute," Jake soothed. She relented and sat on the sofa, her nightgown a tangled mess.

Jake turned to his wife, pulled off his robe, and put it on her.

"You're ripped," he said, and she noticed the large tear in the cloth that exposed her nipple. She took the robe and wrapped it around her. Amanda immediately clung to her mother once again.

A flash of reflection caught his eye beneath the Christmas tree.

He paused and bent to pick up broken ornaments—shards of glass mingled with the fragments of their shattered peace. They cut him and his family with the glass from their own Christmas tree.

"You two stay here. I have to check the basement," Jake said.

"Let me look at her," Teresa whispered, forcing Amanda's chin up.

Jake walked carefully to the basement door. His hand hovered over the light switch, but a silent warning stopped him. Instead, he went back and got the flashlight from Teresa, and used it to light his way.

Jake said, "I'll be right back."

"Honey," Teresa said to Amanda, freeing herself from the child's desperate embrace. "I'm going to get some hydrogen peroxide to put on your cuts."

He watched Teresa go upstairs and turned for the basement.

"Daddy, can I plug in the tree?" Amanda asked.

"Sure, honey," Jake said without thinking as he turned the corner and descended the stairs, the flashlight lighting his path. The smell hit him before he could see it—sharp and suffocating: the unmistakable stench of gas.

He moved cautiously, using the flashlight to illuminate the far end of the workshop.

Glass crunched underfoot. Jake froze.

On the floor lay shattered fragments of a broken bulb. He raised the beacon to the light fixture on the ceiling.

Screwed in, replacing the regular bulb, was one of Jake's sodium lamps—the defective one that produced sparks when used. Jake moved away from the fixture and walked over to the gas meter and shined the light to find a small hole in the gas pipe.

Jake's fingers fumbled for the emergency valve and shut it off.

He shone the beam back to the lighting fixture, then slowly, carefully removed the lamp from the socket.

If I turned that on, a spark would've caused the entire house to blow up, Jake thought, as a fit of coughing from the fumes racked his body.

That's when he heard an alarm and a high-pitched scream ripped through the house—Amanda's scream—piercing, unbearable.

He bounded for the stairs, dizziness and fumes clawing at his lungs.

As he reached the door, Teresa ran down the stairs, panic written deep in her eyes.

"You left her alone!" he yelled, as a terrible smell of burnt flesh struck his nostrils.

Together they ran into the living room, intensely lit by the sodium lamp. Jake took one look and knew what had happened.

Amanda attempted to plug in the tree but plugged in his sodium lamp instead.

They reached the living room just in time to see Amanda's small body convulsing on the floor, the sodium lamp still plugged in.

Teresa shrieked and dropped to her knees, cradling their child.

Jake, blinded by the light, bent over and pulled the plug from the wall. The smoldering bulb had something on it, sizzling and smoking.

His eyes fell on the horror—the black roasting things, which smelled of overcooked meat were two of his daughter's fingers.

"Her hand! Oh God, her hand!" Teresa sobbed, trembling.

"You have to take her to a hospital!" Jake yelled.

"I can't!" she shrieked.

Jake's hand lashed out—slapping Teresa, shocking both of them into deadly silence.

"There's a gas leak downstairs," he said urgently. "I have to fix it. The shadows… they want me. It's safer if you go. You can get help. I'll come as soon as the house is safe."

"But her hand—" Teresa whimpered with tears in her eyes.

Jake looked at the small hand of his daughter. The two remaining fingers and thumb were black as was the palm, with the flesh white and dead around the blackness. Two bony remains stuck out where fingers should have been. Jake turned away, fighting to keep his dinner down.

"We don't have time for an ambulance," Jake insisted, gripping her shoulders. "The shock will kill her before they get here. You have to move now."

Reluctantly she nodded, and Jake carried Amanda to the back door.

The six outside floodlights flared on, blocking out the oppressive dark.

Jake wrapped the burnt hand with torn cloth, fighting nausea.

Teresa scrambled into a coat, clutching her purse.

"Morristown Memorial," Jake instructed. "It's the closest. Drive fast."

"It's so far," she gasped.

"Seven miles from the highway. Hurry."

Tires screeched as she sped away into the frozen night.

Left alone Jake shivered beneath the brutal floodlights.

He ascended the stairs and paused in their bedroom, hollow and ragged. Dressing quickly, he extinguished the remaining candles with trembling hands.

He could not leave—not until he sealed the gas leak.

Down in the basement, Jake found his drill lying among the debris—proof that the shadows had cunning beyond comprehension. He patched the pipe with epoxy resin, holding his breath as the minutes passed.

With a final twist, he reopened the valve and verified the pilot light flames at every appliance.

He even checked the machine in the hall closet that noted passing shapes. The machine registered numbers that began at two AM with the high point of activity being at three-thirty during the attack on Jake and his family.

According to the counter, hundreds of passing shapes filled the hall.

Empirical evidence flashed through Jake's mind. This one slip of paper was proof that the things were not a delusion. He held the paper and realized there was no one he could take it to.

His heart hardened into grim resolve.

He collected every broken sodium lamp bulb from the house and crushed them into dust with a rock, refusing to leave any vestige of that deadly invention.

Still, the image haunted him—the smoking black fingers, the bloodied bone, the final, unfathomable horror of his daughter's shattered hand.

He wanted to rush to the hospital, but the surrounding house stood empty in profound silence, a tomb waiting for its prey. He had to wait until dawn, when the house would be safe before he could leave.

As the first pale light of dawn crept across the sky Jake swung his truck onto the empty road.

He clicked on his headlights out of habit but the oppressive shadows had already dissolved with the coming day. The places where his enemy might have lurked—the dark corners, the hidden recesses—were gone now.

Yet a cold doubt gnawed at him. Did they rest? Did they sleep as he did during the day or were they creatures beyond such human frailties, always watching, always waiting?

The hospital lobby was quiet, the tension in Jake's gut coiling tighter with every step he took toward the reception desk. Behind it sat a woman in scrubs, her skin the rich hue of mahogany, her expression calm but guarded.

"Hello," Jake said, voice taut, "I'm Jake Hurd. My wife and daughter—they're here?"

She nodded with professional kindness. "Of course, Mr. Hurd. I'll get Dr. Klein for you right away." Without missing a beat, she lifted the phone to her ear and said softly, "Mr. Hurd is waiting."

Jake barely had time to process her words before the door swung open.

Two imposing police officers stood in the doorway, their heavy boots thudding softly against the tile.

Behind them came a tall woman with chestnut-brown hair pulled back neatly, her demeanor authoritative yet controlled. And then—hidden partially behind this woman—Jake caught a glimpse of Teresa.

"Teresa?" Jake's voice faltered, confusion and hope tangling together. "Is Amanda all right?"

The tall woman stepped forward, her voice cutting through the room with unequivocal clarity. "Can you identify this man, Mrs. Hurd?"

Jake's heart slammed against his ribs. It appeared that this woman was Dr. Klein.

Teresa's eyes darted around, settling on Jake as she nodded hesitantly. "That's my husband. Jake Hurd."

Jake's gaze sharpened, suspicion flaring. "Teresa, what exactly is going on here?"

One officer advanced toward him, hand reaching for Jake's arm with firm intention.

"Mr. Hurd, we need you to come with us," the officer said evenly.

"No!" The word burst out before Jake could stop it, and he jerked his arm free, stepping back defensively. His eyes pleaded with Teresa for answers. "Teresa, please—what is this?"

Dr. Klein's voice rang out, filled with cold finality. "What this is, Mr. Hurd, is an investigation into spousal abuse and child endangerment."

Jake's mind reeled. "What? That's impossible—I never—"

"You deny slapping your wife?" Dr. Klein pressed, voice sharp as a blade.

Jake's breath caught. "She was hysterical!"

Dr. Klein's eyes didn't waver. "And the bruises? The cuts from glass? Not accidental—meticulously slashed into the skin. Care to explain those, Mr. Hurd?"

The pair of officers moved swiftly, encircling Jake. He wanted to resist, to find words that might unravel this nightmare, but they grabbed his arms, pinning him tight. They slammed him against the wall with a shocking thud, and the steel kiss of metal cuffs encircled his wrists.

"You're under arrest, Mr. Hurd. You have the right to remain silent—"

"TERESA!" Jake's voice broke, raw with desperation, pressed against the cold wall. "Tell them what happened!"

The policeman's voice droned on, monotone and unyielding. "If you give up that right, anything you say can and will be used against you in a court of law."

"Tell them what happened!" Jake pleaded, heartbeat hammering in his ears.

"You have the right to an attorney—"

"Tell them we were under attack!"

"If you cannot afford an attorney, one will be appointed for you—"

"Teresa!" His voice softened, cracking. "Please—tell them the truth."

"Do you understand these rights?" the officer finished.

Jake barely managed a broken, "Yes," as they pulled him away from the wall. Each step felt heavier, the weight of betrayal and disbelief pressing down.

The two officers gripped him firmly as they marched him toward the exit.

"Tell them the truth," Jake whispered, eyes locked on Teresa's face—her lips pressed tight, her eyes cold.

Then, sharp and blazing, came the final blow. "He hit me!" Teresa spat, venom in her gaze.

"Teresa!" Jake's voice was almost a whisper now, anguish pure and raw, as the sunlight of the parking lot felt like a spotlight on his shattering world.

He knew then with crushing certainty, that the house in Basking Ridge was no longer his home.

It would be a place he'd return to only with a police escort, gathering the remnants of a life Teresa would pack up in sealed boxes.

His marriage—a battlefield scarred by his war— became one of the casualties.

HOLIDAYS

33. Empirical Evidence

I sat in the aging wooden chair of the Morris County Courthouse in Morristown on a biting Thursday morning, December 23rd.

Once again, I drowned beneath a tide of yellowing files and bureaucratic drudgery. Every step I took through those echoing hallways summoned fresh bundles of paperwork, each one a fragment of a long-buried court proceeding involving Jake Hurd, Teresa Quinga Hurd, and their daughter Amanda—a minor.

It was all caught in a web far darker than any I could have expected.

Empirical evidence. The phrase Jake uttered repeatedly now haunted me like a dark chant. It echoed in the chambers of my conscience, intertwining with my desperation to uncover the truth.

Behind the marble counter, the woman named Tina had become a familiar fixture in my days—once an impassable wall of office protocol, now something more pliable.

At first, Tina was an impenetrable fortress, a bureaucratic gatekeeper made of cold refusals and clipped answers.

But I found her weakness—her morning coffee ritual—a specific drink that I discovered and brought to her on my visits, just to show I cared. I played my part well, leaning into subtle psychological tactics that would have made Pavlov nod in appreciation.

Slowly she shifted from adversary to reluctant ally, even whispering the name of the key contact who controlled the sealed files I so desperately needed.

"Well, Dr. Lucas," she said today, her gray hair tucked into a more stylish updo than I'd seen before, the faintest spark of festive warmth in her eyes, "I got copies of the final divorce decree and the agreement between the parties."

I grabbed the fragile papers, my hands trembling slightly beneath the weight of decades-old secrets.

"Thank you, Tina," I said, my voice tight with relief. "Merry Christmas."

I slipped out of the courthouse into the brisk December air, settling behind the wheel of my Mercedes and heading towards the town square. By a rare stroke of luck, I scored a parking spot mere steps from the heart of the town.

The town decorated the square as 'Santa's Village'. Giant plywood soldiers and candy canes stood frozen in place, their bright paint dulled by years of winters..In the center, a small, makeshift house held a solitary teenager in a Santa suit. Near a sputtering space heater, his pillow belly budged with each uneasy movement.

There was something achingly sad in the scene.

Morristown's once-bustling shopping district now wore a cloak of quiet resignation as the new millennium loomed. The Bambergers had long since shuttered; many storefronts were dark and forgotten, eaten alive by the sprawling malls.

Epstein's, the sole remaining department store, barely clung to life. Gone were the days of elaborate animated windows, replaced by meager strings of holiday lights.

Mr. Epstein, himself Jewish like me, was a survivor thanks to the patronage of the wider community. Somewhere in that store, I knew a lonely menorah flickered against the encroaching gloom.

Crossing the street, I entered the warm, caffeinated refuge of a Starbucks—not for their drinks, but for the meeting I had arranged.

Public and open ground—a neutral zone.

I found her already seated—a woman with dusky-blonde hair cascading against olive-toned skin that demanded notice for her beauty.

Amanda Hurd.

From the back, she was a striking figure, her presence undeniable. My psychiatrist mask slipped effortlessly into place, a measured smile warming my face as I approached.

My eyes involuntarily flicked to her right hand, curled carefully in her lap. Her right hand was a stark testament to unspoken horrors—only a thumb and an index finger remained, scarred and twisted flesh carrying the fading traces of pain and countless surgeries.

She caught my gaze and lifted her hand deliberately, offering her left in greeting. I shook it gently.

"Ms. Hurd," I mumbled. "Thank you for meeting with me. Can I get you anything?"

"Yes," she replied, voice steady yet guarded. "A hot apple cider, please, Doctor." Her smile was tight, close-lipped—as if it held back storms.

Already, I sensed coaxing her story out would be a far steeper climb than the courthouse records.

I ordered our drinks, hot cider for her, a latte for me. I patted my pocket to confirm that a roll of Tums nestled there.

Returning to our table, I placed the drinks down gently.

"Thank you," she murmured, her manners crisp and graceful—so rare in that restless, cynical age.

Amanda was no ordinary woman. I'd learned she was the head of her own internet business, a self-driven titan running a multimillion-dollar empire. Yet she remained rooted in New Jersey, in stylish Montclair.

She placed her paper cup carefully on the table and looked directly into my eyes. "I don't know how I can help you, Dr. Lucas. I haven't seen Jake Hurd in twenty years, and frankly, I intend to keep it that way."

I hesitated only briefly. "I wanted to hear your side of the events around Christmas 1980. Your father—"

"Don't call him that," she cut me off sharply. "He was an abusive bastard who beat my mother and burned me."

She raised her damaged hand slowly, the twisted fingers etched with scars. "Look at this, Doctor. I'm lucky to still have even these two fingers. I've spent years wrestling with physical and mental wounds. If my mother hadn't dragged me to a hospital when she did, I'd be dead." She drew a shaky breath. "Jake Hurd didn't even leave the house for two hours. Probably needed to sober up."

Her words landed like stones in my chest. I nodded, silent.

"How much do you remember?" I asked softly.

"I was ten years old," she said. "Can you imagine what it's like to suffer this from your own father? Sometimes I wonder why he wasn't locked away as a madman long ago."

"You're angry," I observed.

"Brilliant, Doctor," she replied bitterly. "No, wait—you don't deserve that." The mask cracked; she took a sip and regained calm. "Forgive me. I can't face this with detachment."

"I understand. Do you recall other instances of abuse? Patterns?" I probed gently.

"I must've repressed them," she admitted. "My therapist says that it's common to do so."

"You're seeing a therapist?"

Her smirk was mysterious. "Dr. Anna Quayle."

I swallowed. Dr. Quayle was a post-feminist firebrand, known for her radical view that men psychologically dominated women —a theory that fueled every woman's illness according to her. Amanda's animosity would have found fertile ground there, and I knew better than to question her choice of care.

"Did you ever fear your father?" I asked.

"No!" Amanda's mouth tightened. "That's what made it worse —he abused me, yet made me love him. Dr. Quayle even suggests mind control."

"Mind control?"

"My memories are unreal. That night in 1980— the house plunged in darkness. I remember Mom shielding me while glass cut her, and I felt things, like hundreds of tiny hands were cutting us."

My throat went dry. It was nearly word for word what Jake told me. "Don't you doubt your father did it?"

She shook her head. "Mind control. He shut off all the lights in the house to terrify us." Her eyes grew distant, haunted. "I woke up surrounded by darkness. He probably blacked out the windows to throw me into that nightmare." She sat up straighter. "Psychological torture."

"Could it have been a power failure?" I suggested cautiously.

The smirk returned, sharp and knowing. "Little things hiding in the dark? Don't delude yourself, Doctor. My mother told me all about his paranoia, and how he wired the house with alarms, imprisoning us behind invisible bars." Her voice dropped. "Total dominance. Surprised you didn't recognize it—such a clear, self-serving delusion."

"So you think Jake acted out of a desire for control?" I pressed, curiosity piqued despite the swirl of emotions.

"It fits the pattern," she said, eyes gleaming. "Abusers isolate their victims, crush any outside contact. Then the abuse spirals." She nodded knowingly. "That's what he wanted."

"But your mother went to work, you went to school, you came and went as you pleased. I'm well acquainted with these patterns —from my years practicing at the state mental facility. I see murderers, psychotics, and men who are frighteningly sane but feign madness just to dodge prison. Jake Hurd, in my professional judgment, fits none of those categories. He's neither vicious nor abusive."

Her entire frame shifted, a sudden quiet settling around her as she leaned back slowly in her chair, as if letting the weight of my words sink in.

The frantic energy around her drained, replaced by an unsettling calm. "You know, Doctor, it's easy to take a neat narrative twenty years in the past and spin it into whatever story suits you. I was there. I survived it. And, for once, I was lucky enough to have people who actually helped me."

"Your mother?" I prompted cautiously.

Amanda's lips curved slightly—as if the mention of Teresa softened something inside her. "It wasn't just Teresa." She said it casually, as if dropping a small but critical fact. "There was Dr. Sylvia Klein—the woman my mother was beyond fortunate to find in that emergency room that night."

"I know about her," I replied. "She's now Chief of Pediatrics at Morristown Memorial, right?"

"The same." Pride crept into her voice, and for a moment, she looked almost radiant. "She's the 'Grande dame' of pediatrics these days, known especially for her work with abused children."

I nodded. "Her reputation's impeccable."

Amanda's gaze drifted upward, eyes unfocused, caught in memory's grip. "Six months after... that night, she moved in with us. She was a lifeline—for my mother and for me. She pushed me hard, refused to let me accept my 'accident'—that's what she called it. She wouldn't let me use it as an excuse to quit." She closed her eyes briefly. "Sometimes she even took me to the hospital, showed me other kids like me—kids who needed to be heard. Talking to them was... cathartic, part of the healing."

I nodded slowly, but inside I felt a gnawing unease. No matter the intent, these experiences seemed to anchor Amanda in the victim's role—a label she ought to have shed long ago.

The smug smile returned, sharper this time, like a razor hidden beneath a polished surface. It twisted her features into something calculating, as if she delighted in outsmarting me. The 'I-know-better-than-you' calm was far darker now.

"It's funny," she said, folding her arms, "not until I was twenty did I really figure out why Sylvia moved in. They had separate bedrooms, too."

I lowered my voice slightly, not wanting to miss the subtle cue. "You mean… Dr. Klein and your mother became lovers?"

Amanda nodded, as if revealing a secret treasure. "I put the pieces together in college and just asked them outright. My mother paced and wrung her hands before admitting the truth.. They'd been worried about how it might affect me so they kept it hidden."

"That wasn't unusual for gay couples back then," I offered. "Especially in the eighties with a child in the house. Discretion was everything."

Her eyes gleamed with a mixture of irony and defiance. "I told them to stop pretending. To just be together. And the next week Teresa moved into Sylvia's room. Imagine that—they slept apart for years—because of me." Her voice softened but gained some strength. "By then, I was figuring out my own proclivities."

"Are you gay?" The question slipped out before I could stop it.

That grin—the one that both challenged and taunted—spread wider. "Yes. In fact, when you asked if I was seeing someone… well, let's just say my relationship with Dr. Quayle is far from merely professional."

My breath hitched involuntarily. Her satisfaction at my reaction was palpable—she thrived on disruption.

"Don't you think it's a conflict of interest for your therapist to be your lover?" I asked carefully, striving to keep my tone clinical.

Straightening as if to meet a challenge, she became almost statuesque. "That's exactly what I expected you to say—old-school, male-dominated psychiatric dogma. But Anna and I, we believe it makes her more invested in my wellbeing."

I raised an eyebrow. "If this were reversed—a male therapist and a female patient?"

"That would be about dominance," she dismissed with a carefree tone, like explaining something to a child. "But Dr. Quayle and I are equals. It changes everything."

"Ah." I tried to sound upbeat, though the conversation twisted deeper into uncomfortable territory. "It must be hard for both of you... the way society still views gay women."

She shrugged lightly, almost unconcerned. "True enough." Then, as if stepping up onto a soapbox, she added, "Good thing I had Sylvia Klein raising me, not Jake Hurd. I know how to take care of myself—and win. Despite what everyone else thinks." We locked eyes. "But you're right. Prejudices run deep."

"Do you think that's because people are told things can only ever be one way?" I asked gently.

Amanda's smile sharpened, fierceness returning. "Absolutely. Women can't start companies, can't be their own bosses, can't—on and on. I've proved them wrong every damn time."

"You started one of the largest internet companies on the planet," I acknowledged.

She arched a brow. "Glad you did your homework."

"Meeting you, hearing your side, is far more enlightening than any article I've read."

"Since I knew we were meeting about my fath—" she caught herself. "Jake Hurd, I was expecting a plea to meet with him or —" She snorted. "Help pay for his therapy."

"Jake's being well taken care of by his company."

"Probably to avoid a lawsuit," she scoffed. "No business wants a raving, paranoid, child abuser on the payroll."

"Jake made them a lot of money," I shot back smoothly. "His net worth is in the millions."

The skepticism returned, furrowing her brow. "How could a night guard have that kind of money?"

I slid a page across the desk toward her, the printed figures glaring under the harsh light. "I did extensive research—maybe more than Jake wanted. Here are the records of significant financial transactions made on your behalf."

Amanda snatched the page, eyes scanning. A snarl of contempt crossed her face. "I don't need his money."

"Not now," I said evenly. "But you did. He funded your entire college education—though legally, he was only required to do so until you turned twenty-one."

Her eyes flicked up, raw disbelief tempered only by grudging acknowledgment. "You've done your homework."

"Look further down," I pointed. "When you launched your company, you struggled to get venture capital. Jake supplied the money for your startup."

She frowned, shaking her head. "No—it was a Midwestern venture capitalist."

"Security Investments, yes. But it was Jake who provided the funds. He had a lawyer create a shell company. A bank handled the deal—but the money? It was Jake's. Without him, you wouldn't have gotten the start you did."

The surprise in her voice was genuine. "He helped me?"

"Perhaps you, too, harbor some prejudices. Your mother, Dr. Klein, even Dr. Quayle—they want you to believe things a certain way."

We both stood—she rose effortlessly, even taller than I expected. I tilted my head up to meet her gaze. Her dusky hair framed her face; her presence commanding.

"I want you to know: if you ever want another perspective on Jake..." I offered my business card.".....you can talk to me. Or him, if you want."

"Why should I believe—"

I held up the papers. "The dates, the transactions—they're all verifiable. And there's more. You should learn about Shawn O'Brien. Your half-brother."

Her mouth dropped open in shock. "My half—?"

"Another secret no one told you, I suspect." I allowed a faint smile. "I've only recently discovered it myself. It might just give you a clearer picture of who your father truly is. Good day, Ms. Hurd."

I strode out, not looking back until I was safely across the street, inside my car. I looked through the window to see Amanda Hurd still standing at the table where I'd left her.

She was rubbing her deformed right hand with her left, the way a child holds a favorite stuffed animal for the tactile comfort derived.

As I drove off, she sat and continued to read the papers.

34. Christmas Eve

I drove through Morris Plains on a day swallowed by low-hanging clouds, the dull gray sky pressing down like a weight.

Christmas Eve would arrive tomorrow, and I was seeing my last patients before shutting the office until the New Year. With my children on school break and most patients away on vacation, the silence that would follow felt both a relief and a strange loneliness.

Parking in the lot, I grabbed my laptop and a sheaf of fresh paperwork from the seat beside me and headed inside.

The building's fluorescent lights flickered overhead as I made my way upstairs to my office. I was still ten minutes early for my first appointment, but Anne's reputation as the office's unofficial timekeeper was well-earned—I didn't want to provoke her formidable wrath by being late today.

She was already there when I walked in, seated at her desk with that teasing, almost conspiratorial smile I recognized.

"I know someone who's going to earn a gold star today," Anne said, eyes twinkling.

I raised an eyebrow, returning the smile. "Oh? And who might that be?"

Anne leaned back, crossing her arms with mock severity. "You've been early for every appointment these last two weeks. A seismic shift from your usual timekeeping disaster. I was about to give up hope and shave my head in frustration."

I chuckled. "You're an attractive woman, Anne, but I'm not convinced the bald look would suit you. Besides, I wasn't as bad as all that."

"Doctor," she shot back, "you've always been twenty minutes late—no, make that thirty—since the day you walked in here. But lately? It's like you turned over a new leaf."

"Therapy works—when you want it to," I said dryly, pulling a brightly colored box from my pocket and setting it next to her computer.

Anne's eyes widened as she looked down at the small box. "What's this?"

"A little something," I said, feeling a rare warmth counteracting the day's gloom. "Christmas, Hanukkah, whichever you prefer. Just a thank you for putting up with me lately."

She hesitated, then gingerly opened the box. Inside rested a pair of diamond earrings, each stone gleaming with over a full carat's brilliance. She gasped softly, her breath catching.

"Oh, Sam, this is… far too extravagant."

I shrugged with a smile. "Can't run this place without you. Thought you should know I appreciate it."

Without warning she stood and pulled me into a hug. Her slim dancer's frame pressed tightly against mine. She kissed the top of my balding head, a gesture so genuine it nearly caught me off guard.

"Thank you, Sam," she whispered.

"Thank *you*, Anne," I replied as we parted.

Changing gears I said, "Marcie told me that if you had free time with the office closed, I was to invite you for dinner. You and... is it Gary?"

Anne's expression darkened and she sank into her chair heavier than before, as if the mention of him added weight to her spirit. "Gary's no longer in the picture. No regrets there. Seems I'll be Christmasing alone."

"I get it," I said, trying to sound casual though I felt a tug of sympathy. "Why don't you come over? We'll light candles for the Sabbath tomorrow evening—5:30? You'll be among friends. And Marcie and the kids would love it."

Anne smiled faintly. "I have some visiting to do in the morning. But dinner sounds nice. It's been too long since I saw Marcie and the children."

"It'll give you both a chance to gang up on me," I teased.

"We wouldn't do that—not on Christmas," she chuckled. "We'll just exchange war stories and plot our revenge for later." She stood with a determined nod. "Very well, I will be there. Now, you'd better get in your office and pretend to be a psychiatrist."

"Yes, Doctor," I said with a cheeky salute.

The afternoon slipped by quickly, the sessions unfolding smoothly. Amanda Hurd's appointment filled me with a cautious energy, though I wasn't sure how much to share with Jake. I was slated to see him Christmas morning, a rare uninterrupted session to delve deep into intensive therapy.

I'd uncovered evidence supporting parts of his decades-long obsession, but I still wasn't clear how much was reality and how much mere fantasy. His paranoia was real, but treatment options were scarce.

As my last patient left that late afternoon, Anne reminded me to return a call from Janice Franklin. Within minutes her voice crackled over the line.

"Sam, I asked around like you wanted."

"What did you find?"

"There's definitely anxiety—tons of it—thanks to the millennium buzz. But a recurring complaint keeps popping up: fear of the dark. Worse yet, people say they feel like something's watching them from within it."

I leaned back and exhaled sharply. "Any theories?"

Janice's tone grew sarcastic, even petulant. "Oh, you wouldn't believe the ones they came up with. Every one crazier than the last. Some of our fellow therapists could be inpatients in your funny farm."

"Greystorm is Bill Benning's operation," I reminded her.

Janice softened. "How's Bill?"

"Good. I'll be at his New Year's Eve party next week."

"I never miss it. Damn, I'll have to buy a dress—can't show up looking like I do in therapy sessions, all muumuu and no glamour."

I shifted, feeling the unease creeping back. "So, what's the main theory?"

She shot back sharply, "I thought this was your specialty. I read your paper about anxiety and sleep disorders. Shouldn't you be the one to tell me what's going on?"

I hated to admit it. "Honestly, I'm at a loss."

Janice laughed bitterly at the other end. "It'll all blow over once everyone sees the computers hold up and planes don't crash. Sam, you're not buying into this, right? Media hype chasing doom and gloom. I'll hold your hand on New Year's Eve if you need."

"I'll be fine, Janice. Thanks."

I hung up feeling the knot of concern tighten in my chest. First Jake Hurd's forty-year obsession surfaces, and now it seems to be unraveling more widely—catching on like some infectious disease.

Why were patients from disparate therapists recounting similar delusions? Media sensationalism or something darker? The anxiety in the air was undeniable as the world edged closer to the millennium's dawn, and I feared we were all standing on the precipice of something unknown.

The next morning dawned with a deceptive calm. Marcie dressed briskly and left for St. Clare Hospital, her car's tires crunching against the gravel without a backward glance.

The house, however, remained in a state of lethargy. The kids and I lingered in our pajamas until noon when we finally broke our inertia.

Then, as if woken by some invisible conductor's baton, the house erupted into feverish motion.

I scrubbed the dining room floor until it gleamed, waxing it carefully—a rare indulgence we typically reserved for quieter times. Dust motes fled as I wiped down every surface, the familiar scents of lemon polish and beeswax filling the air.

Even Rueben, normally a reluctant participant in such rituals, emerged from his room with a grunt and pitched in. I caught him stuffing clutter hastily into his closet but I let it slide.

Rachel, muttering under her breath, dutifully took on vacuuming both floors and tidying her own room. The vacuum's relentless hum became the soundtrack of our day punctuated only by my orchestrating kitchen symphony: a golden turkey roasting to perfection alongside a bowl holding gefilte fish, loaves of fresh challah, and my famed latkes, crispy and fragrant, just as everyone liked them.

By mid-afternoon, everyone collaborated to set the table: plates aligned, napkins folded, and silverware—mainly by Rueben, who did better than usual at placing forks and knives correctly.

His tie was my final touch; I smoothed his unruly hair back with enough mousse to hold a small animal in place, the strands gleaming under the steady kitchen light.

Marcie's car slid into the driveway just as I finished the last knot on Rueben's tie. The door swung open, and the kids and I gathered in the dining room—clean, dressed, and bright-eyed. Marcie's eyes sparkled with approval.

"What a handsome family!" she exclaimed.

Rachel grinned crookedly. "Whose, though?"

"Mine!" Marcie declared with a laugh, dropping kisses on Rachel's cheek then Rueben's. She ended with a lingering peck on my lips.

Rachel wrinkled her nose. "Gross!"

"Seriously, stop it!" Rueben echoed, pitching in the chorus with a shrug and mock disgust.

At half-past five Anne arrived, her entrance a burst of warmth and cheer, arms laden with gifts. I insisted the presents wait until after dinner, but Rueben was insistent.

"Come on, Dad," he whined. "It's like Hanukah all over again!"

"I made latkes," I reminded them, watching Anne's eyes light up.

Rachel proposed, "Let's light the menorah for Aunt Anne—she didn't get to see it."

We all turned to Marcie—the ultimate judge of what was permissible on the Sabbath.

She raised her hands in surrender. "You've all worked too hard for me to say no. Just make sure it's before the blessings start."

Although I had packed away all the other menorahs, the large oil menorah remained on the mantle. I found only three wicks left, so I filled the end globes with oil along with the center shammas and lit them. The flames danced atop the oil pools, flickering shadows that seemed to breathe life into the room.

"Beautiful," Anne breathed. "It really makes the evening festive."

Candles were lit at the table and we began the Sabbath seder— prayers and blessings unfolding in a reverent quiet. I tried hard not to rush. When it came time to carve the turkey, I took my time, wanting Marcie to see more than just a meal, but an effort —an offering.

Everyone enjoyed the feast in full. Wine flowed for the adults while the children gleefully tore into their presents.

Rueben revealed a wooden biplane, its carved propeller spinning slightly as he held it up. "Thanks, Auntie Anne!"

"How did you know?" I whispered to her..

"Called Marcie," she murmured with a grin.

Rachel's eyes lit up as she hugged Anne, waving a small stack of CDs from her favorite boy band. "This is just so cool!"

"That's fine, dearie—enjoy them," Anne said warmly.

I exchanged a glance with Marcie, who simply shrugged.

"Okay," I whispered. "How—?"

"I asked Rachel what she wanted," Anne confessed with a mischievous twinkle in her eye.

"Always knew you were sneaky," I admitted with a grin, pouring myself a generous brandy.

"Guilty as charged."

I invited Anne to stay the night, though I feared the den's leather couch might test her patience.

"On that couch?" she replied with a laugh. "No thanks. Besides, I'm off to midnight services at the Episcopal Church— it's the single Christian girl thing to do on Christmas Eve."

So the evening wound down with quiet conversation—Marcie and I sipping brandy, Anne nursing coffee. She helped read Rueben to sleep, spinning a story that softened the boy's restless eyes. At around nine-thirty, she took her leave.

The fire in the fireplace crackled, casting flickering shadows. Marcie's voice softened. "That was really lovely. Anne is such a dear."

"I like her taste in ties," I said, holding up the gift Anne gave me earlier. "She shares your sense of style."

We sat close, watching the flames. "Rueben seemed better tonight," I remarked.

Marcie nodded, sipping her cognac. "I made an appointment for him with Dr. Lesase."

"Good. Lesase is excellent," I agreed.

"I don't think he's going to 'uncover' any false memories of abuse," she sighed.

"That whole thing—so many people getting swept up in it these days," I muttered. "By the way, what do you know about Dr. Anna Quayle?"

Marcie's eyes narrowed. "Oh please. I enjoyed my dinner—I don't want to lose it. She's a psychologist, not a psychiatrist. That means she can practice bad therapy all day long without consequences. What of it?"

"She's been working with Jake Hurd's daughter," I said cautiously.

Marcie straightened instantly. "You met his daughter?"

"I was just gathering background," I explained.

"During a session with Jake?"

"No, I needed—"

"To have your head examined!" she snapped. "You can't have informal meetings with family members—it's strictly off-limits."

I swallowed my annoyance. "Marcie, I'm trying to make sense of what Jake told me. To see if his daughter's memories might match."

"You're dealing with that Quayle witch? Sam, last thing we need is her tearing into you—or the family."

"She's more than a patient," I said, voice low.

Marcie looked at me, her gaze sharpened by dawning realization. "Her lover? That's even worse—it makes it personal. You're doing dangerous things."

She drained her glass in one gulp.

"Hey, you're supposed to sip that!" I protested.

"I'm after the effect," she said bitterly. "Look at you—for the last few weeks you've been better organized, more present for the kids. And now this…" She gestured at me sharply. "Plausible deniability is my new mantra." She rose, swaying slightly from the alcohol. "You're a good therapist, Sam, but not a lawyer."

"But if I can help Jake—"

"You're supposed to help his mind, Sam! Not his daughter, his legal troubles, or even his pet dog!" Marcie snapped.

"He doesn't have a dog," I muttered.

"This is crazy."

"He needs more than a psychiatrist—"

"That's all you are! I thought you were finding perspective. But this? You've gone too far." Marcie pivoted abruptly and climbed the stairs. "I'm going to bed!"

"Marcie—"

"No! We are taking Rueben to Dr. Lesase and he will help him face his fears. You will either help this Hurd guy face his or get off the case and let someone else take over. Someone who knows where to stop." She started up the stairs. "Good night!"

"Shabbat Shalom," I called softly.

"Fuck you!" she yelled back from the landing.

"Marcie, the kids!" I sputtered, but the bedroom door slammed shut, leaving me rattled and alone.

I shook my head, poured another brandy, and sank into the firelight glow. Then I heard it: the unmistakable click of the bedroom lock turning.

I stood, stunned. Slowly, I ascended the stairs and tried the door—locked tight.

"Marcie!" I hissed. "What are you doing?"

Her voice, calm but cold, came through as she leaned against the door. "Sleep in the den. Maybe you'll gain some perspective."

"Now who's the crazy one?" I muttered, pressing my forehead against the smooth wood.

"You are," she said sharply. "That's why you're not sleeping with me."

"Marcie, that couch is torture on my back," I groaned.

"Then maybe it will help you understand *my* position. Good night, Sam."

"Damn!" I cursed, trudging back downstairs to the fire. I poured a double—or was it a triple—of brandy into a snifter and sat down to watch the crackling flames as it burned its way down my throat, dulling the acid clawing at my insides.

I dug out a threadbare quilt from the hall closet, kicked off my shoes, and lay down on the old therapist's couch in the dark den.

The room was chilly, the faint amber glow of the street lamps slipping through the window giving just enough light to see the oil menorah flickering steadily on the mantle. The leather sofa creaked under me as I shifted, chill seeping through my shirt.

I grumbled, too drunk and lethargic to hunt for a pillow, and curled up under the tattered quilt.

If I had known what was about to happen, I would have stayed wide awake.

And kept the lights on…

35. THE DEVIL YOU KNOW

One of my own snores jolted me awake, harsh and unexpected in the suffocating silence. My eyes fluttered open, but when I blinked, the darkness pressed in so thickly it was as if I'd never moved my eyelids at all.

No faint glow, no pinprick of light—only an abyss that swallowed everything.

A jolt of adrenaline surged through me, muscles coiling tight as I sat up in a rush, heart pounding like a war drum. Why was my bedroom so dark? Where was Marcie?

Panic clawed at my ribs. I yanked the blanket from my body and scrambled to steady my shaking hands, groping blindly over my surroundings.

Familiar leather beneath my palms—the rough grain of my old couch. It anchored me, a fleeting lifeline that tugged a memory into focus: the fight, the chaos earlier, retreating here to sleep. But why was the room so pitch black? Had I closed the shades?

The living room door—I always left it open. Were the candles and fire exhausted, snuffed out in the pitch-black silence? Then it hit me, a gnawing sensation slicing through the haze: I smelled smoke.

Something was burning.

I scrambled to my feet, reaching one arm forward, fingers dragging over the couch as I groped toward the door—an invisible maze in the absence of light.

It stung my pride how disoriented I felt. This was my office—my sanctuary. Yet here I was, fumbling like a stranger.

My fingers found the double doors. Cold, solid wood. Closed. It hadn't been—had it? I grabbed the knob and pulled, only to meet resistance.

Locked.

My mind stumbled—no, this wasn't possible. I hadn't locked it. I tried again, desperation clawing up my throat, rattling the door like a trapped animal.

The smell of smoke grew stronger.

Fear pushed past reason, taking hold like a vice as I pounded against the door, frantic and trapped. What the hell was I supposed to do?

My fingers searched the edge, probing for anything—an escape. At the top, my hand brushed a cold metal latch. My heart skipped. I yanked it down, the mechanism moving under my grasp.

On one knee, I reached lower, hands trembling as I found another latch pressing up from the floor. I gave a quick pull; and even with the handle still locked, the doors parted.

What I saw shoved all breath from my lungs.

Hell itself spilled into my home.

I stumbled back, ripping my hand from the doorknob, gasping as the roar of fire escalated. Thick black smoke choked the air, swirling in fierce clouds that blotted out vision, yet the flames dazzled—bright, angry, defiant after the void of darkness I'd just escaped.

Panic seized me like ice water coursing through my veins. My chest tightened until every breath was a struggle. Why was the living room ablaze? Who set this fire? And locked me inside?

My mind raced—not just with fear, but with frantic thinking —rescuing my family, escaping this nightmare.

I stumbled into the hall, pressured by urgency, and sprinted into the kitchen; the smoke stinging my eyes.

My stockinged feet slid on the cold tile as I grabbed the fire extinguisher from its wall bracket. Its weight was heavier than I remembered.

I yanked the pin with shaking fingers, drew in a shuddering breath, and stepped forward.

The thick carpet in front of the fireplace burned with a raging circle of orange and black, fibers blistered and melting. The flames seemed confined, but the heat was oppressive.

I pressed the extinguisher's nozzle to the center and squeezed.

A fierce whoosh erupted sending a blast of freezing carbon dioxide onto the flames.

They sputtered, reignited immediately with a spiteful hiss.

I gripped harder this time, holding the trigger steady, churning out a relentless jet that made the fire recoil, shrinking like a beaten beast.

WHOOSH!

The flames collapsed, vanishing into smoldering tendrils of smoke. But I kept spraying, circling the area and even into the fireplace, hunting any loose embers.

The carpet hissed under the cold assault.

My fingers grew numb from the frigid nozzle. I wiped them on my shirt; the chill creeping up my arms.

Finally, the fire out, I sank into a chair, heart hammering so ferociously it echoed in my ears.

I sucked in jagged breaths, trying to calm the storm inside, but this only caused me to cough from the acrid smoke in the air.

The murky glow of a lamp overhead illuminated a room damaged but spared destruction. Only the blackened circle in the center bore the fire's full wrath.

God, how close had it come to swallowing everything? The couch. The furniture. My life.

Something caught my eye—half-hidden among the charred remains. A frying pan caked in soot.

I stared at it until memory returned. It was the pan I'd used for latkes, hastily abandoned on the stove with oil still pooled inside —olive oil, the same as the oil in our menorah.

My gaze shifted to the fireplace hearth. The large menorah lay toppled, glass globes shattered and strewn like discarded memories. A wick smoldered faintly on the carpet.

Pieces clicked into place with sick clarity.

Someone had doused the carpet with oil. Then, knocked the menorah down, shattering the glass holders—the flaming wick igniting the fire.

The fire could have spread igniting the entire room except for one fact. When Marcie and I bought the house, we'd had the carpets replaced with flame retardant carpeting.

But only Marcie and I knew that one crucial detail. If this had been ordinary carpet—

I lifted my eyes to the ceiling smeared black with smoke..I forced my shaking limbs to calm as I checked the doors throughout the house—for any sign of unauthorized entry.

This fire was no accident. It was arson.

A new dread sank its claws deeper. What if the person who started the fire was still inside?

I stepped through the front door, moonlight spilling over the floor like liquid silver. The street lamp outside bathed the uncovered windows but instead of reassurance an icy knot tightened in my gut.

"No," I whispered breathlessly. I slipped into my shoes and moved toward the back door—locked, the safety chain still intact. Every lock, every barrier secure.

I headed up the stairs; my heartbeat quickened until it thundered in my ears.

I needed to see my children.

Outside Rachel's door I paused, swallowed the knot in my throat, then peeked inside. She lay tangled under her blankets, breathing steady in deep sleep. I smoothed hair from her face and planted a gentle kiss on her cheek.

Across the hall, Ruben's door creaked softly as I entered. He lay rigid, back flat against the mattress, tucked tightly under the covers. Why his sleep resembled death while Rachel's was so restless baffled me for years.

I sat beside him quietly and placed a trembling hand on his flat chest. Up and down. Breathing.

I exhaled in relief through clenched teeth and brushed hair away from his forehead.

"Daddy?" His voice cracked, heavy with sleep.

I turned to him, heart in my throat. "What is it, my darling boy?"

"They were here," he whispered.

"Who?" My voice barely rose above a whisper, dry and raw. A primal chill crept along my spine as if unseen spiders crawled over my skin.

"The dark things. I scared 'em away." He pointed to Jake's disc resting on his bedside table. "They were mad."

No, that's crazy. A delusion whispered sharply in my mind. I swallowed hard, forcing calm into my voice. "It's okay, Ruben. Everything is all right. Go back to sleep."

I kissed his head again and slipped from the room but the cold clung to me. So cold I clenched my jaw, biting back the tremble that threatened to betray my fear.

I crept silently down the dim hallway, heart pounding with a mix of dread and urgency. My fist hovered uncertainly before I rapped sharply on the bedroom door.

"Marcie," I whispered, careful not to raise my voice. "Marcie, it's important. Please."

There was a faint sound—the unmistakable click of the lock turning—and the door cracked open.

She stood there swathed in a peach peignoir that clung loosely, pooling softly at her feet. Her glasses were off, hair a wild tangle around her face, eyes heavy with sleep.

"So, come to bed all ready," she mumbled, already turning toward the bed as if dismissing me.

But I didn't let her go. My hands gripped her shoulders, spinning her to face me, catching her completely off-guard.

"Oh, come on, you're not still angry—"

"Marcie, there's been a fire."

Her eyelids barely fluttered, her body still mostly caught in sleep's fog.

I flicked the light switch hard and the overhead bulb erupted in a harsh glow. She blinked rapidly, shaking her head as if to dislodge the haze.

"What?" Her voice was husky, disbelieving.

"There was a fire. I put it out. You need to come with me—now."

A sharp intake of breath. "Oh God," she gasped, pushing past me. "The kids—"

"They're fine! Put on your bathrobe and slippers. We need to figure this out."

An hour and a half later, Marcie and I sat on the smoke-stained old sofa in our slightly charred living room. The smell of burned carpet still hung heavy in the air.

We cradled steaming cups of coffee, the bitter warmth barely cutting through the chill.

A plainclothes detective, lean and watchful, sat across from us. Outside, two uniformed officers moved in the dark, their radios crackling faintly.

I finished the story, detailing everything I knew, every moment from the fire's discovery to its extinguishment.

Marcie busied herself unlocking windows, shooing the thick haze from the room.

The detective's eyes narrowed thoughtfully. "The whole thing is rather curious."

His name was Walden—the same as the cop who'd interrogated Jake years ago. He mentioned an uncle who served on the Plainfield Police decades back.

A strange echo of the past settled between us—déjà vu all over again, as Yogi Berra might say.

"We need to find out who did this," Marcie said, voice still fragile from the shock.

"I suppose. But according to your testimony, Mr. Lucas—"

"Doctor Lucas," Marcie interrupted sharply. "We are both Doctor Lucas."

"Of course, Dr. Lucas," Walden replied with a half-smile and a glance at his small notebook. His rugged features and casual attitude reminded me of an actor from an old detective show.

"So, some maniac broke in through a locked and chained door to set fire to your carpet with a pan full of olive oil? Odd choice if the goal was to torch your house."

"Maybe he came through the basement," Marcie suggested cautiously.

"We checked all the doors and windows," Walden said, flipping a page.

"Officer, my husband works with people who are criminally insane—"

"Ah, so you think one of them took offense at your style of therapy? And this guy's also an expert locksmith, and silent as a cat?" He jotted a note. "Do I have it straight?"

"I have no explanation," I said sharply, muscles taut. I'd told Marcie it might be a mistake calling the police but she insisted.

Walden leaned back, eyes steady on me. "Run it by me again— why were you asleep down here?"

"My wife and I had a fight."

"Hmmm. And you were drinking?"

"A brandy—maybe two," I admitted, stiffening at the implication.

"What are you implying, Detective?" Marcie's voice was tight with rising anger.

"Nothing more than a suspicion," he said, raising his hands. "You're both respected psychiatrists and I'm just a cop." He rose and began pacing. "But I have a theory."

"We're listening," I said, crossing my arms.

He shrugged. "You had a fight, normal enough. You had a couple of drinks—hell, when my wife and I argue, I'm no stranger to a few belts myself."

I bristled. "But..."

"Maybe in the middle of the night you got up to use the bathroom or get some water, and did the dishes. In the process, you carried that pan of used olive oil through the living room... and accidentally spilled it."

"Why on earth would I carry a frying pan full of oil through the house?" I said.

"It's only a theory. Then, when you tried to clean it up, you knocked over that candelabra—and bam. Fire."

Marcie narrowed her eyes. "Why would my husband lie?"

He shrugged again. "Did I say he lied? No, but if I set my house on fire after a fight, I sure wouldn't want to admit to my wife that I'm an idiot."

Marcie gaze grew cold. "So you're saying I'm being deceived?"

"That's one way to look at it. More logical than any other explanation I've heard tonight." Walden snapped the notebook shut. "I'm going outside to check with the officers. They might have found something. But just FYI—if you file a false report that's a crime."

"What are you—" I attempted.

He cut me off with a raised hand and a smirk. "I'm not accusing anyone. You two decide what you want and let me know." With that, he strode out.

Marcie looked at me, eyes dark and wary. "Is there anything in what he said?"

I met her stare evenly. "If I'd started the fire I'd own up to it. But I have to admit… his theory's the most plausible I've heard."

She slumped against the couch, voice trembling. "It's terrifying. Why would anyone do this?"

I squeezed her hand gently. "So you believe me."

"Of course, Sam. We've been married fifteen years." Her hand was small in mine, but cold—shivering.

"You're trembling."

"I know."

I pulled her close, wrapping my arms around her. "There's another possibility. It's even crazier."

"More insane than a silent pyromaniac who's a locksmith?" she scoffed.

"Yes." I pulled away and paced slowly. "After I put the fire out, I went upstairs to check on the kids."

"Reasonable."

"I woke Rueben. He said… the dark things were there. He chased them away and they were angry."

"The dark things?" Marcie's jaw clenched. "That's just a fantasy —"

"Yes, except Rueben isn't alone. Jake Hurd talks about the same things. I spoke to Janice Franklin—many therapists are hearing about these 'dark things.'"

"You're not making sense."

"What if Jake's telling the truth?"

She backed away, eyes wide. "Sam, you cannot believe this."

"I'm only saying it fits."

She threw up her hands. "I'd sooner believe Jake himself came into the house and started the fire than accept the idea that 'shadow creatures' did."

"Maybe several of them."

"What? They travel in herds?"

"A troop," I muttered.

"What?" she stared at me like I'd lost my mind.

"Jake says they're simian. Monkeys travel in troops."

She stared, mouth open. "If you tell that detective about a troop or a herd or a pride of shadow creatures attacking us, you'll end up in Greystorm, and not as a therapist." She lowered her voice. "I'd have you committed myself."

"Marcie, it's—"

"Enough!" She gripped my arm so hard my skin stung beneath her nails. "We stick to our story. No police report."

"You're hurting me."

"Good! I wish I could knock some sense into you." Her fingers dug in deeper. "Tomorrow, you call Bill Benning and tell him you're off this case."

"It's Christmas. He won't be in!" I yanked free. "And Jake needs me!"

"Jake is a madman, and you're buying into his delusion."

"But if those things were real—"

"That's exactly why you need to stop!" She shook her head, voice rising. "If those shadow things did this, dropping the case is the only way to keep us safe. I can't believe I'm entertaining the idea of a delusion like it's real!"

"But Jake—"

"No! It's the patient who becomes dependent on the therapist, not the other way around!"

I exhaled hard.

"I'll make it simple," she hissed. "Get off the case, or I'm leaving. The kids and I will be gone when you come home."

"But—"

"No 'buts'. You find a replacement now. Or we're gone.." Her arms crossed, a wall between us.

I glanced out the window at the men outside and kept my voice low. "Give me until New Year's, and that will give me a chance to find another therapist and bring him up to speed."

"Fine, New Year's, but that's it. And if you say one word about 'shadow things,' the kids spend their vacation at my mother's."

"O-okay," I whispered.

"Now go shower or something," she waved me away.

Alone upstairs, I stripped and stepped into the steaming water.

Just over a week with Jake.

That would have to be enough.

36. Crunch Time

I drifted into a restless sleep for a couple of hours, my dreams flickering like a malfunctioning light bulb, creating nightmares that were all too real.

When I finally stumbled out of bed I dressed quickly, steeling myself for the grim task ahead. At 7:00, Marcie and I would need to wake the kids to explain what happened—a collision of reality that felt more like a nightmare than the routine of our lives.

As I tried to gather my thoughts I found Rueben, my youngest, drawing hazy shapes in the air with his fingers, his pale face betraying his thoughts. When I told him about the accident, his eyes widened, turning hollow.

"They did it," he whispered, his voice quaking. "They were mad."

The words hit Marcie like a thunderclap, sparking an explosive reaction.

"They?" she echoed, voice sharper than shattered glass, each syllable dripping with disbelief and fury.

"The dark things," Rueben whimpered, his eyes darting to me, seeking reassurance from the man who was supposed to protect him.

"See? See what you've brought into this house!" Marcie's voice crescendoed, a tempest of fury that cracked the morning air.

She stormed from the room, fury trailing behind her like a heavy fog. I sank onto Rueben's bed, trying to mold the fear that gripped my heart into words.

"What makes you think it was the 'dark things'?" I asked, my voice soft, slicing through the tension.

"'Cause they were mad," Rueben murmured, his voice barely above a whisper as he cast a fearful glance towards the door through which his mother had recently stormed.

"How do you know they were mad?" I pressed, wanting desperately to keep the conversation light and safe.

"They said so," Rueben replied, his innocence slapping me in the face.

"You can hear what they say?" The question escaped my lips before I could choke it back. Fear curdled in my stomach.

"I guess," he said softly, wandering around the room. He pointed to his head, the enormity of his words sinking like stones in my chest. "I hear them in here, like whispers."

A chill swept over me and my mind flashed with an image—the bloody knife Shawn O'Brien used on his mother. I had never seen it but the horror felt visceral, igniting my imagination with its bloody aftermath.

"Can I get dressed now?" Rueben asked, breaking the silence.

I nodded, trying to mask my tumultuous thoughts as I rose. Turning back, I dropped to one knee and pulled my son into a tight embrace, desperation choking me.

"I'm okay, Daddy. It's light out now," he assured me, the faith in his small voice a balm amidst my rising dread.

"Everything will be all right, son," I promised, though the weight of his words felt monumental.

"Okay," he repeated, and with that fragile acceptance I left the room, my heart heavy.

In the kitchen we gathered for breakfast, an uneasy silence hanging between us.

Both kids were subdued, the playfulness that usually filled our mornings had vanished. I watched them, longing for their laughter—my heart ached at the emptiness that lay before us like an open wound.

The kids ate and went upstairs to get ready for service. Marcie was a whirlwind, her anger driving her forward, scrubbing at countertops with a feverish determination that bordered on lunacy.

"I think we should sleep apart until you're done with this case," she suddenly proposed, as if the mere suggestion carried the weight of betrayal.

My mouth fell open in shock. "Marcie, I won't survive a week on that couch!"

"Until this is over, you're sleeping downstairs," she snapped, each word punctuated with fury. "That way, you can protect us from any 'dark things.'"

"It's Shabbos!" I protested, desperation creeping into my voice.

Marcie's eyes blazed with a fierce conviction. "I will sleep with you the day you are off this case. Until then, you are not welcome in my bed!"

"This is crazy!" I shot back, anger boiling just beneath the surface.

"Sh! Don't you dare tell me what's crazy. Think of it as an incentive," she countered, storming up the stairs before I could reply, a final slam of the door punctuating our argument as she locked it behind her, the click echoing like a gunshot in my chest.

With my stomach in knots, I left for Greystorm at 7:30. The air felt thick and oppressive, each breath a struggle.

I stopped at Dunkin' Donuts purchasing two dozen donuts and a 'Box of Joe'—a meager offering of normalcy for the staff, a tiny attempt to make Christmas a little merrier.

As I drove a multitude of questions rattled around in my mind, each one sharper than the last. I needed answers from Jake, more than ever.

Upon my arrival Carl brought Jake into my office within fifteen minutes. As he entered I turned to Carl, forcing a smile. "Here on Christmas, Carl?"

He shrugged, his broad shoulders lifting like a mountain. "Just another day, Doc—same for New Year's," he replied. "At least then I'm doing four to midnight."

"I'll likely be in tomorrow to see Jake," I mentioned, conscious of the time slipping away.

He nodded, his bushy beard shaking as he moved toward the door. "You'll have to get him; I'll be off."

"Thanks, Carl," I replied as Jake settled into the chair that had become his throne of sorts.

Jake's eyes were sharp, assessing. "Everything all right?"

"Why do you ask?" I returned, narrowing my gaze.

"You look tired," he stated simply, a stony seriousness cloaking his features. "Word has it you had an incident last night."

"Word?" My temper flared, but I fought to keep it tempered. "Could you tell me where you might have heard this?"

Jake held my gaze, unflinching. "Somewhere in the night."

"Oh! Just whispers in your ear?" I shot back, sarcasm lacing my voice.

"I didn't always hear them," Jake said, his tone as steady as a rock. "That started ten years ago."

"They talk to you, do they?" I asked, my mind racing.

"Like Shawn," he said matter-of-factly, weighing his words. "And your son."

The breath caught in my throat, surprise coursing through me as I realized I had stood up without noticing.

"Goddamn you, Jake! I'm sick of your air of mystery and your 'I-know-better-than-you' attitude!"

Jake merely looked up at me, his expression unreadable. "Rough night?"

I slumped back into my chair, my anger dissipating. "You have no idea."

"I have a very good idea," he replied cryptically.

"There was a fire—"

"A fire?" Jake frowned.

"Yeah, I woke to the street lights out and my house shrouded in darkness." I could feel the weight of my words as I spoke them.

Jake nodded slowly, his face a blank slate, eyes distant. "That sounds like them. What caused the fire?"

"A pan of oil and the menorah with wicks tossed to the floor," I explained, gripping the edge of the desk, searching for the right way to articulate my fear.

"They could do that," he said simply.

"And they locked me in my den," I added, my voice dropping to almost a whisper.

"Locked in?" Jake's eyes sharpened, taking in every flicker of emotion on my face. "Did you lock the door?"

"I don't even have the key," I admitted, unease coiling in my stomach.

A strange grin played on his lips, one side of his mouth tugging upward in a way that suggested a hidden truth. "That doesn't matter."

"I was lucky the carpet was fire retardant," I replied. "The entire house could've gone up in flames."

"Unless it was a warning," Jake intoned, the weight of his words hanging heavily in the air.

I scribbled a note on my legal pad. "Back to your cryptic ways already?"

He shrugged dismissively. "So, what were you doing in the den?"

"Marcie and I had a fight," I said, kicking myself for revealing too much.

"About me?" he probed, eyes gleaming with intrigue.

"What else? She announced to me this morning that I am exiled from our bed until I drop this case," I said, frustration boiling to the surface once more.

"Ouch!" Jake exhaled, genuine sympathy stark against my anger.

"Easy for you. You sleep on a bed—not a couch," I retorted, the bitterness seeping into my voice.

"What are you going to do?" he asked, his expression shifting to something more grave.

"I told her I couldn't get a replacement before New Year's," I replied, sinking into that all-too-familiar knot of helplessness.

He studied his hands, frowning. "That might be a good idea, Sam."

I blinked, taken aback. "You said I was the only one you trusted."

That smile again, tinged with mystery. "After New Year's it might not matter."

"What do you mean?" I pressed, confusion crowding my thoughts. "Are you going to be cured? That would be a psychiatric miracle."

"There is still a lot you need to know," Jake replied, the gravity of his tone sending chills down my spine.

"With what you've told me, Jake," I scoffed, "I don't see how I can consider you sane."

"Then it isn't for me. It's for you. Maybe for your boy," he stated, driving stakes of anxiety deeper into my chest.

"I don't understand," I breathed, exhaustion creeping in around the edges.

"You will," he promised, the cryptic look in his eyes more haunting than reassuring.

I shook my head wearily, letting out a long sigh. "Where were we?"

1990

37. PARANOIA PAYS

··

In early 1981, newspapers across the nation blasted the grim details of the stabbing death of 'Candy' O'Brien. The sensational coverage wasn't just about her tragic demise—it revolved around the shocking trial of her son, Shawn, who killed her citing 'voices in his head' as the cause.

The headlines called it 'The Stripper Slaying,' painting Candy variously as a dancer, a stripper, even a prostitute, amplifying the scandal and morbid public fascination.

Jake was of little help throughout the ordeal.

His recent divorce drained his finances and fighting the fraudulent criminal charges against himself left him unable to afford decent legal representation for his son.

The court assigned Shawn a public defender who quickly had him declared incompetent by reason of mental defect. The unyielding ruling of the judge was the court could not consider Shawn for release until after his twentieth birthday.

Shawn became a resident of Biscayne, the grim state ward.

Meanwhile, Jake's troubles spiraled further—he couldn't afford court costs to establish paternity amid accusations of spousal abuse thrown his way.

Eventually, his lawyer struck a deal through negotiation: Teresa, Jake's wife, withdrew her complaint and the state dismissed the criminal charges.

But the deal forbade Jake ever seeing Amanda again.

His lawyer warned him coldly, "It's the best deal we can get. If they proceed with the criminal charges, you won't be able to work security. Got another career to fall back on?"

Jake had no choice but to accept the terms. He agreed to steep alimony and child support demands, swallowing over eighty percent of his modest security guard salary. He also relinquished all rights to the family home in Basking Ridge.

The house didn't matter anymore. Giving up Amanda was a wound that wouldn't heal.

Clawing by on sporadic repair jobs income, he moved back into his humble bachelor apartment, grateful for the small workshop it offered—a fragment of his old life still intact.

Jake visited Shawn weekly, usually on Fridays. The long drive sapped his strength, forcing him to rest until late afternoon afterward, but the visits gave him purpose. Shawn had grown into a lanky figure well over six feet two, but thin as a skeleton—antipsychotic drugs dulled his mind, and poor nutrition left him ghostly pale with a vacant, haunted stare even during lucid moments.

In early 1987 came an even worse blow. They transferred Shawn from Biscayne to Greystorm.

This was convenient for the state, yet horrifying for Jake. But Shawn was now eighteen and had to leave the juvenile facility.

Jake found out that the state relegated Shawn to the criminal ward and remembered what a nightmare it was.

On his first visit, Jake found Shawn dirty, ignored, confined to a room no better than a padded cell—he'd seen cleaner jail cells.

Haunted by what he saw, Jake increased his visits, bringing food Shawn could tolerate and bathing the boy himself, trying to restore some shred of dignity.

Besides doing his job and building his tinkers, Shawn became Jake's entire world—a focal point around which he swore to build a better future.

That obsession brought Jake face-to-face with his boss and self-proclaimed business partner, Dan Hurley, in the fall of '87.

"Jake, you've been a good sport about this new endeavor," Dan smiled condescendingly from behind the massive mahogany desk in his latest swanky office surrounded by plush carpeting. "But you do not know the expenses we've run into—the manufacturing costs alone!"

Jake sat quietly, offering only polite smiles. Every few months he'd deliver his latest prototypes and blueprints and then endure a ten-minute spiel about financial woes.

Hurley blamed startup expenses, manufacturing delays, advertising costs—always something. But Jake had reached his breaking point.

"I know, sir. I appreciate your hard work."

"Starting any business takes time," Hurley replied smoothly.

Jake nodded, gathered his courage. "I'm short on money, and you've been dragging this out for seven years."

Hurley opened his mouth, but Jake cut him off: "I think it's time I took my future inventions to a company that can pay me."

"Well, Jake, in the long term—"

"In any terms, Dan, I've seen nothing. Your offices get fancier, and I read about warehouses filled with my designs, but I get nothing. I'm seriously considering having our agreement reviewed by my attorney."

Jake was bluffing; after the divorce, he barely spoke to his lawyer, only sending the occasional check to chip away at old fees. Yet Hurley looked taken aback.

"You have a point," Dan conceded, leaning forward. "That's why I asked to meet you today."

"I'm the one who asked to meet, Dan," Jake snapped.

"Oh?" Hurley feigned surprise, then reached into his desk and pulled out an envelope, thick and worn. "This is for you."

Jake's hands trembled as he opened it. Inside lay a check— made out to him for a staggering one hundred thousand dollars.

He rose abruptly. "I don't know what to say."

Hurley laughed. "You mean besides thank you? I've been saving this for you for nearly a year. All I have to do is date and sign it, and it's yours."

"Dan—"

"Now, Jake, go out there and have some fun! You're going to be a wealthy man!"

Jake could barely believe it. Turning the check over and over in his hand, he felt the weight of possibility, of hope. For a moment, loss and failure didn't define his life for the first time in years.

"And remember," Hurley added with a sly grin, "when you finish those next doohickeys, bring them here first. We've got to stay cutting edge."

Jake nodded, stepping into the corridor with cautious optimism—and the heavy burden of everything he still had to fight for.

Jake channeled the money with grim resolve.

First, he cleared his long-owed lawyer's fees then hired him ancw—for a case that would shape the next chapter of his life.

Drawing on the long-forgotten test results from 1980, Jake pressed the lawyer to petition the court to name him Shawn O'Brien's guardian.

It was a gamble, fraught with legal hurdles and resistance, but Jake knew it was his only chance to wrest control of Shawn's shattered fate.

Simultaneously, he waged a quiet war on another front—lobbying Greystorm to move Shawn to better quarters.

The boy's conditions behind institutional walls gnawed at Jake's heart; every request met bureaucratic stonewalls and cold indifference. Yet each minor victory bolstered his hope and deepened his determination.

Starting in 1987, Dan Hurley's checks arrived—sometimes for $25,000, sometimes for as much as the initial windfall of $100,000. These funds were lifelines, fueling Jake's relentless campaign both inside and outside the courtroom.

Amid the turmoil, Jake sought to prepare a sanctuary for Shawn's eventual release. Though his income had risen, the expensive legal battles forced him to make sacrifices. Instead of the upscale neighborhood of Basking Ridge, he settled for a three-story Victorian house in unassuming Plainfield.

The old home featured a turret—its circular room became Jake's haven, a new workshop filled with intricate tinkering. Here, amidst circuits and schematics, Jake pursued inventions he hoped would be his golden goose, financing his and Shawn's uncertain future.

Legal fees, medical bills, and endless phone calls drained his resources, but Jake persevered. His faith in progress, however fragile, fueled every painstaking step.

In late 1989, the doctors at Greystorm declared Shawn stable enough to go on probation as he turned twenty.

The moment was heavy with tension.

Jake orchestrated a careful pre-dawn pickup, evading both the press and prying eyes.

When he saw Shawn, his heart clenched. The boy stood a full six feet three, but gaunt and fragile as a ghost. Clothes hung loosely, revealing a frame so thin it evoked images of survivors from atrocities long past.

His freckles and unruly blond hair, coupled with large, awkward features, mirrored Jake in uncanny ways. Yet beneath the surface was a boy battered by years of isolation.

Back home, Jake transformed the house into a fortress. High-tech alarms, locks, and monitoring systems surrounded them. He patiently explained every device to Shawn, who listened with a vacant gaze—eyes that seemed distant, haunted.

For three weeks straight, Jake took a vacation from his night guard work, staying by Shawn's side day and night.

He found an MD specializing in alternative therapies who made house calls. The doctor began weaning Shawn off years of heavy medication, replacing it with a regimen of regular exercise and wholesome food.

Slowly the boy shed his hollow expression and gained weight, regaining a flicker of life.

They adopted a nocturnal rhythm. Both father and son preferred the quiet of daylight hours for sleep—Shawn needing twelve hours a day to detox his body and rebuild strength.

Communication improved, but not without setbacks.

Often long silences filled Shawn's moments of lucidity. Jake hesitated to intrude, offering him space in those dark hours.

The house's protective systems became Shawn's domain. Learning to operate the alarms and controls gave him a newfound sense of safety and control that neither of his former prisons could ever provide.

Jake had Shawn tested again—IQ, learning skills—and within a month found a tutor willing to take on the challenge of finishing high school and getting a diploma.

Though years of neglect left gaps, Shawn began to relearn, rediscovering a tentative thirst for knowledge.

Meanwhile, Jake's obsession with security grew. He designed electrical systems with multiple backup generators and battery power, determined to defy any blackout or outside sabotage.

The attack at the Basking Ridge house haunted him still. He knew the shadows were never far—sometimes watching him intently with eerie fascination, other times disappearing into the periphery, their inscrutable presence marking the edges of his life.

Despite everything Jake dared to hope. Devoting himself fully to Shawn, he tasted moments of fragile peace. He imagined a future where fear might yield to safety.

Until September 1990.

That month would shatter their fragile bubble and thrust them back into a world far darker than either was prepared to face.

The Star Ledger's headline screamed the same dire message day after day: 'Crisis in the Middle East.' Reporters framed Iraq's invasion of Kuwait not merely as a dictator's land grab but as a brazen affront to the United States itself—a slap in the face to American power. A despotic regime from a third-world nation was laughing at what had once been the most envied military on earth. The tension was palpable across the nation; pride wounded and uncertainty swelling beneath the surface.

Jake drove his old '86 Ford Aerostar down the sun-drenched street, the crisp September afternoon glowing with the warm hues of turning leaves.

The Star Ledger lay folded beside him in the passenger seat, headlines staring back like a challenge.

Yet Jake smiled quietly, a secret smile—a rare moment of peace in a life otherwise overshadowed by turmoil. For once he felt caught up in the world's troubles instead of his own.

Things started looking up. Jake and Shawn were finally getting along. The doctor weaned Shawn off his last medication and the young man mentioned enrolling at the local community college —a small, fragile hope blooming after years of struggle.

Jake had nothing but time this Friday afternoon. He'd slept well and didn't have to work that night.

The light filtered through branches heavy with amber and bronze, the air crisp as he thought about the upcoming meeting. Mr. Hurley was expecting him—time to collect another payment for his inventions and Jake was hopeful it would be more than that this time.

This year, Jake had done his research.

Security Information Systems had just gone public on the New York Stock Exchange. Shares were trading briskly, and Jake expected not just a check but stock options too.

His inventions had made the company a 'sound investment,' 'cutting edge,' even a 'mover and shaker' in financial magazines—buzzwords that meant something real to Jake.

Hidden beneath the newspaper on the seat lay his latest blueprints, inventions he dreamed might revolutionize the world of alarm systems.

The company's sleek high-rise in Somerset gleamed in the afternoon light. Jake parked in the underground lot, took the elevator to the twelfth floor, and walked to the receptionist—another tall, willowy blonde radiating effortless charm.

Jake had long suspected these beautiful women offered more than clerical help.

"Good afternoon, Mr. Hurd. Right on time," she said with a smile that was all business.

Jake followed her to Hurley's expansive office. The man himself was waiting—still trim and commanding though age had crept in: his once-black hair now snowy white, his face lined but sharp.

"Jake! Good to see you," Hurley greeted warmly as they shook hands.

"Thanks, Dan. Glad I could make it."

Hurley grinned, settling on the edge of his desk. "Always have time for you. Miss Conners, coffee please."

"Certainly, Mr. Hurley," she replied smoothly, masking something cold beneath that perfectly practiced smile.

Hurley's eyes lingered a moment too long as she left the room. "She's something, isn't she?" he muttered with a wolfish grin.

Jake stifled a laugh. "Better than your first secretary—a lovely woman called Georgia Trilby, was it?"

Hurley sighed, amusement folding into bitterness. "She was my second wife. Cost me a fortune in the divorce. I don't marry anymore." He lowered his voice conspiratorially. "I've got to watch the harassment stuff but I have a sixth sense for who will play along."

The room shifted as he straightened. "But you're here for another reason, Jake—not to talk about my secretary."

Jake flushed but nodded quickly. "I hope you liked the new designs."

"Brilliant," Hurley said, eyes gleaming. "I brought your blueprints to the guys in R&D—the college grads in their ivory towers. First thing they say? 'This won't work.'"

Jake couldn't stop a faint smile from creeping in. "Really?"

"Yeah. Then I pull out your prototype and flipped it on. You should've seen their faces—they looked like they shit themselves." Hurley laughed, slapping his knee. The sound was loud and raw, filling the spacious office.

Jake laughed too, a rare and carefree sound.

"How do you do it?" Hurley asked, leaning forward.

"Trial and error mostly. I don't draw the blueprints until I know it works."

"That's backwards, according to your Ivy League critics."

Jake nodded confidently. "Worked for Edison."

Hurley smiled in approval. "You've been a rock for this company, Jake—not just with your gadgets. You've been a guard since... what? 1960?"

Jake nodded. "That's right."

"Thirty years, damn. And captain at Murray Hill since before the BT&T breakup—before it became Bellcant."

Jake shrugged. "I'm used to the midnight shift."

"You run a tight ship." Hurley stood, pacing restlessly. "But the actual power? The site supervisor. Farrell's retiring in Whippany. I think it's time you took that spot."

Jake swallowed hard. "Really?"

"There'll be a pay bump, of course. Though frankly, you probably make more from your inventions than the guard's salary."

"Sometimes," Jake admitted.

"If you could make more just from your designs, would you still keep your guard job?"

Jake shook his head firmly. "I'm too young to retire, and I like it."

"Good. Loyalty means a lot. I'm putting you in as site supervisor."

Jake's mind raced. "Do they have office space there?"

"We've got rooms for our use."

"I'd like to set up a workshop—somewhere outside the house to work on inventions."

Hurley smiled broadly. "I support that one hundred percent."

"Great!" Jake said, feeling a surge of triumph.

"And there's more. You've heard about our IPO?"

Jake nodded. "It's in all the financial papers."

"I'm authorized to give you, as a reward for your work, five thousand shares in Security Information Systems."

A shadow crossed Jake's face.

"Something wrong?"

He stiffened. "I appreciate that, sir. I know it's worth close to a hundred thousand dollars. But with Shawn's medical bills… I need cash."

Hurley's expression softened. "I knew about your son's troubles. I took steps to help."

He reached into his desk, pulling out an envelope thick with certificates—and a smaller one. Jake opened the second envelope, his heart pounding. Inside was a check.

He slammed his hand on the desk in shock.

Hurley laughed. "Does that remunerate you enough?"

Jake stared. The cashier's check was for two hundred and fifty thousand dollars.

His breath caught. His mouth was dry. He tried to speak but no words came. Hurley's laughter echoed through the room again.

Miss Conners returned, placing cups of coffee before them. Jake burned his tongue on the black liquid, his bewildered expression triggering another bout of Hurley's laughter.

"Are you all right, Mr. Hurd?" the receptionist asked, concern mingling with her polished smile.

"I—I'm fine," Jake stammered.

"She's worried because you just got the biggest surprise of your life," Hurley said through chuckles.

"Congratulations, Mr. Hurd," Miss Conners added. "We're all grateful for your work."

"You stuck with us through the hard times. Now I'm making sure you get every penny you deserve."

Jake left the building clutching the check and stock certificates as though they might vanish like a fleeting dream.

Driving home, Jake was barely aware of the world around him, nearly a hazard on the road. He stopped to deposit the check, then returned home to do mindless chores—to center himself.

After a decade of hardship and heartbreak, he felt like a man who just won the lottery—new job, financial freedom, and best of all, Shawn back home.

Upstairs in the round room he used as a workshop, he sat beneath the bright fluorescent light surrounded by wires, chips, and circuit boards.

Before him lay a prototype: a combination of ultra-high-frequency sound chips, a tiny amplifier, and a speaker. He envisioned a device that could manipulate sound waves into a feedback loop—a technological 'duck call' capable of coaxing out the shadows.

He'd lost everything once because he hadn't prepared enough weapons to fight back. He vowed this time would be different.

If the shadows dared to come for him again he'd be ready—and he'd send them running afraid him for once.

With steady hands, Jake picked up his soldering iron and set to work.

The battle had only just begun.

38. Adapting

The news of Jake's promotion spread swiftly through the ranks, reaching guards on every shift. Pride hummed beneath their gruff voices whenever they mentioned Captain Jake's new role—site supervisor at Whippany.

To them, Jake was a beacon of steady strength, a man who earned his promotion through hard work and diligence.

Unknown to his crew, Jake's mind churned with a singular, delicate mission—the feedback device he painstakingly developed.

Tonight, he would test it before he took charge of the new, unfamiliar site.

Trembling just beneath his measured resolve was the memory of previous encounters when irritated shadows turned vicious, their wrath spilling over into the real world with merciless ferocity.

He had no intention of provoking a repeat—this time, every precaution mattered.

His plan was meticulous. Drawing on intimate knowledge of the labyrinthine site, Jake chose a dark basement tucked deep within the building's bowels, a favored haunt and hiding spot for those shadowy entities, where he always felt their presence.

Over several nights he set the stage, assembling his equipment piece by piece. The centerpiece was a camera rig outfitted with his own custom infrared system   a lamp flooded the test zone with invisible light designed to pull the creatures into sight where human eyes could not reach.

Jake drilled a hole into the thick floor of a storage room above, threading a cable with painstaking care to link the camera to a videocassette recorder and monitor stationed safely away.

From there, he could watch remotely, shielded by the concrete between him and the dark below.

He fortified himself mentally. This was not like past experiments where the shadows—a name he used but never fully trusted— lashed out by attacking his home.

He checked every alarm and left Shawn armed with a handful of battery-powered lights. Jake also carried two compact units capable of blasting blinding light—his ace against any retaliatory assault.

By the time he walked to the subbasement at 11:30 PM his heart thumped with a mix of nerves and anticipation.

He implanted the sound device—a small box built to capture the peculiar frequencies the shadows might respond to—and secured it to a heavy table using strong elastic cords and metal fittings.

Every detail was accounted for. The room was pitch black once he flipped off the lights and he couldn't see the infrared lamp flooding the basement but he knew it was there.

Hours dragged by as other guards made their rounds. At three in the morning, Jake retreated to the storage room.

The faint green hue of the night-vision filtered monitor flickered before him. Through the headphones, the quiet whir of machinery and silence draped the room.

He whispered, "Ready to go," and eased a light disk onto the floor. With a flick of his remote control, a faint red indicator glow shimmered on the sound box below. On his monitor, it flashed brilliant white.

The box was designed to pick up the subtlest sounds and amplify them, repeating fresh noises or, failing that, increasing volume until its small speaker stretched to the limits.

Shawn had convinced Jake that the shadows communicated. Jake needed proof, and in this haunted basement, he hoped to capture their voices.

Minutes crawled by. Then came a singular, sudden 'whoosh'— an ambiguous sound that made Jake's blood quicken. The box shuddered violently, straining against its restraints. The elastic cords groaned under the assault. Jake's eyes darted between the monitor's grainy screen and the unstable device.

Frustration bit him as he muttered, "I can't see them in infrared either."

Suddenly, the pace and force of the movement escalated. The heavy table seemed to lift, hovered, then slammed down with a thunderous crash that sent vibrations through the concrete.

The red light on the box stayed steadfast; through his headphones Jake caught eerie, unrecognizable noises.

His pulse doubled.

Without warning the box exploded in a burst like a firecracker, shards flying in every direction. The camera's infrared lamp flickered wildly before plunging the monitor into darkness.

The basement vanished from view.

Heart pounding, Jake killed the recorder and yanked the tape free, clutching it tightly. He tapped the light disk on the floor with his foot. A brilliant light blossomed—a lifeline if the shadows tried to emerge through the hole.

He wasn't going down without a fight.

Outside under a swollen sky, Jake sank into his car seat and packed the precious tape into a metal box lined with plastic shielding—an airport film protection bag to guard against any interference. He locked it tight in the trunk, breathing the cold night air with renewed caution.

He waited out the rest of the night at the guard station, eyes heavy but alert. Dawn's pale fingers nudged him before he ventured back to collect the wreckage, both grateful and doubtful.

That morning, farewells were quiet and filled with a strange weight. Jake's hands still trembled when he turned the ignition and drove through a gray, overcast day, clutching remnants of the device—and the fragile hope of empirical evidence.

But his peace was short-lived.

Pulling into the driveway, Jake's breath hitched—Shawn's car was already there. Anxiety prickled his skin before he even opened the door.

Inside an alarm shrieked—a sharp wail that pierced the quiet house. Jake dropped the metal box onto the counter and sprinted upstairs, muscles coiling like springs. The crack of bright light bleeding beneath his son's bedroom door froze him.

Every nerve screamed in warning.

He slammed into the control panel, fingertips flying over the keypad as he silenced the proximity alarm and turned off the brilliant protective lights.

"SHAWN?" His voice cracked as he flung the door wide.

There stood Shawn. Fully dressed, rigid, eyes shut tight. Tears shimmered in the corners, though whether from anguish or the relentless light Jake couldn't tell. The boy might have stood like that for hours, trapped in silence.

"Shawn?" Jake softened, stepping closer, searching for injury.

When Jake touched his son's arms, Shawn flinched, then finally opened his eyes. Recognition flickered. He collapsed into Jake's arms, sobbing uncontrollably.

"It's okay, you're safe," Jake murmured, heart breaking.

"No, I'm not. Nothing's okay," Shawn choked out, voice ragged.

"What's wrong? Are you hurt?"

"Dad... you have to get me to the doctor. I need that stuff again. You've got to—"

The word 'Dad' struck Jake like a thunderclap.

He brushed Shawn's golden hair back tenderly. "Shh, son. What's going on?"

"I heard them again," Shawn blurted. "They... they talked to me. I was reading—or dozing off—and then their voices, they started again."

"They? Who, Shawn?"

"You know who, Dad." His eyes glistened, searching for understanding. "It's not a nightmare. It's real. Like before—"

He broke, grief pouring out in fresh waves. Jake held him tight, soothing him, reassuring him that the alarms and lights had been the right call.

Eventually Jake gave Shawn the prescribed sleeping pill he kept nearby, just in case. Shawn drank it down, lay back on his bed without changing out of his clothes, and drifted into sleep.

With the boy asleep, he walked downstairs, his own breath slowing as he calmed down.

As he reached the kitchen, he froze.

The metal box—the one holding the tape—lay open and empty where he'd left it.

An icy dread slipped under his skin. Outside the sky remained heavy, a dull wash of gray.

Jake whispered to himself, "They can't do anything during the day…"

A dark voice echoed in his mind, chillingly clear: *They can.*

The next morning dawned heavy with a quiet tension. Shawn withdrew into himself entirely, retreating to his room without a word, without a glance.

Jake felt the painful sting of disappointment sharpen in his chest—after all the progress they made it was as if the boy was slipping backward, back into the depths of his old torments.

With a two-week vacation stretched out before him before his new role as site supervisor in Whippany, Jake refused to wait idly.

Determined, he summoned Shawn's doctor to their home and spoke candidly: "Shawn's been hearing things." The doctor's eyes darkened immediately. "We need to run every test we can."

That same day Jake drove Shawn to Essex County Hospital, where a barrage of pokes, prods, and X-rays followed. Despite the invasive examinations, outwardly Shawn appeared no different from any healthy twenty-one-year-old—his body intact..

Inside the cramped hospital office, Jake sat face to face with Dr. Reinholdt, the neurologist on staff.

Reinholdt was a stout man, with a gray hair stretched thin over a balding scalp in a tidy but obvious comb-over, like a fragile lace cap perched on his head.

"I'm telling you, Mr. Hurd," Reinholdt said, his voice low but firm, "we may have to consider psychological factors."

Jake's jaw tightened. "Only as a very last resort, Doctor."

Reinholdt leaned forward, planting his elbows on the desk. "There could be a biochemical explanation for Shawn's symptoms. Our understanding of the brain's functions has grown tremendously in just the last decade."

Jake shook his head, grief and frustration battling within him. "You've seen him. He's distant… like he was back when the facilities drugged him into silence."

"That's classic avoidance behavior," Reinholdt replied. "The hallucinations you describe—the voices—could stem from a brain disorder. It might be a tumor, a minor stroke. Hallucinations can affect any of the senses—you can see things that aren't real, hear voices, even taste phantom flavors. Add to that the effects of long-term antipsychotic drugs he was on as a teen—they might have altered his brain chemistry permanently."

Jake's voice cracked as he asked, "What can we do?"

"There's a new test—It's called an MRI scan—that might give us insight."

Jake's familiarity sparked. "Magnetic resonance imaging, right? Magnetics and radio waves? I know about those."

Reinholdt smiled slightly. "We're fortunate—only a few hospitals in the region have one. It's the best way to look inside Shawn's brain, to find blockages or irregularities."

Jake nodded. "Set it up."

They scheduled the MRI for Monday, and Shawn stayed overnight in the hospital, a concession allowed only because Jake stayed by his side, his small light disk ready at hand.

Hours dragged as Jake kept watch, balancing a drafting board on his knees, refining blueprints to distract his restless mind.

They put Shawn to sleep using an IV drip but he stirred repeatedly through the night, each time Jake moved close, whispering steady reassurances until the boy's body stilled again.

Morning came with a nervous urgency. They introduced a chemical dye via the IV and Shawn accepted the procedure with a vacant, disconnected stare that pierced Jake's heart.

When a petite, energetic nurse pulled Jake aside to review safety protocols, the tension thickened. "Any metal on you? Pacemaker? Pins? Watch?" .

Changing into hospital scrubs, Jake followed Dr. Reinholdt into the MRI room. The machine loomed—a massive donut tilted on its side like a portal to an unseen world.

It was so reminiscent of the device Dr. Goldstein had built decades earlier, that for a moment Jake stared, unable to speak.

Shawn lay on the sliding table that glided him into the magnetic tunnel. The machine powered up with a low hum, abruptly overlaid by loud clanking beats—like a crazed drummer pounding out an erratic rhythm on a metal bongo.

"What's that banging?" Jake asked the doctor.

"Oh, that's the magnets powering up. We gave Shawn earplugs."

"Good," Jake mumbled as Dr. Reinholdt gestured for him to leave the MRI room. "Come on," he said, "we'll watch the images in the radiology lab."

They walked into a small, dimly lit room dominated by glowing screens that looked more like a television editing suite than a hospital. The images flickered alive—the shapes and colors of Shawn's brain swirling in vivid purples, yellows, and reds, each hue representing activity in different lobes.

"That," Reinholdt said, pointing, "is the axial view of the cerebrum—the right and left hemispheres, the frontal lobe, the parietal."

Jake strained to comprehend the vibrant map before him. The room buzzed with silent intensity.

Frank, the technician at the console, grunted noncommittally at Reinholdt's greetings, absorbed in the glowing monitors.

After half an hour of scanning and watching images freeze and shift on screens, Jake's nerves surfaced in a quiet voice. "Do you think he's... all right?"

"Relax," Reinholdt assured. "Nurse's with him. Everything looks pretty normal. Perhaps we should consider psychiatric factors..." His voice faltered as Frank interrupted sharply.

"Activity."

Both men turned to the screen where an area of Shawn's brain was bright yellow on a monitor.

"What is that?" Reinholdt asked, narrowing his eyes.

"Hippocampus," Frank muttered. "Amygdala."

Jake watched the focused examination, feeling the tension spike.

"Freeze that frame Frank," Reinholdt ordered.

Minutes passed as the screens shifted to the sagittal plane. The slow, deliberate work of the machine filled the silence.

"Got it!" Frank exclaimed.

Reinholdt studied the images intently, comparing them side-by-side.

"Tell me what's wrong," Jake pressed, heart pounding.

"It's not wrong," the doctor said carefully. "But parts of Shawn's brain show unusually high activity."

"Is that a problem?"

Reinholdt pointed to a glowing egg-shaped area. "The temporal lobe—the hippocampus. This is where the brain stores short-term memories. The yellow hue means heightened activity, more than expected."

"Memories?"

"Yes. And here," he said, pointing to the amygdala—a similarly bright hotspot. "That structure gives meaning to experiences—it transforms sensations into emotional significance, like pain teaching caution."

Jake frowned. "So why so active now?"

"Exactly. It's puzzling. An overactive amygdala suggests Complex Partial Epilepsy, or CPE. Seizures localized in these brain areas can cause hallucinations and fear."

"Seizures?" Jake repeated slowly.

Reinholdt nodded gravely. "It could explain the voices. The funny thing—there are obscure studies suggesting CPE in this area correlates with ESP—extra-sensory perception—though that's controversial."

Jake swallowed hard. "So... Shawn might be... particularly sensitive? Gifted?"

The doctor smiled thinly. "I doubt it, but it's an intriguing theory. But he wasn't hallucinating in the institutions when antidepressants suppressed this brain region. Is he off meds now?"

"Just stopped recently."

"Then we'll try controlling the activity with a mild anti-seizure medication combined with an antidepressant."

"Preventative?"

"Management. No cure, but control. Drugs, possibly ECT."

Jake's blood ran cold. "No electroshock."

Reinholdt shrugged with a hint of sympathy in his eyes. "I agree. In fact, electric shock can sometimes trigger this kind of epilepsy."

Jake's terror mounted, a dark dread settling like a weight in his gut.

"Wait," he whispered, voice hollow, "I once received a powerful shock. Could that cause me to see things?"

The doctor nodded matter-of-factly. "It's rare, but yes. An electric shock can induce—or control—CPE. It's a rather extraordinary irony."

Jake's mouth went dry, his mind reeling. Could his own trauma have bequeathed this imbalance to his son? Could the shock that he'd received open doors inside his brain—as well as Shawn's?

He watched Shawn lying inside the noisy machine, eyes shut, body trembling slightly. Watching him, suddenly his ears popped sharply.

His senses sharpened. Among the metallic clanging he picked up a whisper—a dry, indistinct rattle like leaves stirring in a weak breeze. Something was there.

They were here.

Jake's eyes scanned the shadowed ceiling and far wall near the door where two presences lurked just beyond sight. He couldn't see them, but he felt their gaze—watching, waiting.

The whispering dry rustle grew faintly louder like voices speaking just out of reach. His heart thundered.

Why were they keeping their distance? The dark room could afford them perfect vantage.

Jake's mind flashed—there was a powerful magnetic field in that room. It was a combination of magnetics, radio waves, lasers, microwaves. It was the same cocktail that opened the original portal all those years ago.

He glanced toward the lurking presences as far from the machine as the room allowed.

Years of fighting them with light and sound failed.

But this—this magnetic force—

Strong enough to turn a doorknob into a lethal projectile—

Maybe that was the key.

39. Fighting Back

Shawn's breakthrough with the combination drug therapy was nothing short of miraculous.

For the first time in months, the relentless chorus of voices dimmed into silence and with it came a surprising lift in his spirits.

The side effects were minimal, barely noticeable, a rare mercy. After just a week of daily capsules the walls of his self-imposed prison crumbled. He emerged from the shadows of his room no longer hiding from the world, cautiously re-engaging with the life he had nearly abandoned.

He ventured outside but his world remained small and cautious—only stepping out during daylight, his visits usually limited to the quiet sanctuary of the library.

Yet as dusk fell, the old familiar shadows crept back. With the sun's retreat, so did Shawn's tentative grasp on the day's peace; he would once again withdraw into himself, as if the darkness could pull him under once more.

Jake watched the change warily, hoping this fragile progress would hold, and gently encouraged Shawn to follow through on his original plan: community college.

"I'm just not ready yet, Uncle Jake," Shawn said, his voice barely above a whisper.

Jake noticed Shawn slipping back from calling him 'Dad'—a subtle retreat that spoke volumes of the emotional distance still between them.

"I won't push you," he said softly, though the urgency beneath his tone was clear. "But I have to start my new job."

Shawn nodded, clutching the fragile hope he held. "I'll be okay. I'll stay in the house at night. And you know I like the library. I can get books."

Jake accepted the compromise though unease lingered.

Meanwhile, he dove headfirst into his own new chapter—the world of Magnetic Resonance Imaging—fascinated by its history, its technology, and the invisible forces at play.

His research pointed out the flaws in Goldstein's design all those years earlier. Goldstein had used copper tubes filled with liquid helium to generate magnetic fields, a method both revolutionary and dangerously unstable.

The method cost Goldstein his life, exploding in a catastrophic surge of expanding gas.

Newer technology evolved: superconductive magnets enclosed within larger containers flooded with liquid nitrogen, outfitted with release valves designed to vent gas safely if something went wrong.

The newer method was elegant, far safer—and they had such equipment at Bellcant's innovative lab in Whippany where Jake would have his own workroom—with both the permission of his company and Bellcant.

At Bellcant, Jake remained on site past his shifts, lingering near the labs as scientists trickled in. He bought coffee, even a pastry or two, offering his company for conversations steeped deep in magnetic fields, superconductivity, and wavelength theory.

The new security site supervisor intrigued the scientists. Here was a man who checked their IDs and discussed and even understood their work on a level matching their own.

Jake absorbed every word, his mind working overtime to piece together what was possible.

The recent unnerving loss of the videotape—a chilling hint at unknown limitations—haunted him.

On the other hand, his newfound ability to hear the creatures lurking in the shadows was a secret advantage, a hidden ace he intended to use.

Armed with this growing knowledge, Jake transformed the small workshop they gave him at Bellcant into his personal fortress.

Drawing on technical journals, he experimented with materials: niobium titanium tubing coiled tightly around iron cores. He discovered that a standard wall socket could power the creation of a powerful magnet if surrounded by liquid nitrogen or helium. In his experiments, the magnetic force soared to astonishing levels.

Yet the genuine revelation was not the magnets themselves—it was resonance.

As he'd always suspected the key lay in frequencies, the way MRI machines used radio waves known as the Larmor frequency through the body. These waves passed through tissues, magnetized hydrogen atoms and altered their speed. The computers translated the received signal into images—allowing a peek inside living flesh without a single incision.

Goldstein's fatal machine combined magnetics, shortwaves, microwaves, and a ruby laser to create his quantum tunnel.

Jake thought differently.

He sought a shortwave equivalent to the Larmor frequency—one that could produce a field not to open a portal, but to exert power over the unseen entities that haunted him.

In his workroom, he left all metal outside its door; day by day he balanced his growing workload—handling schedules, memos, paychecks—with long stretches immersed in his resonant experiments.

He only emerged briefly—to cover the overnight lunch break at reception, to manage morning badge checks, to ensure tours ran smoothly—before retreating again into the hum of his machines.

He started with a small prototype much like Goldstein did. Four upright hoops, two electromagnets at the center, encased in a metal frame capable of containing liquefied gas. Ductwork vented pressurized nitrogen safely outside, a lesson from Goldstein's fatal oversight.

The device which he quietly dubbed the 'Resonant Ring,' rested atop his desk—a paradoxically small machine with a large presence. At home he built another device, a feedback machine he planned to use as bait.

Weeks crawled by, every long night accompanied by the creeping, unsettling presence of the creatures he sought to trap.

He felt their watchful eyes in the corridor shadows near his office, heard their soft rustling—the whispers that spoke of him in their dark language.

Tension hummed beneath every moment, the silence shattered only by that eerie murmuring. Jake willed himself to ignore their calls. For now, he had to stand firm—because he knew the next step would be the most dangerous yet.

"Frequency!" Jake's voice cracked through the quiet of the dinner table, shattering the usual calm. He slammed his fist lightly onto the wood. "They all have different frequencies!"

Shawn looked up from his plate of steak and mashed potatoes, eyebrows knitting in confusion. "What?"

"That's it! That's what I've been missing all this time. The entire problem—frequency!"

Shawn frowned, pushing the food around with his fork, the mashed potatoes morphing into absent-minded shapes. "Uncle Jake, I don't know—"

Jake cut in, hurriedly, sharing his theory, words tumbling out like a violent tide.

Shawn listened quietly, eyes fixed on the food. Suddenly the fork clattered to the plate. Shawn rose abruptly, face flushed, eyes fiery.

"Why are you doing this?" he barked, voice shaking with frustration.

Jake recoiled. "What?"

"It's pointless! You can't win. There's no way to fight back. You just have to give up!" Shawn's voice cracked under the weight of hopelessness.

"Don't say that," Jake said, his tone sharpening. "You don't understand—"

"No, I do! You told me what happened to Amanda, to your wife, to your old girlfriend." Shawn's words stabbed the air. He loomed over Jake who was now sitting, his hands tightening into fists.

Jake's jaw clenched. Bringing up those memories was like opening a bleeding wound.

Shawn caught his breath, covering his face as if to fend off an invisible blow. He raked his fingers through his long unruly blond hair.

"What if all this—the amygdala, the frequencies—they're not the answer?" Shawn's voice dropped to a murmur. "What if... they're demons?"

Jake blinked in disbelief, shaking his head. "Demons?"

"Yeah," Shawn said, eyes haunted yet determined. "Don't they sound like demons? Like the ones in the Bible. Demons have a long history—people have known about them for centuries."

Jake stared at his plate, mind swirling. "Where is this coming from?"

"I went to Saint John's the other day," Shawn admitted quietly.

Jake remembered Shawn leaving Sunday morning but hadn't pressed for details. "The Catholic Church?"

"Yes," Shawn nodded, settling back into his seat, a soft calm settling over him, the fire of anger dampened by the antidepressants—but also something deeper. "It's small, not crowded. The organ played, the priest spoke about protecting ourselves from demons."

Jake shook his head. "Sounds pretty medieval."

"Maybe," Shawn said softly. "But he used it as a metaphor—to avoid the demon of selfishness, the demon of ego…"

"Ah, more palatable that way."

"But it made me wonder," Shawn continued, voice serious, eyes distant. "Voices. Demons. If people had seen what we've seen centuries ago, what would they call it?"

Jake's gaze dropped again. "But these… they're not spirits or ghosts. They move things—they interact."

"Poltergeists do that, too," Shawn shot back.

Jake's face hardened. "You hear them. We both do."

Shawn paused, shaking his head. "To me, they speak full words. What about you?"

"More like the sound of crumpling paper."

Shawn nodded solemnly. "That's how it started with me—the dry, crackling murmurs. Then they spoke." His eyes clouded over with memories.

Jake watched his son fight for control, trying to keep his own emotions locked away.

"You can't win," Shawn whispered.

"But—I have to try. These things hurt everyone I've ever loved," Jake growled.

"Then maybe you have to try a different way," Shawn's voice was eerily calm, unwavering. "Alarms, lights, sirens—they're all science. They don't work. You fight demons the way people have for centuries."

"What? Draw pentagrams? Burn incense?" Jake scoffed.

"At least that would be a fresh approach," Shawn said fiercely. "I was told in Biscayne that the surest sign of insanity is doing the same thing over and over and expecting different results. You react to every attack with more of the same. Lights don't work, so you get stronger lights. Alarms fail, so you make better ones."

Jake's eyes flashed. "And it has kept them at bay!"

"Or made us prisoners," Shawn countered. "I can't wander the halls at night without setting something off."

"The lights won't hurt you."

"Like they didn't hurt Amanda?"

Jake stepped back, Shawn's words cut deep. He gripped the back of his chair, voice low and furious. "That was an accident!"

"I know, Uncle Jake," Shawn said quietly, pausing. Then, more gently, "Dad."

The anger drained from Jake's face in an instant replaced by weary resignation. "So... what do we do?"

"You work on your frequencies and magnets. I'm going to find out about demons."

Jake snorted. "So I should ward them off with a cross, like Dracula?"

"Maybe." Shawn shrugged. "Maybe your machines don't work because God isn't in the equation."

Jake spat on the floor in disgust. "A merciful God wouldn't let monsters like these exist!"

"That's the old question, isn't it? Why bad things happen to good people. I don't know the answer. But if these things are spiritual, then we need spiritual solutions."

Jake rose, pacing the room, his headache intensifying. "They manipulate solid objects—so they must be physical. A magnetic field of the right frequency could affect them."

"You don't know that—"

"Don't you see? We manipulate subatomic particles every day! This is the technology that can stop them—maybe even destroy them!" His steps quickened with passion.

"You're excited about killing them?"

Jake's face hardened. "Shouldn't I be? After everything they've done—to me, to you? They've haunted me for thirty years. Put you in an institution. I want to make them pay!"

"So this is about vengeance?"

"It's about freedom. About feeling safe when the sun goes down."

They looked at each other—breathing heavy, the tension thick. Jake felt his body tremble with a restless fury, as if charged for a thousand battles.

"You do it your way," Shawn said, voice resolute. "I'll try mine." Without waiting for a reply he pushed back from the table and climbed the stairs.

Jake stood alone, the silence pressing down on him like a weight. He took the dishes to the kitchen, letting the storm of emotion fade into the background as he focused on the routine chore—once again burying the fear beneath the mundane.

As he had done his entire life.

40. CAPTURE AND RELEASE

After three grueling days of clandestine experimentation in his cramped Bellcant office, Jake was finally ready.

The Resonant Ring loomed before him on the scarred desk—a formidable apparatus built by his own hand. Dormant power hummed quietly as transformers and a frequency modulator densely packed its heavy metal base.

From that base a thick vertical casing rose, an unyielding enclosure housing the inner hoops. Tonight, he would flood those hoops with liquid nitrogen, turning them into an electromagnet of unprecedented force.

He secured the attached ductwork to vent the nitrogen if a quench occurred—but the risk only intensified the stakes.

Jake's journey over the past few weeks was nothing short of miraculous.

He absorbed and applied arcane techniques that would baffle even the most seasoned physicists. Driven not by academic curiosity but by a fierce desire to instill fear—genuine fear—in his relentless enemy.

For once, he wanted the shadows to be afraid of him.

Across the room he'd mounted a crude plastic control box, his makeshift brain for the machine's operation.

On the floor beside it, he'd fastened one of his powerful battery lights beside a foot pedal, ready to fill the room with blinding illumination if necessary.

He glanced down at his watch: 4:30 AM. The hour was perfect —no foot traffic, no distractions, no chance of interference. Dawn was still a fragile promise on the horizon, and the shadows were usually less bold at this hour.

Jake pulled on a thick protective glove with deliberate care on his left hand, then switched off the overhead lights.

Darkness closed in instantly, except for a faint spill of early morning light filtering through the venetian blinds and a distant fluorescent buzz down the hallway.

The hiss of liquid nitrogen followed as he opened the valve atop the coolant tank, the frigid gas sluicing into the enclosure through the hose with an ominous whisper.

Standing at the control box, Jake unclenched his gloved hand and flicked on the audio feedback device—the bait. He'd painstakingly calibrated it to respond only to a narrow band of frequencies designed to lure the shadows out from their hiding places.

Turning a small dial to '1', he activated the transformers, cooling system, and basic electronics—though the frequency modulator and electromagnets remained dormant for the moment.

Like a predator waiting patiently with a fishing line cast into murky waters, Jake watched the softly pulsing diode light on the box.

The Resonant Ring stood silent in the gloom, waiting to be activated. Minutes ticked by slowly. He heard the faint sounds of the feedback machine—a crackling noise like dry autumn leaves rustling in a restless wind.

They had to hear it. They would come. At least one would. That was all he needed.

Four minutes in Jake's heart suddenly leapt. The subtle shift in the air, the nearly imperceptible disturbance in the surrounding shadows—he felt it before he saw it.

A lone scout had slinked into the room, invisible in the darkness. He sensed an intelligence, wary but curious, sent to investigate this strange human contraption.

Jake remembered the first time he'd recorded one of these feedback sounds—the long pause before a swarm of them erupted into frenzy, tearing his old machine to pieces.

This time would be different.

Slowly, the creature crept in, slipping from the neighboring office through a narrow seam beneath the wall. The movement calculated—skittish, almost hesitant.

Unlike their usual brazen assaults, it skirted the edges of the feeble light seeping from the window, flowing like an oily fluid over the walls. Just a shade darker than its surroundings, it melded seamlessly into the night.

It advanced cautiously toward the Resonant Ring.

Such care was alien to their usual violent nature. Did the low hum of the machine's magnetic field disturb them? Even at low power, the electromagnetic presence might unsettle the creature.

Jake's pulse thundered in his ears as the creature climbed his desk. Paralyzed by a mix of awe and terror, he kept still as one thin, shadowy appendage stretched out, its touch like a finger clad in black latex probing the box perched just past the ring's center.

He clenched the dial with numb fingers, slow breaths steadying his pounding heart. Despite the urge, he didn't intervene.

Patience was critical—he wanted more of them to come.

The presence of a single scout was promising yet insufficient. He had to bait an entire swarm.

Remaining motionless he let the shadow feel safe, drawing it into false comfort with nothing but the sound and silence—this enormous hoop was mere façade for now.

The creature recoiled, releasing a hiss that rippled through the feedback box's speakers—a dry, crackling whisper, faint as a breeze but unmistakably different.

The signal was out. They were coming.

Not in the vast hordes he feared—the ones that once ravaged his family—but enough to make an impact. They flew in fast, impossible to count with certainty as they darted past him on the walls like dark gusts of wind. Angry, reckless, and furious, their intent was clear—to destroy the noisy lure and exact vengeance on him.

The control box shuddered violently as if grabbed and shaken, but Jake had fastened it firmly to the desk.

Come on, he urged silently.

It leapt again and again, held fast against the elastic grip, mimicking their harsh noises over and over—an infuriating game of echoes designed to enrage and expose them.

Suddenly the box violently shook, almost convulsing, as if gripped by an unseen hand.

"Now!" Jake snapped and cranked the dial up to ten.

An eerie blue glow bathed the room as the magnets surged to full power, the ozone tang thickening the air. A desperate, piercing sound—not a scream but something akin to one—flooded the space, echoing through the room.

Shapes lunged at him, whipping past like malevolent phantoms caught in a storm of magnetic fury and radio waves. Their usual ferocity turned to panic: confused, hurt, afraid.

Desperately, they tried to strike back, but their disorientation made them ineffective. Instead, they fled quickly in any way they could.

Jake's chest swelled with triumph. For once he had turned the tables.

Moving carefully toward the ring's hypnotic glow, he spotted the prize—a small shape suspended in the electromagnetic field at its center. It fought, but the invisible forces held it tight.

He'd caught one.

He reached down and lowered the dial by a third. He wasn't here to kill—yet.

His eyes studied the creature trapped within the ring: a tangled, stunted silhouette with twisted limbs and grotesquely malformed features. Its slitted eyes tracked his every movement. The eerie shriek ceased as its twisted mouth closed, leaving an oppressive silence.

Jake scanned the room, struggling to pierce the haze of sound spilling from the feedback box. He flicked a switch and silenced it.

Approaching the captive, he felt an unexpected flush of sympathy surge through him.

Here was a prisoner, a sentient being caught between worlds, trapped in a cage of electromagnetic might.

He wished fervently, that he could speak its language—to warn it, perhaps to negotiate, to understand. Maybe, just maybe, it already knew the gravity of its situation.

Jake cranked the power dial higher, and the creature let out the same rasping squeal—sharp, grating, like nails on metal. He held the setting for several tense seconds, then slowly dialed it back down, watching intently as the thing writhed and strained, gathering its strength like a cornered animal.

"Look at you," Jake muttered, stepping over and sinking into a creaky wooden chair.

His eyes locked onto his captive, the small black shape trembling within the invisible field. He wondered how long it could survive trapped like this. Was it like a shark, condemned to constant movement or death? This one was pinned, desperate, forced to endure immobilization.

Did it hate that?

"So, now I've got a proper look at you," Jake said bitterly, his breath escaping in a harsh huff. "And there's not a damn thing you can do about it, right?"

His mind flashed to Peggy and Sally—lovers lost to these creatures, his life shredded again and again by their terror.

He had to keep that anger alive; it fueled him, gave him the edge he needed—the strength to rip this little bastard apart if he had to.

"How about I keep you here until sunrise?" Jake taunted, eyes narrowing as he watched its futile struggles. "Get a front-row seat to the morning sun, blinds wide open. You think that'd do you in? Burn you up like some damn vampire?"

The creature bucked and twisted against the magnetic field but couldn't budge. Jake's hand hovered, hesitating just a moment before he reached forward. A strange tingle ran up his arm, electric and alive—the shortwave frequencies, the magnets buzzing through the air crawling up his skin. His finger glowed faintly, a bluish aura flickering at the tip.

The creature recoiled instinctively, sliding sideways to avoid his hand—but the force field held it trapped. Jake touched its sooty black skin.

He jerked back almost immediately. The touch was… fragile. Like a rose petal—soft but pulsing with life, delicate in a way he hadn't expected.

The spot where his finger landed shimmered, the blackness giving way to a turquoise glow. The creature's spasms turned more frantic; the brief contact clearly caused it pain.

Jake leaned back. This was unexpected..

Those things clawed and scraped at him for years, yet his touch —powered by his invention—seemed to hurt it. Was it the magnets? The frequencies? Some energy running through his body?

Jake immediately checked the machine's readings. The system was far from perfect. A sudden quench—an unexpected dip in power—and the creature could just vanish from the field, slipping back into the shadows.

He moved to his control box by the doorway, eyes locked on the makeshift gauge. The small needle jittered rhythmically, a silent warning. Minor fluctuations now but they'd only escalate. He estimated he had roughly ten minutes before the system would require a shutdown.

Jake cast a wary glance down the hall. No sign of any of the others of its kind—it was silent, too silent.

His gaze snapped back to the captive. Its small, square head turned rapidly as if seeking a way out, its tiny dark eye slits darting anxiously.

He crouched by the field to examine the spot he'd touched. The turquoise wound remained though now it was darker, like a bruise healing slowly.

"That's what I can do to you," Jake said softly, voice low but firm. "Don't mess with me."

He stood, turning the dial on his control—and the field winked out instantly. Reaching up, he snapped the valve closed on the tank.

He decided this would allow the creature to become incorporeal again.

But instead, the creature collapsed to the floor. The room plunged into darkness, broken only by the faint sound of its fall —a gentle noise like a leaf hitting the ground.

Jake immediately flicked on the overhead lights. No way was he risking an attack from the other shadows emboldened by the dark.

But to Jake surprise, the lights revealed the creature still there, a small flat black shape sprawled on the floor, stunned or disoriented.

It screeched again, that rasping noise, and scrambled to its feet on stubby legs. Without grace it crashed straight into a desk leg and toppled over. It jumped up and darted into the safety of the kneehole beneath the desk, slipping into the protective darkness.

Jake almost laughed at the clumsy escape attempt, but beneath his amusement was pure astonishment.

Moving to the machine he turned a valve and released a vent of nitrogen out the window.

The creature banged helplessly against the wooden backstop under the desk like a bird caught indoors, fluttering toward invisible exits.

Jake approached the desk and knelt, shining his flashlight into the shadows. The thing chirped that terrifying whisper again. He pulled the beam back, then cautiously reached beneath with his bare hand.

He touched it once more. The same fragile, petal-like sensation. Fascinated, Jake pulled back sharply, a sudden stab of pain shooting up his finger. Blood glistened on the tip. Turning the flashlight back on, he caught sight of the tiny red stain near its mouth and the darker blue mark where he'd touched it.

"You bit me, you bastard!" Jake muttered, more amazed than angry. He wrapped the bleeding finger carefully in his handkerchief and flicked off the overhead lights. Slowly, he slid his chair closer and settled in, not hearing a single movement from the crouched creature.

Standoff.

Something inside Jake surged—a deadly urge to retaliate, to punish—to grab the liquid nitrogen and freeze the little thing solid, proving once and for all that it was real. A flash-frozen corpse would be empirical evidence beyond argument.

But the rage ebbed as fast as it came. This was an opportunity —a breakthrough. He had made the impossible happen: he'd made one of the creatures solid, tangible, and vulnerable. How long would the effect last? That question fascinated Jake far more than destruction.

"So, how're you holding up under there?" he said quietly, glancing at his finger: the bleeding had stopped. "You hear me, little guy?"

Outside the sky was brightening. Dawn was creeping in, stealing the night from the room.

A faint crackling sound echoed. The small black form peeked from the kneehole, its shadowy head barely discernible in the growing light.

"Not so tough now, huh?" Jake taunted, a smile creeping onto his lips. "Look at that—dawn's coming. You need a new hiding spot."

The creature followed his finger, watching the light before slinking back quickly into the dark.

"Smart," Jake nodded to himself. "You're not just running on instinct. You think and plan. I always knew that. You couldn't have done all those things if you didn't."

Another whisper, tinged with something almost like fear.

A voice screamed in Jake's head: *Kill it! Now's your chance!*

But no. The creature was hurt, trembling—a frightened animal, raw and vulnerable.

But also lethal.

"If I can catch it, if I release it down in that deep subbasement..." Jake said aloud to himself, weighing options like a trader. Could this be a peace offering? Would they finally leave Shawn and him alone?

But his touch hurt it, and it could bite. He had to protect both it—and himself.

Rising, Jake looked out at the morning horizon, the light spilling relentlessly across the sky.

"Aw, what the hell," he muttered, peeling off his jacket. He slipped on the thick gloves, crouched low, and raised his jacket to block the only exit under the desk.

The creature hissed, panic rising. It slammed into the backboard, its sharp chattery cries shifting into fearful mewls—more heard in Jake's mind than in the room.

Slowly, Jake grasped it through the cloth. It felt weightless, fragile, like holding a newborn kitten.

"Be quiet," Jake whispered fiercely, "I'm going to help you."

There was a large, musty basement in the next building where Jake always felt the creatures. The perfect containment spot until it turned incorporeal again.

Jake went out into the hall and held the moving bundle, only to walk right into one of his guards, Charley Barker.

"Cap'n," Charley said, "I don't mean to bother you—" The man stopped and looked at the bundle in Jake's hand. "What the hell you got?"

"I caught a bird. In my office," Jake said, saying the first thing that came to his mind.

"How'd it get in?" Charley wondered, and tried to take a peek.

"My window was open," Jake explained.

"Cap'n, we gonna haveta send guys off to the gates soon, so you need to come to the front desk," Charley pointed out, no longer interested in the concealed animal. "Normally, you jus' come up on your own, so we got worried 'bout you."

"I'll be right there, as soon as I get this…bird outside," Jake responded as he circled his coworker.

"I'll see you up there," Charley called out as Jake headed down the hall.

Carrying the bundle, he crept down stairs, making sure to turn on the lights as he went. Once in the spacious room, he laid the jacket bundle on the dusty floor.

He powered up his flashlight, turned off the overheads, and pulled the jacket away.

The creature tumbled free, blinking uncertainly in the beam of the flashlight—almost human in its reaction.

It saw the space, decided it was unharmed, and bolted in the darkness with a speed so swift Jake questioned if it had merely melted away.

Not risking it, Jake grabbed his coat, shut the heavy door, and retreated upstairs to the sunlit floors—the safe zones.

He'd found a weapon.

And maybe, just maybe, a way to fight back.

41. There's Nothing There

....

J ake's sleep was restless and shallow that day.

Every hour before work he spent methodically checking the protective devices scattered throughout the house—the sensors, alarms, reinforced locks—anything that might buy them time if the shadows attacked.

When Shawn asked what was wrong, Jake's answer was terse. "Something happened," he said, his voice tight, but stopped short of further details.

"The shadows, isn't it?" Shawn's voice carried a mixture of fear and morbid fascination.

Jake nodded, fingers tightening around the knot of his tie. "Yeah."

"What did they do this time?" Shawn pressed.

Jake exhaled slowly, fighting an irritation he didn't fully understand. "It's not what they did. It's what my tech did to one of them. I captured one of them in a magnetic field and made it solid."

"Made it... solid?" Shawn's eyes widened.

"Exactly. As real as you or me," Jake said, adjusting his collar. "But... if you want to call their forms 'bodies,' they're fragile. You could crush them like brittle glass."

"Did you?" Shawn's voice was barely a whisper.

"No." Jake's annoyance flared. "I didn't hurt it. I set it free—in the basement."

Shawn blinked, confused. "You... turned the other cheek?"

Jake frowned, unsure if Shawn was joking. "What?"

"You know, like Jesus said..." Shawn shrugged. "Turn the other cheek."

"I guess so," Jake muttered, his grumble betraying his uncertainty.

Shawn's eyes brightened. "Jesus also cast out demons."

Jake's temper snapped, sharper this time. "They're *not* demons. Didn't you hear anything I said? I can make them tangible now. They're not all-powerful. Maybe they're gremlins, but I don't think they rate demonic status."

"But if people saw them—"

"We've had this fight before," Jake interrupted, his voice low but firm. "Have you found anything in your church or your bible? A way to stop them?"

"No," Shawn admitted quietly.

Jake's tone lifted, almost triumphant. "Well, I have!"

Shawn started to walk away, shoulders slumped.

Jake's anger melted into concern. "Son, I'm sorry I snapped at you. I know you're trying."

Shawn turned back, searching his father's eyes. "I'm just concerned. What if they come tonight?"

"Retaliation?" Jake asked.

"Yeah." Shawn's voice was small. "Promise me you'll keep the alarms on. That you'll protect yourself."

"I will," Jake assured him. "And I know how to trigger the backups."

For a fleeting moment, as Shawn stood silhouetted against the lamp's faint glow, Jake swore he saw a haze—an ethereal shimmer —around his son's head.

But when he blinked it vanished like smoke. His heart clenched with an undefined fear and urgency. Pulling Shawn close, he grasped him in a rare embrace.

"I worry about you, boy."

"I'll be okay, Dad." Shawn slipped out of his grasp, steadying himself.

Words choked Jake's throat, so instead he forced a steady smile. The haze had to be a trick of the light. "See you in the morning."

"Count on it."

Jake slipped on his outdoor coat over a brown jacket, clipped two small circular lights to his belt, and stepped out into the crisp air. September was fleeing, bringing warm days but chilly nights that crept through the cracks.

Bellcant was unusually lively at the reception center that evening. For weeks Jake buried himself in the back offices but now he was in full view, chatting and joking with the guards—an unexpected change. His presence surprised them.

"Nice to see you out here with us, Cap'n," Charlie Barker grinned. "We thought you slept back there."

Jake laughed. "Not a bad idea."

Charlie glanced at him knowingly. "Did you get that bird out of here last night?"

Jake rubbed the back of his neck. "Yeah. It flew right off."

"Strange it got into the building," Charlie mused.

"Confused in the dark," Jake offered.

Charlie studied him. "And you used the main door? Nearest exit's the other way."

Jake shrugged toward the newer guards milling nearby. "I got turned around." His voice dropped, a touch more serious. "Who's on tour four?"

"I am." Antoine, tall and slender with a Jamaican accent, stepped forward.

"The lights downstairs flicker sometimes. Take a flashlight."

"Yes, sir."

Jake nodded. "I need to check the basement. Call out when you get down there so I don't get stuck in the dark."

Antoine nodded affirmatively.

"We've got tours to do. See you later." The guards dispersed, radios and keys in hand, following their shifts.

Just as Jake headed for the door, Charlie called after him, "Cap'n, what are those things on your belt?"

Jake glanced down at the lights still clipped to his belt.

"Emergency lights I'm testing," he explained—then an idea struck him. "That's why I'm going to the basement. Gonna see how they work in the dark."

Charlie chuckled. "You're always up to something, Cap'n."

Jake smiled but his stomach knotted with unease. The basement was the one place he didn't want to visit—it was where the shadows congregated, where the strange things whispered in the dark.

The bunker-like basement felt claustrophobic and hostile. The cold concrete walls reverberated with mechanical rumbling—air ducts hissing, transformers humming, motors starting and stopping unpredictably.

No windows existed there; only bleak artificial light unable to reach the furthest corners casting long shadows that flickered at the edges of Jake's vision.

He descended the last stairs, heart hammering, and pushed open the heavy metal door.

The cavernous room—maybe twenty feet high—loomed around him, broken only by stacks of dusty boxes and worn storage crates. A narrow path marked with footprints cut through the grime.

Jake slowed, trying to sense the shadows, feeling for the eerie pulse in the blackness. They were here—maybe lurking, maybe watching. His act of mercy last night—releasing the solid shadow —may have changed things.

Had they respected his kindness? Or had they marked him for destruction?

This was no mindless enemy. For thirty years he'd faced a cunning, calculating adversary—and the terror lay precisely in their intelligence.

He called out into the darkness, his voice trembling slightly. "Hello? I'm here... I want to see if you're all right."

His words felt like a plea and he immediately regretted them. What if this were a trap?

Fingers brushed the emergency lights on his belt—clipped firm but ready. In either hand, a gentle tap would unleash a searing brilliance, a shield of light against the encroaching dark.

The machinery's unpredictable noises startled him, wheels turning deep in the shadows, air pumping with unnatural rhythm.

His boots crunched across the dusty floor as he moved carefully off the path. Ahead lay an unfamiliar shape, a patch of impossibly dark fabric splayed on the concrete. As he approached, his breath caught.

It was the shadow he'd freed yesterday—now flat and torn like shredded silk, edges frayed in ragged slashes that looked as if claws had torn it.

He dropped to his knees, wincing against the cold floor, and ran a cautious hand over the oily surface. The residue felt slick but didn't soil his fingers.

Lifeless.

The tiny limbs—fragile and ragged—looked like the carcass of a dead moth.

Had the others torn it apart? Punished it for its difference? Or to send a message?

Jake's mouth twisted in fury and sorrow. They'd left this ruin for him to find.

He gathered the damaged shape, rolling it into a ball. It felt wrong—half cloth, half something else entirely. He shoved it into his pocket, the texture cold and sticky against his side.

Whatever regret he felt, it was now evidence—something he could analyze.

His chest heavy with dread, Jake turned toward the door and hit the lights on his belt. The dazzling circle of light surrounded him and cut through the darkness like a beacon.

Shielded in the unnatural brilliance, he reached the door, closed it behind him, and switched off his lights. His eyes stung with lingering afterimages as he climbed the stairs, heart pounding.

Back in his office he unlocked the door, the Resonant Ring stood undisturbed on the desk. No ambush, no surprise waited for him.

He removed his coat and felt the sticky, oily bundle in his pocket. It left an unpleasant stain, a bitter reminder of the night's grim discovery.

Jake locked the door behind him and headed toward the lab, familiar machinery waiting like old allies.

He needed answers—how the shadow died, if it truly lived—and what it meant for the war he'd waged for decades.

Because one thing was obvious: the shadows were organizing, retaliating, and they had a goal unknown to him.

Jake stood rigid, heart hammering, eyes locked on the blinking machines on the desk.

He went into the main lab and set up his tests. The gas chromatograph hissed softly as it separated compounds, the fluorescence spectrometer pulsed with eerie light, and the electron microscope whirred in precise mechanical rhythm.

Each was running the programmed analyses on the strange sample he'd recovered—fragments of the creature.

He knew every step of the process—the algorithms he'd coded, the scientific minutiae—but that knowledge did little to quell the swirling storm in his mind.

At its core, matter was atoms and molecules—solid, predictable. Yet, this sample defied understanding. According to Einstein's mass-energy equivalence, energy could manifest as mass and vice versa.

Had the magnetic field somehow distorted energy to coalesce into a tangible form? But if so, what kind of mass was this? Stable? Transient? Or something entirely alien?

His fingers drummed anxiously on the desk as the dot matrix printers began spitting out endless lines of cryptic data. He leaned in, peering at the chromatograph's output. Results were maddeningly inconclusive—primarily nitrogen, oxygen, inert gases—the same as the surrounding air. Nothing that resembled conventional matter. A creeping dread crawled up his spine.

Had the sample evaporated? Transformed?

He attempted to peer inside the machine's sealed chamber despite its lockdown protocol, but the sample hid in an impossible void of sterile glass and cold metal.

He moved toward the electron microscope, hope flickering weakly. Fingers danced over the keyboard as he ordered the latest scan. The screen flickered to life revealing a grainy, ghostly image of the sample's atomic architecture. Then, horror froze in his veins —as he watched, entire molecular clusters blinked out of existence, dissolving into nothingness.

"No," Jake whispered, disbelief clawing at his throat. "Atoms don't vanish."

Atoms bonded in intricate patterns—they rearranged but never simply disappeared. Frantically, he commanded the system to save every byte of data as the sample visibly disintegrated on the monitor.

He rushed back to the spectrometer, now silent. Opening its chamber, he found only a void. The mysterious fabric-like remains from his pocket felt… different. No longer oily or soft, it was stiff, brittle—dry as dead leaves. He held the fragile gray fragments gingerly, but they crumbled between his fingers.

Jake stared as the pile of powder shrank inexplicably, as if swallowed by an unseen wind. Within seconds not a speck remained. His breath caught. This wasn't just molecular transformation—this was annihilation.

He shook his head, desperate to reject the impossible.

Matter might alter states—solid to liquid to gas—but to vanish? To have a shadowy entity composed of actual substance evaporate without a trace? The creature held shape for a day after capture. So why now? Had the brilliant light from his safety device caused this? Or was it a deliberate distraction, a cruel trick to keep him occupied while darker forces hunted closer?

The thought chilled him, tightening his chest in cold dread.

He'd been blind, fixated on his office, oblivious to the peril lurking beyond. And the real danger—his son Shawn—was vulnerable.

Jake scrambled for a phone, but fear paralyzed him. Dialing from the lab risked alerting Bellcant that he'd been there. He unlocked the lab door, nerves taut as a wire, and set off toward his office.

Though nearly fifty Jake was in decent shape, but his breath came ragged and shallow as he hurried along the sterile halls. Reaching the phone he dialed home with trembling fingers.

The ringing dragged on—ten rings… fifteen… twenty.

His heart plummeted. The shadows had attacked.

If they could sabotage the power, the phone lines might be down too. His son was alone. He had to get home now.

Straining every muscle Jake broke into a run toward the reception desk, gasping for air. He needed to put Charley in charge, get out fast with the two disks clamped to his belt— perhaps the key to saving Shawn.

His lungs burned, each breath a battle. The lobby swirled in his vision as he slowed to a staggering halt.

"Hey, Cap'n! You look like you saw a ghost!" Charley's voice cut through the haze. The dark-skinned guard grasped Jake's arm, steadying him.

"My… house…" Jake gasped, words stumbling out between ragged breaths. "My… son…"

Another guard, Dave, appeared, alarm thick in his New Jersey accent. "What's wrong, Captain?"

Charley's face mirrored his worry. "You don't look good."

Jake's left arm ached fiercely and a crushing weight settled on his chest. Suddenly, his knees gave way. The floor rushed up fast and unforgiving.

"Call 9-1-1!" Charley shouted, clutching Jake's head gently.

"My… son…" he managed weakly before darkness edged in.

"Don't worry about that. We've gotta get you to a hospital!" Dave said urgently, his fingers dialing as Jake sank deeper into unconsciousness.

Charley murmured with quiet urgency, "You're having a heart attack, Cap'n."

Tears stung Jake's closed eyes.

NEW YEARS EVE

1999

42. Preparation

....

"So that's when you had your heart attack?" I asked, my eyes flicking over my notebook where I jotted down Jake's words—and just as importantly, my thoughts on the silences between them.

There was a heaviness in the air, an unspoken truth pressing down on us both.

Jake sighed deeply, a shiver passing through him as the memory took hold. His eyes glistened with moisture he tried hard to conceal.

"Yeah," he murmured. "They had to do a bypass surgery. But all I could think about was Shawn... I kept begging EMS to come to my house, to check on him."

I leaned in, sensing the tension tightening his chest as much as the heart attack had. "Who found the body?" I asked quietly.

His jaw clenched. "The police only moved after I hounded them relentlessly. Found him... killed by those things. A letter opener driven straight through his heart."

I swallowed hard, trying to keep calm. "What did the coroner say? Cause of death?"

Jake's bitter snort sliced through the room. "Accidental. They say he fell on it. An 'accident' like Peggy's death. Bunch of lies." His voice cracked with disgust and raw grief.

"Is it possible that he fell on it?" I pressed, not sure whether I wanted to hear the answer.

"No." He shook his head, bowing it. "It was them. Year after year—loss after loss." His shoulders sagged under the weight of those years.

Jake's face remained a mask of defeat. No flicker of hope, no sign of the therapy making a difference.

Tomorrow's New Year's Eve loomed like a deadline, and I worried that once our sessions ended, he'd be right back where he started—broken and alone.

At my house the day after the fire had been a whirlwind. On Monday, Marcie sprang into action—calling in a battalion of cleaners who steam-cleaned every surface, replaced all our furniture fabric, and had thick new wall-to-wall carpeting installed before I even walked through the door. The living room smelled sharply of adhesives and fresh carpet fibers—an odd, sterile scent that underscored how much had changed.

True to her promise, Marcie kept the other distance, too. Despite my best efforts to be peaceful and cooperative, each night she locked herself away in our bedroom, barring me from entering.

On Monday night I stood outside that locked door, knocking softly. I started with sweet words, whispered confessions of love and longing. I tried coaxing, shifting to cute jokes, and finally silly pleas, desperate to crack through her defenses.

Not a sound. The door remained shut tight.

I fought down my frustration, retreating to the stiff leather couch that now felt like a prison sentence. I cursed the day I had bought that couch instead of a sofa bed and the day Jake entered my life.

Tuesday and Wednesday passed in stony silence. Marcie and I barely exchanged two words. I was furious, trapped in the den, and she refused to relent.

Locked in a standoff, neither of us was willing to bend.

By Wednesday afternoon, I sat with my own therapist, Janice Franklin, desperate for guidance.

After hearing everything I said, she leaned forward. "Sam, this is a boundary issue. Marcie has drawn her lines clearly."

"Of course," I muttered, "so now you're on her side."

She shook her head patiently. "It's the same problem you had before Thanksgiving. You need to take her boundaries seriously."

"She's pushing me away."

"She feels you're too close to Jake. You're not setting any boundaries with him—so Marcie is setting them with you instead."

I scoffed. "So you think I've gone too far?"

"In a word: yes."

"Great! Why don't you become Marcie's therapist then?" I fired back.

"Because I'm yours," she said calmly. "And you come to me because I tell you the truth."

I let out a heavy sigh, anger simmering beneath the surface—but she was right. When everyone tells you the same thing, it may be the problem is you.

I tried to change the subject. "Any more patients seeing... gremlins in the night?"

Janice caught the dodge. "You're deflecting."

"Just curious."

"Yes, actually. More reports as the year draws to a close. A lot of my patients are having strange dreams." She hesitated, leaned in. "Two of my patients described the same place—a landscape bathed entirely in red."

"No stars in the sky. Creatures you catch only from the corner of your eye?" I asked.

Her eyes widened. "How did you know?"

"One of my patients dreamed that a month ago," I lied. How could I tell her I'd dreamt it?

Janice frowned. "Must be some planetary alignment."

"Isn't Y2K bad enough already?"

With a rueful shake of her head, she said, "I'm surprised you closed your practice for the week with all the fear going around."

"I needed to decompress."

Her smile was small, tired. "I just hope whatever this is, it blows over after New Year's."

On Thursday, December 30, I woke to a searing pain shooting through my back, contorting my body into an unnatural arch.

Each breath was a struggle and with my temper already simmering, I slipped quietly from the house before anyone else stirred. The last thing I needed was an early confrontation with Marcie while my back hurt and my patience was gone.

Jake was the only person during the entire holiday season who showed genuine concern..

When he saw I couldn't stand upright he didn't hesitate. Quietly, he stepped behind me, slipping his arms under mine, crossing them over my chest. With a careful bent back, he lifted me by the elbows into the air.

A sharp crack echoed through the room and suddenly I could sit upright. Relief washed over me along with a creeping tension —our meetings had always been a tightrope walk, but today felt especially fragile.

We settled into our usual chairs, the silence stretching between us before I forced the inevitable topic. The New Year and the prospect of a new therapist weighed heavily in the air.

"I don't need anyone," Jake said sharply, his voice thick with frustration. "Look, Sam, I'm no danger to myself. Just release me and you'll make both your wife and me happy."

My heart raced as I resisted the urge to snap back. "That would be irresponsible, Jake. If I released you and something happened —"

"I'll sign a paper absolving you and the hospital from all responsibility," he interjected quickly.

I struggled to keep my voice steady. "On some level, Jake, you're the sanest man I know."

"That's my point exactly!" he said, a flicker of hope in his eyes.

"But this obsession of yours—it's consuming. Even if everything you've told me is true, you've lived forty years chasing an obsession. Tell me, if you could somehow prove the existence of these creatures you talk about, how would it improve your life?"

His brow furrowed. "What do you mean?"

"Would it bring back Peggy or your son?" I said quietly.

The silence that followed was heavy, palpable. Jake's mouth hung open, words stuck inside.

"Oh, come on, Jake! You mean to tell me you never considered that?" I pressed.

He looked away. "I don't know."

"What does that mean?" I demanded, leaning closer.

His voice cracked. "I drifted after Shawn died. There was little other than work and my inventions. I fell out of life."

"You dropped out years before that. This obsession has ruled you," I accused.

"That's not true!" he snarled, pain flashing in his eyes. "I did what I did because of them!"

"Did you? They left you alone for stretches, but that wasn't enough. You had to prove you were right!"

"It wasn't like that!" Jake's defense was desperate, pleading.

"Then tell me: what was it like? I've heard your story, Jake. You were self-absorbed, shut off from everyone you cared about. This pursuit isolated you." I folded my hands. "In psychiatry, we call it an enabling obsession. When one fixation consumes a person so completely that it justifies everything they do."

His voice rose, cracked and fragile. "It's not like that!"

"Isn't it?" I softened my tone. "Jake, can you see why I can't just send you home? You might function superficially, but you're mentally ill."

We stared at each other in the thick silence that followed. Jake's defenses crumbled.

"I had to—" he started, then trailed off.

"Jake," I said gently, "I don't think you're suicidal, but you aren't coping either. You need to let this go."

His voice was low, weary. "You know I didn't try to kill myself, Sam. After Shawn died, I just... stopped. Hurley told me to keep designing, keep the money coming—for Amanda."

"To start her company, no doubt?"

Jake nodded slowly. "You know about that?"

"I know more than you think."

"Why?"

"Empirical evidence."

For a fleeting moment, a glimmer of vindication lit his eyes. "So you thought I wasn't crazy?"

"I wanted to understand, to help. But—"

"Then let me go!" His desperation was raw.

"Let's talk about your life since 1990," I offered, shifting gears. "What kind of life have you had?"

"A simple one," he admitted.

"Without friends, without companionship, nothing outside your work or your workshop?"

"It was too risky." His voice faltered. "I couldn't bear to lose anyone else."

"That's a psychiatrist's warning sign." I paused, watching him shrink in his seat. "It's a reflection of your disorder."

We lapsed into silence again. I glanced at my legal pad.

"You said these shadows slit your wrists?"

"They tried to kill me," Jake said flatly.

"From what you've told me these shadows have hunted you for a long time."

"They killed the ones I cared about. I thought I was immune —until that night."

"Why?"

"Remember my magnetic device?"

"You said it made one shadow solid?"

"That experiment worked," Jake said with a spark of pride.

"Did you repeat it? Capture more?"

"No," he said, eyes locked onto mine. "After Shawn died, I didn't care. I'd sit in darkness, waiting for the shadows to take me."

I shook my head. "And you tell me this to prove you're not suicidal?"

"I might have been back then." His fist slammed into the chair's arm. "Not now. They stayed away for a while. Then I found a note after Shawn died. It was in his handwriting, and it said, 'It's a matter of faith.'"

"And you assumed?"

"That I had to believe in myself. I had a weapon but was wielding it wrong. I could make them solid—but using it to defeat them would take too long. Think about it; how long would it take to kill dozens or more? Years! But it was more than that. I saw their plan." He paused, eyes dark.

"Their plan?"

He nodded but said nothing.

"So you tried another approach?"

"If I couldn't bring them to me, I'd go to them."

I sat up, incredulous. "You're serious?"

"Dr. Goldstein's invention let them in. Why not use the same to get to them?"

I struggled to process the idea.

He spoke of magnetic energy, radio waves—an attempt to shift himself into their realm and destroy them from within.

I interrupted. "With what, exactly?"

"I thought about that for years," Jake said. "I needed a weapon that would hurt them but not me. Something portable."

"A weapon of mass destruction?" The words escaped before I could stop them.

His smile was odd, almost amused. "More like an automatic weapon. If I could fully bring one here, logically, I could travel to where they exist."

"Another dimension? Another plane of existence?" I scoffed. "How? Click your heels three times? Third star to the left? This is fantasy, Jake."

"It's theoretically possible," he insisted.

"Sure it is! What's next? A time machine?" I said, my voice full of sarcasm.

But there was a heaviness in his eyes as he answered, "I wasn't working in my basement anymore. I was on the second floor. This was real."

I retracted my pen, shoved it into my pocket. "I think we're done here."

His voice cracked with desperation. "We can talk about that night… tomorrow?"

"No, Jake. We're done." I began packing my notes slowly, deliberately.

"You don't mean that," he said, stunned.

"I do. I've heard your story—the entire story."

"But there's more."

"And it will be the same: invisible creatures, deaths, loss, obsession. I can't help you with this. I'm going home to my family. Come Monday, someone else will have to endure your litany."

"You promised to work with me until New Year's!" His plea was raw.

"And I would if there was any hope," I said firmly. "But you're too deep into this delusion—"

"Delusion?" he spat.

"And too invested," I said, bitter.

"Just today and tomorrow, Sam. Let me finish the story."

"We've already covered variations on a theme." I stood my ground. "You won't share your true feelings. If you can't, I can't help."

He looked down at his hands, gnarled from years of soldering and building small inventions. His eyes shimmered with moisture. "I'm not one to beg—"

"Then don't. Let's end this as friends."

"Just until tomorrow," he pleaded, energy renewed.

I studied the man before me—wild white hair, unruly mustache, eyes full of sorrow and desperation. Hardly two months ago he was a stranger. Now, after his four decades of confessions I felt I'd known him forever.

I sighed, dramatic and weary. "I'll try."

His vigilance waned in a heartbeat. "Thank you."

"No promises." I paced to the door. "No more history. I need to know what you feel."

"How will I know you'll come? I have to sleep—" His voice faded.

"I'll call either way. Come on; I'll walk you back to your ward."

He followed silently. Near his room, he grabbed my arm. "Sam, man to man, I like you."

I smiled faintly. "I like you too, Jake. Man to man. Doctor to patient—not so much."

I left him with that.

Was I abandoning him? Part of me wanted to. It was clear he wouldn't get better. My therapist had warned me—I needed boundaries.

Perhaps my initial assessment was right: Jake was simply a raving paranoid.

43. ANALYSIS

I stormed into Bill Benning's office without so much as a knock.

The usual guard—his secretary—was nowhere in sight, the holiday week between Christmas and New Year's leaving the place eerily understaffed.

The air felt heavy, charged with the quiet of the in-between.

"Ah! The promising young psychiatrist," Bill's booming voice greeted me with a theatrical flourish. "What grand accomplishments has the wunderkind unearthed today?"

I dropped into the chair with a thud, immediately regretting it. The upholstery was the same hideous maroon leather as the damn couch at home and it was as equally stiff and unforgiving.

"Lousy," I grunted. "Any word on a new shrink for Jake Hurd?"

Bill's face shifted with a glint of relief. "Matthews should be able to take over starting Monday."

"Good. I've been a total waste of money with Jake."

Bill protested but I cut him off. "No, really, I've been letting him run the sessions—endless droning on about his past. I should have been steering him, pushing him to face his demons. Instead, he's dragged me into the muck."

Bill raised a skeptical eyebrow. "Are you seeing little creatures lurking in the dark corners, Sammy?"

I exhaled sharply. "Not exactly— "

"That's a relief," Bill said with a wink.

"But at the edges of my vision… something. Damn it, Bill, the guy's practically hypnotized himself with his stories, and since I tried to follow along…"

Bill's crooked smile grew wider. "So he's a night guard, an inventor, and a hypnotist? Maybe moonlights with magic shows for kids?"

I grimaced. "I wouldn't put it past him. I've gotten way too wrapped up in this. Even Janice thinks I'm too involved."

Without a word, Bill rotated in his chair and pulled a bottle of scotch and two glasses from a cabinet behind him. He poured a generous slug, offering me the glass without asking. I took it, my fingers trembling slightly.

Bill poured himself a drink and settled his bulky frame behind his enormous desk. "If Janice Franklin says you're too involved, it must be true," he said dryly, raising his glass. "To doctors of the mind. Physician, heal thyself."

I clinked my glass to his and drank, the amber liquid burning a trail down my throat before settling like molten lava in my gut. I dug into my pocket, fishing out a roll of antacids. Three tablets slid into my mouth.

Bill chuckled. "Splendid! Twenty-five-year-old single malt scotch followed by Tums. Classy."

"My belly's getting worse, Bill."

He shook his head, concern creasing his features. "Sammy, I've got twenty years on you, and I'm in better shape."

I snorted. "You look like you're on the fast track to a heart attack."

"Your stomach will get you first. Stress. You carry too much on your shoulders."

"Thanks, Dad," I muttered bitterly.

"Seriously—when will you see a doctor? You're working on an ulcer that's ready to blow. You planning on waiting for a perforation?"

I didn't sip this time. I downed the rest of my drink in a single fiery gulp, feeling the tension knots across my body finally unravel.

"Next week," I promised.

Bill leaned back. "How are things with Marcie?"

I sighed deeply. "Trying to crack through her 'ice goddess' act tonight."

"Still banned from the bedroom?"

"Yeah. The couch is murder on my back, and I haven't gotten laid in two weeks."

Bill chuckled, settling more comfortably. "Sammy, when you get to be my age, it's not all that important. And I said important, not impotent."

We both laughed though his words carried a bittersweet edge.

"It's funny," I said, shaking my head. "When Marcie's available, I don't think about it much. But since she slammed the bedroom door shut, sex has consumed my every thought."

"Classic power play," Bill mused. "Being screwed by a psychiatrist."

I scowled. "Bill, can we have one moment where we just look at life like normal people? Without psychoanalyzing every damn thing?"

Bill grinned. "Sammy, it's what we do. You mull over your actions and their psychological underpinnings, right?"

"All the time," I admitted, finishing my drink.

"Welcome to the curse," Bill said, refilling our glasses. "Forever chained to the footsteps of Father Freud."

I frowned. "This would be great with ice."

"No ice in the office," he said.

I glanced at the massive Art Deco clock ticking silently on the wall. "Ten in the morning. Far too early for whiskey."

Bill shrugged. "What the hell, Sammy? Happy New Year." We clinked glasses again.

I knew doubling down on drinks so early was a bad idea, especially on an empty stomach, but the buzz was a welcome tide of warmth easing the gnawing tension. I drove home carefully, subconsciously trying to balance cheerfulness and sobriety— though all I truly wanted was a long nap.

Walking into the house, I steadied myself, masking whatever wobbly instability I felt.

"You're home early," Marcie noted with polite surprise.

"Yeah, wrapping up Jake's sessions. They're pretty direct nowadays," I lied smoothly.

She studied me, searching for signs of deceit. "You're not just saying that?"

"No. Matthews is officially the doctor starting Monday."

"I'm proud of you, Sam," she said softly, giving me a brief hug and a peck on the cheek. "It's for the best."

Something surged inside me then, a sudden, fierce longing. I leaned in and captured her mouth with mine.

Her startled "Hmm?" was barely a whisper before she pulled away sharply.

"Sam!" she hissed. "You've been drinking!"

"Just one drink with Bill, for New Year's."

I wrapped my arms around her, trying to draw her in again.

"No! Stop, Sam," she snapped, slapping my hands away with practiced precision. "I told you—"

"I've done what you wanted," I whined, clinging to her as she wriggled free. I aimed to kiss her again but she turned her face so my lips brushed her cheek instead.

"Let me go, Sam!" she whispered fiercely.

"But I love you," I pleaded.

"I don't love you when you've been drinking. It's eleven in the morning!" Her voice was low, dangerous.

"Marcie, please," I begged. "It's been days—weeks."

"Months if you don't let me go," she retorted and shoved me away. "Rachel's upstairs!"

"I want to come upstairs with you, without the bedroom door locked."

She shook her head. "You always get like this after drinking."

"I miss my wife. My beautiful wife. I want to make love to you, Marcie."

She put on her sternest expression. "No. And I mean it."

I looked at her, desperate and raw.

"And don't give me those puppy-dog eyes. They're as sexy as constipation." She grabbed her briefcase. "I'm going to work."

"This early?" I asked hoarsely.

"To get away from you when you're like this. I'll do paperwork."

"Can't we kiss and make up?"

She shifted cautiously, like a boxer dodging a stronger opponent. "Sam, you haven't kept your end of the bargain."

"I'll do whatever you want," I offered, voice soft, hope fragile.

She shook her head. "I want a clean house and a good meal."

"Really?"

"Consider that foreplay." Without another word she turned and left.

I stood there, swaying slightly, as she blew me a kiss before closing the door behind her. I stumbled upstairs, poking my head briefly into Rachel's room.

"Rach?"

"Yeah, Dad?" She yanked off her earphones, eyes bright despite the muted TV flickering silently.

"I'm going to take a nap. Can you wake me at two?"

"Sure, Dad." She nodded, slipping her earphones back on, eyes locked on the silent screen.

I lurched into the master bedroom, kicked off my shoes, and collapsed onto the soft bed fully clothed. The weight lifted from my body for a moment felt like salvation—if only fleeting.

I must have been dreaming. It had to be—the surrounding landscape was too alien, too surreal to be anything else.

The earth was no familiar brown or clay but a deep, dark red, the color of fresh blood, stretching endlessly beneath an eternal twilight.

The sky hovered in that half-dusk state between night and day, heavy and oppressive. There was no sun, no moon, no stars—only a faint, ghostly light dim enough to see the twisted shapes that marked this forsaken place.

What I saw was bleak beyond words.

The ground was cracked and gravelly, a barren desert painted in this terrible shade of crimson. Sparse, gnarled trees clawed their way from the earth, leafless and stunted, as if struggling against an invisible weight.

The horizon faded into a black void, the edges of reality blurring and dissolving, leaving me suspended in this nightmarish wasteland.

And yet, this was no dream I could escape.

The air thickened—dry, rancid, and heavy with a dirty metallic tang that coated my tongue. The scent of the scarlet earth invaded my senses, so real I could almost choke on it.

It felt like Hell itself, or *Gehinnom*—the Jewish name for a terrible place of torment. But this was no fiery pit with tormenting demons. No horns, no pitchforks. Only a silent, watching emptiness.

The worst part was that I wasn't alone.

The creatures surrounded me—not in full sight but just beyond my glance, flickering at the edge of my vision. When I turned my head there was nothing, only the barren wasteland stretching into nothingness.

Yet I knew they were there, closing in.

Every step I took stirred the dead soil, and it shocked me to hear the crunch of my shoes on that gravelly, lifeless ground. I walked cautiously, in loops and small circles, relying on my peripheral sight because the direct gaze always betrayed me—revealing nothing.

The shapes were short, squat, with boxy heads and narrow slits for eyes. Their bodies moved like shadows, compact and unspeakably wrong.

The foul stench that clung to the air came from them—a coppery, acrid smell that made my skin crawl.

My heartbeat hammered in my chest, breath ragged and shallow. Sweat slicked over my skin as my muscles tensed, and then it happened—those sleek, smooth limbs grabbed at me like iron traps.

I jerked back but they clung, one hand on my leg, another on my arm. A sudden wild leap and a face lunged at mine with monkey-like ferocity.

I tried to scream but a small, cruel hand clamped over my mouth, muffling the sound.

I clawed at the thing stuck to my face with desperate strength but it held firm, unyielding.

The sudden tug threw me off balance and I tumbled heavily to the ground, the impact rattling my teeth and jolting something deep inside me.

Everything shifted.

The bitter earth dissolved beneath me replaced by the cold hardness of my bedroom floor. The bedsheet wrapped tightly around my face slipped easily from my hands. I was awake—and drenched in sweat, breathing hard, heart pounding a relentless tattoo against my ribs.

I sat up, disoriented and fragile, with the aftertaste of fear and a vague haze of inebriation lingering.

Days it seemed had passed since I'd last slept in this room, and my mind fought to gather itself, desperate for a foothold in reality. Time blurred, slipping through my grasp like smoke.

A glance at the clock snapped me back—the glowing red numbers stared back: 3:30. But was it morning or night? The room was almost pitch black, shadows swallowing every corner.

Marcie had always been sensitive to light and insisted I install heavy curtains— I remembered that now.

Then, like a lightning bolt, the floodgates opened.

Dinner. Foreplay. The words crashed through me with overwhelming force and I was on my feet almost before reason caught up.

I stumbled to the wall switch cursing as I stubbed my toe on my discarded shoes. The harsh light flickered on, cutting the darkness in half. I moved swiftly down the hall and rapped hard on Rachel's door.

She cracked it open, clutching a cordless phone to her chest, eyes wide.

"Didn't I ask you to wake me at two?" My voice was hoarse, cracked and dry like sandpaper.

Her gaze darted to the clock, panic blooming in her expression. "Oh, Daddy, I—I forgot," she stammered.

I kept my calm but my stomach flipped into furious knots. "Finish your call. You're going to help."

She glanced at the phone, ended the call, dropping it back with a heavy sigh. She understood the weight behind my quiet anger—a storm brewing beneath the surface.

"Go downstairs and vacuum the living room. Then set the table. I'll get the bread machine started."

"I'd rather do the bread," she said, the teenage whine coloring her words.

"Rachel, I'm on a time limit here," I said, not raising my voice, but sharp and insistent.

She nodded, wary, and headed downstairs.

"Where's your brother?" I called after her.

"At Timmy's. He'll be back at four," she answered without looking.

"He's helping too." I barked.

Back in the bedroom I slipped on my shoes and started making the bed with deliberate care. The clock was unforgiving, and the pressure mounting—every second counted.

I wanted everything to be perfect, even though an unshakable unease clung to me, a feeling like unseen eyes lurking just beyond my sight, watching, waiting.

I felt the oddest sensation. It was almost as if something followed me back from that dreadful place—something that refused to be left behind.

Despite starting at the late hour of 3:30 we somehow pulled everything together by 6:00. Dinner was ready, the house cleaned, and the kids had pitched in every step of the way. Their youthful energy was a surprising asset even if they weren't the tidiest helpers. Tomorrow night we were heading to the Benning's for

New Year's Eve, so this meal carried extra weight—it was, in essence, our main family dinner of the week.

When Marcie arrived home she surveyed the scene with a look of satisfied surprise, her relief unmistakable that the heavy lifting hadn't fallen to her.

I was quietly grateful. To see it all come together against the odds felt like a minor victory.

We gathered around the table, lit slender tapered candles that cast dancing shadows on the walls, and I uncorked a bottle of wine. Though I had sobered up from that morning's indulgence, the wine's warmth made me a bit more vulnerable, easing the edges of the day's stress.

After dinner we unpacked the Scrabble set. Rueben found it challenging, but his laughter and fierce competitiveness made it worth the effort. We played until the little guy's eyelids drooped and Marcie took him upstairs, murmuring gentle goodnights.

Turning to my daughter I said, "Thanks for the help, Rach."

She shrugged as if it was no big deal, but her voice betrayed a lingering worry. "It's okay, Daddy. I still feel dumb for not waking you earlier." Then, with a knowing smirk, she added, "You were mad, weren't you?"

I smiled, touching her cheek. "Yeah, I was. But you stepping up helped me get over it." I wrapped an arm around her and kissed the top of her head.

Rachel blinked up at me, curious. "You and Mom all made up?"

I sighed, the weight of the day settling deeper in my chest. "I hope so, honey. The den has felt pretty cold lately."

Marcie reappeared on the stair landing just as Rachel excused herself.

"You can't be going to bed— it's only nine!" Marcie said, eyebrows raised.

Rachel just smiled, wiser than her years. "I have a book to read," she replied lightly. "And besides, you two should have some time alone."

As she disappeared upstairs Marcie shot me a curious glance. "What did you say to her?"

"Nothing," I swore, raising a hand like a reluctant witness in a courtroom.

"Well," Marcie grinned, heading to the liquor cabinet to pour two brandies, "how about one more game?"

As we settled back into the game I kissed her softly—surprise flickered in her eyes before she kissed me back, lingering just a moment longer than usual.

Then she put down tiles, forming a word: LUST.

I raised an eyebrow, pulling out my tiles with a sly grin. "Is there a theme tonight?"

"Perhaps," she said, demure but mischievous.

I crossed her S with SENSUAL, which she immediately linked with ASS.

I laughed, "Is that what you think I want? Or how I've been acting?"

"The jury's still out," Marcie teased, her eyes sparkling.

We created the naughtiest cluster of words our limited tiles would allow. Words we'd never say aloud in front of the children. Each placement brought a burst of shared laughter, a welcome respite from the tension still simmering under the surface.

Eventually, Marcie trounced me with a risqué word containing a Q—an unfair advantage, I argued halfheartedly—and we put down our tiles, sipping our drinks.

I stood and pulled her to her feet. "Dance with me."

She chuckled, voice low and throaty. "What could that be poking me?"

"Let me show you," I said, dipping her gently. "I missed you, honey. Let me just be with you."

She sighed, a little resistant. "I said, once you're done with Jake —"

I pulled her close, and she whispered in my ear. "I miss you, too."

"Then let me back in bed," I said firmly. "I'm done with Jake."

"As of Sunday?"

"No," I said, watching her closely. "As of now. He's too deep in his fantasy. I can't follow him down that rabbit hole."

"What brought this on?" she asked, eyes narrowed.

"He's delusional. He believes he can travel to a place where his dark creatures live and destroy them."

Marcie blinked. "You're kidding?"

"Dead serious." I shook my head, frustration thick in my voice.

She moved to the table, twirling her brandy glass. "I thought you were buying into his stories."

"I wasn't 'buying it,'" I corrected sharply. "I was looking at what he believed."

"Oh, come on, Sam! He's leading you around by the nose. He's convincing you his dark night monsters are setting fires!"

"I don't have an explanation for the fire. Or the door to the study being locked, even though we don't have the key," I admitted.

"That wasn't a shadow starting it," she said flatly, then paused thoughtfully. "There are layers to this psychosis."

"What do you mean?"

"Well," she said carefully, "there's a fear of the dark, sure. But those little black creatures? Could be racial symbolism. The stranger—an enemy who can move through walls, under doors, and no one can capture or see? That's paranoia."

I rubbed my forehead. "I don't want to talk about this anymore. Let's be… romantic."

She smiled, moving closer. "Is that so?"

"All I want," I said, pulling her down onto the sofa with me, "is to be in bed with my wife."

"I'm listening," she purred.

"You're more beautiful now than the night I married you." I kissed her lips softly, feeling the old, familiar electricity ignite.

"Lies," she teased, "but well intended."

"You are." I kissed her again.

She sighed, moved back and placed a finger on my lips to silence me. "I'm glad you're pulling away from Jake," she said softly. "It's the right choice."

She kissed me deeply, her tongue tracing mine. Her hips pressed against me and I gasped. She stepped back, leaving me flushed and aching.

"You've earned your way back into my boudoir," she teased. "Give me a minute. I'll leave the door unlocked."

With the practiced grace of a temptress she tossed her hair and disappeared upstairs.

I smiled, tidied the brandy glasses, and carefully boxed up our risqué Scrabble game, mixing the tiles so thoroughly no one would guess what words were played.

A sudden, shaky voice cut through the quiet.

"D-daddy!"

My heart lurched.

"Rueben?" I called, bursting up the stairs two at a time, pulling myself up with the banister.

As I reached the hall an icy dread squeezed my chest—the lights in his room were dimmed.

I ran to Rueben's room, yanked open the door, and hit the wall switch.

Light flickered on—and horror froze me in my tracks.

On top of Rueben lay a small black shape.

The square head. The stunted limbs.

I cried out as it turned slowly to look at me, its slit eyes gleaming in the dim light.

My mind screamed that it must be a nightmare. It couldn't be real. This was impossible.

"Daddy!" Rueben moaned weakly.

That ripped me free from the paralysis of fear.

I lunged at the bed, ready to fight whatever this thing was.

But—it was gone.

Not fading or dematerializing like in the movies.

Just—not there.

I gathered Rueben close, pulling him away from the bed while he clung to me, tears streaming down his face.

The door creaked behind me.

Marcie stepped in, alarm etched across her face.

"What happened?" she asked urgently.

I turned to her, my eyes wild and voice trembling.

"Are you all right?" she whispered, fear twisting her features.

Calming Rueben took more than an hour—long, tense minutes of gentle coaxing and whispered reassurances.

His small body trembled as I carefully swapped out the worn batteries in his light-disk. As soon as I flicked it back on, the soft glow bathed his pale face, and I watched relief wash over him.

Exhaustion finally won; his breathing slowed, eyelids fluttered, and he drifted into a fitful, but much-needed sleep.

Marcie refused to be soothed so easily.

"I know what I saw," I insisted, the words burning from my throat as I poured myself another brandy, the harsh burn grounding me after tending to Rueben.

Marcie's eyes were sharp, skeptical. "We were both drinking. You were tired. You had a hallucination."

But I wasn't fooling myself, and certainly not her. "I know what I saw," I said again, my voice steady and convinced.

I sat across from her at the breakfast table in that bright little room off the dining area. During the day, sunlight spilled through the windows, but now, night swallowed the glass panes whole, transforming them into black mirrors that warped my tortured reflection.

A bitter thought escaped me. "I should've checked those batteries on the disk Jake gave him," I muttered, more to the empty room than to Marcie. "Poor kid, waking up like that."

She shot back, "You don't know if he saw the same thing you did."

"It was right there—right on top of him."

Marcie's frustration cracked in her voice. She stood abruptly. "I'm done discussing this. I'm going to bed."

"Fine," I snapped, "I'm seeing Jake tomorrow."

Her face turned back toward me, disbelief and worry mingling in her eyes. "But you told me—"

"He knows something. Something that makes sense of this nightmare," I hissed. "And I'm going to find out what the hell it is."

Her voice rose sharply. "He's insane!"

"Marcie! The kids," I warned, barely able to keep the edge from my voice.

"And so are you!" she shot back. Her eyes blazed, jaw tight. "You're completely out of your mind. Hope you enjoyed necking, because it's all you're getting this week."

With that she stormed up the stairs, barefoot, footsteps thudding sharply against the floorboards.

I sank heavily into the chair, staring at the distorted figure staring back at me through the window's dark glass.

Alone in the den I left the light on, unwilling to chase away the illusions—and yet afraid to face the darkness entirely.

Sleep claimed me at last, but the weight of what I'd seen—and what was still coming—pressed down like its own suffocating shadow.

44. Battle Plan

A little after six in the morning, bone-tired from too few hours of sleep and carrying a chip on my shoulder the size of Hoboken, I strode into Greystorm with one purpose: to extract answers from Jake no matter what it took.

My jaw clenched, every nerve taut with frustration as I headed to the nurses' station, signed Jake out, and barged into his room.

Empty.

My heart skipped a beat. For a moment I just stood there in the doorway, the fog of exhaustion mingling with disbelief.

Where the hell was he? On impulse, I yanked open the bathroom door without knocking. As empty as his room.

Desperation clawed at me. I scanned the room again, locking eyes on a small wheeled table pushed in front of the bed. Scattered across it were an array of electronics—computer chips, wire cutters, a soldering iron. Atop it sat a peculiar cylindrical device, its intricate circuitry exposed, with a pair of brown reading glasses resting beside it, like Jake had jumped up just a second ago.

"Hi, Sam," came a calm voice.

I turned around, startled and there he was—Jake—standing in the doorway, holding a pair of needle-nosed pliers with his usual bemused expression.

"Jake!" I spat out, the surprise sending a shiver through me. "Where have you been?"

Unfazed he stepped back into the room, perching on the bed. He flipped on his half-glasses and fidgeted with the cylinder. "I have a room down the hall where they let me tinker."

I narrowed my eyes. "Right, and some guy keeps bringing you supplies."

His grin was innocent. "That's all right, isn't it?"

"Bill Benning approved it, right?" I snapped.

Jake looked up thoughtfully, cleaning up his mess. "You said you'd call if you were coming."

"I want to talk to you about—"

"You're angry."

I nodded, voice sharper than I intended. "Yes, I'm angry. They attacked my son!"

Jake's voice dropped to a whisper. "Sam, this isn't a good place for this. Let's go to your office."

I lowered my tone, resisting snapping back. "So now you're deciding where we talk?"

"You came here to ask questions, and I know why." He stood, a rare seriousness in his eyes. "Let's go."

Grumbling under my breath, I trailed behind him. "I sincerely dislike your grandiose statements. As your therapist, I must remind you that's a common schizophrenia symptom..."

He ignored the jab, leading the way into my office. We settled into our usual chairs, the tension thick between us.

"You saw one," he stated plainly.

"How did you—" I stumbled, then cut myself off. "You're a hypnotist!"

His face broke into a grin. "What?"

"That's how I see these things you talk about—you hypnotized me with one of your gadgets."

Jake smirked. "Is that your explanation?"

"Yeah, it all makes—" I trailed off, staring into his eyes, realizing how absurd it sounded. "Jeez, and I'm the one accusing you of being paranoid."

He leaned forward, calm. "Sam, if you imagine someone is following you, that's paranoid. If you really are being followed, then you're just cautious."

I sank back, exhaustion pulling at me. "I don't understand how any of this is possible."

"So you really saw one."

I poured it all out—the dreamscape, the strange, nightmarish place, the hideous thing looming over my son. The words tumbled out raw and unfiltered.

Jake listened, nodding at the right moments.

"I feel bad for the boy," he mumbled.

"Why did you do this to me?" I demanded.

"You said you wanted to share my problem, Sam," he said, his eyes soft with empathy. "But once you know about them, you become a target. I had to tell someone—to make sense of what I do."

Heat flared in my chest, nearly yanking me toward anger again. I wanted to silence him just so the noise in my head would stop. "How did you know—about last night?"

"I heard them. They're not happy you quit on me."

"Why?"

"They think you keep me distracted," Jake said bluntly. "And somehow, you've seen their world."

"You mean my dream?"

Jake shook his head slowly. "More than that. That's their home —the place I glimpsed through the portal forty years ago."

"Don't start with 'other dimensions' again—"

"Do you know anyone else who dreamed of that place?"

I gritted my teeth. "Yes, I do. But how?"

"It's the weakening of the dimensional barriers."

"What are you talking about?"

Jake suddenly got to his feet, pacing. "Do you remember why they attacked me the night I was hospitalized?"

"From what you've told me, it's just something they do occasionally."

"Not that time." His eyes burned with a fierce glow. "It was because I went there."

"I don't—"

"Remember what I told you? About going to them instead of waiting for them to come to me? I did it, Sam."

I took a sip of my now tepid coffee, washing it down with two antacids. "Jake, what does that have to do with—"

"After I trapped one in that magnetic field, I realized it was possible to pull one fully into our reality," Jake explained, settling back into his chair. "Usually they're incorporeal—only able to manifest subtly, to affect small objects. But they can shift forms, adapt while in our world. That's their advantage."

I scoffed. "So even though these creatures kill, you chase them relentlessly. Don't you think that's insane?"

"About as insane as drinking coffee with antacids?" Jake chuckled.

"When did you become *my* therapist?" I shot back.

"We're helping each other."

I glared. "That's rich. You're not helping me. You've dragged my life into that hell I dreamed about."

Jake nodded solemnly. "You dreamed of it because the dimensions are converging."

"What?"

"The night they slashed my wrists, I visited the place you described."

"They found you in the subbasement of Bellcant, not some alien dimension!"

"I chose that basement on purpose. It's one of those weak spots where they can slip into our world."

He explained that certain locations—dark, forgotten, filled with an unshakable feeling of wrongness—served as hidden gateways.

"Evil, Sam," he said quietly. "You've been in such places. There's one right beneath this asylum's basement."

"This is a psychiatric hospital—not an asylum."

"It is now," Jake said coldly. "But it wasn't always. It used to be a madhouse. You can feel the old evil beneath the polished floors and painted walls. They've been feeding off pain and madness here for decades."

"Can we stick to the point?"

"Right," Jake said, leaning in conspiratorially. "The point is, I kept trying to recreate what Goldstein did, making something external. That was the mistake."

"How?"

"It had to be something you could be inside to cross dimensions."

Jake described the vest he'd built, crafted from years of tinkering—compact yet powerful, about the size of a police riot vest. It slipped over his head with battery belts fastened around the waist. Using a tiny tank of liquid helium the device generated magnetic fields exceeding twenty Tesla and confined tightly around the wearer.

"It interacts with my body's electrochemical signals to create the other-dimensional field."

He told how he ventured into Bellcant's lower basement wearing the vest, moving into a massive room with a twenty-foot ceiling. He approached a spot directly under a powerful lamp where he sensed the creatures lurking just beyond the edge of light.

"How?" I asked.

"After years of practice, I can hear them—almost understand their speech."

"Their words?"

Jake shrugged. "More their tone, their chatter. It's a language, and I get the gist. That night, they were buzzing with tension."

"What did you do?"

"I tested all the controls. The wristbands controlled everything, with heavy steel-cased wires running to each wrist. Flicking on the electromagnets made the vest feel lighter instantly."

"Wait, it got lighter when powered?"

He nodded. "Magnetic energy flowed through my body. Then I switched on the wave emitter and heard this ringing in my head —a whining noise."

"You said it was radio waves. You can't hear radio waves."

Jake smiled, eyes gleaming with that mix of madness and brilliance. "I could feel it as soon as I created that magnetic field. My hands trembled slightly as I adjusted the frequency, tuning into the vibrational level I knew was theirs—the ones I'd been chasing. That's when everything shifted. The surrounding room shimmered, the air thickened, and suddenly, I saw them."

"They showed themselves?" I asked, leaning in.

Jake's eyes lit up with a strange mix of excitement and awe. "Not just showed—they glowed. They didn't blend into the shadows anymore. Those small, square bodies stood out like beacons, whether they clung to the ceiling, perched on the generators, or lurked in the darkest corners."

I sat back, mouth slightly agape, trying to absorb the weight of his revelation.

"They were alive in a way I hadn't imagined," Jake continued, voice rising with animation. "Their jagged mouths shifted silently, lips moving. They appeared agitated, even furious. That's when I increased the energy to the emitters and the room didn't just shimmer anymore—it faded away."

I blinked, unsure of what he meant. "Faded away?"

Jake nodded slowly, eyes fixed on some distant memory. "I found myself somewhere else entirely—not inside a concrete bunker anymore, but standing on dusty, barren red soil. The vast landscape stretched endlessly in every direction, flat and desolate. Strange, skeletal shapes jutted from the ground—like dead trees stripped bare of every leaf."

A chill crept over me. A gnawing blend of dread and a haunting déjà vu settled deep in my bones. The clarity in Jake's voice betrayed that he wasn't making this up. He'd seen that terrible place with his own eyes.

"I was alone at first," Jake said, voice almost a whisper now. "But they appeared around me in a heartbeat. In that red place they weren't flat shadows or shifting blobs anymore. They were... three-dimensional. Like malformed dwarfs, with cube-shaped heads and narrow slits for eyes. Their claws scraped the cracked earth, and sharp, jagged spikes filled their mouths."

He swallowed hard. "That's when it hit me—I hadn't brought any weapons."

I held my breath. "What did you do? Did you shut down the device?"

"I started to," Jake answered, voice tense. "But they attacked all at once—biting, clawing, tearing at my gear. I swear, they wanted to trap me there, in that grim, endless wasteland. I fought back as best I could; I flailed my arms and the metal on my wrist connected with one of their heads." He cracked a brief, bittersweet smile. "I won't lie—I enjoyed the solid 'whack' of it."

I leaned forward, heart pounding. "What did you do?"

Jake's expression darkened. "There were too many—too many to fight. They overwhelmed me, tearing into my skin with those claws. I'd built a fail-safe—it shifts the frequency to bring me back. But when I came back, the dark room returned and the red landscape vanished."

He paused, the memory twisting his face.

"I triggered the emergency lights on my belt hoping to scare them off." His voice cracked slightly. "But this time... it didn't work. They tore the lights apart, smashed the glass, yanked out wires. Without the radio's hum I heard them clearly—a crashing, crackling rage that filled the air."

Jake's fists clenched. "They pulled me down, surrounded me. My belt battery pack sparked and hissed as helium escaped. I fought with every ounce of strength I had, but they swarmed me, hundreds of them. Somehow—I don't know how—I switched on my guard radio during the struggle."

He slumped back in his chair, exhausted. "One of them ripped the bracelet from my wrist. Another picked up a shard of glass, dragged it across my flesh. I screamed... and then everything went black. I woke up here, At Greystorm."

I nodded, taken by the distant look in his eyes. "There're worse places than this."

A tired, bitter smile appeared on his face. "Not for me. My father brought me here in the beginning. I visited Shawn here once... And now I'm stuck. Honestly, sometimes I wish they'd finished me in their world."

I hesitated. "It would be hard to explain where you went."

Jake's gaze drifted. "I realized something... while I was studying them they were studying us. They grew stronger and it's my fault."

The room fell silent.

I closed my folder with a soft snap and exhaled deeply. "Well, Jake, my part is done. I'm writing up my conclusions today, and Dr. Matthews takes over on Monday."

He didn't move or respond right away.

"Jake?"

"I'm here," he said, voice faint. "Just... surprised. After everything you told me—about that place you dreamed of, and your boy..."

I placed a hand on his shoulder. "Jake, tonight is New Year's Eve. We're welcoming a new millennium. And it's like you said. If I'm not associated with you, if I am not seeing you. I am not a target. It's time to leave tall this behind."

He stared ahead, eyes reflecting a flicker of hope amidst the fatigue. "I understand, Sam."

I drove home in the daylight, the streets oddly quiet, the weight of the day pressing hard on my chest.

When I stepped inside, the house was silent. Marcie and the kids were out—somewhere, I didn't know where. I felt a sudden, aching loneliness and climbed the stairs without a word, seeking refuge in the softness of our bed.

The hours slipped away unnoticed; when I finally opened my eyes it was nearly two in the afternoon.

I wandered into the kitchen, the warmth of the room contrasting with the chill that settled deep in my bones.

There was Marcie standing by the stove, preparing dinner. Her movements were mechanical, her face pale and drawn, shadows lingering under her tired eyes.

Relief flooded me—so grateful she was here—but then I reached out and hugged her, and she didn't hug me back.

A hollow emptiness opened between us.

"Where are the kids?" I asked, breaking the silence.

"At friends' houses," she said without looking at me. Her voice dropped lower, edged with something I couldn't name: "So, how is Jake?"

The icy sharpness of that simple question was like a slap. Marcie was the only person who could paralyze me with a single glance or word.

"Same as always," I said evenly, forcing calm over the turmoil inside. "I'm not back on his case, I just wanted some answers. Matthews is taking over."

She set a skillet on the stove with a soft clatter, her fingers trembling just slightly. "That's not what you said this morning."

I exhaled slowly, feeling the weight of the morning's argument pressing down again.

"Marcie, it was a rough night. Neither of us got any rest. But I've kept my promise. Tomorrow Jake isn't my patient anymore."

Something shattered between us—something I rarely saw. A single tear escaped her eye and traced a quiet, trembling path down her cheek.

My mouth must have hung open in shock. Marcie didn't cry. She believed in logic, in intellect, in reason above all—never tears. She wielded words like weapons, bullying or debating until she won every fight. Yet here she was, quietly unravelling.

Her voice was barely a whisper. "I just don't know you anymore—" She bit her lip which quivered like she was holding back a flood.

Without thinking, I pulled her away from the stove, took her into my arms, and kissed her—fiercely, desperately, like a man grasping at something slipping through his fingers. I kissed her head, her neck, murmuring soft, soothing words as her shoulders shook and she swallowed hard to hold back the tears.

"Dinner's going to be ruined," she muttered, sounding strangely like herself again.

"I don't care," I said firmly.

"You promised you'd stick with him until New Year's," she said, keeping her distance but her voice softer now. "You should honor it. I shouldn't have made it an issue—you did what I asked."

"I know how much Jake gets under your skin," I said carefully.

"I don't like how he affects you," she admitted. "You've sounded… crazy lately. And last night… what you said you saw —"

I didn't want to drown us in argument, not now. But there was one thing I needed her to understand.

"Remember the dream I told you about?" I asked gently.

"The place with the red soil?" She replied, her brow furrowing with the memory.

"That's it. Jake says it's an actual place."

"Should that surprise me?" she challenged quietly.

"I know how it sounds. But he described it in a way that matched everything I remembered perfectly."

"So now you and Jake are sharing dreams," she said with a hint of disbelief, biting her lip again.

"That's the thing. He didn't dream it. He says he went there. That he… changed the frequency of existence."

Her brow knitted tighter, exhaustion and frustration crashing through her features. "So that's what we're doing wrong? Living at the wrong frequency? I'm too tired to debate this. We're just going to have another argument."

"No, we're not!" I nudged her away from the stove. "Because I'm going to finish making dinner, while you go lie down."

Her eyes brightened slightly. "Would you? That would be heaven. A nap before going to the Benning's tonight would help."

I watched her retreat and a bittersweet thought settled: marriages move in cycles—close, distant, tangled in the mess of children, careers, and all the trivial hardships that shape us into different people. But I hoped silently that the pendulum was about to swing back.

I finished preparing the meal and slid it into the oven to warm. I went to my office, booted up the computer, and wrote—documenting everything about Jake.

Matthews would need every detail, every observation. I doubted Jake could tell him more than I already had. Matthews was stronger, more controlled—he would take charge and steer the sessions where they needed to go.

I typed steadily:

Patient: Jake Hurd
Classification: DSM-IV-TR #295.30
Schizophrenia, Paranoid Type
This patient exhibits unusual intelligence and imagination. Due to intense hallucinations, visual and auditory alike, my current conclusions are—

I pressed on, trying to distill the murky chaos into clarity. The more I wrote, the clearer it became.

Page after page filled with observations and insights. By 5:30 I had ten pages ready to send to Dr. Matthews and Dr. Benning, stopping only to check on the lasagna bubbling in the oven.

A lightness filled me, as if a crushing weight lifted from my shoulders. The new millennium loomed ahead, and I wanted to step into it unburdened.

Jake Hurd would be someone else's problem now.

45. END TIMES

The kids arrived home right on time, and Rachel wasn't alone—she brought her friend Bernadette who was going to spend the night.

I plated up the lasagna, and all three kids dug in.

"How come Rachel gets a friend to stay over and I don't?" Rueben whined, a hint of jealousy in his voice.

Rachel smirked and shot back, "Because you're a squirt who has to sleep with the light on."

"Rachel." I looked sharply enough at her to silence her instantly. Then I turned to Rueben. "When you're older, Rueben."

I looked back at Rachel. "Now, you've got our phone numbers, our beeper and cell, and Bernadette's parents live just down the street—"

"Jeez, Dad, we've gone over this for days—"

"I worry," I said firmly.

"This Y2K thing isn't that big of a deal—"

"Just in case, I want you to have backup plans."

Rachel exchanged a glance with Bernadette and they both giggled, evidently unconcerned.

"We'll be okay," Rachel said with forced confidence.

I wasn't buying it. "And keep an eye on your brother and be nice to him. I'll hear about it if you don't."

Rueben stuck his tongue out at his sister.

"And you too," I corrected, which made Rueben's bravado falter and his face go sheepish. "This is your first year without a sitter and I want all of you to be all right."

"Afraid the shadows will get us?" Rachel teased, her tone light but challenging.

I turned to her, my face so angry and cold that her smile faded and her eyes widened with unease.

"It's all Rueben talks about!" she quickly said, and the defensiveness in her voice surprised me.

I took several deep breaths to steady myself and quietly left the room, clutching at what little dignity I had left.

It was 6:30 p.m. when I went to our bedroom and gently shook Marcie awake.

"Huh?" she murmured, rubbing sleep from her eyes, and I kissed her forehead.

"I don't know why you want to kiss me—I look a fright," she said, fingers absently running through tangled hair.

"You look disheveled. It's sexy. Get in the shower," I said, smiling softly.

She nodded sleepily and stumbled toward the bathroom. I laid out the clothes for the night: tuxedos, thanks to Bill and Helena's insistence, for this one upscale party.

"How are the kids?" she called through the bathroom door.

"Fine," I replied, moving to the doorway where I could peer through the translucent shower glass and watch her naked form as it moved under the water. "Do you think it's okay we didn't hire a babysitter? With the whole Y2K scare and all—"

"Rachel's old enough to watch her brother," Marcie sighed. "There has to be *some* advantage to spacing kids seven years apart."

By 7:30 we were out the door, pressing repeated kisses onto Rueben's cheeks and giving Rachel explicit instructions.

When we got to the car, our breath escaped in visible puffs of steam.

"Do you think they'll stay awake?" I asked.

"The girls will chatter until we get back. Rueben? Maybe nine-thirty if we're lucky."

We drove off toward the Benning's' home. The Benning's live in Summit, close enough to Greystorm for a quick emergency but far enough to get away from it.

Marcie and I have been at Bill and Helena's New Year's party since our engagement—a crowd packed with psychiatrists and psychologists who could read your every move. It's not the place to bring just any date; relationships have to be well on their way to marriage to survive the unspoken scrutiny.

Summit itself is an old-money New Jersey town—not as flashy as Far Hills or Bernardsville but rich with history—and with commuter trains connecting to New York, it has an interesting mix of the working class and the upper crust.

As we pulled into the Benning's' driveway, several men met our car wearing heavy red winter coats embroidered with *CUSTOM VALET* in reflective gold across their backs.

Helena greeted us at the door like a regal hostess. That night she might have been the grande dame of an English castle.

Her flowing aquamarine chiffon gown draped gracefully over her ample figure; her white hair was piled high in a sophisticated updo crowned with a small diamond tiara. Make-up was subtle and elegant.

"Sam!" she exclaimed, pecking my cheek warmly. "And Marcie," she added with a repeated embrace. "You both look wonderful!"

Helena helped Marcie out of her fur coat and said. "Marcie! That dress will have every man at this party drooling!"

"I dried my mouth on the way in," I joked, earning an elbow in the ribs from Marcie.

Helena laughed softly. "So good of you to be the first to arrive. How are the children? Is Rueben all right? I know you had a scare with him last month."

Making small talk she guided us from the entrance hall into the living room.

To call the living room magnificent was an understatement. In the corner stood a large evergreen adorned with old-fashioned, oversized bulbs that had to be screwed in individually—a nostalgic touch from my childhood. Large golden angels nestled among delicate blown glass ornaments giving the tree an elegant Victorian flair.

The wood-paneled walls were rich and polished, crystal chandeliers casting prismatic light. Everything shimmered under the gleam of perfection and the air smelled faintly of lemon-scented furniture oil.

"Helena, you've truly outdone yourself," I said, eyes wide as I took in the room.

She tossed her hair with practiced nonchalance. "Dear Sam, you always know just what to say."

Bill appeared then a snifter of brandy in hand, looking like he'd just stepped off the set of a classic film—suave and commanding, yet moving with surprising grace for his bulk.

Marcie and I drifted through the party, exchanging waves as we passed, surrounded by the soft hum of conversation, the ringing doorbell, and the band's music drifting through the rooms.

Just as I stepped into the kitchen for a soda Bill caught my arm.

"Sam," he said, pulling me toward his study—the one room off-limits tonight.

"What's up?"

His face was tight, jaw set with tension. "There's a problem at Greystorm—with your patient."

My heart sank. "What? Which patient?"

He pointed to the phone lying off its cradle. I grabbed the receiver.

"Doctor Lucas, it's Althea," came the anxious voice.

"Yes, Althea, what's wrong?"

"It's Jake Hurd. He's… out of control."

"What do you mean?" I tried to stay calm. "Did he go ballistic? Hurt someone?"

"He got out of the ward. By the time we found him he'd locked himself in the basement. The door's jammed and he won't let anyone in. I've got Carl watching the door, but—"

I exhaled sharply. "Okay, I'm on my way. I'll talk to him."

"I'm scared, Dr. Lucas. He was working on some electronic gadgets. I'm afraid he might electrocute someone—or himself."

"You did the right thing calling, Althea. I'll get there as soon as I can."

She thanked me and hung up. I went out to the party to find Marcie.

"There's an emergency at Greystorm," I told her. "I have to go."

"I'm coming with you," she said firmly, crossing her arms.

I tried to keep my composure. "It's Jake Hurd."

"I said I'm going."

I considered her for a moment. "It's been a long time since we worked together."

"Are you sure you can handle it?" she raised an eyebrow and I smiled despite myself.

"It'd be good to have someone with your training," I admitted.

"Thank you, Sam. So, we agree on the diagnosis, Doctor?"

"It would appear so, Doctor."

She headed off to get our coats.

"I'll get the valet to bring the car around," I called after her, my mind already racing toward the crisis I knew awaited us at Greystorm.

We were ten minutes out from Greystorm. The city's pulse had quieted with the late hour—most people safely tucked away where they belonged—which blessedly kept traffic to a minimum.

The streets stretched ahead, empty and indifferent, as we sped through the night.

I turned to Marcie, eager to lay everything bare. "Let me fill you in," I said, voice tight with a mix of urgency and exhaustion.

I told her the conclusions from my report on Jake, ready to spill it all out.

She met my gaze, eyes sharp and attentive, inviting me to speak.

"Any sign he was planning something this... this catastrophic?" she asked, her voice a low probe.

"Yes, damn it," I snarled, the frustration bubbling just under my skin. "He dropped hints all over the place—said I'd 'cure' him after New Year's, claimed he wouldn't need a new psychiatrist. Then, this morning, I found him wandering the halls like some restless ghost. The problem is—he's always so damn cryptic. It never felt more than background noise, just another one of his strange tics."

Marcie nodded slowly. "Anyone could have missed it, Sam."

"That's the worst part. Whatever he's planning, I'm betting on tonight." My stomach tightened. "The old millennium to new—there's symbolism there, a point of passage."

She considered that, voice steady but dark. "It's the perfect night for madness."

I swallowed hard, memories pressing in. "These months with Jake... it was like he pulled me into his nightmare, dragging me through every dark corner."

Marcie's eyes darkened with concern as we pulled up to Greystorm's security booth. "That nightmare might end up destroying him."

At Greystorm the guard, expecting me, nodded curtly and waved us through. We drove up to the main entrance—no other door was open at this hour. Behind the receptionist's desk another guard eyed us warily.

I walked in holding up my ID. "I'm Dr. Lucas."

His eyes flicked from my tuxedo and overcoat to Marcie, swathed in her elegant fur, before stepping aside without a word. The dimly lit corridors stretched ahead, bathed in subdued nighttime lighting. The elevator doors slid open and we hurried up to Jake's ward where Althea was already pacing nervously at the nurse's station.

"Dr. Lucas!" Althea gasped, eyes wide with unwelcome news. When she spotted Marcie confusion furrowed her brow.

"This is my wife, Althea. She's a doctor, too," I introduced.

"Pleased to meet you, ma'am," Althea said briskly, then turned back to me. "You're going to need all the help you can get tonight."

Marcie and I exchanged a concerned glance.

"Doctor—uh, Doctors," Althea corrected herself. "He's in the subbasement. Take the elevator to the basement. Carl will meet you there."

A thin smile touched my lips. "Thank God you were here, Althea."

"Carl!" Althea barked into her walkie-talkie so loudly I nearly winced. "Dr. Lucas is heading down. Meet him and—handle our problem."

Marcie and I got in the elevator and it rumbled downward; tension filled every creak and shudder of the old building.

"You okay?" I asked Marcie quietly.

"We've dealt with worse," she said, nerves steeled, "but let's see if we can pull Jake out of this."

The elevator doors opened to reveal a bleak, concrete corridor lit by a solitary swinging bulb. Marcie gasped involuntarily as a large figure emerged—Carl.

"Where's Jake?" I demanded.

Carl gestured down the grim, shadowed hall. "This way. Hope you can talk him out, Doc, because if you can't, you're gonna need a bomb to get him out."

Marcie's eyebrows rose sharply. "Why's that?"

"Lowest point in the building," Carl explained gravely. "Stone foundation, over a hundred years old. No windows, only one reinforced door. No way in or out except through that."

"Sounds like a prison," Marcie muttered, pulling her coat tighter.

We passed room after room—wood and iron doors with small barred windows swung open to reveal concrete cells stuffed with old gurneys and forgotten files draped with faded fabric. The air reeked of mildew and musty paper, thick with neglect.

"How did he even get down here?" I pressed.

"The old bastard just rode the elevator," Carl said, disbelief edging his tone. "Made multiple trips, bringing all his electronics down bit by bit. We never realized he was missing."

We came to a massive wooden door. Carl pushed it open with a grunt; rusted hinges screamed their protest. A wave of decay hit us, stronger here in this new passage. Marcie paled.

We stood at the top of a stairway leading down into utter darkness.

"Must've known every step," Carl said quietly. "We don't check on Jake much—he's always the calm one."

I nodded. "He played us perfectly. Got us to give him exactly what he needed."

Marcie shivered, voice low. "What was this place?"

Carl flicked a switch and a cavernous stairwell emerged from the gloom. "Subbasement storage normally. But these rooms? This was where they kept the criminals back when this was a prison for murderers."

I glanced back down the narrow hallway. "It was a prison... and Jake told me stories about it. The place where they did electroshock, frontal lobotomies. He said... evil lived down here."

"I'm staying up here," Carl said firmly. "Unless you really need me."

"That's fine. We got this," I reassured him.

"Just go to the bottom. The door's there," he indicated the descending stairs.

I glanced at my watch: it was 11:50. I gripped Marcie's arm and started down. The uneven stone walls pressed close, mortared roughly at strange angles. Marcie lifted the hem of her black dress, now dust-streaked at the bottom.

At the foot of the staircase stood another massive wooden door reinforced with thick metal brackets and framed like a vault.

"How gothic," Marcie whispered.

"All part of Jake's fantasy," I muttered. "The perfect setting for his delusions, like a twisted horror set-piece."

I raised my fist and pounded on the door.

"Jake!" my voice echoed off the damp stone.

A ragged voice came from the other side. "Who's there?"

"It's Sam. We need to talk."

Metal scraped. The heavy door creaked open a crack, revealing Jake's head, gaunt and pale.

"Who's with you?"

"My wife."

"Of course." He opened the door fully, stepping back into the dim light. His frame seemed larger somehow, bulky beneath wires that snaked from his wrists to his chest.

Marcie and I exchanged a quick, uneasy glance and followed him inside.

The ceiling was low with pipes snaking overhead. The rough stone walls bulged ominously suffocating the cramped space. Jake moved to bolt the door behind us.

I saw his attire—thick padded vest, a belt rigged with what looked like battery packs, and heavy wrist devices blinking with soft red and green lights.

"So, you must be Marcie," Jake said smoothly, acting the perfect host. "I almost feel like I know you."

She returned his controlled smile. "And I feel like I know you, Jake. You've been… a part of our lives lately."

Jake glanced at a large LED display strapped to his wrist—an alarm clock-sized device glowing ominously: 11:53.

"I'm glad you could make it, Sam. Sorry about the manipulations."

"That's what you call all this?" Marcie asked, voice icy.

Jake's smile never faltered. "Nurses and orderlies never suspected; I was very careful. I brought my equipment down over a week. No one knew I was gone until tonight."

"But why? Why are you doing this?" I demanded.

Marcie's voice cut in, firm and cold. "Shutting yourself away won't fix anything."

Jake's smile widened—something fierce gleamed in his eyes. "Maybe not… but it might change everything. When I crossed into their world I understood the stakes. Sam you asked why they spared me—they weren't sparing me—they were learning. Learning everything about us."

His enthusiasm was unsettling, a dangerous fire burning in his gaze.

"Why, Jake?" I pressed. "You chased them, but why did they want you?"

"Convergence," he replied, eyes gleaming.

"What?" Marcie whispered.

"They waited, growing stronger, biding their time to cross over and attack us. All of us."

He moved toward a scratched table, lifting a long metal staff covered in wires and flickering electronics.

"What's that?" I asked, heart pounding.

"Remember what I said?" Jake's smile twisted into something darker.

I swallowed hard. "A weapon?"

"Oh God," Marcie breathed, clutching at me. "He's got a bomb."

"I don't think so," I murmured at first, the words barely escaping my lips. Then, gathering courage, I spoke louder, my voice sharp with disbelief. "Is that what you've been working on? Explain—what's the purpose behind all this?"

"To save the world," he answered, his tone flat and steady as if stating a simple fact rather than a grandiose claim.

"Oh, great!" I exploded suddenly, unable to hold back the sarcasm. "So now you're our messiah?"

"No, Sam. I'm a warrior." His eyes darkened, the weight of his conviction shifting the air between us. "You're not the only one who's dreamed of the red place. There are others—people like you, and your boy too. They're breaching our world. And I believe an attack is imminent."

"Attack?" I grunted, the word heavy and monstrous in my throat.

"Yes. Tonight. At midnight." His voice lowered, almost a whisper full of dread. "All those fears about Y2K, the Millennium Bug—that isn't just paranoia. There's a weakening of the barriers between dimensions. It's breaking down and they'll cross over like an invading army."

"The convergence?" I demanded, heart pounding.

"Exactly." He stood taller, the contrast between his slight frame and the armor he wore making him almost ghostlike—a knight from another age, armed with modern tools instead of swords but no less ready for battle.

He continued, voice grim: "If I can stop them at one point, I can force them to retreat, disrupt their plans. Then I'll hunt them, just like they did to me and my family."

Jake glanced down at his wrist display, then flipped a switch on the battery belt strapped around him. With a practiced motion, he reached behind his back and opened a valve on a small tank nestled beneath his left arm. A sharp hiss escaped and the tubes connecting to the device frosted over in an instant, white as bone.

Marcie cleared her throat, slipping into her calm, measured psychiatrist's voice. "Why don't we all just go upstairs? We can talk, toast the New Year—"

Jake only smiled, eyes fixed on the digital clock now ticking down: 11:59. He pressed a button, and an ominous hum filled the room.

"I figured it out, Sam," he said quietly. "They need us. They feed off powerful emotions."

"What?" I asked, confusion and alarm washing over me.

"They feed on fear." His gaze hardened. "That's why they come into our world and hide in the shadows, why everyone's terrified of the millennium. They're like leeches, Sam—drawing strength from our panic."

"Jake," I said, voice dropping. "What if it's all in your head? What if this is a delusion? Please—let's go upstairs."

He faced me then, a rare softness breaking through his warrior's mask. "Sam, what else is there for me? What's left to live for here?"

Marcie spoke up quickly, logical and firm. "Suicide is never the answer."

"Who said anything about suicide?" Jake snapped, a sudden blaze in his eyes. "I'm going into battle." He pushed another button on his gauntlet.

It began—an eerie crackling, like dry leaves crushed underneath boots but far stranger. I glanced at Marcie; her eyes widened—she heard it too.

The hum intensified, crisp and electric, carrying the sharp smell of ozone.

Marcie's hair suddenly lifted as if a thousand invisible fingers grabbed it. There was a piercing metallic ping as something flew off Marcie and struck Jake.

"Your hairpins!" I yelled, yanking her back toward the door as the small shimmering objects flew from her hair.

The heavy door's bolt rattled, jiggling violently in the lock.

"How?" Marcie breathed, panic rising in her voice.

"It's Jake!" I said, eyes fixed on him. "He's generating a magnetic field."

Her hair flared upward in more places, and she yelped sharply when another hairpin shot out, drawn toward the glowing armor on Jake's chest.

I stared as the pins clustered glowing blue, the faint aura spreading casting an eerie light that bathed the room.

"I saw it—the haze," Jake said softly. "Around my own head… every time I looked in the mirror. Like the others before me. I knew it was coming."

"What's he talking about?" Marcie demanded, stepping closer, her voice trembling.

I already knew. The haze was how Jake sensed death approaching.

Suddenly, the shrill sound snarled inside my head, unbearable and searing. Marcie pressed her hands over her ears but I knew it wouldn't help.

The first one appeared, materializing beside us. Its form was as black as ink, though now rimmed with a faint, glowing outline— blue shifting from the dark shadow of its body. It seemed stunned by the light defining its once-invisible form, staring at its peg-like arms in disbelief.

Marcie screamed, stumbling backward. The creature twisted away, trying to escape into the shadows, but the glow around it betrayed its every move.

"Oh God," she cried as more flickered into existence around the room's edges. She grabbed me fiercely. "Get us out of here, Sam! Please!"

"Stay calm," I urged, heart hammering as the glow slowly deepened, transitioning now to a sinister red. The room shifted, morphing all around us.

My mouth fell open in shock; Marcie shut her eyes tight in desperation. "You have to see this."

"I don't want to," she moaned, voice barely audible.

The walls shimmered like liquid glass, glowing scarlet and turning transparent. Pipes overhead faded away. The once-solid floor beneath us felt soft and earthy—red soil, not concrete.

Beyond the fading walls was a barren landscape, stretching for miles in every direction. The horizon was black, menacing, endless.

The heavy steel door behind us remained our fragile tether to reality.

"This can't be," Marcie whispered, clinging to me.

The creatures shifted too. No longer flat silhouettes their bodies expanded into full three-dimensional forms. Their heads were blocky cubes with no necks—yet they twisted with a grotesque independence that was impossible to understand.

Some froze, stunned by the transformation, but others—emboldened by the familiar red terrain—boldly approached.

One creature neared, slit eyes fixed on me. A hiss slipped from its powerful jaws, revealing rows of sharp teeth built to crush and snap. Its square jaw and taloned three-fingered hands were terrifyingly precise weapons.

I shoved Marcie behind me, raising my leg and kicking out hard.

The creature recoiled but quickly returned, backed by two more.

"JAKE!" I shouted.

The monsters closed in a ring around him, but he moved with deadly grace, spinning his metal staff and striking powerfully.

One creature exploded in a burst of fiery orange light, collapsing instantly.

"Sam!" Marcie cried, but before I could reach her two creatures seized her, dragging her down.

I lunged forward, claws raking down my leg. Fire swept through me like a blitz of angry ants.

I fell, struggling to evade another strike.

A second creature's claws grazed my head, burning like molten flames scorching my scalp. I rolled violently, anger and adrenaline fueling me.

Adopting a crouch like in my high-school football days, I roared and charged blindly.

I slammed into a figure as tall and solid as my son Rueben. It rocked back, dodged swiftly, claws grazing past me.

I scrambled back up, ready for more—only to see Marcie pinned beneath a creature.

With all my might, I kicked at the monster's chest.

A sickening crack radiated up my leg.

The creature flew off, landing yards away.

I collapsed forward, the fierce pain in my foot sharp and unforgiving.

I had broken it.

Dragging Marcie up, I balanced precariously, bracing for the next attack.

The creatures stood still, all eyes locked on Jake.

Or rather—on the staff glowing fiercely in his hands.

It wasn't just blinking lights now; it pulsed with energy so raw I could feel it crashing against me, wave after wave.

Underfoot the floor trembled like an earthquake, and the creatures' bodies vibrated with the force.

Jake stood unmoved—tall, proud, the eye of the storm.

The black creature nearest me doubled over, clutching its head and letting loose a horrible howl—a sound drenched in despair and agony, the cry of the damned.

The room twisted and churned around us with a sickening lurch.

In Jake's hands the staff ignited, roaring alive with fierce orange flames that gutted the shadows engulfing us. The creatures writhed, their grotesque forms convulsing before collapsing like deflated balloons, slipping lifelessly to the cold, hard floor.

Marcie's scream cut through the chaos, raw and desperate as the nightmarish figures crumpled.

In an instant the red-hued landscape shattered like glass, dissolving into nothingness.

We found ourselves back in the cellar. The air was heavy and damp and beneath our feet sprawled hundreds of flat, oily black shapes, motionless and strange, plastered across the floor like spilled ink. Jake was nowhere to be seen.

A sudden thud pounded against the sturdy door.

"Doc, you all right in there?" a voice called out muffled but urgent.

Marcie and I exchanged a grim glance, blood trickling from the deep, angry scratches lining her cheeks. She staggered weakly and I limped alongside her to the door. Together we unbolted it, pushing it open to reveal Carl's concerned face framed by the dim hallway light.

"Jeezus, Doc! Heard yelling and some awful racket. You two okay?" Carl's brow furrowed as his flashlight swept over the black shapes strewn around us. "What the hell is that?" he muttered, stepping forward cautiously.

He crouched beside one of the dark forms, the beam piercing it sharply. Smoke hissed and curled upward, wisps of smoldering ash rising as the shape disintegrated beneath the light. Carl's startled cry echoed in the confined space, then he stomped hard on the burning silhouette. It scattered instantly, reduced to nothing more than fragile ashes that drifted like dust.

Carl shook his hand to brush away the particles and looked up sharply. "What happened, Doc?"

"We… fell," I said simply, though the meaning weighed far more than my words implied.

Carl's gaze swept the room again, landing on the pale faces of Marcie and me. "Where's Jake?"

Marcie let out a hollow, manic laugh that sent a chill through me.

I swallowed hard. "He's gone. There must be another way out."

"Want me to head back and look for him?"

Marcie shrieked a wild, disturbing cackle. I grabbed her arm before she spiraled further.

"Carl, we're hurt. She's bleeding."

"Jesus. What the hell did you get into?" Carl's flashlight bore down on the deep scratches across her face.

"My foot—it's probably fractured. Can you help us back upstairs?"

Without hesitation, Carl bent his broad shoulders, looping one arm under my armpit. Supporting us both, he helped us clamber slowly up the steep stairs, down the hall, and into the cold metal elevator.

Back on the ward, Althea's eyes widened as soon as she saw us. "I'm calling Saint Clares. We need an ambulance now." She snatched up the phone, urgency razor-sharp in her voice. "We don't have an ER here."

"Althea," I interrupted, shakily steadying myself, "I need a release form."

She frowned briefly then opened a cabinet swiftly and pulled a form from a file. Wordlessly she slid it over.

I felt the tension in the room rise.

Marcie sat in a wheelchair Carl found, fingertips brushing her raw cheek. I touched her hair gently before pulling out my pen, scribbling frantically on the form as Althea treated the ugly gashes on my head and leg. She peeled off my shoe, her face tightening.

"Ah!" I jerked back as she tested my toes—the pain searing, sharp.

"You're going to need X-rays." Althea's nod was grim. "I can tell already, Doc. It's broken."

I handed the completed form back just as Carl returned with a second wheelchair, his face tight with worry.

"Make sure this gets to Dr. Benning's office first thing," I grunted, sinking onto the vinyl seat with a wince.

"I will. Now keep quiet 'til the ambulance arrives."

Carl and Althea pushed us through the empty halls toward the front door.

The wail of the ambulance pierced the silent air and soon whisked us away to Saint Clares.

In the sprawling Emergency Room, a pale, much-too-young doctor did his best, running tests and X-rays with the bare minimum of staff.

At about 2:00 AM they moved us off out of the ward and into a room with two beds, Marcie lay down and fell asleep.

Exhaustion seeped into my bones, but I forced myself to call Anne. Her voice was sharp with irritation at the hour, but she agreed to go to our house, use her spare key, and watch the kids.

I dozed briefly as I could. I wanted to remain near Marcie in case she woke.

At 4:00 AM I heard a groan from Marcie and she bolted upright. She looked around and rubbed her head on the spot she clunked against the concrete.

I rose, hobbled to her bed, and touched her arm. She saw it was me, then grabbed me in a tight hug.

I murmured, "It's all right."

"My head hurts," Marcie whispered, voice brittle.

"You have a concussion."

"With unconsciousness?" she asked, fear threading her words.

"It's minor the doctor said. But they want to keep you for observation, maybe an MRI in the morning." I squinted at her eyes—her pupils matched. "Though honestly, that doctor looks like he's still in high school."

"Should I stay awake?" she asked.

"He said it's okay to sleep."

I stretched out on the bed next to her with barely enough room for us to lie side by side.

"This is nice," she murmured, snuggling closer.

"You're the one with the locked door," I teased softly.

She laughed—a soft, tired sound. "All this seems like a lot of trouble just to get me in bed with you."

"That's putting it mildly."

Silence settled between us, thick and unspoken.

"How much of it was real?" she finally whispered.

I shook my head. "I don't want to know."

"Neither do I," she breathed.

We clung to each other, the strange night pressing in as we drifted into a restless sleep, the shadows of what we'd faced lingering just beyond the door.

46. TRAVELER'S PRAYER

B right and early the next morning, the nurses swept into our room like a storm, gently but firmly shooing me away from Marcie's bed.

They needed her for tests and there was no time to argue.

I stumbled back to my bed, collapsing onto it with a heavy sigh. For ten agonizing minutes I lay there, heart pounding, mind spinning.

Then—just as I was trying to steady myself—a fresh group of nurses appeared, this time to take me away for my foot to be cast in plaster.

I wore one of those mortifying hospital gowns, the short, thin kind that left me feeling vulnerable and exposed. There I was—an overweight, middle-aged man with his ass hanging out for all to see.

I clenched my jaw and tried to ignore the humiliation as they worked.

By the time Marcie and I returned to our room, we arrived side by side but worlds apart. She looked worn to the bone, her face pale and drawn, shadows under her eyes that hadn't been there the night before.

Yet somehow, in that fragile, stripped-down state, she looked more beautiful than ever—more real, more undeniably her.

It was a beauty no make-up or glamour could replicate, the raw imprint of a woman who had just weathered a storm.

At eleven o'clock, Anne showed up with the kids in tow and the neurologist emerged with news: Marcie was clean—no concussion, only minor trauma.

Relief washed over us but beneath it, a quiet undercurrent of unease lingered.

The hospital released us and we all piled into the car to head home. Anne driving, me in the passenger seat and Marcie and the kids in the back.

Anne did her best to lighten the mood. "Well, thank goodness. Except for you two, Y2K ended up being a big nothing."

I couldn't shake the nagging thought of what might have been —if it weren't for Jake's decision.

"Sorry if we worried you all," I said, glancing at Rachel and Rueben in the backseat.

Rachel shrugged, her brow furrowed with lingering confusion. "We didn't even know until Auntie Anne woke us this morning. And it was weird… last night at midnight there was this red glow in the horizon—just for a few seconds. No one knows where it came from."

Rueben clung tightly to Marcie, practically sitting on her lap, caught somewhere between fearless and fearful. "They went away, Daddy," he said quietly.

I turned my head, peering over my left shoulder toward the back seat. "Who did?"

Rueben hesitated, glancing at his mother with a guilty look. Then, in a voice barely above a whisper, he leaned forward and said, "You know."

"The dark things," Marcie said from the back seat, her voice barely audible but heavy with fear. Our eyes met briefly. "Yes," she murmured. "I hope to God they did."

Back at home, Rachel jumped right in, helping with dinner and house chores as if she'd been waiting for a chance to do something useful.

Despite whatever plans she might have had, Anne settled into the den and transformed into an all-in-one nurse, nanny, and housekeeper. I kept thanking her until she finally snapped, "Enough. Go to bed."

Later that night, Marcie and I lay in our bed, the room shrouded in darkness with curtains drawn tight to block the cold, clear light of New Year's Day. I turned to her, holding her hand in mine, the lingering tension thick between us.

"So here I finally get back in our bed," I said softly, "and I can't deliver."

She squeezed my hand gently. "That's okay," she replied. "You were right."

"About what?"

"About those things," she shuddered, her voice barely a whisper. "Seeing them."

Silence stretched out between us, heavy and impossible to break.

We'd had so many silences since the ordeal began—each one filled with unsaid words, fears, and questions. That day we did little more than sleep, each of us lost in our own thoughts.

But after dinner, once the kids went to bed and it was just the two of us again, Marcie's hand found mine, pulled me to my feet and led us upstairs.

"Are you sure?" I asked, hesitation in my voice.

"Yes," she said. "I think we need it."

It was awkward with my foot in plaster, but quietly, carefully, we removed our clothing, lay down and made it work.

Afterwards, as we held each other close, I felt a slow unwinding of the tension that had gripped both of us.

She was right—we needed it.

More than just the physical closeness we needed the reassurance, the connection, the simple human touch to anchor us after the storm.

Days later, driving was impossible without a usable right foot, so Marcie took the wheel and brought me to Greystorm that Friday morning.

The weight of what lay ahead pressed down on me as we entered the building. Bill Benning was waiting, his expression tight, ready to dive into the mystery that haunted us all—the disappearance of Jake Hurd.

We settled at Bill's desk, the sterile office illuminated by the cold hum of fluorescent lights.

He wasted no time. "Jake left several papers behind," Bill said, shuffling through a sheaf of documents with practiced efficiency. "One document transfers all his savings and property straight to his daughter, Amanda."

I nodded slowly. Amanda—the only family Jake had left. Losing her must have torn him apart, but from the shadows he fought; this inheritance could be her chance at a life far removed from his darkness.

Bill's gaze sharpened, locking onto both Marcie and me. "You two were the last to see him. Right, Sam? Marcie?"

"I saw him," I said, steadying my voice. "He was in the basement. Then the lights... they flickered erratically. Marcie and I lost our footing. When we looked again Jake was gone."

Bill pulled out a green folder and flipped it open. "Sam, you had scratches on your leg. Marcie, the marks on your face—they're fresh." Marcie's fingers glided over the scabbed trails, shallow but vivid enough to fuel questions. "Did Jake put up a fight?"

She shook her head, voice flat. "Only our own clumsiness."

Bill's eyes narrowed. "If he'd attacked you—if there was any violence—the police would have to be involved."

That's when the pieces clicked in my mind. "You have the release forms I signed for Jake," I said quietly.

"Yes," Bill admitted, brow furrowed. "I still don't understand why. You were leaving his case—"

"He was free to go," I interrupted firmly. "You don't have authority to hold him or continue searching."

Marcie leaned in, eyes sharp. "If he broke the law, or attacked us—"

"We're a hospital, not a prison," Bill said, his indignation barely concealed. "But if he's dangerous we can call in the police. Nobody knows where he went. And Sam—why did you sign those release forms? Althea brought them upstairs."

"It's better this way, Bill," I said. "Let Jake go."

Bill's shoulders tensed, sweat beading at his hairline. "There's more going on here than you realize. The security company might sue us—"

"He wasn't insane," Marcie interjected, and Bill stared at her as if the mere notion was absurd.

"We still don't know where he is!" Bill pressed on. "In his room, we found designs of a device of some kind, though I can't make head nor tail of it. If it's valuable—"

"It belongs to his daughter, like the rest of his things," I said, voice steady but resolute.

"The security company won't like that one bit," Bill grumbled.

I shrugged, unwilling to justify any further. "As his therapist, I believe Jake was ready to move on."

"Move on? What kind of prognosis is that?" Bill's tone was incredulous.

"The best possible." Marcie's voice was firm. "He'd had enough."

Bill's gaze fell. "Move on... where?"

"A new town. Another state. Maybe even another plane of existence," I answered quietly.

"That's hardly a concrete answer," Bill said, deflated.

"It's all we have to offer," I said.

Marcie nodded firmly. "I was there, Bill. Jake was ready to leave."

I glanced at Bill one last time. "I'm sure you can find some way to protect the hospital and secure your fees."

Bill shook his head slowly, searching our faces. "There's something you're not telling me. Marcie, I can't believe you'd be part of a cover-up."

She met his eyes without flinching. "I support my husband, Bill. You should too."

As we moved toward the main entrance, a stubborn pull drew Marcie and me back down to the basement—urgent, unspoken. We took the elevator quietly; the dread settling low like a stone in my chest. No one caught us; no one questioned. But something had to be done.

In the dim concrete corridors I pulled the small flashlight from my pocket. We pushed forward, descending the narrow, uneven stairs to the subbasement. Maneuvering with crutches was awkward but I managed, ignoring the sharp sting in my leg.

Marcie's voice dropped to a whisper. "I'm scared, Sam."

"You stay by the door," I said, trying to sound braver than I felt. "I'll go inside."

The door still hung ajar from our last visit. I flicked on the switch and both of us gasped. The floor was littered with shattered remnants of black, shadowy forms—grotesque specters sprawled lifelessly like spilled ink.

"Look at all of them," Marcie breathed. "Where do you think Jake is now?"

"I want to believe he's exactly where he intended—hunting those creatures in their own domain, protecting humanity from the unseen," I answered.

"That place looked like Hell," she whispered.

"It did," I agreed, as a shudder went down my spine.

"Let's get on with it," Marcie said with a weary sigh.

I pulled the smooth disk from my pocket placing it carefully on the cold floor. Stepping close I told her, "Close your eyes."

Marcie covered her face with trembling hands. I clapped loudly and the disk flared to an astonishing brilliance, flooding the dark room with searing light. I instinctively shielded my eyes, seeing a pinkish glow bleed through my lids.

Turning my back, I clapped again. The glow slowly faded. I waited, eyes shut tight, until the heavy darkness reclaimed the space.

"Alright," I said. We opened our eyes in unison. Only faint wisps of smoke lingered. The black shapes were gone, melted away by the light.

Retrieving the disk, we retraced our steps in silence, back to the elevator. As Marcie drove us home, I asked her to stop at Adath Shalom before the synagogue gift shop closed for Shabbos.

Inside, I approached the woman at the office and asked if we could purchase Mezuzah cases and scrolls from the gift shop. She smiled warmly, more than happy to help.

"I thought you didn't believe in superstition?" Marcie said as we walked back to the car.

"Maybe," I said, "but sometimes you take every protective measure you can."

I bought enough Mezuzahs for every door. Together, Marcie and I spent the early afternoon placing them carefully, chanting blessings for each one—a small but sacred shield.

That night, as we lit the Shabbos candles, I prayed the soft glow would wash away the darkness that had crept into our lives.

Just as the light from that disk erased the shadowy forms in Greystorm's basement, so too might these flames cleanse the heavy night around us.

Across the table, Marcie and I exchanged a glance—quiet, understanding, yet fraught with unspoken fears.

During the seder, I added one more blessing: the *Tefilat HaDerech*, the Traveler's Prayer. Its words, filled with hope and protection, poured from my lips as a quiet plea for Jake.

May he reach his destination safely, guided and guarded by God's hand.

Never have I prayed with such fervor, such desperate hope that the prayer might reach him, wherever he was.

THE END

AUTHOR'S NOTE

Greetings, Reader of the Odd;

Kept In The Dark is a weird book, even for me.

It is based on my own short story, *The Dark*, which was published in H.P. Lovecraft Magazine Of Horror. It was my first horror tale, and the fact that it sold and I was given money for it was a thrill.

However, this novel is in some ways my most personal novel, which made it a struggle for me. My first job out of high school was as a night guard. Many of the situations Jake faces are like situations in my life, and I feel almost swept up in the hopelessness Jake faces. I can understand his inability to get ahead as something is always forcing him down, bigger and stronger than himself.

Yet, in the novel I also admire Jake, because he never gives up and faces the finale of his tale as a fighter, as a warrior, even though life has taken far more from him than it gave. He fights on, with faith that he will win, that he can succeed, despite the numerous setbacks he has faced, and the loss of every person he ever loved.

Characters in novels often puzzle the author, and Jake is no exception. There is a nobility in the character I could never hope to attain myself. I've been lucky that the good things in my own life have far outweighed the bad.

So, I would like to think this book salutes the people who keep going, even when things look bleak. It should be a reminder to us all that there is no life without challenges and that it is always darkest before the dawn.

It's how we handle our challenges that makes the difference.

Ghost Writer

A Supernatural Suspense Mystery

ARJAY LEWIS

MIND
BENDER
PRESS

1. THE BEQUEST

I t was Franklin D. Roosevelt who said, "I think we consider too much the good luck of the early bird and not enough the bad luck of the early worm."

That day, I understood how that worm felt.

I've had plenty of bad days, but as I glared at Chandra — my second wife — across the court tables for our divorce proceedings, I felt it was just one more indignity piled on top of all the others.

I was hungover, and I couldn't even have a little of the hair of the dog, because they frown on you showing up in court with liquor on your breath.

Of course, this was the last step. Lawyers had parsed the details of our agreement as if it were of biblical origin. The lawyers investigated and deliberated over each sentence to find its true meaning.

Chandra's lawyer, the Shark, was there, smiling like she'd taken down Al Capone. My own ineffectual lawyer was there as well, a cordial enough man recommended by my publisher. On the first day of negotiations, the Shark had chewed him up and spat him out.

I bought a house ten years ago, restored it, and paid it off with my royalties and book advances, so I owned it free and clear.

Now after five years of marriage, my ex owned it free and clear.

The case was simple — it was the State of New Jersey. I possessed a penis; therefore, I must pay.

We had no children, so no child support. She accepted the house instead of alimony, accompanied by a large cash settlement, which dwindled my savings greatly.

I was currently living in a tiny cottage in a crowded neighborhood in Lake Hopatcong. One tiny bedroom, a bathroom with a shower stall, a minuscule living room, and a kitchen.

Not that I had much to put in it. All my good furniture stayed in the house that Chandra now owned.

Except my leather recliner. I had to have my recliner.

As she signed the divorce papers, Chandra looked up at me and winked.

I clenched my teeth so hard, it's a wonder I didn't crack a few of them. One more indignity.

I hated her, and at the same time, I desired her so badly it was surprising I didn't become aroused right there in the courtroom.

That was the thing with Chandra. She was bad for me. She was poison. All I had to do was see how she treated a waiter with her condescending attitude.

But, my God, the sex.

She was a fire I couldn't quench. I wanted her, and I wanted her badly. That was the one thing the divorce didn't change.

I drank to control my lust for her, especially as our marriage fell apart. She encouraged the drinking so that I would keep writing.

After all, you don't want to kill the golden goose, not until you receive a few more golden eggs.

Once the judge had approved the agreement, Chandra, me, and our lawyers stepped out into the hall to finish signing the paperwork

"You're off to your uncle's funeral," Chandra said as I finished signing. "Joe, give my best to the family. I always liked Rick. I'm sorry he died."

As a writer, I should have a great retort. Something worthy of Oscar Wilde, Mark Twain, or Dorothy Parker. But I wrote stories of spies, guys, and willing ladies. Lacking a comeback, I muttered, "Yeah, sure."

Brilliant! I missed my calling as a stand-up comedian.

She did like my Uncle Rick. He'd been beneficial to her, or at least to her plans. Richard Riley had been a renowned literary agent, and when I wrote stories as a child and teen, he encouraged me. We were a family of readers, and I was fortunate enough to grow up in the 80s and 90s when people still read books.

He helped me sell my short stories to magazines, and when I wrote my first novel, A Man Called Soul, he gave me excellent pointers and guided me to a content editor who brutally ripped the tale apart and had me rewrite it several times.

By the time of publishing, the book was so polished, it all but glowed.

Uncle Rick sold the book with a fair royalty for a new writer. I was thrilled, and taking my gains, I started the second book in what became a profitable series.

My lead character, Soul Mason, was a CIA agent helping to stop terrorists and evil plots. In the latter part of the 2000s, with terrorists as the bad guys, a brave, chisel-jawed CIA agent was just the sort of thing people wanted to read.

The second book in the series, Body And Soul, got me the money to buy my house, now the property of the ex-missus Riley.

She announced to me during our divorce negotiations that she would keep my last name. Since her maiden name was Crapanzano, I don't blame her. Riley is much easier to spell.

I left the Morris County Municipal Court a much poorer and bitter man, and my next port of call was Uncle Rick's funeral.

Chandra had been fond of Rick. She started working for him about six years ago as his assistant. I had dated no one seriously since my first marriage went bust before I sold my first novel.

That lasted only one short year. That must have been a long year for my ex, Elaine. I was a troublesome man to live with, struggling with my desire to write and my frustration at what I produced. I was an angry, sullen would-be writer.

There was no monetary settlement, and I remained in the New York City apartment we had shared.

Years later, once I was writing and sold some books, I got out of the city and bought the house. Six years ago, I showed up at Uncle Rick's office with a new book ready to go — and there was Chandra.

After six months of dating and the most mind-blowing sex I'd ever experienced, I proposed. We married a few months later and Chandra quit her job.

"I have to, Joe," she explained. "This way, I can help you with the next book. I'll fix your errors and help with the editing. I'll be your muse."

She was my muse alright, and I thought things were good, as we blissfully fornicated and she lubricated me with alcohol into a state of passivity.

But by the time I wrote Soul To The Devil, I realized my wife was living well beyond our means ,and I did not know where my money was going. She had taken over the finances so I could, as she put it, "focus on writing." Dummy that I am, at the time it seemed like a good idea.

It was about that time, six months ago, Uncle Rick informed me my book advances were going to be less.

The ebook revolution had gained momentum and was devastating the publishing industry. For years, the agents and publishers kept the riffraff at bay. But with the gatekeepers silenced, and the gates broken down, anyone could publish.

To the Stephen King's, the James Pattersons', and the Nora Roberts' this was no big deal. They were worth millions and their multi-million dollar advances, as well as the royalties, would keep rolling in. To a middle-of-the-list guy like me, it meant my income was going to go down.

I sobered up, figuratively and literally, and tried to figure out what happened to my money, which Chandra always referred to as "our money."

Which apparently meant "her money."

I moved out of my carefully restored house into a crummy little shack, hired a divorce lawyer and a forensic accountant, but they found little of the money. She siphoned it off slowly and cleverly, and boffed me into a state of unawares. Then she hired the Shark, who plucked my house and half my remaining savings.

The Shark argued I was still at the height of my productivity as a writer and would probably see much more money in the future. She said it was right to make a claim on future royalties as her client, "Was a vital part of the creation of Mr. Riley's very successful books."

Even my lame lawyer got that thrown out.

Of course, Chandra and the Shark knew something that my lawyer didn't. My latest book, tentatively titled Lost Soul, had netted me a small upfront advance, but I wouldn't get the rest until I delivered the book. In the past, I delivered a book or two after the requested deadline.

The due date for the latest book was two months away.

I had written exactly ten pages.

Chandra may have only been looking out for herself in our marriage, but she was correct: she was my muse. Her offerings of steady sex and booze kept me going, kept me working.

For the last few months, I'd done little writing.

All of this whirled through my mind as I arrived at the Stanley Funeral Home in a town called Clinton. It was a large, stately house, a Victorian converted for business use.

Uncle Rick's services were to be held in the largest room.

I arrived just as people were being called to sit down for the service. I saw my older cousins, Robert, Liam, and Ashley. Neither of my brothers came, which was fine by me. We had never been close, and they lived far away. Growing up, I was always closer to my cousins than my brothers. To the cousins, I was a fun visitor. To my brothers, I was the annoying baby of the family, and either a pain to deal with or someone to be bullied.

Walking in, I could see the open coffin at the front of the room. Uncle Rick looked as he did in life, a tall and lean man, around six foot-two with an excellent physique. His white hair gave him an air of maturity and wisdom. They had combed his hair neatly, and dressed him in one of his expensive suits; he looked ready to get up and take a meeting.

Uncle Rick was the last of that generation, as my parents died in a car accident when I was thirty-seven. Now, it was just me, my brothers, and my three cousins. That was all the family I had left.

But it wasn't like we all got together and hung out for the holidays.

I was still fighting a headache and wishing I had brought something with me to take a little nip, just to clear my head.

As I sat, a reverend spoke comforting words at the front of the room. From the gist of it, this eulogy could have been a prepared speech made from a template or thrown together by an AI program.

When he finished his opening tribute, he asked people to get up and talk about Rick.

Robert was the oldest son, so he rose and gave an excellent speech. I figured all those years working as a real estate salesman and investor gave him skills as a speaker.

When he finished, his younger brother Liam got up. Despite being in his late forties, Liam had yet to establish a solid foundation for his life. He was a chain smoker of cigarettes and pot, as well as imbibing in other substances, and squandered his nights away on alcohol and questionable company.

Not that I could judge, considering my ex-wife.

He constantly relied on others for money, with promises to pay them back that never came to fruition. I knew from experience, having given him about a thousand dollars by this point. I was smart enough to say it was a gift, because I knew there was no way in hell he'd ever pay me back.

Liam rambled his way through an unprepared speech, and all of us were thankful when he finished and sat.

My youngest cousin, Ashley, got up to speak, and to my surprise, she started reminiscing about summers in the Poconos in my uncle's rustic cabin. Growing up, all of us, my parents and brothers, my uncle Rick and aunt Betsy, and the cousins would all hang out for a couple of weeks there in the summer. Thinking back to all those people in the one cabin, I wondered how we all fit.

Whispering Pines.

That was the fanciful name Rick had given it.

Nestled in a national forest, the cabin stood out like a beacon among the towering trees. There were acres of woods and we had a dock on Sandy Rock Lake, large enough that we could swim and fish.

I recalled those times as she spoke. Memories of long-forgotten laughter and carefree summers flooded my mind, thoughts of sun-dappled days and warm nights.

From a young age, I looked forward to those annual trips to Uncle Rick's cabin.

It gave me a taste of life disconnected from the modern world. Back in the 90s, we didn't have screens and smart phones so we had to actually go outside and play, like kids are supposed to do.

All of us, brothers and cousins, slept in sleeping bags on the main room floor, while the adults had the two bedrooms.

I was the youngest of all my brothers and the cousins, and Ashley, like a little general, made sure the older boys included me in everything that was going on.

God, I adored her when we were kids, a mix of hero-worship and awe. She was six years older than me, with blonde hair and a powerful personality. We played games, roughhoused, and ran around those woods like little savages, all orchestrated by Ashley.

Then, as the sun dipped below the horizon, we would all gather around a crackling campfire. The adults shared stories as laughter echoed through the trees, and the scent of pine trees and freshly caught fish mingled with the aroma of wood smoke.

It was listening to these stories that made me want to be a writer, to tell stories to other people, and make them feel like I did on those nights.

My current life didn't have any of the peace or joy I felt when we stayed up in that cabin.

The service ending brought me back to awareness as everyone started getting ready to get into their cars and form a caravan to the burial site.

I just wanted to get a drink.

"Joey?"

I came around to see Ashley approach. She pulled me into a hug, the first hug I'd received from a woman in months.

"Hey, Ash," I said. "I'm so sorry."

She pulled back, and her short, chestnut-brown hair framed her face, her bright blue eyes wet. As usual, she dressed impeccably in a black pantsuit with a gray satin blouse. "At least it was quick. Not like Mom, slowly eaten away by the cancer. This was a shock, but it was almost easier."

I nodded sagely. What could I say? Is there ever a good way to die?

"Are you coming to the burial?" she asked.

"No, I've got other things," I said, avoiding the question as best as I could. "I divorced Chandra this morning."

Ashley's expression changed, and the tears were gone. "That bitch," she murmured. This was a stretch for my cousin, as she never used coarse language about anyone. "She took you for everything, didn't she?"

I lifted my shoulders in an attempt at a shrug. "She got the house."

Ashley shook her head, and I saw the fury in her eyes. My protective older cousin. She'd fought my battles as a child and looked like she would happily do it again. "I warned you about her. Didn't I tell you to get a prenup?"

I hung my head. "Please Ash. Today's been rough enough."

She put her hand under my face and lifted my chin. "All right, Joey. But don't be a stranger."

I nodded and forced a grin.

Other guests pulled her away, and a hand slapped me on the back. "Hey Joey."

My oldest cousin, Robert, pulled me into a bear hug. He was about fifty at that point, stocky with his dark hair showing traces of grey at the temples. He pulled back and looked at me. "You holding up alright, Joey? You look terrible."

"I divorced Chandra today," I said with a sigh.

"Ding-dong, the witch is dead," he murmured.

That got a grin. "Heard from her? I understand she called my brothers."

Robert shook his head. "She probably was looking for people to take her side. No, I was lucky enough not to be on her call list. How did you make out?"

"I got screwed, lost the house. My lawyer said if we went before a judge, I'd get screwed even worse. Her lawyer would portray me as a rich writer who was bad with money—"

He frowned. "I thought Chandra handled the money?"

"My first mistake. They'd make me look like a drunk kept solvent by my loving spouse, who deserved everything I owned because of my spendthrift ways." I shook my head.

Robert smiled his real estate agent smile. "I think we can help you take your mind off the situation. Come to the wake."

"Will there be food and booze?"

"An Irish wake?" He easily slipped into a fake brogue. "What else would ye have, Joey, me boy?" He dropped it and glanced around the room. "It'll be tonight at the Shamrock's Embrace Irish Pub right here in Clinton."

"Could they give it a more cliché name?" I asked.

"I would have gone with the Leprechaun's Asshole, but that's me," Robert grinned. "Look, I'm staying at the Holiday Inn right on the outskirts of town. I've got two beds if you want to crash."

I nodded. "That would be good. I need a release."

Matt glanced over at the door. "Looks like the convoy for the burial site is getting ready. I'll see you tonight."

I waved at my other cousin Liam as he headed for the door. Most of the people were strangers to me, and I tried to decide whether I should start drinking now or wait until the evening.

Maybe it was time to make a change and fight my impulses.

A voice said, "Are you Joseph Riley?"

I faced a man about six feet tall with a lean build, neatly trimmed salt and pepper hair, and a meticulously groomed beard. He wore a suit that looked like it cost more than my last book advance.

"Not if you have a subpoena," I said. I meant it as a joke, but with the way my day was going, it could have happened.

The man made a facial expression that suggested a smile but was far too practiced and fake. "I'm Benjamin Clarke, with Bayson and Clarke."

He didn't offer a hand to shake, and neither did I.

"I'm representing Richard Riley's estate," he said in a clipped tone. "I take it you received our notice about the probate and release of the will?"

I tried to appear wise. "I've been in the middle of a divorce, so my mail might not get to me," I explained. That wasn't the truth. I hadn't been looking at my damn mail. I'd been on a bender that had started about a week before. "What does that have to do with me?"

"There is a bequest for you in the will," he said, handing me a business card with a local address.

I stared at the card in my hand. "A bequest to me?" I repeated.

He seemed nonplussed by my response. "Yes. We are meeting after the burial, as we need all the heirs to sign releases. Could you be at my office at 5 PM today?"

"Sure," I said, and glanced at my watch. It was two-thirty, and where did I have to go?

"I'll see you then," he said with that rigid smile, and followed the group out to their cars.

I stood staring at the card in my hand, my mind racing.

What could Uncle Rick have left me?

2. YOU GET WHAT YOU NEED

I was the first to arrive at the lawyer's office at 4:30. I used the time between the service and the meeting to visit my cousin's cafe, Brew Haven, in the heart of Clinton.

Ashley created this about five years ago, converting a charming, historic building, once the town's general store. It had a rustic charm, with exposed brick walls and large windows. She'd transformed the space with local artwork, handmade pottery, and whimsical decorations.

I didn't know when Ashley had become an expert with coffee, but it showed in the latte prepared by the barista on duty. My beverage was fantastic, dark and hot, yet not overpowering. A perfect blend, and it was the first thing that helped ease my headache.

I sat and had coffee and a freshly baked scone as I puzzled over what Uncle Rick had left me. He knew about my divorce from Chandra, and that she was bleeding me dry. I know it troubled him, as she had been his employee when I met her.

Perhaps he left me a tidy sum to tide me over the next months until I could finish the book.

Or to tide me over if I couldn't finish the book.

He didn't know I'd only written ten pages of Lost Soul.

I would not let my agent know I had writer's block, even if he was my uncle.

I sat there sipping coffee, forty years old, divorced twice and unable to work. Yeah, my life was just peachy. I envied Uncle Rick. Maybe I should take up golf and try for a massive coronary.

Uncle Rick had looked a lot happier in that coffin than I felt.

By 4:45, all three of my cousins had arrived. While Ashley talked with a secretary, I sat with Robert and Liam. Robert was still in one of his 'power' business suits, black for the funeral, with a strong black tie.

Liam looked like an unmade bed. He wore a baggy and rumpled black suit, his shoulders hunched from a lifetime of slouching. His hair, an unkempt mess of dark brown curls, fell haphazardly over his forehead, obscuring his narrow brown eyes. His appearance was further worsened by his scruffy facial hair, which he unsuccessfully attempted to grow into a beard. A perpetual smoker, he smelled of tobacco from several feet away.

At 5:00 precisely, a junior secretary escorted us to Mr. Clarke's office. We went into an empty room, and the four of us chatted about the funeral.

Mr. Clarke came into the office with a sheaf of papers. "Please remain seated."

I wondered what I was doing there at all.

Mr. Clarke went through a bunch of legalese and how he was the executor of Richard Riley's estate, et cetera, and he would supply each of us a copy of the will. He also expected us to sign individual releases in order to receive our inheritances.

"Now, I am sure you've all seen on television where the lawyer dramatically reads a will," Clarke explained. "That's not accurate. I have a copy for each of you, and I have only asked you all to be here in case there is some confusion about the bequests, or in case a conflict may arise."

"What would Dad have in the will that would cause a conflict?" Ashley asked.

"Actually, it is the bequest to Joseph Riley that may concern his other heirs," Clarke said, and all eyes went to me.

"I have no idea what this is about," I muttered.

"Why don't you all read the will, and we can discuss it," Clarke said.

The entire will was only a few pages, and most of it seemed straightforward. He was leaving his investments to be split equally among the three children and created a trust for Robert's two kids for college and beyond. The family home in Clinton was to go to Ashley as she lived in the town. There were several charitable donations, and specific monies designated for longtime secretaries and staff people who worked in his office.

Then I reached a paragraph that read: "I leave my cabin in the Poconos, named Whispering Pines, to my nephew, Joseph Riley. It always brought him great joy when he visited there, and I believe he could use more joy in his life."

I sat there stunned. I spent most of the funeral service lost in thought about the cabin. Oddly, this made a shiver run up my spine.

I met Mr. Clarke's eyes. "Uncle Rick left me his cabin in the Poconos?"

"Yes," Clarke said, and glanced at the others. "I was not entirely sure this would be agreeable to your relatives."

"I think Joey would love it there," Robert said.

"I don't know," I said. "Ashley, you always went hunting with Uncle Rick."

"Damn straight," Ashley said proudly. "He taught me to shoot. But I'm too busy with the restaurant to go on a retreat."

Liam nodded. "Yeah, I just hope you'll invite us once you've fixed the place up."

"Fixed up?" I asked with concern. "Is it in disrepair?"

"No one's stayed up there in, like, a decade," Liam pointed out.

"But Dad kept the place up," Robert said. "He had a property management company watch over the place."

I frowned. "A property management company?"

Robert nodded. "Yeah, some place called Pocono Pines Property Care. They sent out a caretaker every few months to check the place out. They hired workmen to do repairs and made sure the pipes didn't freeze."

"Are you three okay with me inheriting it?" I asked, still unsure.

They looked at each other and nodded, and I saw Mr. Clarke relax.

"Very well. If all of you sign your releases, we can move the will to probate first thing Monday."

And yet, a part of me felt uneasy. Wasn't a lonely cabin in the woods the beginning scene of every horror movie?

At the Shamrock's Embrace Irish Pub, it was quite a party for Uncle Rick. In true Irish tradition, my cousins wanted a grand farewell at his wake. Friends and family from near and far gathered together, sharing stories, laughter, and tears. A live band played traditional Irish music, filling the room with a sense of warmth and belonging. Guinness and whiskey flowed freely as those gathered raised their glasses to toast the life and legacy of Richard Riley.

I was still in shock. The idea of losing one house and gaining another on the same day was enough to make any man dizzy. At least I could finally have a drink, but so far I'd stuck to the beer.

I was savoring my second pint of what they call a 'black and tan', a blend of Guinness stout and Bass pale ale, watching the crowd of revelers and the band. Observing people was something I always did as a kid. I think it was part of what made me an excellent writer. I spent so much time watching people, scrutinizing how they acted, how they talked, until I had an ear for dialogue and a sense of how people behaved and how to describe it.

Finally, Liam came over. He was already two sheets to the wind, much drunker than I was.

"I heard you dumped the bitch today," he said in lieu of a greeting.

"That's true." I said.

"Good on you," he said, and attempted to focus. Then, out of the blue, he said, "Your mom hated Chandra. Told my mom all about it."

I looked at him, shocked. "This is a fine time to tell me that."

He shrugged. "When was a good time? We all knew how you two were in the early days. To you, she was the one. There was no talking you down."

I shook my head. "My mom liked everyone."

"Except Chandra," Matt said. "She wouldn't say anything to you because she hated interfering mothers."

The band broke into an old Irish tune, The Wild Rover.

"You know, I always wanted to play Irish music," Liam said. "Of course, I'd have to learn to play an instrument first."

He wandered off to get closer to the band.

Ashley approached with her own half-finished pint of black and tan sloshing around in her glass.

"I thought you'd be ordering champagne," Ashley shouted in my ear to be heard over the music. "Lose a viper and gain a house."

"It's all overwhelming," I said.

"Are you going to move out of that tiny house in Lake Hopatcong you told me about?"

"That dump," I chuckled. "It's so small, I have to step outside to change my mind."

"When you put the key in the door, do you break the window?" Ashley said with a grin.

"Yes, and all the mice are hunchbacked," I said, hoping this would end the jokes.

"So you're really going to go live in Whispering Pines?" she said. "Out in the middle of nowhere?"

"I think I am," I yelled back. "I have only a card table, two folding chairs, and my recliner. If I can get them in the back of my truck, I can do it."

I was driving an older Ford F150. When I moved out of my former house, I single-handedly manipulated the recliner into the truck bed and hoped I could repeat the process.

"All the old furniture is still at the cabin, beds and everything," she said, and appeared troubled. "But I don't know about living there. The last time I went there, the place had a weird vibe."

I leaned close so she could hear me. "When was that?"

She shook her head. "I dunno. I haven't stayed up there since I was in my twenties. But I've gone up a few times recently to check the place for Dad." She shuddered, as if the memory was unpleasant, and looked at me blearily. "I'm worried about you. There's nothing for miles around."

"Writers like solitude," I said. "Besides, there are towns within driving distance, and even a mall or two."

"You're alone on ten acres and the lake," she said. "I don't know. I think I would find it creepy. Are you switching away from heroic secret agents and taking a stab at horror?"

"Taking a stab at horror?" I repeated and shook my head. "You're a regular comedienne."

"Just be careful if you go, little cousin. There are bears out there, you know."

I knew. As kids, we saw them all the time. They were mostly brown bears and more scared of humans than we were of them. But you had to be careful if there were cubs. Protecting a cub could cause a mother bear to charge.

Another guest pulled her away, and I lifted my beer in salute as she went.

Robert walked over to me. "Hey, Joey."

"Robert, are you sure you're okay with me getting the cabin?" I asked, still talking loudly over the music. "The last thing I want is to cause friction in the family."

"Who else could he leave it to?" Robert said, answering my question with a question. "I have a vacation house — on the Jersey shore, thank you, and Ash never wants to be far from her restaurant. Dad could've left it to Liam, but I don't think that would work out well. Liam barely gets by now. How would he do out in the woods without us to borrow money from?"

"He got a pretty good inheritance from Rick's will."

"It'll be gone in six months, if that long. He'll put it in one of his schemes he thinks will make him rich. Trust me, he'll flush it all away." He stepped closer so that he could lower his voice. "But look, if you don't want to be saddled with an old place like that, I could see what the market will take. Believe me, I could get you a good price for the place."

I frowned, confused about the direction he was going.

"I mean, none of us have been up there since we were kids," he went on. "All those memories we have of the place, we're just fooling ourselves. It wasn't much then, so it won't be much now."

"I'd like to try," I said. "Maybe fix it up. I'm not completely broke."

"From what I heard over the years, the locals avoid the place."

"Avoid it? Why?"

He glanced around to see if anyone else was nearby. "The rumor is that it's haunted."

"Haunted?" I repeated as I felt a shiver run up my back. "What do you mean?"

Robert shrugged. "Strange noises, flashing lights, people seeing shapes in the windows. A couple of neighbors heard screams in the night and called the police. They thought someone had broken in."

"Did someone break in?"

"Maybe, who knows? But the police found nothing, and they called the caretaker who comes around to check the place. Get this, the guy tells the cops he won't go in there at night and tells them where the spare key is."

I thought of the cabin nestled deep within the heart of the woods, the same place where I spent multiple summers and created countless memories. That it was now tainted with such a strange reputation was completely foreign to me.

Several people pulled Robert away, and I headed to the bar to switch my drink to whiskey. I felt I needed it now.

I sat alone in the dimly lit corner of the pub as music played and people chatted. I found my fingers tapping restlessly against the rim of my glass. The amber liquid swirled inside, mirroring my own tumultuous thoughts. People thought ghosts haunted my uncle's cabin, which was now mine.

Of course, any place that stands empty develops a reputation. But why wouldn't the caretaker show up at night?

And what if a restless spirit wandered around the place, longing for solace? Wasn't that what I wanted to do? Return to something I enjoyed in my childhood and bring some peace after my ruined marriage? Plus, maybe the place would inspire me. If I could get to work, I should be able to knock out a rough draft in two months. Hell, that was less than a thousand words a day.

I have a skeptical nature and have always scoffed at tales of the supernatural. But tonight, with the idea of living on my own deep in the woods and Uncle Rick in his grave, I found I fought to dismiss the chill I felt.

After all, I was a rational being, not some frightened child hiding from monsters.

Wasn't I?

To Be continued
In

Ghost
Writer

ABOUT THE AUTHOR

Known as the "Wizard Of Odd," Arjay Lewis is an actor, magician, and multi-award-winning author.

I write tales of the strange and the horrifying.

I have spent my life as an entertainer, amusing people as a street-performer in the 1970s; a Broadway and casino artist in the 1980s; a party performer in the 1990s and 2000s; a cruise ship performer in the 2010s.

Stories have always been in my mind, and I have been writing since the 1990s. My reason to write is simple: to entertain. I write the type of books that I like to read: murder mysteries, strange tales of unnatural gifts, odd happenings and horror.

Please visit my web site and sign up for my mailing list to be "in the know" for upcoming books. Visit me on Facebook, Twitter, or my Amazon Author page.

And thank you for reading. You are the reason I write.

www.arjaylewis.com
www.facebook.com/arjaylewis
www.twitter.com/arjaylewiswrite
www.amazon.com/Arjay-Lewis

ALSO BY ARJAY LEWIS

Doctor Wise Series
Fire In The Mind
Seduction In The Mind
Reunion In The Mind
Haunted In The Mind
Devotion In The Mind
Asylum In The Mind
Specter In The Mind
Vengeance In The Mind
Echoes In The Mind
Infection In The Mind
Justice In The Mind
Ritual In The Mind
Vanished In The Mind

Horror
The Muse
Kept In The Dark
The Vanishing
Digger
Ghost Writer

Romantic Suspense
(with Debra Snow)
A Study In Murder

NYPD Wizard Detective
The Wizards Of Central Park West
The Vampires Of Greenwich Village
The Werewolves Of Washington Square

www.ingramcontent.com/pod-product-compliance
Lightning Source LLC
Chambersburg PA
CBHW021330070726
47496CB00016B/18

* 9 7 8 1 7 3 2 6 5 9 3 9 1 *